FAMOUS
LAST WORDS

a novel

by

Timothy Findley

Penguin Books

Penguin Books Ltd., Harmondsworth, Middlesex, England
Penguin Books, 625 Madison Avenue, New York, New York 10022, U.S.A.
Penguin Books Australia Ltd, Ringwood, Victoria, Australia
Penguin Books Canada Ltd, 2801 John Street, Markham, Ontario, Canada L3R 1B4
Penguin Books (N.Z.) Ltd, 182-190 Wairau Road, Auckland 10, New Zealand

First Published in Canada by Clarke Irwin & Company Limited, 1981
Published in Penguin Books, 1982

Manufactured in Canada by Webcom Limited

For: Phyllis Webb and
William Whitehead;
Alec McCowen and
Margaret Laurence;
and
in memory of
Thornton Wilder

"... one does not know what one knows, or even what one wishes to know, until one is challenged and must lay down a stake."

Thornton Wilder, *The Ides of March*

ACKNOWLEDGEMENTS

I am deeply indebted to the following people for their assistance and professional advice during the writing of this book: Nancy Colbert, Stanley Colbert, William Hutt, Juliet Mannock, Diana Marler, Charles Taylor, Dr. R. E. Turner, Dorothy Warren and, as always, William Whitehead.

Finally, my thanks to the Canada Council for the invaluable assistance of a Senior Arts Grant received during the completion of this work.

T.F.

1910

When Mauberley was twelve years old, his father took him onto the roof of the Arlington Hotel in Boston and said to him; "I've always loved the view from here. Cambridge across the river. The red bricks of Harvard. . . .The Swan Boats in the public garden. The gilded dome on Beacon Hill and all the people walking on the grass. . . ." And it was so. His father had spent much time up there alone on the roof of that hotel where Mauberley was born. Mauberley, too, had come to love these things. "I love the tops of the trees," his father said. "And the smell and the sound of the horses passing by. . . .When you were born, it snowed. And I came up here that night and threw a snowball all the way across the avenue and hit George Washington square in the face! I meant no disrespect. I only wanted him to know. It was late, you see, and there was no one else to tell. . . ." His father smiled. There was a pause in which the two of them looked out on all these things and then his father said; "but the world is too much with us. That's a quote and you can look it up some day." There was another pause and then; "I love you, Hugh. You can't look that up anywhere. But I ask you to memorize it, just the same. The thing is—I'm afraid I haven't been able to love your mother as I should have since she was ill. You'll understand that failure later on, when some of what you love has turned to stone. You'll leave your mother too in the course of time. As children do and should. But every husband doesn't leave his wife and I want to be sure you understand I do not blame your mother, and I beg you not to blame her either, for the failure of our marriage. Your mother is herself—that's all. And I am me. Do you understand? You might as well blame a person for surviving birth, and blame their heart for keeping them alive, as blame them for the fact they are themselves. . . ." Mauberley's father stood up very tall and sighed. "But the fact remains, your mother is the most unhappy woman I have ever known. And some of that has been my fault—and even, sadly, yours." He smiled at his son. "Because we're here. . .and have intruded in her life. And because—" the smile began to fade and his father turned away "—not all the caring in the world will mend her mind or the bitterness that's come with her failure to be whole. And I wish. . ." He stopped. "But no. I've spent my whole life wishing. Don't ever wish for anything. Want everything, Hugh—but wish for nothing."

Now his father looked across the Charles to Cambridge, shading his eyes against the sun. "Tomorrow," he said, "you will read in the papers I have been let go from Harvard. This, again, is something you will understand when you are older. The simple explanation is: I had too much to say they didn't want to hear. My students have been very kind and there is talk of protest. But I won't go back. I can't go back. There's nothing left to teach that's mine: unique. And so," he smiled, "it's over. And a whole new life awaits us." Mauberley's father laid his hand upon his shoulder and took him on a guided tour of all the views. He smoked a cigarette and reminded his son of secret cigarettes they had watched the servants smoking down below in the side yard of the Sears' Mansion. "They thought they were getting away with it— and all the time, we saw!" They had a good laugh together over that, and the time the Fishmonger came and kissed the Cook and she slapped his face in the same side yard. And the day when President Taft fell down in front of the Ritz Hotel and it took eight men to lift him up. Mauberley's father took off his jacket, then, and laid it neatly folded on the parapet. "All these years, eh, Hugh?" he said, "of staring down at the world. Now; look at all the people staring up." And then he clambered onto the ledge and—waving at the sky—he leapt down fifteen stories to his death.

In the pocket of his father's jacket—hung for many weeks like a wreath on the back of Mauberley's door—there was a soft, flat leather bill-fold with a clasp. Inside, there was a pencil made of silver and a message addressed to *Hugh Selwyn Mauberley: my son.*

"*He who jumps to his death has cause,*" it said. "*He who leaps has purpose. Always remember: I leapt.*"

ONE

March, 1945

The age demanded an image
Of its accelerated grimace. . .

Ezra Pound

About ten weeks before the end of the war, Mauberley went up out of Italy to hide at UnterBalkonberg. This was in March of 1945.

His journey began at Rapallo.

All he took with him was his notebooks: some of them packed in his attaché case, others jammed and crammed into a cardboard valise whose corners and handles were riveted with brass. Time and panic had already taken their toll of his possessions and most of what he wore was scrounged:

an oversized greatcoat; a pair of army boots; a peasant's cap and a blue suit tailored in Verona. His underwear had rotted at the armpits and his socks, by journey's end, would peel away with the skin from between his toes. His shirt was the only vaguely decent thing he wore—a nondescript and over-mended plaid, his parting gift from Ezra Pound.

Mauberley wore no tie and, although he had begged for one, Ezra had refused to give up the only one he owned, having already planned to wear it himself on the day of his arrest.

"But you never wear a tie," said Mauberley.

"That's right," said Pound. "Ergo: to wear one is to say I have surrendered."

Mauberley, all his adult life, had been a fastidious dresser, famous for his suits of Venetian white and his muted English ties. The open collar nearly drove him mad, and his hand kept going up as if a pressure point had given way and he needed a tourniquet. In the end, he accepted the bootlace offered by Ezra's wife, Dorothy, and tied it firmly around his neck. This made him feel complete. It also made him look like Dorothy's Scarecrow.

"Suits you," said Pound. "It goes with the straw in your head."

"And you can go to hell," said Mauberley.

All they did, to the last, was argue.

Dorothy watched and listened from the sidelines; finger-ing her worry beads, worn in a loop at her waist. She felt she was cut adrift and lost in a very small boat with no one else to row but two sick men. And she was tired. Her only consolation was her memory of the shore. Otherwise, she fed on fear for Ezra; sadness for Mauberley; apprehension for herself.

This was the end of the exile they had chosen.

Twenty-six years before, in 1919, when the other war was over, Mauberley had come to Europe from America—just like Ezra before him—a boy with a sheaf of poems in his hand. And Ezra had become his mentor. ("Ezra! Ezra! Everyone's mentor!" Dorothy had said. "The world is full of Ezra's protégés.") This had been in England. Then the exile moved by stages down from London into Paris then to Rapallo in Italy—everyone's ultimate choice for exile—where they settled by the sea. And Ezra had predicted Hugh Selwyn Mauberley would become the greatest writer of his time.

And was wrong.

(Dorothy put a quarter cut of cheese, a stick of bread, a jar of soup and a string of onions into an old cloth bag and handed it to Mauberley.)

Not that it mattered now that Ezra had been wrong. Infinitely more important things had come to govern their lives in Italy. Ezra had said: "I am giving up poetry for politics. . . ." Poetry maybe: writing never. And Dorothy could count the events that had ensued with the brevity of telling her beads. *Click:* Mussolini. *Click:* the Fascists. *Click:* first Ezra, later Mauberley, had joined. *Clack:* their writing had followed.

(Dorothy took a bottle of wine and bumped its cork with the palm of her hand and shoved it down inside the bag beside the stick of bread.)

Still, looking back, it was sad about the writing; sad when she thought of all the protégés and promise and success. And the failures. So many wars had come and gone through the 1920s and '30s, each interlocking with the next—Mauberley's "boxed set of wars"—and with them down went all the old necessities for literature; all the old prescriptions for use of the written word; all the old traditions of order and articulation fading under the roar of bombast and rhetoric. And Ezra, somehow adoring it, had said: "You see? There's no place left for a man who writes like Mauberley. Mauberley's whole and only ambition is to describe the beautiful. And who the hell has time for *that,* any more? No one. Beauty will have to describe itself from now on. Words have more important work to do. . . ." And he set about doing it— Ezra: pouring through a dozen languages, phrase books and dictionaries piled up around him. Buried at his desk. "Somewhere in here," he had said; "is what we know already; forgotten and ignored. And I mean to find it." Digging like an archaeologist.

6

Sometimes with dynamite.

But Mauberley would not take part in this dismantling of the past. The past was where he lived; or wanted to. He wore his whites and wrote his careful books; he invested his mother's fortune and took up residence in all the best hotels of Europe: the Savoy in London; the Meurice in Paris; the Grande Bretagne in Venice; the Bristol in Vienna. He began to cultivate a taste for people Pound could not abide. He came back, from time to time, and Pound went on receiving him. Fondness prevented a total schism. Fondness or admiration; loneliness; fear of what was coming; or something. Dorothy called it love—and Ezra spat on the floor.

(Dorothy, rummaging, found an old cotton pair of gloves and put them into the bag.)

Now, in the face of capture, both men having been denounced as traitors to their country, they were in hiding on the hill above Rapallo: guests at Sant' Ambrogio in the house of Ezra's mistress (click) Olga Rudge. Miss Rudge had retired from the present scene and was standing out in her olive grove watching through binoculars for planes. The Allies were dropping bombs on Genoa across the bay and only a fool could not foretell the end of this. But Ezra was determined he would brave the ending out.

"I may be hiding from their bombs," he said; "but when their soldiers come, I won't be hiding then. No sir! I shall bid them welcome. 'Welcome, Fellow Americans!' Eh? And maybe I'll holler it, hunh? WELCOME, FELLOW AMERICAN SONS OF BITCHES!" he roared. "That oughta make 'em jump."

(Dorothy closed the handles of the bag and walked away into a corner, where she sat beside Miss Rudge's cat—the cat asleep, impervious.)

"That oughta tell 'em who I am." said Ezra.

But Mauberley could only think of escape.

Anywhere neutral would serve his purpose and his first idea had been to make a dash across the south of France to Spain. Others had done this before him early in December and succeeded. But Mauberley had put it off too long and by the time he was prepared to run, the route to Spain was closed and the railroads north to Lugano and Switzerland had either been destroyed from the air or were under attack from Partisans. The only way to avoid the Americans now—and the British—lay in the hope he could somehow get across the Lombardy plain and through the Brenner Pass to UnterBalkonberg in Austria.

"Thing is," said Ezra Pound, "you got more enemies than me and it's Nazis you got to be afraid of just as much as the others. . . ."

Mauberley had even offended the Germans with his writing.

"You should've stuck to one side," said Ezra. "Made up your mind and stuck to one side."

"I did," said Mauberley.

Dorothy winced. "Take food and go," she wanted to say. "Be gone. It's late." But was silent, making a fist around the worry beads.

"Did, eh?" Ezra snapped. "Well—no you didn't, arsehole. What you did was stick yourself in the middle, right smack damn in the middle of everybody, and now you've got 'em coming down like the Whores of Ghengis Khan on top of you. Ghengela Cohen," (Ezra could not resist it) "leader of the Lost Tribes of Israel and, after Moses, the first expansionist Jew. Yes—yes? Yanks and Huns and Brits all coming down on top of poor old Hugh Selwyn Mauberley—arse-eyed traitor to the whole world!" He laughed.

Mauberley did not appreciate the laughter; he was mortally afraid. Pound, of course, knew this but refused to play to fear of any kind in anyone. It was one of his taboos. "Now," he said, "since you went and made an enemy of everyone, you got to go out there and pray that no one will recognize your puss. Fat chance. Your face may not be pretty but it's potent: ready to explode. Soon as one of them enemies of yours gets a sight of it—bam!"

Yes.

"Bam!" Pound made an explosion with his fingers, jabbing at Mauberley's face with its worried eyes, its pursed and careful lips, its well-known expression of apprehensive disdain. "You might as well carry a big white flag, my friend. Might as well advertize."

Dorothy thought of all the photos over the years of Mauberley printed in the papers and the magazines. Seen with this one and that one and everyone. He'd wanted that. And got it. Now he would pay for it.

"Couldn't we say goodbye with less antagonism, please?" asked Mauberley.

"Please, hunh?" said Ezra.

"Yes."

They stared at one another.

"*Please*. Well, well. . .I like that. *Please*, he said."

Dorothy held her breath.

Ezra scowled and worked his jaws and turned away. Sunlight and silence. One whole minute. Ezra wandered— bearded, old—across the floor. There was dust on the leaves of the potted geraniums. The windows needed washing.

Finally Ezra made his way to Mauberley. Mauberley sat rigid. Dorothy hooked her fingers tight in her lap and waited.

"One more generation and you might've worked out," Ezra said to Mauberley. "What a pity you never had children."

Dorothy watched, ashamed. Ezra's venom was like a snake's. If he bit himself, he'd die.

But Mauberley was used to it. "Yes," he said. "I wish I had." And smiled.

Olga's cat sat up and scratched its neck.

Ezra said; "I've never kissed a man. So this is only what they call a soldier's farewell. From one who stays. . ." he paused ". . .to one who goes." And he leaned down, brushing the top of Mauberley's head with his lips. And was gone.

Mauberley sat completely still.

Goodbye.

"You did have children," said Dorothy, at last. The cat was purring, reaching to play with the worry beads. "Some of the best I've ever read."

"Thankyou."

Sitting.

Then rising.

They knew they would never see each other again. But people do not say such things out loud.

Instead there was just a touching of hands—and Dorothy let him go.

On the hill above Rapallo Mauberley could smell the cordite miles away at Genoa mixed with the stink of dogs and garbage tangled in the wires along the beaches down below. Stepping forward, he walked through a world transformed by violence and fear into a place where all the landmarks learned by heart had disappeared and every face might hide an enemy.

Later, having crossed the Po and come to Cremona hoping to find a train, he found instead the city was a shambles of blown-up houses and candy factories. Red clay dust obscured the sun. Smoke obscured the ruins of the station. Nothing remained of the Telephone Exchange and the other public buildings. No one could tell what lay ahead along the roads. The soldiers of the *Wehrmacht* shot at you today, and, tomorrow, it might be the Allies.

Mussolini was in retreat at Salo by Lago di Garda. It was not, of course, being called a "retreat" but the new seat of Government: the German-sponsored *Republica Fascisti* of which Mussolini was the figurehead. Two months before Ezra had gone to visit him there and Mauberley had tagged along in the hope that Ezra might persuade *il Duce* to provide some means of their escaping into Switzerland. Or a piece of paper, at the very least, absolving them of conspiracy against their own kind and country. Everyone was seeking such pieces of paper. Mussolini himself was drafting rebuttals: ". . .I did not mean. . .I did not want. . .I did not intend. . .it was not my ultimate goal. . ." Just as later at Nuremburg so many others would say; "*I did not know. . .*"

Now Mauberley must decide which route he would take

into the mountains. Going around the western shores of Lago di Garda would cut at least a quarter of his journey; maybe a third. But he dared not risk the formidable concentration of German troops surrounding Mussolini's encampment.

So it was that Mauberley turned eastward and made his way to Mantua, thinking for certain the rail lines would be open to Verona and the north.

He arrived at Mantua on the 8th of March. On the 7th the bridge across the Rhine at Remagen had fallen into Allied hands. The panic brought about by this event swept down through the *Wehrmacht* all the way to Italy. Visions of being killed in a country they had come to hate seized the Army of Occupation with a frenzy of rebellion. The breaching of the Rhine defences was an atavistic signal that Germany was done for. Wives and children were in jeopardy. The attempt to maintain the *Republica Fascisti* had been hopeless to begin with and the "fight to the death" being called for by their leader would be meaningless so far away from Germany. The only place for such a death was at home. And home they went; by the thousands.

Nothing, it seemed, could stop them. It was a rout without precedent. Officers as well as men took part—though not a single enemy soldier pursued them. Only the Partisans, who struck from ambush. Three battalions, each swollen with Austrian and German civilians, were at the core of this retreat and they commandeered everything that rolled on wheels to get them to the north. Their immediate goal was the Brenner Pass—almost a hundred and fifty miles away through the mountains rising into Austria. Mauberley arrived at Mantua to find that all the world had joined him in his journey.

His first mistake was in taking the train; his second in wanting so much to get out of the cold that he bribed his way into a compartment instead of riding on the top of the car. Anonymity was guaranteed up top by the fact that everyone must shut his eyes against the wind and every face was covered with scarves and turned-up collars. Not that he might not have fallen from the top, as one man did; or been frozen, as several were; but at least he would not have been seen.

In the compartment—which was grossly overcrowded—
Mauberley was able to remove his cotton gloves and warm
one hand in the palm of the other. The valise and attaché
case he carried on his lap, the handles turned against himself
so no one could grab them and run away. Dorothy's old cloth
bag was rolled in his pocket against the chance he might be
able to buy or steal enough to make himself a portable larder.
He hadn't eaten since the last heel of bread and the last of
the onions downed against the cold that morning, followed
by the last gulp of wine. He would buy something more
when they got to Verona. In the linings of his clothes there
was a fortune in lire and Reichsmark, suitably muffled in
cotton wool so it wouldn't "talk" every time he moved. In
his pocket there was a modest amount of other monies, ready
to be drawn against the need to bribe his way here and
there—as he had when he got on the train, as he might when
the next opportunity to sleep beneath a roof appeared. For
the moment, he was happy just to sit and be warmed by the
pressure of the people on either side and the comfort of
knowing someone else was in charge of his destination for
a while.

They sat this way, beneath the canopy of broken glass that
had been the station, for the next three hours, while the air-
raid sirens screamed and moaned and the B-24s flew above
them into the north and northwest to drop their bombs on
Brescia and Milan. Then—at last—the whole train gave a
series of kicks and lumbered off to the east and the first blue
hint of the mountains. Everyone sighed. There was even
laughter. They were free. They were going home.

Mauberley's first awareness of being followed did not occur
until the train was about to make its first stop. He had been
snoozing, pleasantly warmed, rocking gently from side to
side. Suddenly someone called out; "*schau mal!*" Look! And
pointed through the glass of the compartment, out through
the windows beyond the people in the corridor. Mauberley,
coming very slowly to his senses, tried to understand what
all the commotion was about: people rising to peer above
each other's heads and pressing down on one another's

shoulders. It was difficult to tell if there was anything to see
at all—until there was a jolt and some of the people fell
towards one side.

Then it could be seen: the rest of the army, with all its
bicycles and horses, all its stragglers marching on foot, those
who had started out in the night or even the afternoon before.
The road ran parallel to the track for several miles. And
every mile was black with soldiers and overloaded transport,
the transport moving at a snail's pace; stalling; moving; stalling; moving—the train, too, losing its momentum. It was
plain they were coming to some sort of junction or perhaps
a town. "Wo? Wo?" "Villafranca."

Mauberley was catching as many fleeting glimpses of this
scene as he was able between the crowded bodies, when he
became aware he was being watched. One of the people in
the corridor—a severe, unsmiling woman who wore a ratty-
looking moleskin coat—was leaning against the glass, staring
in at him through narrowed eyes. Her hair was cut like the
hair of a man. Her hands, laid out along the sleeves of the
coat, were strong, and the fingernails bitten. But the most
alarming thing about this woman was her expression.

Clearly, she knew who Mauberley was—and clearly, she
hated him. Even when she saw he had seen her, she was so
engrossed in this hatred she could not bring herself to look
away.

Mauberley tightened his grip on the valise and the attaché
case. He couldn't breathe.

The woman lifted her chin, bit at one of her fingers and
spat out a piece of nail against the partition. She might as
well have blown him the kiss of death.

And then she was gone.

Her place was taken by a soldier with a pack whose shovel
screeched along the glass and made a series of marks like
the graph of a heart attack.

Mauberley sat there unable to move. Finally, looking down,
he had to tell his fingers one by one: *let go.*

After that, the train rolled into the station yard at Villafranca, where it took on water and coal and let a few more
soldiers onto the tops of the cars and shuffled away into the
winter afternoon and the wooded approaches to Verona.

Mauberley dared not sleep again. Or think of sleep. Or even watch the others sleeping and dozing all around him. Instead, he sat up very straight, with his eyes on the passenger opposite—a gaunt, unshaven man whose lips were cracked and whose mouth was set as if about to bite on glass. This was the only other person wide awake besides himself. When the man stared back at him, Mauberley realized how rude he was being and smiled. And it was then—as the smile was being returned—he saw it was himself he had been watching, caught in the trick of a lopsided mirror hanging between advertisements for *Aqua di Silva* and German fortitude: *"Der Führer erwartet dein Opfer!"* Eau de cologne and sacrifice—and a trainload of deserters. A fitting way to go.

Someone began to sing. A soldier's song. The whole car took it up and doubtless the passengers in other cars as well. When the song was over there were cheers and shouts of: *bitte! bitte!* More. More. Another song was sung and another and another. Finally, silence. Out of this silence someone else began to sing—a woman singing all alone. She sang with a full contralto voice, taking her rhythm from the train. *"Wien, Wien, nur du allein sollst stets die Stadt meiner Träume sein."*

Everyone listened, each one caught in some private dream of home: Vienna, Munich, Berlin. . . .At least there were some with cities to which they could return. For Mauberley, the cities of the past and all the people in them might as well have been the cities and the citizens of stars.

Suddenly there was a raucous hullabaloo of brakes and wheels and thudding cars, and all the men and women sitting opposite came hurtling across—all in slow motion—all with the sharpest bang that Mauberley had ever heard.

Something or someone pushed down hard against the back of his neck and he fell under everything down on top of his attaché case and the cardboard valise.

A dreadful stillness followed. And a pause—like the intake of a breath.

The next thing he heard was the sound of steam and the

clanging of a very distant bell and even more distant voices. Then a burst of gunfire.

Slowly—far too slowly—the people on top of him began to rise. Someone stepped on his hand.

"Don't cry out. . ." they said in German, whispering. "Don't cry out."

Mauberley desperately tried to do as he was told and was silent—but the pain was terrible.

Everyone rose.

At first, they only got to their knees.

The gunfire continued somewhere further down towards the head of the train.

"What is happening?" a woman asked, sitting with her hip against the floor and her back against the seat. "Did we hit another train?"

A man, quite young, a civilian and perhaps a minor official from one of the consulates, let down the window, allowing a blast of cold air.

"Yes," he said. "There is another train. But there's a barrier of some kind, too."

Gunfire.

It was getting dark.

Mauberley checked the locks on his valise and attaché case and put on his gloves.

"Why are they firing? Don't they know we're Germans?"

"Maybe it's the Partisans."

"No," said the man at the window. "There are soldiers coming down over the barrier. And there are trucks all along the road. Army trucks. Ours."

Suddenly a searchlight was thrown on, sweeping the train from end to end, and all the people covered their faces as if afraid of recognition.

"Why are they doing that?" said the woman. "What if there were a bombing raid? We should all be seen and killed. Are you sure they're Germans?"

"Absolutely, meine Frau, I promise you. I can see the helmets. I can hear them talking."

"Then who are they firing at?"

"Us."

"Why?" the woman asked. She was outraged. "Germans firing on Germans? Why?"

"Don't be a fool," said another man, who had not said a word till then. "We have all deserted our posts. We are traitors."

"But all we're doing is going home," the woman said.

"Yes. Against orders."

"I'm afraid," said the man at the window, "he's right. They are coming, many, many soldiers now, along the road. I can see them very clearly. Units of the S.S."

"Dear God—they have been sent to stop us; sent to cut us off."

"Well, they won't cut me off," the outraged woman said. "I am a German citizen. I am on a German train and I have a German destination." She got to her feet and stood in the glare of the light. She brushed her clothing and poked around in the scattered luggage for her suitcase and her handbag. "If I'm going to die, I mean to die in Munich with my husband and my children." She was brisk, and not the least hysterical. "I shall go outside and speak to their Commandant. And when I get home I shall write a great many letters of complaint."

On the very tail of the word "complaint", she pushed aside the man at the window, threw the door of the carriage open and stepped down onto the cinders.

Maybe she took the step and maybe she did not. She did raise her arm and call out: "Please be good enough to advise your officers that. . ." And Mauberley thought it was the most "English" thing he had ever heard a German say. But she failed to complete it. She was cut in half by a burst of automatic rifle fire from about twelve feet away. She fell without a sound except a rather startling sigh which emerged from her wounds.

The young man reached out carefully and swung the door back in towards the train.

They waited.

All the soldiers who were travelling out in the open on the tops of the cars were told to dismount and stand in single file along the rows of coaches and wagons-lit. The civilians on the roofs were told to lie down flat and cover their heads.

The searchlight, now augmented with one or two others as darkness fell completely, played along the length of track. The sounds of little bursts of steam from the air brakes mingled with the sounds of shuffling feet on the cinders and the muted voices of the soldiers climbing down.

Mauberley and his compartment companions huddled as far away from the door and windows as they could get—but they could not move out into the corridor, since it was blocked with scores of other passengers crouching below the glass partitions.

They could see, quite distinctly, the tops of the soldiers' heads beyond the windows, some of the soldiers pulling off their woollen caps, others unwinding their scarves, throwing down their helmets; none of them turning away from the lights. It was clear that all of them were waiting to be shot.

"Why must we sit here and let this happen?" someone asked.

But no one answered.

"Why must we sit here. . .?"

Rising, the voice was suddenly drowned in burst after burst of machine-gun fire.

All the bare, blond heads beyond the windows banged against the glass and fell away from sight.

Smears—frozen instantaneously—took their place.

Now the cantankerous man who had said they were all traitors said in the same cantankerous way; "they are going to kill us all." As if it was merely an act of insolence.

"Everyone out! Everyone out!" a voice began to call from the dark. "Down! Down! All you people on top get down! Everyone out of the carriages! Out!"

The doglike voices and the deadly words had been heard for years by every passenger aboard the train. But only in their dreams of Jews and their nightmares of the future. The S.S. always came in the dark for others. Now, they were splitting open the dark, reaching in through the dreams for the dreamers. Down. Out. Down. Out. It was terrible.

No one could tell how many machine-guns might be waiting in the night beyond the searchlights. No one could tell how many S.S. troops were there or whether, as rumour was always saying, someone insane was in charge of them. No one could tell if the children amongst the passengers would be killed, or the women, or the men in civilian dress or just the soldiers. One old woman lay outside the car already, underneath the bodies of the first contingent to die.

In the corridor the man whose shovel had made so many marks against the glass spoke up and said, "I am armed. There must be others who are armed. Why don't we open fire. . .?"

"No. Don't," a woman said. "Please. If you do. . ." her voice trailed off. "Please."

"EVERYONE OUT!" (Bang, bang, bang on the doors.) "EVERYONE OUT AND EVERYONE DOWN!"

No one could look at anyone else. Some looked away. Some closed their eyes. Some did the most extraordinary things. One woman, rising, straightened her skirts and dusted her knees. A man took out his watch and held it up to his ear. Another blew his nose and said; "excuse me." Mauberley also heard, distinctly; "well—have you got everything?" and turned to see two women sorting baggage.

Someone opened the door.

The bodies of all the blond soldiers lay directly in their path, like stepping stones, but a man got down and helped the women out and over the corpses—everyone lost and having to shield their eyes from the sweeping lights. Even the children were silent.

Mauberley stepped back.

He had a vague awareness he was in the way—or something. Not letting go of the attaché case or the cardboard valise was causing a problem for the others, and instead of moving forward through the door, he was crowding back into the corner, holding his luggage over the seat and letting the others pass like a man whose floor has not yet been called on an elevator ride.

Meanwhile, there were hundreds lining up in the floodlights. People were scurrying overhead on the top of the car and still there were the cries, outside, of "OUT! OUT! OUT! DOWN! DOWN! DOWN!" In the waters of the dark, the sharks of the S.S. had begun to swim in Requiem packs.

In about ten minutes—maybe less—the carriages were almost empty.

Mauberley stepped around the glass and into the corridor.

He was not alone. Ten, maybe fifteen, others were crouching down below the lights. Mauberley got down with them.

Nobody spoke.

Mauberley kept the valise and the attaché case between his knees.

Beyond the train, there was firing. Someone had tried to escape.

Then silence.

Mauberley looked along the corridor—left, then right. Others were doing the same, though still without a word. The one small chance for freedom lay at either end of the car where doors led out onto a brakeman's platform from which a person might leap down into the darkness on the northern side of the train.

All of the ten or fifteen people crouching in the corridor must have been thinking, just as Mauberley was: *let someone else go first—and then we'll know if it's safe;* for no one moved a muscle. Mauberley's knees and thighs, spread wide to protect his luggage, were killing him.

"Señor Mauberley. . .?"

He turned towards his name.

The searchlight flashed along the coach and threw down bright reflections from the glass, which lit both Mauberley and the woman—now alarmingly close to him. Striking distance. Less.

He could see the black, black hair; the moleskin coat; the undersea complexion and the eyes. And then the light had passed and there was nothing but a shadow, crouching at his elbow. *Señor Mauberley. . .Spanish. . . .*And then he knew precisely who she was and why she had come for him.

Mauberley rose and ran—or began to run—the valise and attaché case almost at once preventing him by banging with a sickening reverberation into the face of the soldier with the spade.

And then, in a spate of confusions, there was a bright new

light directly in his eyes; a rifle butting through the glass; a banging of doors and shots. One and then another body fell beneath his feet. A great, grey soldier with a submachine-gun raised his arms above his head and shouted. Something struck—a knife?—at Mauberley's neck and there were hands around his ankles, trying to pull him down amongst the arms and legs and faces jerking and kicking underneath him.

All that Mauberley knew was that he ran through all of this, while his wrists were battered back and forth against the walls of glass by the weight of his attaché case and the valise. And the adrenalin shot so sharply through him that it burned and make him sick. But, at last, there was air and space and darkness through which he ran until the only thing he heard was his breathing and the train was a quarter mile—a half mile behind him, shining in the searchlights like a toy.

He was in a place with trees.

He vomited.

The taste of onions filled his mouth.

He washed his face and mouth with snow. Even though he had no memory of falling down, he realized now that his knees and the palms of his hands were pitted with cinders and he could feel the cold, clean chill of the wound on his neck—the sort of wound a razor makes, a pair of parted lips from which the blood has withdrawn in shock. Mauberley packed it with ice in order to kill the pain.

Looking back, the scene from which he had fled seemed strangely distant: a miniature diorama, the figures barely visible. Just as the young civilian had said, there was a second train. It was four coaches long and the locomotive, bulky and armour-plated, sat behind a barrier of logs and rails with two great flags streaming in the rush of steam and light. Nothing could be seen of the markings or the colours—just the bright, pale cloth against the dark. But the ten cars of the train on which he had made his escape from Mantua were lit so brightly by the searchlights they were almost silver.

Along the road, which ran about a hundred yards or less from the track, he could see a neatly laid-out convoy of trucks from which the searchlights shone, and each of the trucks was reeling in a pale grey line of people. All that he saw seemed part of a clockwork display.

His "place with trees" was in fact a wood of some dimension. Not that he could tell this in the dark, but he could sense there was no habitation near him. Nothing that gave off warmth or welcome, though the shelter of the trees was welcome enough.

It began to snow.

Mauberley ached all over. Ached and was hungry.

Maybe it would snow enough to hide his tracks. At any rate, he had to stop and rest. He stumbled to the nearest congregation of pines and a few minutes later drew their branches down around a scooped-out sleeping place.

Once, he was wakened in the night—his body made of boards—and heard the sound of what appeared to be a battle over by the trains, and later still, his sleep unregained for an hour or more, he saw the sky light up with the aura of exploding engines. Last thing of all, the sound of one lone truck escaping up the road that ran past the trees, and then the deep and muffled silence of the snow that fell like a dream of snow—with flakes the size of coins straight down out of clouds so low they tangled with the pines.

In the morning there were shrouds of mist, like remnants hung from the branches. Mauberley had come to the foothills of the mountains and surely, now, he was safe. Unless the trees were enemies.

Ezra Pound, in one of his regular broadcasts over the Fascist network, had taken special aim at President Roosevelt as one of those "who think you can get through hell in a hurry." And all through what remained of Mauberley's journey— walking; lying flat on the tops of trains; crawling in and out of the backs of trucks; wading through water one day, snow the next—Mauberley thought of these words and was grimly amused. The image was so clear in his mind of Ezra, hunched and glowering above his microphone, fingering his pages like the pages of a menu—*à la carte or table d'hôte: what shall I feed you today—all you out there who are starving for my wisdom?* And sometimes he ladled it with silver spoons and other times he mounded it, gross, on forks; and sometimes, like an animal that feeds its young by force, he chewed it up and spat it out across the airwaves: all his warnings—panaceas—blasts—pronouncements. . .

Well.

If Mauberley could speak with Ezra now, he would tell him categorically; *you cannot get through hell at all.*

Every inch of the way—from the woods at Verona to the forest at Merano—Mauberley sensed he was being followed by the woman in the moleskin coat.

He knew of course what she wanted. It was the contents of the cardboard valise and the attaché case—the only thing of value he possessed: his notebooks, his years and years of jottings and annotations.

Whatever else he was, Hugh Selwyn Mauberley was a compulsive witness. In all his life he had never been able to refrain from setting things down on paper, recording the lives of those around him, moment by moment—every word and every gesture instantly frozen in his private cipher. To those who knew of their existence, Mauberley's notebooks were feared like a morgue where the dead are kept on ice— with all their incriminating wounds intact. Not that it would matter greatly if the men and women lying there were name- less. But Mauberley's friends were anything but anonymous. All his testimony had been drawn from years of privileged relationships with people whose lives could now be ruined— or ended—by the information contained in his notebooks.

The woman in the moleskin coat wanted not only to kill him; she wanted to kill his words as well.

But in whose behalf? Whose creature was she? Was she von Ribbentrop's? Or Schellenberg's?. . .Or worse. . .

When Mauberley had left Rapallo, he had presumed his route would lie through the Brenner Pass. But now, within striking distance of the Brenner, he realized that was the last way he should go. To begin with, it would be clogged with the retreating army. And it would be the route to safety expected of him.

The unexpected route to safety would be to turn where he was, strike out across the foothills, and tackle the face of the mountain.

The Grand Elysium Hotel stands over UnterBalkonberg in the Tyrol looking down eight hundred feet into the emerald waters of the Ötztalsee. Ten thousand feet below it on the other side is the valley of the Adige winding off towards the Gulf of Venice. To the east, the Brenner Pass; westward, the mountains standing in the way of Switzerland. Balkonberg itself is known as the southern *esplanade* of Austria, rising fourteen thousand feet above the floor of Italy. The old hotel provides a spectacular vantage point from which to view these distances and, before the war, its Rhenish turrets and its Gothic towers, its terraces and palisades had been the subjects of a million photographs, magazine covers, travel brochures and even of a postage stamp. Isadora Duncan, Greta Garbo, Somerset Maugham and Richard Strauss had all come up the famous tiers of marble stairs, crossing the lobbies to sign the registry and collect their keys. Edward VIII and Mrs Simpson had danced incognito in the Winter Garden. It had been in those days that Mauberley had known the hotel first. He had been there twenty times. Or more. He could not remember. What he could remember was the place; the scent of its trees; the sound of its waterfalls; its walls of windows blazing in the sun; the terraces with chairs and tables; the great, winding drive by which one normally arrived to be greeted by Herr Kachelmayer, the concièrge, who made a point of greeting everyone. And by the time you were half way up the steps beneath the portico, Herr Kachelmayer had told you who among your friends was in residence and who among your enemies. . . .

Now at the foot of Austria, all Mauberley could see before him was the great stone face of the Balkonberg, fogged and clouded, mellowed in the foreground with trees. This was the climb he must make.

It snowed. And underneath the snow there was mud. Mauberley's skin had not been dry in days. And behind him was the woman, waiting to pull him down—with her razor in her pocket. And he could not climb. He could not even think of climbing. For one thing, the cardboard valise was already beginning to disintegrate and turn to mush and the metal corners of the attaché case had become his enemies. And even if he could climb, even if he got there, nothing would await him but the old hotel itself. Just a vacant, frozen star—with private room and bath.

But if I destroyed the notebooks now, he thought, I could bring the whole pursuit to a close. I could climb out of Italy— free. I would be left with nothing then but my mind. And no one can have my mind. She can't cut it out and put it in a bag and carry it away. She can't make it speak or spill its contents. Not if I spill the contents first—and burn them.

So he waited in the snow beneath the trees, feeling like an animal deserted by its herd, left ailing for the wolves to find.

But no wolves came and well after nightfall he went back out towards the nearest road where he stole some petrol from a German army truck that had sunk to its axles in yesterday's mud. Its driver sat behind the wheel, iced over in the moonlight, dead of a heart attack brought on by rage. It was this man's helmet Mauberley used to carry the petrol back to his hiding place amongst the trees.

Quickly he dumped the notebooks into a hollow he had made in the snow. Mostly it was the backs of the books he saw, but he saw some pages, too—imagining their shorthand scrawl, the cipher he had devised of signs and symbols and his own private way of telling the date. He closed his eyes and fell to his knees and poured the petrol over the books.

One swift gesture would do it.

Matches.

There were two.

He fumbled the first and watched it fizzle in the snow.

He removed the cotton gloves that Dorothy had given him

24

and rolled them carefully—slowly—into a ball and stuffed them into his pocket.

Then he prayed. And struck the second match.

When it caught, he watched it burning for an instant before he threw it down amongst the pages.

Nothing.

And then a "pop" and a great, green flame shot up against the palms of his hands and his hair was on fire.

Mauberley rocked back onto his heels and fell away towards one side. His mind was burning: twenty-five years—a quarter century of private thought. Suddenly he flung himself—like a sack of earth—onto the flames.

For half an hour he lost all consciousness—and when he woke there was darkness everywhere and not a trace of fire. Beneath him, once he had dug down through the numbness of his hands, he could feel whole pages at his fingerends and the bulk of volumes that seemed to be either complete or partially so. He drew himself up and sat with his feet in the ashes and knew both he and the books—some part of each—had survived.

He sat that way all night.

The next day—and the next—he climbed into Austria, sleeping one night on the mountain, and made his way successfully into the courtyard of the Grand Elysium Hotel, where he found the concièrge, Kachelmayer, sitting in a blanket in the sun.

"Is it you, Herr Kachelmayer?" said Mauberley, setting down his cases on the ice, but unable to uncurl his fingers.

"Yes, but of course it is me," said Herr Kachelmayer, rising, clutching the blanket. "Just as I trust that is you, Herr Mauberley."

It was.

Mauberley noticed a certain nervousness in Kachelmayer. He also noticed a certain amount of "scurrying" off in the background, whether of people or of dogs he was not quite able to tell.

"You have come from the *mountain* side," said Kachelmayer. "You have come without a motorcar. . . .You have come without your chauffeur, your friends. . ." Kachelmayer had what is known as an eye for the obvious. "Are you all right?"

Mauberley said; "is there any chance we might go in? I have been in the cold a very long time."

Herr Kachelmayer was hesitant.

"The Hotel Elysium," he said, "is closed for the season."

"Nonsense, Herr Kachelmayer." Mauberley was already stooping, picking up his cases with his fingers already shaped to hold them. "I want a suite of rooms—as always—on the second floor." He began to cross the courtyard, making for the well-remembered steps, the great glass doors, praying that Kachelmayer would follow him.

He did.

"But Mister Mauberley—Herr Mauberley—sir—"

Babble babble babble.

In the end, they struck the bargain Mauberley had all along intended. He would pay to live almost alone in the great hotel, and Kachelmayer would have the five thousand Reichsmark Mauberley had set aside for just that purpose.

There were bonuses as well. It seemed that Kachelmayer had been keeping a store of the best of his wines and brandies and Schnapps, together with a hoarding of everyday foods such as eggs and milk and sausage, even some vegetables, in the expectation and fervent desire that someone of rank— a colonel, or a general—might turn up on his doorstep wanting somewhere to rest or even, God forbid, to hide. Many troops had already been withdrawn through the valleys but the Hotel Elysium was out of the way of the retreating army and it would take a personage of rank to know of its existence. . .a personage of wealth.

Mauberley thought of a fat Uriah Heep as he watched Herr Kachelmayer's performance in the middle of the grand lobby. The hands did not even pause to change direction once they had started their twisting and turning: round and round and round. He might as well have spent the energy in kneading bread or wringing out sheets as waste it on Mauberley's ego. The one thing he did not ask—and the one thing he should have asked, of course—was how it was that Mauberley could be in Austria. . .the American writer. . .the great American expatriate. . .the great American. . .before the *Americans* had arrived. But perhaps he did not want to ask. The answer might retard the advance of the five thousand Reichsmark.

Mauberley heard, once again, the strangely disconcerting noise that sounded like a dog—or, rather, like a pack of dogs.

"Are we alone, Herr Kachelmayer?"

"But of course. . . ."

The noises were repeated; something scurrying out of sight; something falling with an awful series of bumps like a sack of potatoes emptying its contents down a staircase.

Herr Kachelmayer shrugged and smiled.

"*Die Ratten. . .*"

"Rather loud rats, aren't they?"

"*Ja.*"

A small, white face appeared very close to the floor near the edge of the registration desk.

"And rather large," said Mauberley.

Kachelmayer made a gesture with his arm—"*whisht, whisht,*" he said. And a child aged four or five, perhaps a girl, made a dash across the marble towards the kitchens.

"How many are there?" said Mauberley. "Please, don't tell another lie. I haven't the patience or the time."

"There are four, Herr Mauberley."

"Four. . . .And who are they?"

"My children."

"Aside from that, are we alone?"

"There is my wife," Herr Kachelmayer said, apologetically.

Kachelmayer turned and went across to the desk—rather too quickly, Mauberley thought—and rummaged for some keys.

"You may have the suite you have always occupied. Third door down on the left. It will take some time to open the pipes and restore the water service to the second floor. Perhaps by this evening. . .As for light: you must draw the curtains just in case. . .and. . ."

"Food."

"Yes, at once."

"And drink. I will have some brandy and some wine as well. . . ."

Mauberley started over towards the lift, as if by habit. But when he saw its doors with their metal designs and the bars enclosing the shaft, he decided to walk. He must beware of cages.

He began to climb the stairs.

"Herr Mauberley. . .?"

"Yes?"

Herr Kachelmayer was standing in his blanket, right in the middle of the empty lobby, looking up at him. Smiling.

"It is so good to have you come back," he said.

"Thankyou, Herr Kachelmayer. Thankyou. It is good to be here."

After he had turned the key in the lock and had opened the door, Mauberley put his arm across his face and closed his eyes—more afraid of seeing who might kill him than of being killed.

But there was no one. Of course, there was no one. The fear was habit.

The salon was empty. The windows had not been opened for weeks. The air was as dry as a biscuit tin. The carpets smelled of civilized dust and the chairs and sofas, though covered with sheets, had all been arranged for conversation—not confrontation. In the bathroom, one of the gigantic taps was already banging—dripping real water into which Mauberley dipped a finger, licking it like someone finding honey in the bottom of a cup; and in the bedroom was a bed—under which he could hide when the walls began to fall.

It was heaven.

Later, after about an hour, Kachelmayer appeared himself with a smallish blond boy in tow who carried a tray.

The tray was set on a table and the sheets removed from the chairs and sofas.

Kachelmayer handed the boy some towels and a bar of

soap—already used, but nonetheless a bar of soap. He waved the boy away towards the bathroom, watching him go: a very well-made boy, if rather thin, of maybe twelve or thirteen years. His hair was almost white, it was so very blond.

Once the boy had gone, Herr Kachelmayer stood for a moment in the alcove of windows, staring at the marvellous view as if he had invented it himself. Then he turned to Mauberley and beamed.

"Fifteen marks a day—the boy."

Mauberley was more amused than affronted.

"Are you selling me your son, Herr Kachelmayer?"

Kachelmayer fumbled around for a proper response, Mauberley watching fascinated all the while.

Finally, Kachelmayer made his choice.

"It is true he is not my son."

"I see."

"Very clean, this boy; a most useful servant. He will bring your food; he will run your errands; he. . ."

"And how many of the fifteen marks a day will he see, this boy who is not your son?"

Herr Kachelmayer shrugged. "Maybe five."

Mauberley just stared at the concièrge, in order to shame him. But this was impossible.

"He must be fed," said Kachelmayer. "And I must feed him. And—if he is to be your servant—then he will require an extra ration. Fifteen marks. Yes—or no."

The boy himself was standing, now, in the doorway to the bathroom watching and listening. His face was completely without expression.

Mauberley thought of the others in the cellar: die Ratten. This boy was so very pale, so very blond he was almost an albino. So he christened him die weisse Ratte. Later he would discover the boy's real name was Hugo.

Mauberley nodded at the boy and said he should go along with Herr Kachelmayer. "I will ring when I want you," he said. "Do the bells still work, Herr Kachelmayer?"

Kachelmayer shrugged.

"Will they work for another five marks a day?"

"But of course."

Kachelmayer pushed the boy from the room.

"Now tell me," he said to Mauberley, every trace of the unctuous man he had been but a second before having disappeared, "how much trouble are you in?"

Mauberley thought about it: not the trouble, merely what to say. Then he said, "I am in every kind of trouble you can think of. On the other hand—" he looked Herr Kachelmayer straight in the eye "—I am not in any trouble at all that you are not in, now that I am a guest in your hotel."

Kachelmayer swallowed.

"Have you been followed?"

"Aren't we all?"

Kachelmayer drew his blanket around him.

"How long will you be with us."

"Until it is over."

Kachelmayer nodded. "The war."

Mauberley looked away. "No. Not the war, Herr Kachelmayer."

Kachelmayer regarded the attaché case and the cardboard valise with a new kind of interest. Perhaps an arsenal. . .

He said no more, and went away afraid.

Mauberley looked across the room at the tray of food. An egg. Three carrots. Cheese. A piece of bread and a bowl of cabbage soup. On plates. With a napkin. Silver utensils and a bottle of *Montrechat*.

He burst into tears.

Later in the bathroom, he turned on the taps and picked up the bar of soap and held it to his nostrils. It smelled of something dark and warm, like moss. Mauberley closed his eyes and drew in the scent as deep as he could make it go, unable to believe he was standing in a bathroom—safe— with a bar of soap in his hand. Opening his eyes, the first thing he saw was all the bright towels hung up along the wall, three of them suspended from a silver rail. Dazzling. On the floor the tiles had been set in an intricate design by hand and he wondered when it could have been that people had the time to labour over something casual as this—a floor of blue and white octagons laid out like waves for some transient Aphrodite to stand on.

After the first few days of paranoiac seclusion, during which he slept with the attaché case and cardboard valise in pillowslips beside him in the bed, Mauberley ventured into the hallways not quite certain he was the only ghost that haunted them. Every sound and every smell evoked both fear and sadness. Every door along this corridor had opened to him, once, revealing friends and laughter; cocktails and evening dress; orange juice and tennis whites; mulled wine and Iceland sweaters. From his own room he could see the terrace down below with its low stone wall. Now these were only summer memories on the Alpine edge of his mind: Isabella, with her pale red hair swept back and her furs laid up against her cheek and her hand making shade against the sun; both of them smiling, staring off through the valleys towards the city where they had met—the only city in the world whose name could still make Mauberley's senses quicken. Venice. The distance here, in his mind, was indefinable; all the horizons hidden in the haze of river mists and brilliant rains that never fell.

His suite of rooms had always been the same: third door on the left of the second floor—and across the hall might sometimes be the Allenbys or the Hemingways and Shirers, or Willy Maugham with his drunken Gerald. The Hemingways and Shirers were mostly winter visitors; the Allenbys and Maugham exclusively *Sonnen und Sommerkind*, basking on their balconies, feeding on salads and marching out in boots too large for English feet to struggle up the mountainside on paths that had been cut by goats. It had always been a laughing time and the talk was always gossip, never work and never, never politics—the politics being audible enough in the faces of the German and Italian tourists and the marked proliferation of the uniforms from year to year. But the atmosphere was mostly one of slightly giddy laughter: the joy of high altitudes, brought on by lack of oxygen and the presence of the most exciting and talked about people in the world. The richest woman in the world, for instance, Marielle de Pencier, had a penchant for the northern prospect and would book the whole of the "Austrian" side of the hotel for two weeks every June and install the most outrageous people in its rooms and suites: circus performers dangling from the terraces above the Ötztalsee; midgets and dwarfs sliding down bannisters; a great detective, once, who organized a game of "murder" involving all the guests; and another year, a pair of nude adagio dancers dipped from head to toe in gold who collapsed at the end of their performance due to the fact their skin could not breathe and one of them nearly died. All this besides the fact that Marielle de Pencier brought along her lover and his lover and his lover's "friend" so all night long there was a scuttling in the halls and the pipsqueak scurrying of midgets and dwarfs and of monkeys on chains. And, once, Greta Garbo took up residence next to Mauberley and Mauberley—shameless— listened to the walls, though all he heard was hours and hours of coughing and a telephone that rang and rang until Garbo answered it and all she said was; "no" and hung it up.

Now, there was nothing but the wind that whimpered for admittance at the doors and billowed under the carpets making a patterned sea to walk on, while the chandeliers called from overhead in muffled voices like the echoes of the midgets and the dwarfs long dead. And Mauberley would take up candlesticks provided by Herr Kachelmayer and wander out amongst the shadows—not quite brave enough at first to knock upon the doors and certainly not brave enough to open them. He stood, one night, emboldened by his wine and brandy, daring the staircase into the lobbies, but something real was there, *eine Ratte* maybe, so he turned again and locked himself inside his rooms. But in the end he could not bear the absence of his friends and went to seek them in their rooms. Fortified with a five-point candelabra, he drew his fingernail across the surface of Isabella's door and turned the handle, pushing it open.

The room he entered was the salon, furnished with remembered chairs, a littered desk, some tables and a Recamier

couch. The carpets were rolled against the furthest walls
and the drapes had all been stripped away from the windows. Everything smelled of slightly perfumed dust and the
frost on the panes had the look of Venetian lace, all rucked
and torn in places by the breath of birds that had been
trapped inside the room and lay along the windowsills like
stones. And there was a gramophone.

Mauberley walked across the floor on tiptoe, fearful the
gramophone would disappear before he reached it. On the
table, close beside it, was a pile of records, some of which
were broken, most of which were not: Schubert, Mahler,
Brahms and Strauss—a Viennese concert. Not that he dared
to play them: but he stood and stared and touched them
with his fingers—just the labels—running his mind around
and around the grooves until the music rose up like a hand
and pushed him into a chair. But the chair did not restrain
him and he left it several times on journeys to the past where
he lounged with his father on the roof of the Arlington Hotel
in Boston, waded with Ezra in the pond at Rapallo and
danced with his mother in the corridors of her asylum at
Bellevue.

That night Mauberley got so drunk he fell asleep on the
Recamier couch—almost setting fire to the hotel because he
forgot in his drunkenness to blow out the candles. When he
woke in the morning there was a large red welt where the
wax had scalded the back of his hand.

But he was not alone. *Die weisse Ratte* was asleep across
the room on the rolled-up carpets, lying under the brocade
drapes. After Mauberley had awakened him by reaching out
and knocking over his empty bottle, the boy said; "you were
making noises in your sleep."

"Oh?" said Mauberley—wary. "What sort of noises?"

"Music," said *die weisse Ratte*. "Waltzing." He smiled.

"I found these records," Mauberley said. "I wonder whose
they can be."

"No one's," said the boy. "I do not know." A lie—and
Mauberley could see the lie quite plainly written in the pale
blue eyes with their pink, unhealthy rims.

Die weisse Ratte sat up frozen on the mound of carpet,

drawing the brocade curtains over his head and shoulders.

"My mother," Mauberley told him, thinking he just might draw a confession from the boy, "was a musician; very fond of music such as this. She was a pianist, you know. I spent my childhood—all my childhood—listening to her play."

Die weisse Ratte shuffled his feet and edged along the carpets, seeking a softer place to sit. But was silent.

Mauberley fished in his tatters, fumbling with his buttoned layers, finally producing money in a folded lump and holding it up for the boy to see.

Die weisse Ratte stared at the money like a starving child at loaves of bread spread out in buttered slices on a plate.

Mauberley knew what he had to say, but had never uttered such words before.

"I need a friend," he said. "I mean someone who will help me."

Now, *die weisse Ratte* smiled. *Friend* was the word he had waited for. *Friend* would be certain to produce money from Herr Mauberley's mitt. *Friend*, in *die weisse Ratte's* whole, and only, concept of the word, was just a synonym for cash-and-favour. Not that he knew any better, for in all his life, he had never had a friend who had not crossed his palm in order to gain his favours. Now Herr Mauberley was opening up his mittens and showing more money than Hugo had ever seen.

Friend.

Die weisse Ratte brightened. Even the pink of his eyes grew more intense.

But Mauberley knew this look too well to be fooled. He smiled. "A friend—in times like these—and if I find one—must be mine alone. He can have no other friends, not even Herr Kachelmayer. Do you understand?"

Hugo began to nod, which brought a certain colour to his cheeks, white on white.

Mauberley needed to know how far his new-found friend would go to play this game. He removed two banknotes from his mitt. "I want a gun," he said. "Can you get me a gun?"

Nothing.

Three banknotes.

The boy stood up. The brocade fell aside. He walked across the room until he stood so close to Mauberley that Mauberley could smell him. Sour—like soup. Then, with a gesture only a child could make and get away with, the boy pinched the money, still held up in Mauberley's hand, and squinted at it. Real; not counterfeit. He took it.

Mauberley watched *die weisse Ratte*, amused and wary. The boy was very bold to stand so close, to take so much proximity for granted. Bold and dangerous—reaching for the bills. They stood so close together, part of their clothing touched. And then the boy undid the buttons of his shirt, exposing for an instant one pale nipple and a flaunting exhibition of his skin so raw that Mauberley wondered what might be going to happen next and how this gesture would end. But when the boy withdrew his hand, it held a small, bright nickel-plated gun of the sort that women carry in their handbags: snub-nosed and cold in spite of its recent resting place. All this seduction was silent: not a word being spoken. Now *die weisse Ratte* said: "it's loaded," and handed the gun to Mauberley.

Mauberley was forced to take a step away. Almost to his surprise the gun went with him. Never had he held a thing so icy cold.

The boy was folding his money.

"Thankyou," said Mauberley, losing all the rest of what he had meant to say in the shock of the gun's so sudden appearance.

Die weisse Ratte started to make his retreat towards the door. "I shall be wanted in the cellars," he said. "I shall be wanted to bring your breakfast. Herr Kachelmayer will be waiting for me. . . ."

"Wanting the news of how I spent the night?" Mauberley's distrust of Kachelmayer was suddenly absolute. "It was him, wasn't it, who sent you here. . .?"

"No," said the boy, who had got as far across the room as the gramophone. "I sent myself."

Their eyes met; shifted; parted.

"You were singing," said the boy.

Mauberley smiled. "And you wanted to hear the music?"

Die weisse Ratte shrugged.

"No one ever sings any more."

"I see."

"I will bring your breakfast," said the boy.

Mauberley nodded and *die weisse Ratte* departed, first unlocking the door—a fact which Mauberley noted, silent, with alarm. All this time, all through the night, they had been locked inside the salon, Hugo holding the key.

Mauberley stood there sweating wine and brandy, listening to his new-found "friend" departing towards the stairs beneath the bags of chandeliers that rattled, like his brain, with gagged and indecipherable warnings.

A generation of children he thought, that carries guns. . . .He had never even seen a gun when he was Hugo's age, unless it was up on the screen at the Bijou or the Nickelodeon. Movie guns and movie killers. Bang. With little puffs of pale white smoke that looked so harmless and innocent. Death at the end of a silent white cloud. And the printed word: *Bang!* With an exclamation point. Which was why, in his solitary games, he'd never made the noise of guns. But always said it: *"Bang!"* Walking home through all those summer Sundays—church in the mornings, movies in the afternoons. Choirboys and cowboys. Anthems and gunfights. Gone.

It had been a very long walk indeed from the Bijou, this time. Mauberley smiled. And what a tale to tell. If I could only tell it, he thought. If there was only time and I could tell it all. Oh well. The journals; the notebooks would have to suffice. Except they were like the title cards of a silent film—without the film itself.

Mauberley noted the brief, white clouds that came from his mouth as he breathed.

"Bang, bang," he said. But without exclamation points. The air was too cold to breathe that deep.

He wandered in his blanket over towards the windows, looking down at a frozen bird whose eyes were mercifully closed and whose claws were withdrawn in a gesture of resignation. Either it had starved to death or broken its neck against the glass.

If I could only tell it all. If there was only time.

He stared through the little hole his breath had made in the frost and he saw it was a frozen, sunny day—quite beautiful.

He put the gun in his pocket and took it—suddenly—out again. Something was wrong. And when he looked inside the chambers, he was shocked. So shocked, he could not breathe at all. The chambers were empty. Every one.

TWO

May, 1945

*Elysium, though it were in the halls
of hell. . .*

Ezra Pound

Mauberley was found by strangers.

"Here's another," said a boy called Annie Oakley. "Dead maybe weeks. . . ." Annie was a private in the U.S. Seventh Army. He was standing in the doorway carefully staring down at the back of Mauberley's neck, mistaking the bruises and emaciation for decay. Annie was very young and the only dead he'd ever seen had been his victims. He was a sharpshooter; toppling Germans out of trees and windows was his specialty. "Don't go near 'm," said the Sergeant, elbowing his way past Annie's pack and entering the room. "He could be dangerous."

Mauberley was leaning forward into a corner not unlike a man at prayer. One arm was crumpled under him and broken: the other twisted back with its hand, palm upward, clutching the silver pencil.

"Looks like he's froze," said Annie Oakley. "Even in spite of all them clothes."

Mauberley was dressed in scarves and other bits of wool, with a blanket pinned at his throat and drawn around his shoulders over his greatcoat. Underneath, he wore a suit with all its pockets ripped away and its lining hanging down in strips. But this could not be seen till later. Now, it was only clear that—indeed—he was "froze". The fires had all gone out and the snow had drifted in across the carpet till it touched his feet. Some of the windows had been blown open in the last assault by storms. Frost had formed on the mirrors. Even the ashes in the bathtub had a kind of crispness to them not to do with fire and the water spout was jetting an icicle the size of someone's arm.

"I'll stay here," said the Sergeant. "You go get Lieutenant Quinn."

Annie Oakley went away disgruntled down the corridor, down the stairs and into the lobby with its marble tiers piled high with gear. He wanted the silver pencil. Now it would go in the Sergeant's collection, not his own. Loot had become increasingly difficult to come by during the latter part of the campaign. Most of the civilians they encountered now were destitute and starving. Every watch and ring and brooch, it seemed, had been bartered away for tins of yellow horsemeat sold by retreating soldiers of the *Wehrmacht*.

The war had gone on longer here than elsewhere in Europe. Innsbruck—fifty kilometers north of the Grand Elysium Hotel—had been the last of the Austrian cities to fall. Four days later, the war had ended. Now there was nothing left in the army's path but hordes of unhoused, unfed refugees fleeing from the Russians who had entered Vienna; the endless parade of barefoot prisoners straggling out of Italy; the mud in the valleys giving way to the ice on the hills and the blizzards in the mountains. And the fear that some new horror like the shock of walking through the gates at Dachau might reach out from underneath the snow to catch a person unaware.

Not that Annie Oakley was afraid. Annie hadn't gone through the gates at Dachau. His job had been to shoot the dogs that had been trained to kill and he'd done that out in the woods, alone. And afterwards he'd made a fire and burned the bodies. Meanwhile, one of his friends had bagged himself a German officer waltzing off with a suitcase full of diamond rings and watches. Not that his friend got to keep them. Still, if Annie Oakley had been there. . .

So Annie's fear was different from his fellows'. Annie's fear was of spending the rest of his military life being sent to shoot the dogs or to find Lieutenant Quinn and of missing out on the silver pencils and the diamond rings.

Left alone, the Sergeant—Rudecki—took no chances.

"Never trust a corpse," he said out aloud, pointing his Browning down at the back of Mauberley's head, watching the hand with the silver pencil. Some of the dead, in Rudecki's experience had been alive while others had been booby-trapped. The handsome silver pencil was a good example of the sort of trap that blew your balls off, shot you in the face or tripped a wire that brought down the ceiling. "Don't touch a thing till Quinn is here," he said—just as if Mauberley could hear him and obey. "Don't touch a fuckin' thing."

Lieutenant Quinn was their demolitions expert. He was efficient and ambitious. His hair was always combed; his breath was always peppermint fresh and the moons always showed on his fingernails. Even when he had dysentery, his underwear was always clean. And he kept a special kit apart from all his other stuff with a bottle of antiseptic inside and a bar of Castile soap. He was even good at his job. It wasn't fair. He looked like Tyrone Power. Still—he was only a lieutenant. No one had bothered to learn his first name.

Coming up the marble stairs with Annie Oakley in tow,

Quinn balanced his fingerends along the rail and said; "this ranks among the great hotels of Europe. Did you know that, Private?"

"No, sir."

"Poor Scott Fitzgerald used to get drunk in the bar down there."

"Good for him, sir. Who was Poor Scott Fitzgerald?"

Quinn—who was walking first—gave the slightest hesitation and made a little sigh. "He wrote," he said, "books."

"I'll remember that," said Annie Oakley, looking back across the lobbies past a pair of glass doors and into the gloom beyond—presumably the bar where Poor Scott Fitzgerald got drunk. Oakley thought how nice it would have been to join him there for a Pilsner. He wondered if there was any chance Poor Scott Fitzgerald would be returning, now the war was over.

"No," said Quinn. "He won't be coming back. He's dead."

Some German sniper got him, maybe.

Arriving at the mezzanine, Lieutenant Quinn could feel the draught and he pushed the tails of his khaki scarf a little deeper down against his chest.

"Now you say there's another body?"

"Yes, sir. Just up here."

"What with those others we found before that makes six or seven. . . ."

"Eight."

"And there wasn't even a battle here. I simply don't understand. . . ."

Up on the second floor, Lieutenant Quinn was puzzled further by what he saw. A long thin drift of snow stretched down the length of the corridor before them. Over their heads, the chandeliers in canvas bags made all the shapes and motions of a torture chamber. Crystal corpses: tinkling bones and swaying shadows. One or two doors stood open, giving off the echoes of the hollow rooms beyond—everything lit with a pale, filtered light that smelled of ash.

"Third door down on the left," said Annie Oakley.

Quinn felt the old familiar twinge of apprehension. *Third door down on the left*, he might be blown to pieces.

"Sergeant Rudecki?"

"Yessir."

"And what have we here?"

"A body, Lieutenant. Maybe booby-trapped."

"I see."

Quinn pressed forward, drawing on his leather gloves. Annie hung back in the doorway. Rudecki, who was loathe to cross the floor in case it got him in the balls, stood off a single step, his Browning automatic rifle still at the ready.

"Watch that silver pencil, sir," said Rudecki.

"Thank you, Sergeant. Don't forget I've done this sort of thing before. It's why I'm here," said Quinn.

"Yessir. I just want to keep you here, that's all. . . ."

"Your concern is very touching—"

Annie Oakley smiled. Rudecki's kiss-ass concern was oh so very touching. Hah! Maybe the silver pencil would blow the fucker's hand off. No one would get the pencil then. Good. And Quinn maimed for life in one of the great hotels of Europe.

Quinn got down on his knees beside the body.

Mauberley's head was turned away into the corner.

"He's starved to death," said Quinn "or had a heart attack. I can't tell." He sniffed. "Funny. There isn't any smell but fire and smoke."

"Could be the devil, then," said Annie Oakley from the doorway; smiling.

"I mean there isn't any smell of death," said Quinn, chagrined and sitting back on his heels.

"I told you. He's been froze. Nothin' froze has a smell."

Logic, thought Quinn, is always in the smallest package. "Private Oakley, please shut up," he said. "I have to listen now."

Quinn leaned out across the body, turning his head from side to side like a doctor listening for the shale-fall of illness in beyond the patient's clothing. Rudecki put his free hand down and gathered his testicles under the protection of his fingers. Oakley, unaware he did it, whistled through his teeth, "Don't Fence Me In."

Mauberley was bent in such a way his right ear touched

the floor. The back of his neck was exposed and twisted. Otherwise, he was a sack of cloth. Quinn made a thorough inspection with his ears and eyes before he laid a hand on anything. Nothing ticking; nothing whirring; no wires leading anywhere. "He's safe. . ."

Gingerly, Quinn made a cup for Mauberley's chin with his gloved right hand. He was afraid—though he maintained his poise and silence—Mauberley's ear or nose or even his head might break away, being frozen. Still he had only seen that once and then the victim was alive. A lad whose ear had come away in his helmet. This was different. This was death. He wanted first to see the face and then to roll the body over onto its back. And cover it.

"Oakley?"

"Yessir?"

"Take his feet. Everything's fine. . .we're just going to turn him. First on his side and then on his back. . . ."

Annie put his rifle down against the doorjamb. Rudecki went even further off across the floor, since now the floor was presumably safe.

"Maybe best to hold him by the shins till we get him on his side," said Quinn, whose hand was still supporting Mauberley's chin. He laid his other hand against the shoulder of the twisted arm that held the silver pencil. Oakley was now on the floor by his side.

"Okay?"

"Okay. . ."

They pushed, very gently—Mauberley "toppling" under the pressure further onto his broken left arm, his back now hard against the wall, his knees drawn up, his toes hooked back: a child, asleep.

Rudecki turned away and was sick.

Oakley got to his feet—but Quinn was unable.

After a moment, Rudecki went out into the corridor and threw up again.

Quinn said, "Go bring Captain Freyberg, will you?"

Annie said; "yessir" but didn't move.

"Tell him there's someone here important. Tell him to come as fast as he can."

"Yessir."

"Don't say a word to anyone else."

"No, sir."

"Quickly, Private. Quickly, damn it."

"Yessir."

Rudecki, in the corridor, covered his vomit with snow and turned away while Annie passed. He was ashamed of what he had done, angered by his weakness.

"Better get back in there, Sarge. Clean up the rest of your mess," said Annie, departing. "I'm to get Freyberg—an' you know what that means. . . ."

Annie sort of bounced as he walked away—like a kid. Where did all that adrenalin come from? Finding corpses? Maybe Rudecki was getting old. The prospect of Captain Freyberg's arrival did not please him, either. It meant the body was dangerous after all. It meant the war, that was over, wasn't over and had just been given one more chance to kill him.

Down in the lobbies, Annie Oakley slung his rifle over his shoulder and made his way across the marble, heading for the courtyard. Freyberg, he knew, was out there tagging the toes of the other dead and making one of his famous lists. Annie turned his collar up, put on his gloves and straightened his helmet. There before him were the great, blank doors that opened into the Kristall Salon. Annie stood, like one in reverence, gazing at all the fallen glass on the floor— conjuring the warmth and music that must have been and the pale gold light and the famous clientele. Maybe Dooley Wilson sitting at the piano; Ingrid Bergman over in the corner smoking a cigarette, with her hat pulled down across one side of her face; Humphrey Bogart standing in the shadows and the music sad and perfect. Annie pulled his gloves on tighter: watching—listening—making movies. "Well—here's lookin' at you, kid," he said. And the music swelled. . . .

Turning away, there was one last vision. The ghost of Poor Scott Fitzgerald shunted along the bar in Annie Oakley's movie, making way for the Corpse of Someone Important to belly up beside him: One Eyed Reilly, blinded with a stick and his brains all pouring down his cheek.

> *Too-ri-oo-ly, too-ri-i-ly*
> *What's the matter with One Eyed Reilly?*

Lieutenant Quinn, still kneeling, wondered what he should do. Propriety and decency demanded Mauberley's face be covered and that thing removed from the eye. But the company commander—Captain Freyberg—would only complain. "Don't touch a thing," he would say. "I want every single clue to be left intact. There are Nazis hiding everywhere, and every one we find and every thing we find may lead us to something or someone more important." Freyberg had spent the latter part of the war, ever since they had crossed the Rhine, looking for something and someone "more important". Yes, it was his job, Quinn thought. Freyberg, being an Intelligence Officer, had to chase a lead if he found one. But he was positively a fanatic when it came to Nazis. Dachau had stunned him and withered his ability to think of anything else. He had given up even the pretence of rationality. He moved alone. He sat alone. He ate alone. He would not even talk about "going home". He was traumatized. "The war isn't over," he would say. "The war is not over here." Freyberg was not going to let it end.

If he smelled a rat outside his jurisdiction, he would even go so far as to commandeer another unit's Intelligence activities, drawing them into his own private sphere on the bold excuse he was some kind of expert. He spent all his time compiling dossiers and setting up a private filing system that required a Section of clerks and a truck to move it about as a part of his personal entourage. Most company commanders only had five or six officers to push around. Somehow Freyberg had acquired two more. But in spite of all this, he was liked and respected. He hardly ever raised his voice. In fact he could barely be heard. His rage was silent and he pursued his obsession like a man collecting butterflies. The only problem was—he had so many nets. Every single flutter was investigated and he demanded first examination rights of anything that was found. And now, in this room, there was cause for yet another examination— yet another dossier. Photographs would have to be taken, new lists begun and nothing touched or moved until it had all been scrutinized and given an accounting.

And why not? Quinn sighed. Certainly, there must have been a madman here. The means of achieving this death were appalling. Even a bullet through the eye would have been saner than this. . . .No wonder Rudecki had been ill.

Quinn said a prayer for Mauberley, crossed himself and got to his feet. He decided that, under the circumstances, he could allow himself one cigarette. He removed his gloves in order not to fumble the package and the striking of the match. His hands were not allowed to shake: not ever. Nothing must ever be dropped, nothing knocked over. Nothing must fall. It was a rule.

He selected a Philip Morris and wetted his lips so the paper wouldn't stick. He struck the match and lit up, rounding the gesture by extinguishing the flame with his first exhalation. Perfect. If only someone had seen.

On the other hand, the match. Where does one put a burned-out match in an empty room?

"Lieutenant?"

Quinn put the match in his upstage pocket.

Sergeant Rudecki was bulging in the doorway.

"Sorry I was sick," he said. "I'll clean it up."

Quinn turned away. He was not unfond of Rudecki, but there were moments when his ingratiating tone, his incongruous thoughtfulness got on his nerves. As if a hippopotamus were asking pardon for stepping on your foot.

"Any sign of Private Oakley or Captain Freyberg?"

"No, sir."

Rudecki set to work—the work made easy by the fact that everything had frozen. He kept his back to Mauberley.

"What do you think happened here, Lieutenant? Who was this guy? You said he was important."

"He was important. And still is." Quinn gave the corner a glance. "His name was Hugh Selwyn Mauberley—and, we are told, he was a traitor."

"Who to?"

"To us."

"But you don't believe it?"

"No."

Rudecki went over to the window and threw out part of the mess like a flapjack off the end of his bayonet.

"What makes people say he was a traitor, then?"

"The company he kept."

"Like who?"

"Like Ribbentrop and Mussolini. . ."

"Go on! This tramp?"

"What tramp?"

"Well—look at the way he's dressed, for Chrissake."

"He wasn't always dressed like that."

"You talk like you knew him."

"No. But I read every word he ever wrote. And his picture was always in the papers." Quinn felt sad as he remembered the pictures of Mauberley smiling with his friends on terraces; strolling over summer lawns; lounging in a deckchair on the Lido; waving from the entrance to the Hotel Meurice. . . .

"What'd he write, then? I never heard of him?"

"*Stone Dogs. Crowd Invisible*. . ."

"Oh yeah. *Stone Dogs* they made a movie. Bette Davis."

"Well. There you are, then." Fame.

"Jeez. A famous writer." Rudecki almost made the mistake of turning around to look, now that he knew the corpse was a true celebrity. "What's his name again?"

"Mauberley," said Captain Freyberg.

He was standing in the doorway; six feet plus and stooped at the shoulders. How long had he been there?

Rudecki and Quinn both shot to attention, Rudecki's bayonet rattling to the floor.

"Stand easy," said Freyberg.

Quinn went over to the window and flipped his cigarette out.

"Well," said Freyberg, barely audible, squinting into the corner. "So this is where the son of a bitch was hiding."

Twenty minutes later Quinn was standing back against the furthest wall he could find.

Freyberg was checking out the bathroom and Quinn could see his lanky shadow passing back and forth across the tiles.

Rudecki had been dismissed. Oakley had not yet reappeared.

The light was shifting. Late afternoon was approaching. Quinn's whole mind was on the ordeal of what would now take place as Freyberg began to poke and pry and dig.

Mauberley was dead in a corner; murdered; wearing rags. And surely this was sad—unjust—no matter what he'd done; so long as you considered who he was. Though doubtless Captain Freyberg would not agree. Freyberg never spoke of justice. *Justice* was civilized, so how could you speak of justice in the context of Dachau? All that remained for Freyberg was vengeance. After vengeance, maybe—just maybe—justice could be reinstated. Freyberg could speak for hours about this—never once raising his voice—and his arguments were lucid and persuasive. Not that he was eloquent. "How the hell can eloquence come into it?" he would say. But he was articulate; blunt and unwavering. Quinn had no argument with Freyberg there. His fear of Freyberg lay entirely in the fact there was no way in past the Captain's defences. Every route to Freyberg's reason—and reasonableness—was mined, and beyond the mines, there was the barricade of Dachau. And Freyberg stood in the cloisters there and would not—for anyone—come out to parley or to listen. He was deaf.

Quinn, too, had suffered—as every soldier had—the trauma of being confronted by the horror of what the Nazis had done in Europe. No one could escape it who was there to see it. But Quinn's sense of shock had not left him. Quinn could still look around him and wonder how these things had been accomplished by the race of which he was a part. All his life in the army since his induction after Pearl Harbor, Quinn had been deeply suspicious of the propaganda machine into which he was thrown with all his fellow soldiers. "We" and "they" were words about which he was paranoid. So when Quinn thought of Hugh Selwyn Mauberley, it wasn't good enough simply to say "he was one of them". It didn't help Quinn understand how Mauberley, whose greatest gift had been an emphatic belief in the value of imagination, could have been so misguided as to join with people whose whole ambition was to render the race incapable of thinking. . . .

Misguided.

That was the word Quinn chose to use for Mauberley. Not traitor. "Traitors" could only be defined in a court of law. And here the only court was Freyberg's roped-off arena into which he was determined he would herd the first and the last of the Nazis—and all the others in between.

Quinn looked over into the corner, Mauberley staring back at him, one-eyed and grotesque. The assailant, it seemed, had been rage itself.

In the bathroom, Freyberg sneezed and blew his nose and coughed. With his handkerchief in hand, he came and stood in the doorway, dabbing at his nostrils.

"Going to want this room roped off," he said. "No one's to go in this bathroom, either."

Yes. The Arena.

"You hear me, Quinn?"

"Yes, sir."

"I'll want a picket. Top of the stairs will do. And I don't want anyone to come in here without an order. Understood?"

"Yes, sir."

Freyberg turned and looked at the body.

"H.S. Mauberley. Well, well, well. . ."

"Yes, sir."

Freyberg blew his nose again and put away the handkerchief, fumbling it into his pocket amongst his lists, his paper tags with strings, his candy-bar wrappers and his extra pair of gloves. The most appalling example of dress that Quinn had ever seen in an officer's uniform.

Quinn made a sigh; unintentional.

Freyberg caught it and smiled—misunderstanding, perhaps.

"This is quite a *coup*, of course," he said. "Our finding Mauberley. There was some concern he might have escaped."

"Surely there's nothing he did to warrant so much concern."

"You think not?" Freyberg's voice was as icy as the room in which they stood.

"No, sir," said Quinn. "And I think it only fair to tell you, Captain Freyberg, I do not agree with you about this man. He was not a son of a bitch and not a traitor."

Quinn was somewhat alarmed to discover he was trembling.

"You're saying you admired his writing?" said Freyberg.

"Yes, sir. In part."

"And what else?"

"Well—look at what they've done to him, sir. Jesus Christ. Look what someone's *done*."

"Yes. I can see what they've done."

"Well. . .?"

"Well what?"

Quinn looked over at Mauberley. "It seems to me," he said, "if we're going to be *concerned*, we should worry about finding whoever killed him. I mean—that is not the work of someone sane."

Freyberg's expression did not even alter. "And you feel you're exclusively qualified, do you, Quinn, to point out for those of us not in the know, what is sane and what is not? By way of killings, I mean."

"I didn't say that, sir."

"Oh. Then you mean you feel you're qualified to tell us *who* is sane and *who* is not. Have I got it right yet?"

Quinn coughed.

"If I may be permitted to speak, sir. . ."

"Of course."

Quinn said. "I think the implications of your question are extremely dangerous." He looked over sideways at the Captain. "It's not that I'm personally affronted," he said. "It's just. . .You're saying that—somehow—killing Mister Mauberley is understandable, and the method excusable. And I think you're wrong."

Freyberg turned away.

"Well. I'm sorry you think so," he said. "I really am very

sorry." He fished around for his extra pair of gloves and put them on; a woollen pair over the leather pair already being worn. "I guess the problem is," he said—not turning, not looking—"you think of insanity as being the exclusive property of madmen." He turned. "*Which it ain't*," he said. And smiled.

It was then that Sergeant Rudecki burst in.

His face was red. He was greatly excited; almost speechless.

"Sir," he said to Freyberg, "I think you better come."

"What is it?" said the Captain.

"I found something. Honest. You better come right now." Rudecki's eyes were like the eyes of a man who has just discovered gold. It was a wonder he could see.

"What is it?"

"Honest, Cap'n, I can't explain. You gotta come see it—" He turned to Quinn. "*Please.*"

"Where is it?" Freyberg asked, still unperturbed and not apparently the least excited.

" 'cross the hall. Two whole rooms of it. . . ."

Rudecki was already leading the way—and when they got to the corridor Oakley was coming along it, whistling through his teeth about the Chatanooga Shoeshine Boy.

Freyberg was brief. He jerked his thumb and said to Annie; "anyone goes near that body in there but you till we get back, I'll brig you six months."

Annie knew the Captain meant it and wheeled, without so much as losing a note of his tune, and went inside to Mauberley.

The silver pencil.

There it was.

His.

In the room across the corridor into which they were led by Rudecki, the first thing Quinn and Freyberg were aware of was the smell of plaster dust.

It was darker here than on the western side, but not so dark as to obscure completely what had so excited the Sergeant.

It was the walls.

Every single inch of space had been covered with writing: all of it in pencil. Etched. And thus the smell of plaster dust. No one spoke.

Freyberg and Quinn and Rudecki had never seen the like of it.

Finally, Freyberg said; "and there's another room as well?"

"Yessir," Rudecki said. "Through here. . ." And he pointed to a door within the room.

Walking like pilgrims—loitering just to stare at the walls—Freyberg and Quinn allowed themselves to be led across the dusty carpet to a door already standing open.

Freyberg went through first, then Quinn, who walked through backwards, with his eyes like a child's on the words they were leaving.

Here, in the second room, there was still some furniture. A table and a chair; a writing desk and gramophone. The desk, the chair and the gramophone were all in the centre of the room. On top of the desk there was a pile of records, some of them chipped, some of them cracked, all of them covered with a fine white dust. The table had been set against the furthest wall and on it sat a five-point silver candelabra, all its candles burned away to crooked stubs, as if the wind had guttered them. There were bottles, too, on the floor in rows, each meticulously emptied, nothing but the faintest stain remaining: brandy and some wine. And down beside the chair, a great blue bowl of cigarette butts set out like after-dinner mints; about two pounds of them.

The walls here, too, were a mass of words.

"Well I'll be damned," said Freyberg in his muted way.

Quinn turned around and saw the room.

Even its ceiling was adorned. There were animals there. And birds. And stars. And a handprint drawn with candle smoke.

"I don't see how it's possible," said Freyberg—and got out his handkerchief. "One man. . ."

Rudecki said; "didn't I tell ya?" Beaming. "Didn't I *tell* ya?"

"Yes," said Freyberg. "Yes, you did indeed. Congratulations."

But Quinn was the first to see the epigraph.

He crossed the carpet almost running, moving towards the candelabra on the table like a man who after many years has seen a friend.

"What is it?" Freyberg asked, alarmed. "What the hell is it?"

Quinn could not reply. All he could do was shut his eyes and wait for the noise of the words inside his head to stop.

Freyberg noted the lift, the oddness in the set of Lieutenant Quinn's shoulders. He guessed there would be no answer so he went across himself, though not so far as Quinn had gone, and he read—unable to prevent the sound of it from reaching his lips—aloud:

"IN THE SAME HOUR CAME FORTH FINGERS OF A MAN'S HAND, AND WROTE OVER AGAINST THE CANDLESTICK UPON THE PLAISTER OF THE WALL OF THE KING'S PALACE. . ."

After maybe thirty seconds, Quinn said: *"and the King saw the part of the hand that wrote."* And turned, with a smile to Freyberg and said; "with a silver pencil?"

Freyberg nodded.

"Well," he said. "At least now we know what he was doing here."

"And—maybe—why he was murdered," said Quinn.

"And—maybe—why he should have been," said Freyberg.

Quinn exploded.

"Jesus. God damn it, sir!" he said. "I mean, why the hell. . .? I mean—look at what we've just discovered here! Look at it! Two whole rooms of *evidence*. Not even classified. Not even *read*. And you're so god damn sure he's guilty, you might just as well have put that thing through his eye yourself! What are you so god damned scared of? He might be innocent, for Christ's sake? Might not be what you want him to be?"

"Are you through?" said Freyberg.

Rudecki was looking—one man to the other—astonished. Quinn had never blown his stack like that before. Freyberg had never let him, had never let anyone get out of hand like that.

Freyberg began to fold his handkerchief, making it as small as something he was going to hide in a matchbox—a specimen, perhaps, for his collection. "Think about it," he said. "There's all this writing on the walls, all very neat, all very ordered, all lined up in rows, all very. . .careful."

"He was an artist," said Quinn.

"That's right. An artist." Freyberg looked around the walls. "Something of a con-artist, too, for all we know. *The bigger the lie, the more we are bound to believe it*. . .didn't one of them say that? Something like that? And *twice told lies become the truth*. . .Years, we've had of it now. The Nazi con-game. . . ."

"Mauberley wasn't a Nazi."

Freyberg just smiled and went on smoothing and folding his handkerchief, turning it over and over in his hands.

"He hated Nazis," said Quinn.

"Mmmmm-hmmm. . ."

"He did."

"Yes. Yes. I'm sure he did." Freyberg's smile was pinched and demeaning. "Why, from what I hear, they *all* hated Nazis. Didn't they? I mean, I hear that every day. And if I was fool enough to believe it every time I heard it, I'd have to believe there weren't enough Nazis to form a quorum. Were there, Quinn? And the war never happened. And Hitler was just an actor with a moustache made up to look like Charlie Chaplin. So, when Charlie says we should all fall down—we all fall down. . . .Pratfalls. *Yes*? And no war. How wonderful. Just to walk out into the lobby and leave it all behind us on a giant movie screen. With the music playing and everyone applauding. . .I'd like that. I really would." Freyberg squeezed the captive handkerchief tight between his palms and walked away to the windows, his features fading until there was nothing left but silhouette: a boy's head and bones and six feet of rumpled coat got up to look like a man. "But I'd also like this movie to include the scenes at Dachau, Quinn—so you could walk back through the gates and tell me nothing happened there. Tell me that all those people were only extras, paid to starve themselves. . .paid to lie down and play dead. Yes? Hansel and Gretel lying in the ovens. . .and maybe somewhere a gingerbread house. Playtime. Movie time. Make believe." Freyberg turned to look at Quinn. "You think you might be able to arrange all that?"

Quinn could only look at his feet.

"I assume your answer is no, Lieutenant?"

Quinn put his hands behind his back and waited, still looking down. He was aware that Freyberg had begun to cruise along beside the walls and would soon be behind him. All Rudecki did was hang in suspended animation, barely breathing over by the door.

"Really, you disappoint me, Quinn. After all the training you've been given—all the skill you have with words and ideas. 'Such a fine mind!' as Colonel Holland says. 'What a pity to waste it on a demolitions expert. . . .' "

Freyberg came and stood at his shoulder. Quinn looked up. Freyberg was smiling at the hanky in his hands. "Colonel Holland thinks so highly of you, Quinn. And I do, too. We talk about you all the time. And we're afraid some booby-trapped wall is going to blow up in your face—and then we'll lose that fine, fine mind—ka-boom!" He gave a false and patently exaggerated shrug. "And maybe it will, one day. Some wall. Go boom." Freyberg's breath smelled of peanuts and chocolate—even of candy wrappers, stale and dry and faintly sweet. "But I'll tell you what. You look at these walls here. . ." He laid his hand out flat in the air. "And maybe Mister Hugh Selwyn Mauberley, traitor and propagandist, can teach you a thing or two about storytelling. Yes?"

"Sir," Quinn began.

And Freyberg reddened. "No," he said. "No, Quinn. No. This—" he gestured at the walls "—whatever story it tells, will end with an apology. I absolutely guarantee it. Tell us, he may, the truth—the whole truth—and nothing but the truth—but in the end, he will apologize. And in the end, because he has apologized, you and twelve million others will all fall down on your knees before these walls and you will forgive him." He held up his hand to prevent Quinn from speaking. "You will forgive him, Quinn. And once you've forgiven him, you will forgive all the others too. And that, my bamboozled friend, is what I mean by propaganda."

"Damn it all, sir," said Quinn. "You don't even know what's written there."

"Don't I?"

"No, sir—you do not."

"Okay. All right," said Freyberg at last, as if conceding defeat. But then he grinned and added; "just as you don't know what I found in the bathroom, back across the hall."

"What's that?"

"The bathtub is full of ashes."

"So," said Quinn. "He was freezing to death. There wasn't any heat. He made a fire."

"No," said Freyberg. "It's not that simple, much as I'm sure you'd like it to be. In fact, Lieutenant, I'm sure you'd like it very much if everything but what you approve of here would go away and leave you alone. Then we could all get down to the proper business of a eulogy. . .burial and martyrdom. Yes? Well, that isn't going to happen. Not while I'm here."

Quinn began to panic. The Captain, after all, had developed his own procedures, based on his own priorities and prejudices. Freyberg's whole existence, ever since Dachau, had been a search for clues. He had seen so many ashes. Sifted them. Blown them off the backs of his hands. Kept them in packages. Knew what they had been. "He burned some handwritten notebooks in there," he said. "A great many handwritten notebooks, in fact." He walked in closer to the walls and gave the words a glance. "You know—I have to wonder why a man would burn so many books if what they contained was essentially the same as what he took so many pains to lay out, oh so very carefully, here on these walls."

Quinn fumbled for excuses.

"They were notes," he said. "And what he's written here is larger. Expanded."

"Maybe," said Freyberg. "Maybe. But then, why burn them?"

"I told you. He was freezing to death. He wanted fire."

"Wanted fire—and did not burn this table? And this chair? This desk?"

Quinn said; "well—he needed the chair to stand on. Look how high he's written."

Freyberg actually laughed. "You don't know what's written here, either," he said. "But you're already holding up his arm to help him write it. Jesus Christ, I bet if I introduced you to Hitler, Quinn, you'd call him *sir*. I'll bet you'd even *bow*."

"Captain," said Quinn. "The war is *over*."

Rudecki was relieved to hear it.

Freyberg regarded the small white thing he had made with his hands; crumpled it tight and let it fall open.

Then he turned and began to walk away from the room.

At the door, he stopped. "I'm giving you a job," he said to Quinn. "I want you to read every word of this. And I want you to keep me abreast of what you're reading—just so I can check it against a little research I'll be doing on my own. But do, please do be careful; and if you hear it whirring and ticking, just be sure you stand well back and warn the rest of us. I don't want to be buried in rubble like that, and I don't think you do either. Anyone found in a garbage heap is suspect, I always think. Don't you?"

Annie Oakley's Crystal Saloon was beginning to fill up.

The bodies—five from the courtyard, one from behind the counter in the lobby and one from the stairs—had been tagged and bagged and placed in a row on the floor against the wall where Ingrid Bergman had been sitting when he first looked in through the doors. There was a candle on her table. Annie had put it there.

Freyberg had given him charge of the corpses. Perhaps because he was such a good shot—and the corpses needed protection. Annie had kept the silver pencil in his pocket, together with the Iron Cross from that Colonel he'd shot in the latrine at Innsbruck and the one and only piece of "precious" jewelry he'd managed to collect thus far: a ruby ring (or just red glass) in an antique setting taken from the woman who had died on the road to Umhausen. That was all. But the pencil was the best—because it was famous.

And every minute the pencil got more and more famous. Every time Quinn or Freyberg or Rudecki came down the stairs, there was some new development, shocking and intriguing. More and more writing was appearing on the walls. Its content seemed to be more and more "alarming" (to Quinn), "damning" (to Freyberg) and "fuckin' fantastic" (to Rudecki). Freyberg had ordered the whole Elysium Hotel off limits except to classified personnel, and he was moving Quinn and himself into rooms on the second floor.

But Annie was the Keeper of the Morgue.

His only fear was that Freyberg would tell him to take the bodies out and burn them, like he had the dogs at Dachau. No one could be buried yet. The snow was still too deep up here and the ground still frozen. But maybe if he got lucky (for a change) someone would come and take the bodies down the mountain into the valley where they could be given some kind of so-called decent burial. Churchbells and stuff and someone saying prayers. There hadn't been too much of that with all the dead he'd seen. Mostly it was just the dogtags looped on some guy's arm. He'd tip them all into a cardboard box and hand them to the Chaplain, twenty, thirty or forty at a time—and a truck coming and the body-bags all driven off, looking so lumpy and strange and not as if there were human beings inside at all.

Annie looked over at the candle on Ingrid Bergman's table and began to hum "As Time Goes By."

Freyberg had started negotiations for a generator. It was promised for tomorrow or the day after. This was standard vocabulary for "when we get to it," meaning: "okay, let's bargain." The way was now open for communications between Freyberg's Quartermaster and the Quartermaster down in the town. Freyberg's QM came up with one case of Scotch for two cases of Liebfraumilch; twenty Panatellas for five hundred Camels; six jars of Vaseline (no questions asked) for eighteen gallons of kerosene. And finally; "your Betty Grable for my Rita Hayworth." Result: "An absolute guarantee, sir. We'll have a generator tomorrow." Meaning the day after.

In the meantime: candles.

Immediately after Freyberg had left, Quinn and Rudecki had discovered two more rooms—all the rooms with the writing sharing the opposite side of the corridor to the suite where Mauberley's corpse had been found.

Quinn had put his cot in the room with the gramophone and the candelabra; moving in with a sense of relief and exhilaration. He was absolutely certain he would exonerate Hugh Selwyn Mauberley. Freyberg simply didn't understand. It was a question of interpretation, and this was Quinn's forte.

Evening was upon them.

Down in the valleys Quinn could see green, heightened by the vivid emerald overlay of water on the ice of the Ötztalsee. Here, however, on the heights the wind and the cold prevailed. There was frost on the windows, sparkling now in the increasing light as Quinn lit more and more candles to augment the single kerosene lamp he had been allotted.

Taking the last of his candlesticks, Quinn went over and opened the door between this room and the next. He could still not believe what Mauberley had done; accomplished. Four whole rooms of it—sixteen walls of meticulous etching, every word set deeply in its place, all the writing clearly cut and decipherable. Yet, surely, some of it must have been written in haste. And under whatever threat, since death for Mauberley had been murder, and he must have known it would come that way—very sudden—quick—and the end of all words forever. Yet even in spite of terror—absolute clarity. So after years of silence, Mauberley was a writer at the last. And here was his book—his testament entirely made on walls.

THREE

1936

O bright Apollo. . .
What god, man or hero
Shall I place a tin wreath upon!

Ezra Pound

Quinn had thought to begin his reading of the walls where Mauberley himself had obviously intended—over to the right of the epigraph from the Book of Daniel. But his eye was caught by a second epigraph, inscribed on the ceiling: a sentence scrawled outside the disciplined alignment of the others and set there like a bear trap to catch the reader unaware.

"*All I have written here,*" Quinn read, "*is true; except the lies.*"

Quinn smiled.

He loosened his scarf, removed his cap and lit a cigarette. (If Mauberley had smoked two pounds of cigarettes, then so would he: a new kind of hero-worship.) And he began to read by the light of candles, kneeling on his cot beneath the words *"except the lies"*.

At once, he was in another time, another idiom. And the voice he heard was hoarse with the distance it had journeyed in order to be heard.

* * *

Dubrovnik: August 17th, 1936

The heat was merciless. The whole of Dubrovnik was turned like the palm of a hand against the sun, squinting through its fingers at the sky. The Adriatic light was white, the air translucent and the sea a remorseless sheet of green-tinted glass. If Icarus had fallen here he would have bounced.

H.S. MAUBERLEY, ESQUIRE, read the cable in my pocket, HOTEL GRAND BRETAGNE, VENEZIA: NAHLIN ARRIVING DUBROVNIK NOON SEVENTEENTH. MASQUERADE IMPERATIVE. WE ARE COMING INCOGNITO. LOOKING FORWARD YOUR COMPANY. LOVE. W.

One was left, of course, no leeway to refuse this invitation. Still, it would be madness to complain of being commanded to join the King of England's progress through the Isles of Greece—one of a dozen hand-picked guests. The wire had said "we are coming incognito"—he as the Duke of Lancaster and she as Bessie Jones from Baltimore—so my intention had been to wait as unobtrusively as possible. Consequently, my rented Daimler and its chauffeur had gone straight back to Venice and I had hired a boy from the marketplace to trundle my bags on a cart.

By three o'clock in the afternoon there was still no sign—

no signal. Nothing on the horizon. I was sitting halfway down the town, having chosen a café terrace from which I could see the harbour and the bay beyond. In spite of the overnight rain, the atmosphere was stifling and breathless. The terrace on which I sat and the buildings around it were bleached a blinding grey that hurt the eyes. And there was a sound—a humming, arid sound I could not trace—of insects or of birds. It was like a kettle boiling dry. Yet there was nothing here completely wilted or dead, as one might expect. Every window box was filled with scarlet geraniums and nearly every upright surface crawled with magenta wallflowers. Some of the stones, in fact, were split apart with yellow shafts of broom and pungent aloe swords the colour of a peach. And the scent of all these blossoms mingled with the cobble dust to produce a kind of powdered, aromatic drug that settled over everything. The whole population— dogs and cats and people—was drowsy. Everyone moved through the streets as if afraid to wake. Even now my boy was asleep on the stones of a nearby wall and my steamer trunk was hunkered down in its cart beside the curb, dreaming of its contents—all my new white suits and coloured shirts and handmade underwear from France.

Dubrovnik is a very foreign place where everyone wears black—so I'm certain I looked, in my Venetian whites and Panama hat, precisely as I felt; a misplaced, bad-tempered tourist.

I was over-tired from my hectic journey—over-anxious lest I be detected and recognized and greatly over-excited thinking of my impending rendezvous. As a consequence of all these tensions the first thing I did, sitting down, was to tip the dregs of the previous customer's wine across the cloth; after which, with my usual excess of nervous nonchalance, I set myself on fire while lighting a cigarette.

A man in a fez was staring at me from another table. Not a pleasant experience. An ugly man and I was fairly certain he belonged to the police—though whose police I could not say. He might even be an Englishman, I thought. Englishmen loved the fez and all that wearing it implied of erotic sophistication. They wore them, I suspected, to bed. Alone.

This man wore it wrong, however. Surely it should not cover the ears.

I wondered if he knew who I was. Or was I just another *turista* seeing the sights. Of course, the intensity of my gaze made him nervous, since I stared so meaningfully at the harbour that I must have appeared to be memorizing the details of the town's defences (nil) and the comings and goings of all the ships (twenty-two since dawn). Perhaps, if he was English, he thought I had come to kill the King. A Bolshevist assassin. Princip updated—who had killed that other foreign prince and his morganatic wife a handful of miles from here. And of course, the king of *this* country, Alexander Karageorgevitch, had been murdered only two years ago at Marseilles. Ports of call were dangerous for kings.

And yet I liked this coast—its legendary cast. This place was once *Illyria*, Lady. *Mythic*. Well chosen for the king in hand, since this was where they had deified Pan. Well chosen, too, for my sake, I thought—since somewhere south of Dubrovnik was the cave where Cadmus had been transformed into a serpent (dragon?) who was made the guardian of myth and literature. . . .Folklore had it that Cadmus was the Phoenix, or a sort of lizard-Lazarus, rising from the flames of some forgotten human rebellion; an assurance that, in spite of fire, the word would be preserved. And it was then I decided what my disguise might be for that incognito rendezvous. I should play the serpent's part.

Closing in on suppertime I became aware of a genial but throbbing commotion in the streets surrounding my café. People began to lean out of windows pointing towards the bay while others rose from nearby tables, including the man in the fez, to get a better view.

"What's going on?" I asked the fez—damned if I'd risk my neck trying to stand up on my chair.

"Ships," he said, with a tilt of his chin at the harbour.

And ships there were! With the sun beginning to sink beyond them into the Adriatic—two magnificent British destroyers in full regalia, gliding into view. And sandwiched in between them, very slightly to the rear, was a long white graceful ship much larger than any *yacht* I had ever seen. The *Nahlin*.

Every bell in town began to ring and every signal known to sailors round the world broke out across the waters. Great whooping sounds like operatic birds and horns like prairie trains: the most glorious fracas I have ever heard.

Incognito, indeed!

Only the *Nahlin* came into harbour, the other ships remaining out beyond the bar, and the whole town rose and gave it a standing ovation.

Boys and girls and men and women, little children, dogs and cats began to run. Babies were hoisted onto their mother's shoulders: not even they would be allowed to miss this sight—because the golden king had come from heaven bringing his lover with him—icons walking on the earth—choosing the people of Dubrovnik to bask in. This was the new mythology, I thought. Homer might have written it.

And as night began to fall, they filled the streets with lights and shouts, all the young men carrying torches, all the young women shouting: SMIRT MRAKU! DEATH TO DARKNESS! DZIVELA LJUBAV! LONG LIVE LOVE!

The press of people was so great I was afraid I should not be able to reach the quayside in time to get on board the motor launch. I had expected the whole event would be a whisper. Now this pandemonium. And my hired boy—long since awakened—was standing on his wall and dancing with excitement.

"*Avanti!*" I called to him, using all my languages at once: "*Trasmiti! Vorwarts! Go!*" I screamed; having to scream it to be heard above the bells and all the shouting. At last I had to pull him from the wall and force him into place behind the cart. And all the while he kept on saying over and over and over again "Eduardo! Eduardo!" as if it was a spell.

Thus it was I found myself with my attaché case in one

hand and my black umbrella in the other, inexplicably raised against the moon, rushing and pushing, being pushed and rushed among ten thousand others down the winding streets of this Dalmatian Camelot with my steamer trunk thundering behind—the boy and it full tilt on wheels at my heels. All this to greet and be greeted by the legendary Prince of Wales, the idol of a whole generation—the Boy King of England, Edward VIII and his lover, Wallis Warfield Simpson, with whom I had been in love myself in the way dogs have of loving the feet at which they lie. And when Wallis greeted me she said; "It was so good of you to come." And I said; "No. It was good of you to come." After which we all stood leaning on the rail, watching the whole dark mountainside light up with bonfires.

And the man in the fez? He too was on board, asleep already in a cabin beneath us. He would be departing tomorrow, for he had come to perform, in the strictest secrecy, a relatively easy task. English he was, after all—and a very special agent of the King—whose job it was to measure Wallis Simpson for the Crown.

* * *

Quinn sat down.

He was shaking.

The candle guttered, threatening to go out, and it was only revived when he set it on the floor beside his cot.

It wasn't that he hadn't known—as everyone had known— there was a flashbulb-gossip-column friendship between the writer and the Duchess.

It was the shock of seeing it pulled from the impersonal distance of newsprint into the focus of "me" and "Wallis".

And the awareness—like a draught—that a door had just been opened way off down a darkened corridor. And the fear of where it led.

No. Not the fear; the certainty.

Mauberley was lying with that thing in his eye, on the

floor across the hall, and the beginning and the ending had already been joined.

Quinn got up and went across the room to the candelabra, reaching out to touch the stalactite of wax that was hanging down towards the base. He couldn't help thinking that Mauberley's fingers must have performed the same gesture. It was one of those irresistible things people did—automatic as smelling a paper flower or standing back from a painting. All the time he stood there, Quinn thought; *Mauberley was here; he stood right here, like me; he felt this wax; he could see the same view; he could raise the same dust as he crossed the floor*. It was a painful thought that all these things, mere things, had had the privilege of being there with Mauberley during the final days of his life and could never tell of it.

But Mauberley himself could tell—so long as Quinn went on with his reading. And began at the beginning.

Looking up from where he stood, he read; "1924". The figures were beautiful and formal. The nine had a great rococo loop spreading out beneath the one and the four had a great, high cap riding back towards the two. "1924": written over against the candlestick upon the plaister of the wall. . . .

This then was where it began. Quinn felt the same as he had when he made his first parachute jump—suddenly confronted with the enormity of space and the death that might await him at the bottom. He closed his eyes and held his breath. And then he opened them—and read.

*   *   *

China: August, 1924

> Tell her that sheds
> Such treasure in the air,
> Recking naught else but that her graces give
> Life to the moment,
> I would bid them live
> As roses might, in magic amber laid,
> Red overwrought with orange and all made
> One substance and one colour
> Braving time.

Wallis is sitting in my mind as I saw her first in the lobby of the old Imperial Hotel in Shanghai.

This was in the middle-age of her youth.

She had already married once and had come to China to pursue her husband. He had deserted her; not for another woman, but the bottle. He was someone of importance in the United States Navy: someone having something to do with aeroplanes; a man called Spencer. My theory is he was a homosexual. Not that it matters. So am I—from time to time. The thing is—he left her.

She was lost.

The lobby of the old Imperial Hotel was crowded far beyond its capacity. A great wave of people washed back and forth between the pillars and the palms, one half attempting to depart, the other half attempting to arrive, neither half succeeding.

There were plain too many bodies in the city. Shanghai was then the crossroads of the world: known as the Charnel House of the East because the bones of so many cultures had been hung out to dry, to be sold in her streets. She was also known as the Golden Whore of the Orient.

Boats and trains brought daily hordes of foreigners: South Americans, Russians, Europeans, Mexicans—Americans from Boston and Baltimore; all of us in flight. Many were in flight from wars and revolutions; some were in simple flight from the past; some were in flight from one another.

I, too, was "lost" as Gertrude Stein said, with the rest of my generation: "lost" meaning not, as so many seem to think, astray, but destroyed. Perdu. And if we wandered, what we wandered in was the aftershock of a great catastrophe. An earthquake had tumbled everything known to all the generations leading up to ours. My father, even in 1910, had felt the early tremors of this quake and I've always counted him among its early victims. What he cried against before he leapt to his death was the raucous and wilful repudiation of civilization by industrified America. And when he spoke against it down he went, "the enemy of progress". I always see in my dreams the counter image of Henry Ford, who is seated on my father's casket, wielding his magic scissors; cutting out miles and miles of paper motorcars—creating, single handed, the United Fabricates of America.

Early in the 1920s Ezra Pound became my surrogate father. It was on the impetus of his encouragement that I had found my way to China, much as a child will dig through the earth of his parents' garden to discover if the people are walking upside down. I had begun by then to try my wings outside of verse and called myself a "serious writer". Shanghai drew me like a motherlode of dreams and I thought I had found the ultimate source, the wellspring of every fiction known to man. It was there in that massive, visible throng that I found my Crowd Invisible, and thus my first success.

This was the age of the Treaty of Versailles when half the countries of Europe disappeared overnight into the gullets of the other half who woke up suffering from indigestion.

In Shanghai I met so many German, Austrian, Bohemian and White Russian refugees I was able to learn their languages (the White Russians all spoke French). I also made my living, for a while, teaching their children English.

It was a dreadful time; there was so much dissolution of the past and fear of the future. Nothing to stand on, nothing to reach for. Almost every day there were killings and suicides. Sometimes parents would murder their children. Others gave their children away and shot themselves. Other times, families were slaughtered by the agents of a revolution taking place far away. It seemed grotesque that anyone should travel halfway round the world to slit a woman's throat and drown her babies in a bathtub. Not in some hovel out beyond the pale, but always in some embassy or sumptuous hotel. Even though it was a frightening time nothing could have dragged me away, because I recognized that in this microcosmic hell the age I lived in was being defined, and if I wanted to write then I had to force myself to become a witness to these lives and these events and to this place. Looking back, I think Shanghai was all a dream. Which is why, perhaps, its images return so poignantly at night in sleep.

Wallis was sitting in the lobby waiting, as I was, for someone who was late. In the crush, I could see her figure perched very still on the edge of a chair up against a wall. There was a mirror behind her. Intermittently I could see myself in this mirror, flashing on and off like a nervous white light as strangers passed between us. Out beyond the revolving doors, the sun was shining and I think it must have been teatime—four or five in the afternoon. Wallis was so composed in the midst of all the commotion that once I'd caught sight of her, I couldn't stop watching. She was like a child who had run away and was caught in the adult world when the curfew bell rang. *If I sit like this and wear white gloves and fold my hands, I shall pass for at least fifteen. . . .*

She had not yet begun to affect Chinese dress as she later did, and was wearing a very "American" cotton suit. Her hair, pushed back and up, was severe yet elegant—like angel wings. It was covered with a pale blue veil and the veil came down to her chin. Her mouth was very red; her eyes, though blue, had darkened against the intrusion of so much light and her whole face carried, even through the veil, across the fifteen yards or so of lobby like a mask. There was not a trace of emotion written there—only: *I am here and if you break me you must pay for me.*

I was waiting too: for one of my students, Dmitri Karaskavin.

Dmitri Karaskavin's parents had engaged me to teach him English. They wanted very much to go into exile in America. I warned them about this, but they would not be dissuaded. Everything was contingent now on their passports being endorsed by the proper authorities. Also on the arrival of two other children, lost somewhere on the journey through Manchuria. It was all very complicated. Masses and masses of money were involved. Everyone who lifted a pencil or carried a rubber stamp had to be bribed.

Sun Yat-Sen was dying of cancer. China was about to burst into flames. There was nationwide political unrest and intrigue, much of it fostered by the Reds in Russia. It was not, therefore, a good time to be a White Russian in Shanghai. So many knives were out. So many hands. There was speculation Dmitri Karaskavin's sisters were being held for ransom. His parents, of course, were frantic. But pragmatic also, to the degree that while they waited for the past to catch up to them, possibly even to murder them, they went on planning for an American future in which Dmitri Karaskavin would be their interpretor. I was to provide him with the language.

We met in various places, including the lobbies and gardens of other hotels and even in the ante-rooms of brothels. Sometimes our lessons took place on foot as we tramped around the city or climbed the nearby hills to stare at the Yellow River and wonder where the ships were going and had been. And on more than one occasion, Dmitri Karaskavin hired a motorcar and we drove out into the country.

I had been in Shanghai for more than three months by the time this scene took place in the lobby of the old Imperial Hotel: long enough to have written one whole draft of Crowd Invisible; long enough to have fallen in love with Dmitri Karaskavin. Long enough to have begun to know who I was—independent of my father and of Ezra. I had even begun to wear white suits.

I was standing. Wallis was seated.

The whole world passed between us, shuffling and pushing over the famous tiles (long since, I fear, destroyed) replete with their fiery dragons, winged messengers and monkeys.

The lacquered chair on which she sat had an inlay of mother-of-pearl chrysanthemums. Time, as it does in dreams, went by without the hands of clocks. Hours, days, years. I was alarmed. Dmitri Karaskavin was a wild boy, accident-prone and capable of gross misjudgement. He might have stopped on the street somewhere, caught up in his passionate concern for other people, listening to some conniver's story. Always in the back of my mind there was fear that one of these would harm him: trap him and blow him out of my life. So much political intrigue lay in wait to swallow him. He was only eighteen and had spent the whole of his early life in a world of inviolate privilege and then, all at once, was a fugitive from men whose murderous hatred he was incapable of understanding. He wanted just to be in the world, in all of it—but he'd never been able to grasp that more than half the world was his enemy.

I was just about to give him up that afternoon when I saw him pushing through the lower part of the lobby. It was quite impossible not to see his hair, blond and windblown as the hair of a child and cut too long for a boy; it even touched the nape of his neck. I began to step forward, thinking how I should admonish him for being so late—eager to bless him for being alive and unharmed. I had never told him how I felt—I never would—but I ached for his presence. He knew he didn't have a better friend in the world than me. He was always happy to see me. Sometimes, bursting with Russian enthusiasm, he would take my hand or embrace me, even laying his lips along my cheeks. One of his greatest pleasures was to sit among the whores at Madame Liu's, whose company he introduced me to, and incite them to riots of laughter with his imitations of Charlie Chaplin.

As I walked towards him, pushing through the people, I began to raise my arm in greeting. But in this dream my arms are always frozen and I cannot move them—knowing what will happen next. All my movements lock. I am weighted to the floor. The riotous storm of people increases.

Dmitri Karaskavin doesn't even see me. His hand is lifted, too, to wave—but not at me. He is striding—weightless—pushing his way past boatloads of people setting off for

America, waving their Stars and Stripes, singing their anthems as obscene limericks. Wilfully ignoring where he walks, Dmitri walks across the faces of the monkeys and the winged messengers oblivious of everything except his destination.

Wallis sits in her lacquered chair. In the dream there is silence—slowly broken open by the moaning of a long black wave of curling water pouring down the steps and over the moment of their greeting.

Wallis extends both hands in Dmitri's direction. He kisses them. One, its white glove shining, rests for a moment on his cheek and leaves its mark indelible forever. She was then a woman of twenty-eight. He was a boy of eighteen. I cannot tell what really happened, having no access to the dreams beyond the doors they closed. My jealousy had access there, but not my eyes. I only know her power to move him to his manhood was embodied in the way she greeted him that afternoon: seated; veiled; her white hands extended; her feet implanted in a dragon's mouth; her eyes upon his gesture, not his person. Vigilant. Wary. Refusing to rise until he had made his obeisance and kissed her hands.

I forget what I did that afternoon. It was not till sometime later—weeks—that Dmitri introduced "my teacher to my lady". I did not (how could I?) like her at all. I had to presume she was a courtesan: how else could someone "old" attract someone so young and hold him for so long? I had noted, too, that since their liaison began, her appearance had improved. Which is to say, her wardrobe. Dmitri's family had money. Much of it. Now I presumed it was clothing this woman.

Maybe six and maybe seven times the three of us were together. Once, we drove above the city so far back into the hills we had to spend the night in a stone hotel. We had strayed into that pastoral China seen on plates where the willows bend and the bridges disappear into the mist.

Sometimes we laughed. It would not have been possible to live in Dmitri's presence never laughing, never smiling. He played Charlie Chaplin for Wallis, Mary Pickford for me. He would play whole scenes with flowers and tea-cups. Sometimes, he brought a Victrola with him and we danced in the dust of the courtyards. Other times we sang the songs. But still, I could not address the woman by her name. I called her—strangely, now I think of it—"ma'am".

And then one day it happened. As it must.

We waited. He did not appear.

Our tea grew cold. The wind blew. There was no news. Nothing.

Finally, I telephoned. No answer.

Then we made our way to where he lived. Even the servants were gone. There was blood on the doorsill.

Twice we drove out along the winding roads to find him. Far back into the hills. Far down the river to the sea. No sign.

In the lobby of the old Imperial Hotel, we took up our final stations. Wallis sat in her chair. I hovered in the mirror.

Dmitri never came back.

He died. Was killed. Or killed himself. Was drowned and swept away. We made up our minds together he was in the river, perhaps because the river reached the sea. This made his death less difficult—acceptable. No, not acceptable. But credible. He could be in the river. He could not be in the earth.

"You loved him," Wallis told me.

"Yes."

"I loved him, too," she said.

I looked away. It seems, in memory, I looked away at tea-cups. Blue ones. And white. I didn't speak. She placed her hand on top of mine.

"I loved him, Mister Mauberley," she said. "But I was not his lover."

How could I believe that? I turned and watched her mouth. I could not bear to see her eyes. I refused to speak. She withdrew her hand and placed it underneath her chin, the palm turned down as if to signify its emptiness.

"He wanted me to marry him."

"*Marry* him? He was a child. . .!"

Wallis studied her fingers. "You wanted him."

"Yes. But *he* did not want *me*. At least we were not grotesque."

She looked away.

I should not have said grotesque.

There was a long, long silence—somehow held in her hands—and when she opened them, it was to confess her marriage to Spencer, of which I had been unaware.

Then, looking off into the crowd around us, she also confessed her virginity. I sat immobilized, alarmed. Women—certainly none that I had known—did not "confess" their virginity. They proclaimed it.

"It isn't fair," she said, "Mister Mauberley. All my life there have been such fine beginnings. And such rotten endings. Everyone I love is swept away downstream. What is a person meant to do?"

She withdrew her hands into the territory of the tea-cups, touching them very lightly on the way as if to mark their whereabouts.

She did not speak again until she had regained complete control of her poise—and then she said; "it seems to me, Mister Mauberley, this world is nothing more than someone's revenge. We are led into the light and shown such marvels as one cannot tell. . ." I watched her staring off towards some view to which I was not privy. "And then. . .they turn out all the lights and hit you with a baseball bat."

Now she withdrew her hand into her lap, and fumbled for her handkerchief. "Well," she said, blowing her nose and beginning to repair the damage of her tears, "we have to fight back. Don't you agree? We have an obligation to fight back." Smiling. "Even if it means we have to pick up baseball bats of our own. . . ."

Her fingers, I noticed, however much they shook, were brisk as they made their repairs. It is only now—after twenty years—that I see her face as lacquered; only now that I realize she has never lived without the application of a mask. There is a mole you would never see, for instance, down by the corner of her mouth, which I saw that day for the first and last time. As she worked—she was an expert: her mouth, her eyes, her hair were masterpieces of illusion—she went on speaking through her teeth; her voice as sibilant as something from behind a screen. "That boy we loved is dead," she said. "You wanted him; I wanted him; Now—" she drew a thin red line along her upper lip "—what we have is each other."

She snapped her compact shut, giving off a punctuation mark of pale pink dust, and said; "I like you, Mister Mauberley. I will be frank. You are not Dmitri. You are not my *beau idéal*. But then—in your eyes—I am not Dmitri, either."

I smiled.

"Very well. We can be friends."

I nodded.

She dropped the compact back into her purse. Done.

"Then," she said, "there are practicalities, Mister Mauberley. If I am to have my life, I must find some means of sustaining it. The same, I assume, applies to you."

I agreed. All I had was my tutor's fees, and few enough of those.

"One thing I had from Dmitri was an entrée to that other world where money floats more freely than it does down here. I do not mean that was the basis of our. . .relationship. Only one of its side-effects. But one I shall sorely miss. . . ." She toyed with her gloves. "And the same might be said for you. Am I right?"

It was true—though not so great a concern for me, being a man, as it was for her, a woman and alone.

"We shall strike a bargain, then," she said, assuming my assent, "by which we can both achieve the goals we have in mind. You will have a woman—let us say *'of mystery'*—on your arm." A smile. "'Mister Hugh Selwyn Mauberley and Mrs. Winfield Spencer were together *again* last night!' And we both know how gossip of that kind works in this society. Why they will positively *fly* to your side to know what I'm about. That is, the ladies will. While the gentlemen will sort of *amble* over in my direction, mumbling into their shirts it's a wonder they never laid eyes on me before and *where* have I been hiding myself?" She laughed. "And it will work, I promise you. I've seen it work a hundred thousand times. And here comes the bit about the money, you see. . ."

I held my breath.

What *did* she have in mind?

"As for you," she said, smoothing out one glove and making a perfect hand of it, "all those ladies have sons and daughters. Or, most of them do. And, once they hear about your expertise in languages, why, take your pick and name your price!"

It made sense.

"As for me—" and here she smoothed the second glove, face down on top of the other "—it may come as some surprise, Mister Mauberley, but one of my talents happens to be a very great expertise with a deck of cards. In fact it is not too boastful to claim my poker skills are a match for any man's. And I stress the word *man*. Because it is the men I want to play. It is the men who have the money. It is the money that I need. It is. . ."

She waited.

Then she smiled the saddest smile I've ever seen and said: "I only want one thing. I only want my life."

She is renowned—and justly so—for her smile.

In those days, it was battered out of tin. Now gold. But battered, nonetheless.

When this is read, remember that: the hammer blows. The baseball bats.

This now begins to fade.

I do not know when I became her lover in my mind; as I had been Dmitri's lover in my mind; and countless others' since. In my mind. I do know this: it was her audacity that won me. Her ruthless stillness, seated in her place in the lobby of the old Imperial Hotel, with her feet in the dragon's mouth, waiting to be seen; her awareness, even then, that she had a place in time. And yes—she was debonair: the first to laugh; the last to weep; the best of company. And brave. It was not and it has not been a fearful thing to watch her climb.

"I want my life," she had said.

And, since my father died, I had been waiting for some-one—anyone—to say those words out loud.

*   *   *

At this point, Quinn got down from the chair on which he had been standing and sat with the candle in his hands and closed his eyes.

His neck was sore. He was not even sure how long he had been standing on the chair—almost falling over backwards, shifting the candle from hand to hand, squinting at the writing, losing it in and out of focus.

At last he got up and set the candle in the centre of the desk and lit yet another cigarette. The whole room smelled of smoke and candle stubs—much the same, he imagined, as it must have smelled to Mauberley at work on his "frescoes".

For a moment—and perhaps it was his own shadow—he caught a vision of the writer writing: pinned in his blanket, with his hair all matted with plaster dust, his fingers jetting out of fingerless gloves and the silver pencil never pausing, gouging out the words. But Quinn, disoriented, looked up and saw not words but pictures: animals drawn on the ceiling above his head. Deer—bison—stars—the moon and Mauberley's handprint. Maybe he had needed to create an-other image of the world: innocent and shining, like the one the Duchess of Windsor had intended when she said; *"we are led into the light and shown such marvels as one cannot tell. . .And then. . ."*

Quinn turned. He looked at the words that Mauberley had written on the walls.

And he thought; *"we have an obligation to fight back."* And he went on reading.

*   *   *

Ezra Pound has one mad eye: his left. And there were times I thought he saw the world through it alone, as if the other eye were blind. But now, as I write this here, I think about the world outside these windows and I see it as being the world that Ezra always saw: the world of chaos, fire and rage. I never heard him once remark upon the beauty of the world, the stuff of other poet's dreams—of *splendour in the grass;* but only of the human world, whose beauty all was lost or passed.

Ezra will be condemned, I know, for what he's said and done: his broadcasts and his writings. But he will only be condemned because the world cannot acknowledge that the mad have visions of the truth. Ezra will be destroyed for no better reason than that no one wants to be seen by a mad-man—lest the madman call him "brother". It will be some-body's job to pull him down and say he was the cause of madness; thus disposing of the madness in themselves, blaming it all on him. "We should never have done these things," they will say, "were it not that men like Pound and Mussolini, Doctor Goebbels and Hitler drove us to them. Otherwise, we should have stayed at home by our quiet hearths and dandled our children on our knees and lived out lives of usefulness and peace. . . ." Missing the fact en-tirely that what they were responding to were the whispers of chaos, fire and anger in themselves. All of which Ezra could see from the very first with his one mad eye.

Rapallo: March 7th, 1936

Ezra is feeding the cat. He tosses little bits of goatmeat at it where it sits on the roof. Most of the pieces of goatmeat roll down off the tiles and land on the grass, but the cat won't come down after them. It just sits there, stupefied by heat and flies. Ezra thinks this is all very amusing—rolling meat into tight little bullets and firing them up at the cat. But I find it rather irritating, since I'm desperate to concentrate

on the pile of newspapers down beside my deckchair and
the notebook balanced on my lap and the fact that every
single piece of lead I insert in my pencil is determined to
break today, no matter how many times I fill it. Maybe it
doesn't want to write. Maybe it has the same sense I have—
cum sybilla—of impending doom.

They've done it. The Germans. Hitler, rather. He sent in
the *Reichswehr* to occupy the Rhineland. Yesterday. In spite
of all his promises, he just went in and did it; no fuss;
nothing. Not a word from France or England. Mute. The
murder of Dollfuss; the invasion of Abyssinia. Now this.
Games of chance. And it makes me very nervous. I say so
to Ezra.

Ezra says; *"the world is too much with us"* and flings
another ball of meat. Amen. My father said so too.

"But what if there's a war?"

"Then good."

"Good?"

"It's what the Boche do best, ain't it?" *(Dialects.* Everything is a joke.) "Better a var—vot? Oddervise ve got a rheffolution. . .hunh?"

My mouth hangs open. Damn him. He doesn't care if they
pull it all down. The whole precarious structure.

"We have their assurances," I remind him. "Their promises. *No more wars.* Hitler and Mussolini. . ."

Ezra's eyes glaze over. His mouth moves. Silence.

"Listen," I say to him, "don't you understand how fine
the line is here?" I lean out towards him, clutching my
notebook, stabbing my wrist with my pencil. "All we're
asking for is a bulwark against the Bolshevists! Not 1914!"

"Bullshitists, please."

I refuse to laugh. "They're changing the definitions, Ezra",
I say to him. "Hitler and Mussolini are changing the definitions. Breaking their promises. It's. . ."

"Ids da Joos vot done it. *Dey* vas da Bolsheveki. Nod da
Rooshun pipple. Jus da Joos. Hidler gonna kip a promis mid
a Joo? Ya crazy! So mek var! Good an goddam var. Dat vey
ve got kaput! No more rheffolution."

All I can do is sit back and stare at him: my knees together, rubbing my wrist with its purple puncture. My pulse is racing. My mind goes blank. Ezra really doesn't seem to understand. He makes me so angry, shrugging the way he does: totally unimpressed, even though the headlines are six inches deep, even though Dorothy's radio positively shouts it from the house. From Ezra, nothing. Just another ball of goatmeat, lobbed against the tiles.

At last the cat has finally caught one and sits there chewing, with its head on one side.

"But think of the chances he's taking," I say.

"Who?"

"Hitler. What if the French and the British respond to one of these moves of his?"

Ezra fires off another salvo and winks at me and says: "be less afraid of movement than of standing still." And he puts his fingers (farmer's fingers) up against his temple, tapping the veins. "*All things are a flowing,*" he says. "So says Heraclitus."

Heraclitus: for whom all things began with fire. Maybe he sat too long in the sun like Ezra and the cat. Dreaming with their heavy-lidded eyes. Disconnected. Floating, when dammit, the world is real and vulnerable.

"Let them march and make their wars and get it over with," says Ezra. "Then we can finally come to the only subject that matters: *money.*"

Dorothy's radio stutters in the living room. Static. Hitler is speaking: far away, as always.

Ezra has fallen silent. His face is like a bearded beet. His jaws keep moving. Words unspoken. Odd. He frightens me. Sometimes he'll say things: just the middle parts of sentences. Then he expects you to know what he's talking about. And when you don't—and say you don't—he scowls as if you'd only half a brain. "You never pay attention," he says.

Pay attention indeed! He owns half my mind. I have a dozen notebooks filled with his advice. So must nearly all the writers writing now in English: "*stand in the middle of your work; throw out half of what you've got; write the way you talk—like a twentieth-century human being. . . .*"

And now look at him. Can a poet come to this?

All his ideas are stolen from somebody else's game preserve. An intellectual poacher, that's what he is. Hunting in the Dark Ages. Bringing home trophies so exotic they're extinct by the time he gets them through the door. A tour of Ezra's mind is like a tour of that room at the Hemingways' where Ernest's game is displayed on the walls—all those mounted heads and horns and hooves *without bodies*. . . .And the gun racks. The arsenal of personal furies. . . .

Ezra never speaks but that he spits a bullet from a dove's mouth.

"Going to put a pond right there," he says pointing down the yard. "Pound's Pond. You like that?"

I can't even smile. Half my mind is marching into the Rhineland, wondering what will happen when the cheering stops. "Where will you get the water?" I ask. The lawn has died for lack of rain, even now in the rainy season.

"Out of the earth—where else? You think the ground is a Jew and can't be made to give?"

I don't really want to talk about it. Why would I want to talk about the digging of a pond when the careful world we've made is tottering along the edge of chaos?

"Not too deep a pond, of course," he says. "Not any deeper than that"—and he shows about three or four feet of depth by slicing the air with his hand. "Just enough to float the moon in." He laughs. "You ever hear that story?"

I shake my head.

Ezra throws another pellet at the cat.

"Chinese poet, Old Man Li Po, went down off his porch one night—dead drunk—and drowned in his pond." He began to roll more meat in his palms. The smell was appalling. Ezra didn't seem to mind it at all. "Wanted to embrace the moon, you see? Thought it was down there waiting for him in the water. Drunk as an old goat. Fell in love with the moon. So goes the legend. Fact is, he probably thought it was some young lady's behind. . . ." He laughed. "Got a great hard-on and thought, I'll just go down there and creep up behind her. . .see how she feels, this pale, round-bottomed lady. And drowned." He hits the cat. "Bull's eye!"

The cat doesn't make a sound, but only narrows its gaze.

I wait   for Ezra to explain the story. Nothing is forth-coming. Finally, I say; "so now you want a pond of your own to drown in. Is that it?"

"Mebbe. Lots of poets drowned over time. . . ." He sticks out his lower lip as he thinks about it. "Shelley down the coast. Viareggio."

Yes.

"All washed up," says Ezra, chuckling. Then he falls silent working his jaws so hard I can hear his grinding teeth.

"Ezra. . .?" I rattle the papers. I'm concerned. I'm supposed to be writing a series for the London *Daily Mail* about the success of Mussolini's regime. I can write about the success of Fascism, yes—but not about a regime hell-bent on war. "Ezra?"

"No," he says, his eyes half-closed. "You want to talk about the world—and I don't want to hear it. All my life I've talked about the world. Broke my teeth, chewing the world's ear. Now screw 'em. Fuck 'em, my friend. Let 'em go march and get it over with. . ." He stands up. "Me? I will bide my time. I have the answers all locked up in here. And one day, mark my words, the call will come. Benito Mussolini will march back home from Addis Ababa, dust himself off and lay down his sword and say to someone: '*bring me Pound*.' You wait! It's coming. There will be a knocking at the gate—and I'll be here."

"Sitting on your porch—or lying in your pond?"

He doesn't like that. He looks right at me and says; "at least I am not impeccable: stiff from spats to collar. And I don't wear gloves when I undo my flies. And I am not a flit."

I cannot breathe.

Finally, he says: "that God damn cat is crazy, baking up there in the sun. So I will do it a favour and bring it down."

He goes towards the lean-to where he keeps the garden tools. I still cannot speak or breathe or move. Dorothy looks out the window. She has turned off her radio now and can hear her husband rattling all the rakes and hoes and shov-els—and she sees me sitting pale as my suit in the yellow deckchair.

"What's going on?" she says.

"God damn neighbour's cat is on the roof," says Ezra, muffled inside the shed.

Dorothy looks at me. I do my best to shrug. "It's been there all day," I say.

"It's up there every day," says Dorothy, leaning down out of the window, shouting at Ezra. "Why can't you leave it alone?"

Ezra re-emerges with a bamboo stick in his hand. "Ever kill a cat?" he says to me, ignoring his wife.

I'd never killed a thing. And I say so.

"Flit—flit," says Ezra. "You done pretty well with your words. Seems to me I've seen a few corpses floating in your wake from time to time."

Dorothy says; "you two fighting again?"

Ezra says; "we two are parting." He clambers onto a table under the window. "Mauberley cannot bear the world of men at arms," he says, "and I cannot bear the world of men in white linen suits."

He begins to jab at the cat. Dorothy runs out through the door. "Leave it alone!" she cries.

Ezra pokes the stick at the cat—but the cat is three feet further up the tiles than he can reach.

"Leave it *alone!*" says Dorothy again. "Dear one. . .Ezra. . .Please!"

The cat looks down at Ezra and the stick. I am compelled to stand up. All my papers fall to the ground.

Dorothy tugs at Ezra's sweater. Ezra goes on rattling the stick and banging it against the tiles. "God damned cat!" he says. "God damn you, cat! Come down!" Bang! Bang! Bang!

And then the one thing happens no one has bargained for. The cat makes a leap at Ezra's face.

Dorothy screams. Ezra falls back. I run forward.

All of us land on the grass in a heap, and the cat takes off across the lawns and up the nearest tree and over the wall.

Dorothy untangles herself and hurries away to bring a cloth and some lemon juice to rub on Ezra's wounds. He is bleeding profusely. Most of the cuts and scratches are superficial. Only one, drawn down lengthwise over his skull and through his hair, is serious. I put on my hat. My bare head makes me nervous. Then, having brushed off my trousers, I cut up the lemons—handing them to Dorothy, watching her clean up Ezra's face and beard.

"Thought I was going to drown in blood," he says in his best dove's voice, all smiles. He is sitting like a child, his legs spread wide apart and Dorothy kneeling beside him. "One more bleeding poet drowned, eh, Hugh?"

I cannot even nod. I feel as if I might never speak to him again. I truly hate him. But then, I've hated him before, and loved him since, and will, I am sure, another day. Nonetheless, I do not speak.

"God damn neighbour's cat," says Ezra, smiling. "God damn cat." And he lifts up Dorothy's hand and kisses it. "Tomorrow," he says. "Tomorrow I will kill it."

I turned away. That's right, I think. *First you feed it, then you kill it. Like your mind.*

And mine. If I let you.

* * *

"What a prick," said Freyberg—reading the end of the encounter with the cat just as Quinn reached it himself. "What a prick."

Quinn turned around, surprised he was not alone. "Who?" he said. He was still somewhat lost in the spring afternoon he'd been reading on the wall.

"Take your pick," said Freyberg, "excepting, of course, the cat. Cat had the right idea—and you should pardon the pun, but I wish to hell he'd got the bugger's tongue instead of just his face."

Quinn went over to the table and pretended to look through the records. He wished that Freyberg would go away and let him read, instead of barging in and shooting his mouth off. If Freyberg didn't want to know the story and hated all the people so much, why not just go out and commandeer a sledge-hammer or a stick of dynamite and bring the whole thing down? Not that Quinn believed for a moment the captain would. He was rather like Pound in that: he needed the wall to rail at—just as Ezra had needed the cat.

Freyberg said; "one thing Pound says I kind of like, however."

"Oh? What's that?" said Quinn.

Freyberg was leaning in—up close to the wall so he could read the words. "Pound's just called Mauberley a fag and then he says; 'it seems to me I've seen a few corpses floating in your wake from time to time,' " Freyberg turned and smiled at Quinn. "Nice assessment, eh?"

"Maybe you'd better tell me what corpses you think he had in mind," said Quinn.

"Oh. . .I think by the time you've finished reading you'll find out who they are."

Freyberg's smile was infuriating: and the more so because Quinn had no comeback up his sleeve.

Freyberg dropped a candy wrapper neatly into the centre of the floor and began to walk away. "Good reading," he said.

When he had gone, Quinn looked down at the wrapper. His instinct was to pick it up and put it somewhere out of the way. But, instead of that, he left it sitting there: the perfect reminder of the mind he was up against.

* * *

Venice: May 5th, 1936

In Venice I was crossing the foyer of the Hotel Grande Bretagne, certain I'd got through Europe without a trace of recognition, when suddenly I heard my name being called very loud across the lobby from the furthest distance. It was Edward and Diana Allenby, just come south themselves to see her ailing father, "Old Redoubtable" Wyndham, who was dying in his mistress's *palazzo* on the Via d'Aquila. Lord

Wyndham once had given me the privilege of reading Disraeli's original manuscript of *Coningsby*.

"You've been very naughty," said Diana, linking her arm through mine. "I read those dreadful pro-Fascist pieces you wrote in the *Daily Mail* and debated burning all your books. Still, you're very talented—and I couldn't bring myself to do anything Herr Hitler might approve of."

Ned looked slightly rumpled. He was limping more than usual and having to use a cane. He hung back.

"Hello, Ned."

"Hugh."

Yes, there was a coolness there—but I would have to suffer it. I offered to take them into the bar and buy them a bottle of wine.

Perhaps if we had been in London, Allenby might have declined. But in a foreign place, an Englishman never refuses an acquaintance. He did not say yes. He merely turned towards the bar.

"Neddy hates Venice," said Diana, chipping away at the ice between us. "Dampness plays havoc with his legs."

We sat at one of the tables with a view of the Canal and I ordered a bottle of Pernod. Until it came, we sat quite silent, smoking Abdullahs—even Diana—staring through the awninged windows, trying not to see each other. When the Pernod was delivered, I dismissed the waiter and tipped the liquor into the glasses myself. As I poured the water over it, Allenby broke the silence by saying; "all these years in Europe and you still don't know how to do that."

I sat back and thought; *oh dear. He's going to criticize everything I do.* "All right," I said. "What am I doing that's wrong?"

"Toss that back and I'll show you."

"Thank you very much," said Diana. "But no thanks. I'll drink mine just as it is." And she raised her glass in my direction. She, at least, was prepared to forgive me for what I'd done. But Ned. Was it the pictures in the press of me and Mrs Simpson? Or was it the pieces I'd written: Mussolini and co.?

I handed the bottle to Allenby.

Diana said; "I do hope you aren't going to drink it neat. It destroys the brain, you know, just like absinthe. Deadly."

"I can think of lots worse ways to die," I said. "All right, Neddy. Show me how it's done."

Allenby filled each glass with about three fingers of water from the pitcher and then said: "now. You have to do this very carefully." And he raised the bottle of Pernod and tipped it slowly, letting the liquor fall from about eight inches height. There was barely a sound: like the pouring of oil. "Watch," he said. "Watch."

All of us watched the marbling of the waters: green; yellow; white and then very slowly a paling off into milky clouds.

"How beautiful," said Diana. "Beautiful. But, surely it tastes the same as mine."

Allenby lifted his glass and drank. "I doubt it," he said.

"Why, dear? Why? It's the very same mixture."

"Anticipation makes it different," said Allenby. "And the fact one cares enough to do it right. One is just a ho-hum drink that makes you want to spit and the other is a work of art." He looked at me. "Sort of like the difference between your articles and books."

So that was it. My political sympathies after all.

"Oh dear," said Diana. "Are you going to argue? Not today. Please."

Allenby put out his cigarette and immediately lighted up another. He looked around the room. The clientele was almost entirely English, with a few Americans thrown in. "I've always felt slightly uncomfortable coming here since the war," he said. "In those days, the Italians were our allies. It rather made sense to come here, then: give them our money and our patronage. . .swim from the Lido. . .learn their language. . .revel in their art. After all, they gave us the Renaissance. Even he can't quite obliterate that."

"Even he?" said Diana. "Who, dear? What are you maundering on about?"

"The Fat One; the Great One; Zio Benito."

"Are you tight?" said Diana.

"No. But I will be. Soon I hope."

Allenby poured another glass of water, oiling it with Pernod from an even greater height than before, holding the bottle almost a foot above the glass.

"I'm afraid my presence is making you unhappy, Ned," I said. "Perhaps I'd better leave."

"If you stand up to go, I shall trip you with my cane," said Allenby, meaning it, having said it without a trace of humour.

"I already seem to have fallen on my face so far as you're concerned."

Diana laughed. Allenby didn't.

He oiled his glass with another inch of Pernod and rolled the ash from his cigarette against the edge of the enamelled dish in the centre of the table. "Seems to me, Diana, you and I have come here to take part in more deaths than one," he said.

Diana winced, but didn't speak. At least she was somewhat reconciled to her father's death, since he was very old (in his ninety-second year) and had lived abroad for a very long time. They were not estranged, but had lived entirely different lives for over twenty years. She was more concerned, I think, for me and Ned. We'd been friends a very long time. But Ned, when he got in this mood, was apt to say things unretractable.

A party of Blackshirts entered the bar. Four of them, with two very handsome women. The maître-d' and several waiters made a great fuss as these officials were seated. Diana watched them. So did I. Allenby, pointedly, did not.

"As I was saying," he continued, raising his voice, staring at his cigarette, "we seem to be taking part in more deaths than one. One old man. . .one old culture—one old continent and—one old friendship."

"Don't," said Diana. She even touched my hand. "That isn't fair."

"Hugh understands," said Allenby. "Don'tcha, Hugh." Allenby narrowed his gaze and spoke through the smoke. "I'm fifteen years your senior," he said. "I've known you ever since you came to England, Hugh. All I'm exercising now is the privilege of years. Seniority. I know you—maybe not entirely inside out, but better than you like to think. I suspect you like to think there isn't *anyone* who knows you. But I do. You're some kind of pilgrim looking for a faith." He winced a sort of belch, carefully hidden behind a fist. "Only thing I don't understand about you, dear old friend— what I positively bloody *hate*—is that you've started looking for it under rocks. . .for instance, over there at that table with those four young men sticking out their chins."

"Don't dear, they'll hear you," said Diana.

"Lady, dear lady," said Allenby, smiling at his wife, taking her hand, raising his voice another decibel, "I'm sure you would say that if Hitler were sitting across the room."

"I just hate embarrassment," Diana said. "That's all."

"Yes. You do, don't you. Yes, you do. And on your way to the concentration camp you will probably apologize for falling down when they push you through the gate."

"What concentration camp?"

"The one we shall all end up in if things keep going the way they are." His voice kept getting louder and louder; and some of the individual words were shouts—like rifle-fire.

"Now I know you've had too much to drink. And I think we should go," said Diana.

"Not before I say one more thing to Hugh, because. . ."

But he was interrupted.

Out in the streets, out on the canal, out in the hotel lobby— everywhere, it seemed—there was a shout: a great, wild-firing boom of exultation, just as if a gigantic display of fireworks had reached its climax and all of ten thousand spectators roared their approval.

"What in the name of hell is that?" said Allenby.

Diana turned as white as a sheet. She reached for Allenby's hand, but it wasn't there. He was fumbling for his cane and knocking things over in the attempt to rise. All around us, in fact, the whole room was turning, rising, running onto the terraces, waving. It was crazy.

Somewhere, a drum was being beaten; somewhere a bugle was calling; somewhere there were people singing. Out across the canal, a gigantic Italian flag—the largest flag I have ever seen—appeared to descend from the heavens and cling to the side of the building there.

"*Che cosa? Che cosa?*" I kept repeating. How could everybody know but us?

And then we heard it. The meaning and the jubilation all in one name: Addis Ababa.

The city had fallen. The war in Ethiopa was over. Mussolini had his empire.

Neddy apparently gave up his attempt to recover his cane. He was rigid in his chair, with his tie askew and his hair falling forward onto his forehead, revealing its sparseness and its dampness. He looked like a man with a fever and his eyes were very slightly glazed.

Diana looked at her lap and then at me.

I reached down, thinking it would be easier for me to retrieve the cane, but Ned said; "you touch that stick and I'll have your head." Not even raising his voice.

We sat that way for another twenty minutes, while the ructions around us died away to mere celebrations and the drums and bugles faded off towards St Mark's and the singing into another part of the hotel.

Allenby poured himself a very large, utterly undiluted shot of the Pernod. Diana brushed a few imaginary things from her lapels.

A waiter came—thank heaven—and picked up the stick; but Ned denied it was his. It was handed, instead, to me.

"*Grazie.*"

Diana made a motion with her shoulders, meaning it was time to get poor Ned away.

"I still have one more thing to say to Hugh," said Allenby: precisely as if the past half-hour had not even happened and the very sentence that had been on his tongue before the fall of Addis Ababa came up out of the rubble like a survivor only very slightly dazed.

I took a deep breath and said; "all right. Go ahead."

Allenby looked at me; and then away. But he did reach out and take Diana's hand—which gave me hope.

"You know you can come and visit us at *Nauly* anytime you like," he said, each word spoken separately like a completed sentence. "We've been friends so many, many years—and I don't like losing friends. Besides. . ." he took Diana's other hand "I think my wife is in love with you. A little.

But—" he made a desperate attempt for just the right words "—what I really want is just to know how it ends, you see. I mean your story. *This.*" And he looked around the room at where we were and all the people there. "We have to get beyond this awful moment, Hugh. Beyond this awful time. And we won't—if people like you give in. And you have, you know. You have. If it wasn't for people like you, this awful moment wouldn't be here. Do you see?"

He was nearly breaking Diana's hand in two with the force of the tension inside him and I became quite alarmed. He stood up, pushing down very hard on her hand and on the table—having to support himself without the benefit of his cane—and I thought he was going to fall over backwards.

I rose.

Diana and I supported Ned on either side and we could feel him give away a little—easing very slightly in towards her shoulder. Diana motioned for the cane and I gave it to her. Ned didn't even see this. He was shaking so much his eyes had all but closed.

Diana reached across and touched me on the cheek and smiled at me—desperate—and said; "you know, dear, he was right when he said I am in love with you a little." And she drew me forward and kissed me somewhere south of the ear—but really only so she could whisper to me; "please; be patient; understand. You are far from being the only cause of this unhappiness. . . ."

Then—stepping back—she stood beside her husband and gave her famous smile that is seen in all the Beaton photographs and said to Neddy; "ready to march, dear heart?"

And they left, without looking back.

And now I must tell what followed.

After they had gone, I sat for the next three-quarters of an hour at the enormous table, sipping what remained of the Pernod. On the other side of the room, the Blackshirts made a great show of their presence, laughing a good deal, making much of their African victory, flashing what seemed to be an inordinate display of strong white teeth, exuding an aura of masculinity that caused an imbalance in the atmosphere as if something quite invisible, but huge was taking up more and more space between the tables.

At one point one of them stood up—very tall—not more than twenty-two years old and wearing boots and a wide brown belt. I could hear him excusing himself and I knew this young, exuberant man would have to pass my table. And I began to perspire. I wanted so desperately to follow him, but I could only think of what Allenby had said; "you are some kind of pilgrim looking for a faith. . .under rocks."

And yet I turned in my chair and watched that young man going away. And I went away with him—in my mind. And knelt before his strength. And his victory.

Once I had escaped from the Bar, I waited in my rooms, for nearly twenty hours. And in all that time the bands were marching through the streets and the songs kept rising through the floors and the rockets flew up into the sky obliterating all the ordinary stars with stars of green and yellow, blue and red. But I would not go out; I could not. I could not admit the bands were mine and the songs were mine and the rockets flying up into the sky were celebrating my victory. . .and my defeat.

I couldn't eat. I didn't want to think. I only wanted to be drunk, like Ned. I was ill.

I bathed. I lay on the bed beneath a shroud of netting. I bathed again. I covered myself from head to toe with *Knize Ten*. I bathed again. I thought; I will bathe myself to death if I can't get rid of the smell. But of course, the smell was only in my mind. At last, the next night, after dark I had a perfunctory call from Ned. "You might want to come and say your goodbye to the old man. The Palazzo d'Aquila. . ."

I was shaky still, but knew I must say yes. For Diana's sake, if not my own.

So we all went out together, riding across the lagoon in a motor launch and slowly down the far canal to the Via d'Aquila, where footmen bearing torches met us at the steps and ushered us inside past rows of official mourners, officers, ambassadors and princes of the Church.

The room Lord Wyndham lay in smelled of incense and roses. The bed was raised on a dais and had a canopy of thick brocade and drawn-back netting. Along one wall, there was a fresco, chipped and faded, showing a pageant of worshippers and eagles. Two nuns, one of them a nursing sister, sat on chairs by the windows, sipping water and lemon juice, telling beads. A cardinal hovered by the bed.

A tall, blonde woman—forty-eight, maybe fifty years old— came down the length of the room to embrace Diana. This must be the old man's mistress. Lady Wyndham had been dead for years.

Allenby kissed the woman on both cheeks rather formally and brought her over to be introduced to me, while Diana went and knelt beside the bed and kissed the cardinal's ring and held her father's hand.

The gold-headed woman was the Baronessa Isabella Loverso. She spoke impeccable English. She told me she had read my books and had long ago met Ezra, when he lived in Venice.

As she spoke, she stared into my face as if to tell me something else, unspoken. As if she wished to literally impress herself upon my mind. But then she turned away and walked with Allenby across the room to introduce him to the cardinal.

Diana spoke in her father's ear.

I could hardly bear to watch. (But I always do.) I saw him move his hands to find Diana and watched him touch her face and then reach out to find the other woman.

"Presto! Presto!" someone whispered.

The room filled up with the sound of rustling clothes, like wings, as everyone fell to their knees. Falling down myself, I realized I was kneeling more in awe of history than of death. For the old man dying on the bed had knelt himself, as a child, to kiss the hand of Wellington. There we all were in the midst of the twentieth century, but now his daughter and his mistress kissed his hands, through which time flew to Waterloo and Bonaparte. Somewhere a clock was striking.

The reigns of Victoria, Edward, George rose up and fell away in seconds.

Then there was a sigh. And death.

We waited there all night. And in the morning the Baronessa Loverso, standing with me on the steps beside the water, said; "I have read what you have written in the London *Daily Mail*. You are right, you know, when you say that we need a new kind of leader—not the leaders we have. I have friends with whom I think you should speak. Would you mind—would you object, if one day, once this mourning is over, I wrote to you and arranged a meeting?"

No. I would not object at all. I found the woman charming. Isabella Loverso stood at the edge of another age, retaining its dignity and serenity in spite of all the harassment of the modern world. I was impressed.

"You are one of us, I think," she said—and smiled. "Though of course you don't know what I mean by that. But I am very glad we met."

I kissed her hand and we parted.

In the motorlaunch, I said to Allenby; "what can you tell me of her?"

Allenby pursed his lips.

"She comes from a very important family," he said. "Though not of rank. She's a niece of Admiral Ciano."

"That's where she gets the handsome features, then?;" I said.

"Yes. And the dreadful politics."

I was about to ask for details but Allenby gave me a look that told me the conversation was over. I should have known better than to think that Ned and I could ever talk of politics again.

About a week later, Allenby and Diana left for England— taking with them all Diana wanted *in memoriam*: the pillow her father's head had lain against when he died.

I telephoned the Palazzo d'Aquila but was told the Baronessa Loverso was in Paris. She had gone away quite suddenly "on business"—but with no address.

"You are one of us, I think," she had said. *"Though of course you don't know what I mean by that."*

But I thought I could guess. It must have to do with where she got the handsome features. And the politics.

* * *

Quinn had now made his way around the walls from China, 1924 and had arrived with Mauberley at the moment in which he was preparing to join the King and Mrs Simpson aboard the *Nahlin* in the summer of 1936.

He sat on his cot and wished it was as warm in this room as it was above his head in Dubrovnik. He turned his collar up and wondered why there hadn't been a call for chow. Freyberg, no doubt. The last thing on his list was always the Mess, one reason being that Captain Freyberg lived on candy bars and Coke and never really gave much thought to proper food.

Way off down the hall, Quinn could hear two people talking. Rudecki, more than likely, nattering with the picket at the top of the stairs. Just two ordinary voices, barely audible. Just two ordinary men way off down the hall polishing the butts of their Browning Automatics and shifting the weight of the hand grenades that wouldn't be there on their belts if it wasn't for the writing on these walls.

* * *

The *Nahlin*: August, 1936

It was unnerving at first to have the King so close. I never knew where to look, and was always staring him straight in the eye. He was wary of this and avoided it at all costs and I thought for certain I had made some dreadful gaff in protocol. In the end, of course, I came to my senses and realized that very few conversations with anyone are held "eye-to-eye" unless one is trying to intimidate the listener—or perhaps if one is making love. People's eyes so rarely meet in the normal course of events, it can be quite alarming when it happens and I think the King must have thought I was somewhat peculiar at first. I was known as *that man who stares*, Wallis told me—and then we all had a good laugh about it. It was, I explained, a writer's prerequisite to stare—and they accepted this.

The King had a charming smile and his colouring was vivid and exquisite under the sun, which he revelled in—though his lips, I noted, tended to pale if he stayed too long in the heat. He was otherwise tanned and golden and he wore the briefest kahki shorts I have ever seen on a grown-up man and an open shirt with a brace of crucifixes round his neck on silver chains. He literally shone from head to toe, so you could pick him out a mile away in any crowd and this *shining* was so pronounced and unique that I ultimately found myself believing in the magic "inner lights" of which one hears superior beings are possessed.

But in spite of the shining and in spite of the smile and in spite of the glorious times we had and the marvellous reception given the King and Wallis everywhere we went, the last few days of the *Nahlin*'s cruise were tense and ambiguous. The King withdrew from his guests and even scowled when we passed him on the deck. He was not bad-tempered, merely melancholy—and our final meals together were eaten in silence, though Wallis played a good deal of music on her gramophone. Nothing, however, helped—not even "Dardenella", which had been our anthem throughout the trip—and one night Wallis made the fatal mistake of absent-mindedly putting on a recording of Fred Astaire and Ginger Rogers singing: "A Fine Romance".

> *A fine romance, my friend this is;*
> *A fine romance, with no kisses. . . .*

At this point, the King got up and left the table.

The cause of his melancholia was plain. As soon as he disembarked from the *Nahlin*, he would be parted many

weeks from Wallis. And he was not going home to the best
of situations. He was going, instead, to confront his first real
crisis as King and a test of wills between himself and his
family that would set the pattern for the rest of his reign.
He would have to tell his mother, his brothers and his sister
he was determined to marry a woman they each had refused
to accept.

All the King wanted was to make Wallis Simpson happy—
and a marriage, in time, was not completely out of the question. But the King and Wallis wanted more. Their intention
was now quite clear she should be his consort. For the last
three weeks of the cruise they spoke of it openly. People
began to defer to Wallis even to the point of bobbing when
she passed. This in turn led her to assume an air of hauteur
which a person might otherwise have smiled at, were it not
that it now took on an edge of ugly grandeur when she dealt
with those "beneath" her. Going into public places soon
became an embarrassment, since Wallis always raised her
hand to be kissed and held people off by the length of her
arm as if she expected them to curtsey. She even did this
to the mistress of the King of the Hellenes—a woman, in-
cidentally, whose real name was Jones.

Then, too, there was a heat wave and the war in Spain—
which lent an air of delicate unease to the whole of Southern
Europe. This was like a hot wind with sand in it—a sirocco
full of tiny shards of glass. German battleships sat offshore
from Barcelona—harmless enough, but blond and out of
place. There was the sound of aeroplanes all day. It was time
for all of us to head back north and for the King to go about
his business.

Nonetheless, it proved an impossible wrench to simply
pack one's bags and entrain for the rains of London. Having
been so long on display in the sun, our bodies demanded
a measured withdrawal into the shade, in the manner of
addicts who pare down their intake of alcohol by one glass
a day. Consequently, stepping onto the quayside, the King
begged Wallis to go with him to Vienna—which of course
she did; but not without the companionship of her dogs—
two canine and myself.

We stayed at the Hotel Bristol, an old haunt of mine and, as it turned out, the King's as well. He knew the doorman's name and the wine steward's too—which rather threw me. Not that he shouldn't know such things. It was just that he was so very familiar, it made me wonder how much of his time had been spent "incognito" here and elsewhere. I was not yet used to Royal ways and had always thought, along with everyone else, that princes lived entirely apart in a world that had no border with my own. True, I might enter their world by invitation, but they never entered mine because they had no need. Unless they were pushed, of course—as Dmitri had been.

In Vienna there was music of which the King approved, and Wallis put away her gramophone. There was dancing noon and night and cocktails every evening: long hours and rich meals. We dined, it seemed, on an endless diet of cream and cake. There was nothing we ate that did not arrive in a torte or some kind of pastry. The King, I think, was feeding his courage.

There were other signs, too, he was testing something—growing in some new direction—feeding other appetites than his own. He wanted to see what could come of the image of himself and Wallis if he pushed it to its limits. He became completely careless of the Press. Photographers were even encouraged to cease their lurking in doorways and wingback chairs and to come out into the open so their pictures might present a less furtive look to the King and Wallis; and Wallis began to smile less shyly; and she glittered more and wore more jewelry. Indeed, she had more jewelry to wear.

There was something in those photographs worth re-marking on—a kind of signal only seen and recognized later. I saw it in myself, at first, more vibrantly than in the others. I had never looked better, never looked happier, never looked more fit. I did not even guess why this should be, though I suppose I thought it was just the age, the times, the ex-citement of the moment. After all, I was younger then; I was relatively famous; I was poised on the lip of great expec-tations; my future was secure; I knew who I was and I had my health. We had all been out in the sun and now we were dancing in the limelight. Everyone in all those pictures taken then was smiling; everyone was radiant; everyone was infallible. It was all a lie, of course. The fact was, we were being used to shore up the King and his reluctant confidence—used as the symbols of the public approbation he needed so desperately before he could broach the subject of Wallis and himself to his family. Given time and coverage, he could finally point to names and faces far more telling and prominent than mine and say: "But look! The people approve!" As if the Duff-Coopers and the Prince and Princess of Hugelstein were the people. . . .So this was why we smiled. We were all so willing to be there; thinking ours was the ultimate face of the age. And perhaps it was.

The King eventually left us there in Vienna and in our own time we departed together, bound for Paris aboard the Orient Express, a large and very gay party. But it was not till we had passed through Venice that Wallis took me aside and said; "when we arrive, I want you to stay with me a while at the Meurice. I have a most unpleasant thing to do— and cannot possibly do it all alone. . . ."

The King had unpleasant things to do as well, for it was now he must put his case before his family. His "family" meant, pre-eminently, Queen Mary—and he found her having a picnic tea in one of the drawing rooms at Marlborough House.

The fact she was having a picnic tea and wore a bibbed apron over her dress was not entirely eccentric: Queen Mary was in the process of moving all her possessions and her staff of over sixty servants from Buckingham Palace down the Mall to the traditional residence of heirs presumptive, where she had lived so happily twenty-five years before as the Princess of Wales. Some other home might well have been assigned, but now that her still unmarried son was King, her second son, the heir, had established a family residence elsewhere and did not care to leave. So Marlborough House had been given over to the Queen.

The heir—"Bertie", the Duke of York—was a private man whose only wish was to be left alone with his wife and his children; standing on the edge of things but never at the centre. "David" was at the centre and had always been at the centre and, having survived into kingship, would surely continue to be at the centre now and for evermore—*amen*. The Duke of York was in fact a paragon in this—and the rarest of princes because of it: there was not an iota of ambition in his veins and he shunned the Crown as anyone else might push away a basket of snakes. The very thought of it repelled him. Kingship would kill him; his nervous spirit and his shyness would simply not bear it. Besides which, he stammered and could not say "King".

The Queen, in her cotton apron and pale mauve hat, was seated before a makeshift table eating a crustless sandwich of which a dozen more were piled on a plate.

"Have one," she said. "They really are very nice." The Queen, though English born, still bore the faintest traces of an ancestral German accent that had endured unshaken though modified for many generations.

"No thank you, Mama. I'm really not hungry."

"But David, you must. I cannot sit here and eat alone."

The King set his hat and his gloves aside on the lid of a packing case full of swords and sat down and sighed. He picked up a sandwich and peeped inside and found it was not to his taste. Sliced tongue.

"Mrs Moore," said the Queen, referring to her housekeeper, "had them made especially for you when I told her you would be here. So eat."

The King turned the sandwich over in his fingers several times and finally laid it back on the plate without his mother seeing. The Queen was busy munching and had turned away to stare into the green recesses of the room in which they sat.

Packing cases, open and shut, some of them spilling their marble contents over the floor, gave the place the look and feel of a mausoleum—and the fact there were not yet curtains or drapes at the windows added a cold, hard light to the scene. The Queen began to pick at the crumbs that were scattered over her apron, eating them one by one with a reverent, distant look in her eye. "You can surely not fail to recall," she said, "this house when you were a child."

"Of course not, Mama."

"We were here seven years. And you were already sixteen and the Prince of Wales when we left."

"That's right." The King was looking grim and his jaw was set. His mother's sole bad habit—irritating and sometimes even maddening—was her tendency to litanize. If a cousin's name was mentioned, out would come a string of genealogies. If a date was given, every week and month and year preceding it was struck with a tick mark—verbalized and embroidered with detail. She could name every child of every child of every child of Queen Victoria, and even Queen Victoria herself could not have done that.

"Do eat. Please do," she said.

The King picked up and palmed another horrid sandwich, placing it, once his mother's gaze was averted, in his pocket next his handkerchief.

"Your grandpapa was here, heaven knows, a century before he was King. And your grandmotherdear, before and after being the Queen, and before them both, Queen Adelaide-the-Grump. . . ." Queen Mary smiled. "She was very bad-tempered, you know. And she would have been your great-great-great-Aunt. I never knew her, but certainly my mother did and she always said. . ."

"Mama?"

"Yes, David?"

"Please. No history today."

The Queen picked over the sandwiches and held one near her lips, prepared to bite. "I am only thinking," she said, "of where we are and what we do. It is almost a hundred years since Queen Victoria came to the throne and in all that time this house has been the house of a Princess of Wales or a Dowager Queen. Before and after the throne, we must all lie here in waiting. . . ." She trembled inadvertently and tried to eat the sandwich, but could not. Her lower lip retreated and she bit it—hard—as she always did to prevent the onset of tears. Queen Mary never wept. It was a rule.

At last she placed the sandwich—whole—in her mouth

and ate it as if her life depended on it. "Eat," she said to her son. "You must." And she handed him the plate, which he could only stare at and put in his lap because it seemed ungrateful to hand it back to her. And when he looked up, he saw that she was looking at him strangely, as from another time. It was perhaps the afternoon light that caused this effect and the gentle, silent rain that misted the windows. And a veil of dust intruded between them, raised by his mother's servants moving in a cortège behind a row of monstrous packing crates being carried through the great saloon towards the double tiers of stairs beyond and his mother chewed her sandwich and watched and waited a very long time before she spoke to him again and, when she did, her eyes were misted. The King was quite alarmed. . .until she spoke. "I got the end of Mrs Moore's mustard pot that time," she said and dabbed at her eyes with a double damask napkin hugely embroidered with the letter G. "Just as I seem to have got the end of the mustard pot," she went on, "with the news I hear of your recent trip abroad. . . ." And she bit decisively into a piece of ginger cake, with her eyes snapping blue like two brisk flags in a rising wind.

The King was overwhelmed with sorrow and anger. Anger at Mrs Moore's vindictive mustard pot and her ginger cake and her damned impertinent sliced-tongue sandwiches; sorrow at his mother's words. And he opened his mouth to speak, with an intake of breath that was an overture to violence, but his mother raised her hand and said; "please don't explain. I do not want to hear this woman's name. No. Do not speak it." And the King, who had come such a long, long way to inform his mother of his plans for the future of her line, was forced to look away into his lap, with his mouth still open. . .staring down at the spiteful sandwiches on their Ludwigsburg porcelain plate. And he tried with all his might to speak his mind, but his mother's presence was just too great to overcome and he could not even raise his head. There was something dreadfully wrong, all at once, with the back of his neck.

The Queen at last said; "come, there is something I wish

you to see." And they both stood up and began to leave the room. The King looked back at his hat and gloves where they sat like carved, forgotten things on top of their box of swords. The plate of contentious sandwiches sat beside them, carved as well, though out of malice, not of stone. But the King dared not go back to retrieve his things, since his mother's stride was already leaving him behind and perhaps he thought he would turn into something carved of stone or malice himself if he waited there too long. So he turned and hurried after, both of them passing the rows and rows of royal portraits Queen Mary had made it her business to collect—all of them shrouded, all of them leaning back against the walls, unhung, and some with a single eye exposed to watch them as they passed—the Queen and her son—the King and his mother—pattering heel and toe across the great uncarpeted saloon with its painted battle scenes raging on the ceilings overhead—all the great and glorious victories of the Duke of Marlborough for whom Sir Christopher Wren had built this house in 1710—and all the Queen's servants and all the King's movers nodded and bobbed as best they could beneath the weight of the giant boxes and trunks and wicker hampers flowing unceasingly through the doors and up the stairs and the King and the Queen took up their place in the procession—climbing all the way to the top with unbroken step and marching along the gallery as if in the lead of troops till they came to an open door through which the Queen propelled the King and closed the door behind them. Click.

There was instant silence.

"I don't remember this," said the King, as his eyes adapted to the light.

"You were never allowed in here," said the Queen. "It was always locked when children were about."

Standing dead centre of a narrow, ill-lit room was a dressmaker's dummy clothed in a long white shift. It was raised on a dais two feet high, with a step running all the way around. Its other salient feature, besides the shift and the dais, was the fact that, unlike the rest of its kind, it possessed a head and the head, which was made of white kid leather, was crowned with human hair.

"Is it you?" said the King.

"It is the Queen," his mother said.

The thing, indeed, had the very shape of the Queen and even its coiffure was so well made it gave the approximate shape of his mother's hair; but its leather facelessness disturbed the King a good deal more than he could say. Somehow, it frightened him, standing there so still and utterly bound to its place as it was. Its round metal base was nailed down tight to the floor of the dais, so nothing could topple it over and the King could see that it plainly had neither arms nor legs—which added, somehow sadly, to its poise since it stood so forthrightly there, as if such things as arms and legs were mere encumbrances. Nothing would be allowed to make it afraid, no matter how defenceless it seemed. But of course it was only a thing and all these thoughts of "silence", "stillness", "poise" and "defencelessness" were nonsense.

The Queen had been watching her son to see what his reaction might be to this apparition, and now she turned and faced her other self as if it were her twin. She reached out and touched the cotton shift, adjusting here and there an unbecoming fold until it fell just so. Its bows and pale rosettes all wanted putting up and fussing with, but she would come some other time and do that. For now, it was simply pleasant to see again an old respected friend.

All down the sides of the room the Queen's royal gowns and robes were hung on racks, a hundred pieces of clothing and more and each one bearing a number pinned discreetly to its sleeve. On a lectern near the door, beneath a naked pink electric bulb, there was a large, much used and very old ledger bound in leather. Every occasion on which each gown and robe had been worn was entered there and all the corresponding hats and shoes and jewels described and numbered, too.

Queen Mary looked around the room and smiled with deep and genuine pleasure. "You should know," she said, "that I came up here the day your grandfather died—and curtsied to my sawdust sister here."

The King was now watching his mother's face and he saw how deeply moved she was by the thought of that historic day so long ago when the old world passed. And the evening light in which that scene had taken place must have been the very same as this that flooded now between the corridors of robes from the windows at the western end of the room.

"As I waited here," Queen Mary said, "for the call to take my place, do you know that Grandmotherdear had just let Alice Keppel in to say farewell to your Granpapa?" Mrs Keppel had been the last and most enduring of Edward VII's mistresses—and Queen Alexandra had had the heart and the decency to bring her in to say goodbye. She had even left the King and his mistress alone for their final words. "There is nothing we cannot do or bear," Queen Mary said to her son, King Edward VIII. "If we are the lords of the realm, we must."

The King looked away.

"Mrs Keppel is still alive," Queen Mary said, "with all her happiness and memories intact. And Grandmotherdear passed on the Queen to me. . . . Do you see? Do look," she said. And she ran the palm of her hand across the leather shoulders of the figure on the dais. "The Queen has had a most extraordinary life. And she will, I am sure, be here when I am dead for many years."

The King was speechless now—deprived of every word he might have used to tell his tale. And if Wallis Simpson's name had not crossed even his lips, it would certainly never cross his mother's.

There was a burst of sunlight, then, and the King and his mother turned towards the windows. "Look," she said. "We can see the tops of all the trees in St James." And she went along between the robes and opened the doors and stepped out onto the balcony. "No more rain," she said. "It has all gone by and the sky is as clear as a bell. Do come and see." She held out her hand to her son and the King went out and joined her, overlooking the gardens. The balcony was very small and only large enough for three or four to stand there comfortably.

In the yard below, where the gravel and sand abutted the grass, an enormous congregation of birds was gathering. Pigeons and rooks and sparrows from the Park. And there was Mrs Moore with the Ludwigsburg plate in her hand and all the remains of the uneaten sandwiches and she was breaking them up into tiny, tiny pieces and mingling these with the crusts the cook had earlier cut away and also, perhaps, with a crumb or two of ginger cake and scattering all of this with a wide and generous gesture of benevolence over the grass so that all the birds—every one of them—might eat. And the Queen, on seeing this, looked over at her son and said; "is there nothing in your pocket that you think you might throw down?"

She was smiling. Damn. She had known all along he had palmed that sandwich and put it there beside his handkerchief—so it shamed him having to reach inside and take it out.

"You should break it up, as Mrs Moore has done," said the Queen, "so as many will receive some parts of it as possible. Do."

So the King threw down his sandwich—morsel by morsel—onto the grass and the pigeons, rooks and sparrows made a very happy racket, scrabbling around to find it all and his mother said; "there. It is all they ask. Just listen to them sing!" And she turned and went inside and left the King alone on the balcony. Moments later he went inside himself and, closing the doors behind him, he stood ostensibly alone in the wardrobe room. His mother was gone but the ledger remained with its pages and pages of legends neatly inscribed, and all the numbered gowns and robes made a rustling sound as he passed—and the Queen was still in her place, nailed down forever. Her eyeless gaze was like a pressure on his back as he went through the door and left her there in the dark. But this was more than he could bear, so he turned again and opened the door again so the light from the gallery fell on the hem of her long pale gown and the oval of her white kid face could just be seen. It was easy enough, he thought as he watched, to understand the power of the mystery that had drawn his mother to her knees before this image all those years ago. He would kneel himself, if he was not her King. But he was her King and he must not kneel.

Paris: September, 1936

The moment Wallis and I appeared in Paris there were photographs; American reporters; invitations from the French, the Spanish and the forty-eight Russian Pretenders. We became a curious "item": scandal bait—without a hook.

This, however, was only in the evenings. By day there was genuine scandal afoot—but all of it was private. It began the very day we arrived.

The unpleasant thing that Wallis could not do alone was to meet in secret with her husband. This meeting occurred downstairs in her suite where, fascinated, I hung in the background with the other dogs and watched while Ernest Simpson crossed the carpet to be greeted by his wife's extended arm and noticeably ringless fingers.

Simpson, impeccably dressed in pin-stripe blue, had come to effect, if it were possible, "a reconciliation of mutual intent" (as his lawyer had obviously told him to put it).

"Why?" said Wallis. "What for?"

Ernest Simpson mumbled something that incorporated the phrase "past happiness". It was all I could hear.

There was something vaguely Oriental about the way the scene unfolded: Ernest Simpson standing in the centre of the carpet, almost at attention, bobbing from time to time, and Wallis seated on a silk divan, with her feet precisely touching at the ankles and her back as straight as a ramrod—while I hovered, (the Shanghai ambassador) in the background, holding a tiny dog in the crook of either arm and watching, of necessity, through slitted eyes because the light was pouring through the windows, cutting across the room between the suitor and his wife.

The suitor pled for himself. He pled for his wife. He even pled for the King—for the "honour of the King and all he stands for". Still she would not be moved.

It went on and on, until at last they broke for lunch like actors being released from rehearsing a scene they did not know how to play.

I retired to my own suite. Paris was slowly being ruined. I read the latest pronouncements of Aldous Huxley in the newly-published *"Eyeless in Gaza"*—none of which pleased me once I had read that "chastity is the most unnatural of sexual perversions". Damn it all! Is nothing sacred? I slammed the book into the wastebasket. *Rubbish.* From an upstart!

All through the rest of the afternoon, Ernest and Wallis did their best to extricate themselves from history alive and sane and physically unwounded. The tension in the rooms became so great that one of the dogs threw up, while the other lifted its leg against a Louis Quinze table (luckily an imitation).

In the end, Ernest Simpson informed his wife she was not the only infidel abroad that summer and hinted he was falling in love with her best friend, a woman called Raffray (which I thought made her sound like an Irish tout).

Wallis made a face and eased one foot from its shoe. I was certain she would laugh. But she controlled herself.

"Have you slept with her?" she said.

Simpson said; "of course not"—positive proof that he had.

"Well—what are we to do?" said Wallis, allowing me to light her cigarette.

Ernest said; "I implore you to return to my bed and board."

Now, Wallis let go and roared with laughter. *"Bed and board?* It sounds like a rooming house!"

At this point, Ernest Simpson grew very red in the face and shouted at his wife; "damn it, woman, I would sue you in a second if I could!"

"Why don't you, then?" (Knowing full well he didn't have the nerve.)

"For the simple reason the law does not allow me to name the King as co-respondent."

Wallis paled, I think. At any rate, the back of her neck was livid.

"Oh." (The first *small* sound she had made; the first admission history might have aces up its sleeve.)

Just when I thought he might win if he kept up his attack, Ernest Simpson suddenly sagged. He gave up.

"Very well, Wallis," he said. "Tell me what you want?"

I waited for her to say; "the Crown." But all she said was; "a divorce."

108

"When?" said Simpson.

"Just as soon as it can be arranged."

Simpson hesitated just one second and then, for the first and only time in their whole encounter, he smiled. "And do you want it arranged *with* or without publicity?" he said.

It won me to him completely.

But I must admit her answer was very winning, too.

"Without knives," she said.

And so—they, too, were parted.

Nauly: September, 1936

It was a perfect English afternoon, resplendent with flowers and insects, seedcake and cucumber sandwiches. After their tea, Charles Augustus Lindbergh asked the Honourable Edward Allenby to walk with him across the lawns at *Nauly*, in Kent. "There's something I want to say," said Lindbergh. "Alone."

It was as if they had wandered into a verse of Victorian poetry, illustrated by Tenniel. Civilized by seven generations of Massies, the Jacobean manor house and its estates had fallen to Edward Allenby only because his eldest brother, the present Earl of Massie, preferred to live in town and, out of season, in the South of France.

There were arbours overgrown with roses, a yew walk, a knot garden filled with herbs and a round pond down the slope that was hung beneath a willowed shade. Over to one side, visible but increasingly distant as they walked, Lady Diana and Mrs Lindbergh and a dozen others sat on a terrace continuing their tea while children played with a dog on the grass and a gardener wheeled the deadheads from some roses past their prime toward a compost heap. Budleia bloomed— all blue—beside the paths and a bees' grove of lavender drooped in a raised stone bed.

Allenby was just past fifty, rounding, but still very handsome. He was currently Parliamentary Under-Secretary of

State for Foreign Affairs and the member for Justin-Beeches.

Lindbergh—only recently returned from the German Olympics where he'd been an honoured guest of Reich-marshal Göring—was thirty-four years of age and spare of mind as he was of form: thin as a walking photograph; weath-erbeaten as a prairie bone. Allenby, on the other hand, was compacted like a well-wrapped English parcel—everything spruce and neat, with all the awkward corners nicely turned and folded under. When Lindbergh walked, he led with his shoulders, and standing still was apparently impossible. Some part of him was always in motion—his wrists, his hands, his elbows. Allenby in England (where it was not quite so damp as Venice), still had a noticeable limp but could discard his cane. The cause of the limp would be best described as the Somme.

Lindbergh and Allenby had known one another for several years—though never so intimately as Allenby and I. Lind-bergh, being shy, would not let people in. But they were genuine friends, not mere acquaintances.

They had met in the worst of conditions, in America where Allenby had gone as part of a diplomatic mission back in 1932, the year the Lindbergh baby had been kidnapped and murdered, an event from which Lindbergh never recovered. In a sense, it had driven a part of him "mad". He became like Orestes—driven by furies. Some say the Furies are flies—or a swarm of bees—and they torment their victims both with buzzing and with endless bites. For Lindbergh these Furies were his fellow countrymen, in particular the Press, whom he hated with an all consuming rage that has been described as "demented".

Allenby thought of this dementia as a great and debili-tating tragedy: "that one so revered by his countrymen, who had done his countrymen such credit and brought them so much honour, should turn so vehemently against them." Vehement was something of an understatement. Lindbergh once described America as having the bloodiest form of government on earth, because it indulged and encouraged people's lust for violence by tolerating freedom of the press. He called this form of government "degenerate democracy".

But he and Allenby were standing now on an English lawn, bathed in sunlight. They were not on that American lawn, in the awful darkness with the ladder propped against the window, crying; *I am gone forever: dead*. Still, it did not seem to matter. When Allenby looked at Lindbergh from the corner of his eye, he beheld the same demi-mordant man he had known all along—with thinning hair and a thinning mouth and an ever-thinning sense of tolerance. It could well be, of course, that Bruno Hauptmann's execution in the spring of 1936 had brought the horror back in ways that only Lindbergh would ever know. Merely to kill the killer of his child did not kill the killing. It extended it.

Lindbergh, his wife and son Jon had come to live in England, in the Harold Nicolsons' old farm house, which more or less made them neighbours of the Allenbys. The distance between them was only eight miles. Lindbergh was given to "wandering over" in his motorcar and even, on occasion, walking. In spite of a happy marriage he always seemed lonely. Always seemed as if there were something he was about to ask—but never did.

They reached the Round Pond and Allenby sat, to relieve his legs, on a small stone bench and lighted up a Turkish cigarette.

"All right, Gus. We won't get more alone than this," he said. (The terrace with its people was about five hundred yards away.) "What can I do for you?"

Lindbergh had already laid the groundwork for what he'd come to say to Allenby by delivering, as they'd walked across the lawns, a sort of "eulogy" to Hitler's Germany that in fact was rather commonplace and therefore not too much of a shock to Allenby. He'd heard it all a dozen times before from a dozen other "converts": not unlike an actor's audition piece, spoken entirely by rote and more often than not with a total failure to connect the words to their meaning. Lindbergh's version might have rated a C-minus. Whatever genuine passion he invested all came within that part of the speech that had to do with air power.

Now, by the pond, Lindbergh came directly to the point: what to do with the future once it had been captured. Kidnapped.

He spoke of a world divided: halved. "We all know the greatest menace is Bolshevism," he said. "And in order to counteract its encroachment, our half of the world must act in concert against it."

"Led by Germany, no doubt," said Allenby—blowing smoke. How disappointing that Lindbergh was becoming just another boring Nazi evangelist.

"No," said Lindbergh. "Not led by Germany. Led by us."

Allenby looked at him sharply. "Us?"

Lindbergh didn't even blink. "That's right."

Allenby might not have understood what he was hearing. He looked up across the lawn, because he wanted to see his wife and children—just to verify their existence. "Us?" he said. "Who do you mean by us."

"You and me." Lindbergh's voice was like a child's describing what it was going to have for supper. "You and me. Our friends. . ."

Allenby narrowed his eyes. "What friends? Which ones?"

"Oh, come on, Ned. We both have friends in Germany. . .here. . .America. . ."

There was a very slight pause and then Allenby felt constrained to say; "you and I are friends, Gus. But not political friends. Surely to God you know that."

"What are you, then? Some sort of Communist?"

"Don't be childish."

"Well then, what are you? Tell me. Give it a name."

"Can't we have some other—*any* other conversation? Something pleasant. Something grown-up."

"No. I want an answer. I'm making a point."

"All right," Allenby said. "I'm in the centre, where you know damn well I am. And where, I might add, all sane people should be in this hopelessly juvenile world of yours. God, Gus—don't make me angry. I can't bear it." He rubbed his leg.

Lindbergh didn't respond to Allenby's anger at all. What he did was brush a fly from the back of his hand and then said; "there is no centre."

Allenby laughed.

"There *is no centre*," Lindbergh repeated, flaring, red-faced. "There's nothing now but two halves: right and left.

If the world were a lemon," he said; "and someone cut it
with a knife, it would lie there like this—" he used his hands
"—in *halves*. Them and us. Nothing in between."

Allenby felt belittled. Degraded; his political sophistication insulted. Undergraduates had more sense than to talk
of *halves*—as if the world were black and white. "Gus," he
said, speaking as to a child, "my friend, there have been
parties of the centre since time immemorial. Why? Because
they are the only civilizing, saving grace we have with which
to stave off those two halves you keep talking about—*bar-
barism and complete élitism*."

"Maybe once," said Lindbergh. "Maybe once there was
a centre—but not any more. Now there's just. . ."

"If you say 'two halves' once more I'll hit you." Allenby
tried to laugh.

The laughter wouldn't quite come, but Lindbergh had
sensed it was there and it altered his features, moulding
them into an ugly, paranoic mask that was not only unat-
tractive but shocking. And with it came an unfortunate,
bullying tone of voice. "I've started to tell you something,"
he said. "And I mean to finish. . .by which I mean I insist
you hear the end of this—because if you don't, you'll regret
it."

"Is that a threat?"

"Maybe. But I'd prefer to call it advice."

Allenby sighed. He lighted up another Abdullah—elegant
and oval; evocative of other, better times than these; the
early days of his marriage. . .the linden trees in the Wilhelmstrasse when he'd been a comer, making his mark in
the Foreign Office. . . .*Was it that?* All that time he'd spent
in Berlin? The German connection? Had someone drawn a
dreadful, dreadful conclusion; dead wrong and damaging?
Had someone thought he could really be converted to the
present German cause and sent Gus to do the dirty work?
Was that it?

Then he saw Lindbergh's eyes through the smoke, with
their menacing light that impelled attention. Yes. Whatever
this was, it was dangerous.

He looked away. Far off across the lawns, his wife and

Mrs Lindbergh and all the other guests were seated in their places—actors in a scene they didn't even know was taking place. He waved, just to make contact. But no one waved back. Surely only because they hadn't seen. Nonetheless, it made him feel appallingly alone.

"All right; I'll give you five minutes," he said. "Finish it."

Lindbergh now became very quiet. He folded and made a knot of his hands. For the next few moments, as if it was a vital condition of what he had to say, he was utterly still.

"You have been chosen," he began, "among a few others, to be given a chance to save your country. . . ."

(Chosen, Allenby thought. Chosen? Dear sweet God, he sounds like a Buchmanite, or one of Aimée Semple's simpletons. Any minute now, he'll froth at the mouth and fall down.)

Lindbergh went on. "When I was in Berlin," he said; "I had the privilege of watching the German air force in action. I've seen its size. I've seen its power. I've seen its potential." He paused. "Ned, England mustn't ever draw its fire. Never. They can bomb you out of existence."

Allenby's mind went ticking over everything he knew about the Lindberghs and the Germans. Hermann Göring was their friend. And Hess, who was Deputy Führer. And von Ribbentrop, in London, often entertained them. Who else? Robert Ley? Goebbels?

He looked at his children playing with the dog. He could hear Diana laughing. Oh God, he thought. This man here used to be my friend, and now he's trying to blackmail me: frighten me into submission, so I'll say what he wants me to say in the House. . . .

"If there were to be a war right now," said Lindbergh; "England would lose it as surely as you and I are sitting here beneath this sun. They can cut you off from the whole of the British Empire. Nothing would reach you. Nothing. All the convoyed ships would be sunk, and you would starve." He looked at Allenby, who was sitting more and more dejected, slumped on the bench. "I hope you believe me, Ned. I mean every word of this—and, of course, I'm saying it all for a reason."

Allenby didn't dare speak. But he did nod.

"Someone has to prevent there being an English war," said Lindbergh. "And that someone has to be us."

Allenby looked up then.

"So that's what you mean by 'us'? A sort of peace movement?"

"No. Not quite."

Allenby looked away. "You know, this has an awful ring of conspiracy to it, Gus. I like it less and less and I like you less and less for making me listen to it."

Lindbergh lowered his head. He seemed acutely aware of the others on the terrace—even given the enormous distance between them. His next words were almost a whisper. "There's more at stake than England," he said. "And more at stake than Germany." For the first time, he looked directly into Allenby's eyes. "And more at stake than America."

Allenby went pale. He could feel the colour draining down towards his heart. What. . .? What was this? What could it be about?

"Tell me exactly what you mean," he said, driven himself to a whisper. "*Say* it."

Lindbergh sighed and folded his arms—his wings—and twisted the upper half of his body away from Allenby; the gesture of a boy. Then all the way back, his arms hanging down against his sides. "There is more at stake than nations. And more at stake than governments. More than parties and regimes and systems."

Allenby wondered what was left when you took away nations and governments; parties, regimes and political systems.

"Us," said Lindbergh.

"God damn it! Tell me who you *mean* by us?"

Lindbergh lowered his chin against the knot of his hands. "You, Ned; and I—and others like us—can control what happens, even when governments come and go, even when nations fall."

"Dear Jesus God. . ."

"And I'm telling you, we must."

A bee buzzed—drowning in the pond.

"There are others," Lindbergh said, "who want to see all this destroyed: that house, these lawns, the pond, you and me, that terrace and its people. . .your kids. . .my son Jon. . .even that dog."

Allenby bowed his head.

"You know who they are, Ned. So do I. Eating at us from within. Eating at us here, and in Germany, and all over Europe, and in America. So why should it surprise you that someone means to prevail against them?"

"But that's why we have political parties," said Allenby. "That *do* prevail against them."

"No, they don't," said Lindbergh. "And you *know* they don't."

Buzz—buzz.

Allenby stood up.

"So I have been chosen for this?" he said.

"Yes. There's a very small group already. . ."

"And they want me, too?"

"Yes."

"WHY?" Allenby was finally outraged, and he yelled.

Lindbergh, maybe inadvertently, looked towards the terrace. Allenby followed his gaze. Everyone was staring at them, having heard Ned's cry.

"You want my friends," said Allenby, hoarse. He felt ill.

Lindbergh was calm. "They would be useful. Yes," he said. "And your voice in the House."

Allenby sat back down. He looked at the pond and tried to concentrate on the bee. He took off his shoes. He began to roll up his trousers. For a moment, he simply couldn't speak. He took off his socks, and then said, very carefully; "This small group you speak of. . ." He stood back up. "Who are they?" He started to walk towards the pond.

Lindbergh said; "I'm not prepared to tell you that."

"Oh?" The pond was cool. The water reassuring. Allenby got out his handkerchief. "You want me to join, but you won't tell me who with." (He floated the handkerchief under the drowning bee.) "But I presume, because I'm Parliamentary Under-Secretary and because of my friends up there on the terrace, you want me to exert my influence to offset the possibility of war between Britain and Germany." (The bee caught hold of the cloth.) "And therefore I presume this small group of yours holds its meetings in Berlin. Am I right?"

"Not at all."

Allenby seemed to catch on fire in his stomach. Panic. He tried very hard to be calm, at least to sound it.

"Oh?" He waved the bee away across the grass towards the roses—watching it, shading his eyes and squinting, giving an excellent imitation of nonchalance. "Not in Berlin, eh? Where, then?"

Lindbergh thought about it and decided all he could afford to say was: "*there are common factions everywhere whose interests have to be protected come what may.*" (Allenby was certain these words had been memorized, which meant that somewhere there must be some of this written down. Maybe a manifesto.)

Allenby sat and put on one sock, one shoe. Some of the scars could be seen on his left leg. "So. Not a purely German thing?"

"No. It is not just German." Lindbergh was watching what he could see of the wounds. "It goes beyond mere Nazism, Ned," he said.

Allenby was holding up the second sock, dangling it over his toes. His mouth opened. But there wasn't any voice with which to speak. *Beyond mere Nazism. . .*

Then, at last his voice came back and he put up his hand. "Gus," he said, "say no more."

"But. . ."

"No, Gus! Not another word! *Amen.*" Allenby was shaking. "You son-of-a-bitch," he said. "You god damned son-of-a-bitch!" And that was the end of it. Allenby just stood up, wearing one sock and one shoe and carrying the others, his trouser leg still rolled, and limped away.

From the centre of the lawn, he turned back and shouted "Gus, I pray to God, one day you can come to me and tell me what it is that can possibly go beyond mere Nazism. Really. I'd be fascinated. Does it have to do with human beings?"

Lindbergh didn't move.

"One day, Gus. I pray God!" And Allenby was gone.

Finally, Lindbergh sat down. But not on the bench provided. He sat on the grass and stared at the pond. For an hour. Till dark when the bees at last were silenced and the flies crept under the leaves and the moths came out, attracted by the whiteness of his face and hands. And the lights in his eyes.

Edward Allenby never again let Lindbergh come to *Nauly*.

Once—ten years before—he had thought so highly of the young man's courage and daring as to call his own son Charles Augustus. And he had grieved for both Lindberghs with all his heart when their baby had died. The birth of Gus's second son had been celebrated at *Nauly* as it had been at *Englewood*, where young Jon Lindbergh was born. (Only Allenby of all Lindbergh's English friends ever called him 'Gus'. It had been his way of trying to break down Lindbergh's shyness.)

Allenby lay awake in his bed for many hours that night, deeply troubled by all that had been said in the afternoon. Much of it puzzled him, but more of it frightened him. He was not quite sure what it was he'd been asked to join, though he guessed it was a sort of cabal whose power was greater than that of governments. He wished he had been more tolerant of listening to it all, for he now felt cheated by his anger since it had prevented him from hearing more and understanding more. He hadn't told his wife, though she had guessed something traumatic had happened. He was silent all through supper and hadn't laughed when she'd repeated the afternoon's jokes. At midnight he came and sat on her bed, but he still didn't speak.

The moonlight streamed through the windows and Diana thought how subtly his profile was changing with time. He was such a good-hearted man. Sentimental. Kind. Ugliness of spirit in other people bewildered him. He had his weaknesses, but she was confident his integrity would hold against whatever troubled him. Her father, "Old Redoubtable", had

been the same. In a political crisis, no one was more reliable.
But if the toast was burnt or one of the children scraped a
knee, he fell to pieces. "God. . .!" he would cry, with a great
Victorian shout at Heaven. "Why is my toast always burning,
God? Answer me *that*, if you can!" And Neddy was the same.
Neddy might scream blue murder when she told him she
was expected in town tomorrow, but he would survive the
Lindbergh crisis—whatever it was.

"Do you want to talk?" she said, sitting back against her
pillows.

He tightened his grip on her hand. "Not really," he said.
"Just please don't go to sleep."

"No."

They sat like that for another fifteen minutes, both of them
looking out through the window at the moonlight on the
pond and then he said to her, "Do you remember, when Gus
first came to England, what it was he was doing?"

"Trying to forget his troubles, I should think."

"No, no. I mean his work. Don't you remember?"

"Yes, yes. Oh, that!" Diana laughed. "He was working
with Alexis Carrel. They were trying to invent a mechanical
heart."

"That's right," said Ned.

"What about it?"

"I think he's succeeded."

All this happened on the 8th of September. On the 9th, Diana
went up to town and had lunch with Juliet d'Orsey, this
having been arranged many days before. Coming home that
evening, she was somewhat surprised to discover Neddy
gone, though he'd left a note that told her he was suddenly
called to Paris "on account of business with Maximus" (his
brother, the Earl of Massie). But none of this was true. The
fact is he had gone to Clerkenwell to speak with Eden and
he did so, over the next two months, on at least four more
occasions. None of these meetings were recorded in his Parliamentary blotter. They were not of an official nature. Nor
did he ever speak of them to Diana. Maximus, however, was

,warned to be prepared to back up the lie about the Paris rendezvous, which he did with good grace, being often used in this manner whenever his brother needed a "blind" for conducting delicate missions in behalf of the Ministry.

On September 14th, six days after Lindbergh's visit to *Nauly*, a coded message was received in Berlin from London. It was addressed to Deputy Führer Rudolf Hess and it was signed by Germany's Ambassador to the United Kingdom, Joachim von Ribbentrop. It read: PLEASE BE ADVISED ALLENBY DECLINES.

There is no reply on record. Of course, it is possible no reply was ever sent. It is even possible no reply was required. One thing is certain. Edward Allenby was never to hear of "us" again.

He died with his son Charles Augustus, when the car they were riding in failed to brake at a corner on the winding road to *Nauly*. The funeral occurred on Friday, December 11th, 1936—but the news of it was superseded by the fact that Edward VIII had abdicated the throne of England and was going into exile in Austria.

There were not as many at *Nauly* as should have been, though all the best of them turned up. But I felt Ned was cheated of honours due him because of the Abdication, an event he would surely have abhorred. Indeed Baldwin later did a theatrical number-in-one in the House that had the ring of Neddy's voice in it, which suggests the PM may have had some discussion with Ned on the subject. I too found the Abdication intolerable—but for quite another reason. Poor Wallis. Not to be Queen.

I sat there that night in the semi-dark with Diana, Maximus, Harold, Vita and a few others listening to the King on the wireless—all of us down with Ned and the boy in their graves—and I saw that halfway through the speech, or near the end, or wherever it was when the King said; "I now quit altogether public affairs, and I lay down my burden. . ." Diana reached to the table beside her and took up a photograph of Neddy in her hand, framed there in silver and held it, not as if she watched him—but was letting him watch her. And then the King said; "it may be some time before I return to my native land, but I shall always follow the fortunes of the British race and Empire with profound interest." And as he said this, Diana laid the photograph back on the table—face down.

Every one of us valiantly tried to get drunk, but none of us managed.

The funeral itself was dire. Sometimes, there can be at least some sense of being uplifted into a community of mourners. But not that day. Poor Diana, having just put down her father—now her husband and her son Charles Augustus in one gesture. And of course it rained, and of course there was all the unavoidable buzz of the Abdication and, of course half the people who should have been there weren't.

Someone did come, however, who was not expected. I was first aware of his presence in the churchyard, after we had gathered there for the throwing down of the earth. I was standing off to one side, opposite the principal mourners—Diana, Freda Massie, Maximus and the others—when I noticed someone moving behind them.

At first I thought it was just someone come late, until I saw by his behaviour he was not a mourner, but an observer of some other kind. A policeman? Scotland Yard? Definitely not a "friend of the family". He was on a scouting expedition, never standing still for a moment, making a circle of the mourners, walking round the outside, keeping his eyes on this one and that one (myself included), his hands in his pockets the whole time. And I don't think I would have noticed him, other than just to be aware that someone was moving while the rest of us were still, if it hadn't been for his extraordinary appearance.

I had never seen a figure of such compelling menace. I had no idea who he was or why he might have been there but I do know that whenever I see that funeral in my mind it is dominated by his figure, dressed as he was in a teeming leather coat, hatless, no umbrella, with rainy hair curled against a skull like a Roman marble, and skin Italianate in colour. . .not quite six feet tall, I should say. And, even in spite of the rain and mud, wearing his shoes uncovered with either rubbers or galoshes. The ugliest pair of shoes I have ever seen. Shiny shoes; glossy shoes; sensual shoes, if such a thing exists—but appropriate, I suppose, for walking in the mud. Alligator shoes. And looking up at one point after I had forced myself to look away from him and concentrate on Freda Massie and Maximus standing either side of Diana, each one holding up the other, I noticed him watching me and it made me shiver, as if the rain had suddenly all poured down my back. Not only had he this pair of alligator shoes but also, in spite of his beauty, alligator eyes.

Paris: December, 1936

I was boarding the steamer for Dieppe—the Boulogne runs were booked for the next twelve months because the late king had passed that way and people wanted to stare at the water over which he had crossed—when I was confronted by Julia Franklin, asking if I could help her find a porter to get her things on board. I suppose she must have known me well enough to realize that no matter what she had written and said, I would still feel constrained to play the gentleman. I should have known better. Julia Franklin, for all her well known emaciation, is about as helpless as a shark in a school of mackerel—Julia, with her rawboned arms and her hipless legs which she covered with trousers like a man.

This was during the time when every word that Julia Franklin wrote was gospel to the leftist movement, and her pieces on Spain had practically been enshrined. She had also written a devastating attack on Ezra, which had caused a sensation. No one else had yet begun to recognize the fact that Ezra, the man, could be as much a target for attack as Ezra, the literary lion. The tradition had been, until Julia Franklin appeared on the scene, that the private lives and personal views of literary figures were sacrosanct until there was a death under which a line could be drawn. No one, for instance, while Virginia Woolf still lived, would have dared to print such a sentence as "Mrs Woolf has bouts of serious depression" let alone "Mrs Woolf, from time to time, goes mad." Julia Franklin would—and did—write sentences such as that, though she wrote them not about Virginia Woolf—but Ezra Pound.

It must be said, however, if I am to make the point about this woman I intend to make—because she had a very real impact both on myself and on the events that follow—that Julia Franklin never wrote such things as I have suggested here merely to hurt or merely to be destructive or merely to elevate herself and her own importance. She wrote with commendable directness—never "pussy-footing" and never currying favour with either her subjects or her readers. Her deviousness was all confined to method—never to matter.

This is not to say that Julia Franklin was a paragon—or infallible, and could not be wrong. It is only to say she never knowingly lied. Which is why, to certain people, myself included, she could be extremely dangerous. All her truths were told from a single stance: she was red—without apology —and the publication of everything she wrote was eagerly awaited.

Ezra had been her latest victim. I was to follow. It was dreadful—and not at all unlike being tracked and trapped by a kind of sainted killer: for no matter the political persuasions of her individual readers, everyone applauded when Julia Franklin drew blood. I think this had as much to do with the age as anything else. It was, after all, the decade of the tabloid and a time in which the Press had the power to madden and drive a man like Lindbergh out of his native land—and even to turn him against it.

What then was I thinking of when I agreed to find Julia Franklin a porter at Newhaven? Perhaps it was simply that something in me knew she could not, in the long run, be avoided. And I might as well get it over with. Maybe, too, I was thinking if she met me while the world was distracted with the Abdication, I should not perhaps suffer too greatly from the exposure. That I should have known better is no excuse. I walked in freely. And then she shut the door and struck—though I was not to know how hard or with what effect for another week after we had crossed together into France aboard a very rocky boat.

There was then in Paris a great deal of rain; the weather, in fact, was as foul as any I can remember. Paris is no place to sit out the winter but it had been my choice because I wanted to write and needed a closet, so to speak, in which to do this. Not too many distractions. At first, the writing went well—but slowly. Paris got to me. Paris in November and December becomes more grey than is bearable; its leaves all underfoot have turned to mush; its pigeons are more than ever mournful in the eaves. It is every bit as doleful and depressing as a chapter from *La Dame aux Camellias*, the story of that desperate woman who perished in Paris of winter and aloneness, curtained and cut off in a world hermetically sealed and utterly airless. Deserted even by laughter. And by charm. Strange, how that Paris of the mid-1930s rang with so many echoes of itself a hundred years before. Dumas could have written the very room I sat in, to say nothing of my mood and my exile. Looking out, I could see his Paris and my own in one unaltered view. The rain. The rain. The rain. And the people. Looming. Glowering. Argumentative. Bedraggled. Rebellious. Shaking their fists at one another, even from a distance. The bleakness of it all.

Winters teem with French rain and rudeness. Slush—which they call there a *demi fondue* of snow—and a kind of hectoring social unrest which I call *demi fondue* of the brain. I suspect the winter French are the most bad-tempered people in the world. On the streets, ill mannered; in the cafés and restaurants, intemperate; in the salons, intellectual bullies; in the Chamber of Deputies, lions with false teeth. As for French politics, they are based entirely on emotion—rabble-rousing *faits et gestes* and the corruption of the moment, be it money, real estate, peddled foreign influence or women.

I had not had a single invitation since my arrival, though the reason was plain enough. It had to do with my relations with Wallis, and all my usual horde of hosts was waiting to see whose stocks would rise the furthest—the King's or Mister Baldwin's. Having appeared triumphantly September last with Wallis, I was presently in no man's land. Not quite pariahcal (since it was still quite possible my horde of hosts might be required to rush to my side and embrace me) but still not acceptable as a guest at any table where my presence one night might prove embarrassing the next. And to think that in September I was turning down three or four invitations a day. The French upper classes are the world's worst snobs and it is surely not for nothing *clique* is a word universally employed without translation.

Then, late one evening, the telephone rang. The caller was Isabella Loverso, whom I had not heard from since the death of Diana's father. She would not disclose her whereabouts.

"But how did you know I was here?" I asked.

"You have not seen the *New York Times*?"

"No." My heart sank. "No. I have not."

"You will require your best sense of humor when you do," Isabella told me. But there was no sense of humour in her voice when she added, "You have been pinioned, as I believe they say in English, by a lady who is making quite a name for herself. . ."

Julia Franklin.

"Really?" I tried to sound as if I had known it was coming. "So she's been as harsh with me as she was with Ezra?"

"Yes. I'm afraid she has. You are—what do they say in England?—the latest victim of the Ripper. Never fear, however. You are not alone and the company she promises is good."

"What do you mean by the company she promises, Baronessa?"

"There is to be a whole series," Isabella explained, "of

what she calls Portraits of Expatriates—meaning expatriates of the American persuasion. Ezra Pound, as we know. Yourself. Mrs Simpson, Lady Astor, William Joyce. . ." (who was then nothing more than an agitator, but who later would become Lord Haw-Haw) ". . .and also my friend that I want you to meet, Mister Charles Bedaux."

It was hard not to ask at once what Julia Franklin had written about me, but I didn't want to appear over anxious. So, for the moment, I followed Isabella's lead. I had never heard of Mister Charles Bedaux—this man she wanted me to meet—and was in the embarrassing position of having to say so.

"Never fear, Mister Mauberley," she told me. "Charles Bedaux is not of your circle, but an industrialist. It is most unlikely you would hear of him. However, the purpose of my call is to inform you of his wish to meet you and to place for him an invitation at your feet."

I thought this a quaint and charming way of putting it and told her I would be delighted to accept. The appointment was for Friday at Tattinger's for lunch. I asked if Isabella Loverso would be present.

"I most certainly shall," she said, "since I must perform the introductions."

"I will be glad to see you," I said, which was true. I was intrigued by the mystery that surrounded her activities—her sudden departure from Venice following Wyndham's death; her absence from Neddy's funeral.

Then she reminded me (as if she had to!) "Take your good sense of humour now and go downstairs and obtain a copy of the Paris edition of the *New York Times*."

I was halfway down the stairs when I saw the lobby was filled with reporters. Thinking they must be there to catch my reaction to Julia Franklin's diatribe—for such I was sure it would be—I turned and was about to rise again when I was met by the sound of a familiar name drifting up from below.

"Señor Hemingway! One moment, please!"

Ernest? Here at the Meurice? I crept down a few steps and peered into the lobby. The crowd of reporters had now sorted itself into two focal groups, one gazing hungrily at the sight of Ernest Hemingway and the other turning to stare at a tall, magnificent woman who was breeching their ranks to draw closer to Ernest himself.

"Señor Hemingway!" she called again, as she strode across the marble. She looked to be about sixty years of age. Red furs hung down like garlands from her shoulders and her piled red hair was like a modern version of a Pompadour, sweeping upward from a wide, pale forehead and heavily powdered complexion. Every eye was now on her. She removed, as she strode, the glove from her right hand and placed it in her left, where it remained like a major's swagger stick.

Ernest, by now, had turned. I could see the lights in his eyes flare up at the impertinence of being so publicly hailed and then die down and soften when he perceived it was a woman of obvious importance who might be importuning him for some good reason, not for ill. I was shocked by his appearance, for he had aged in the year since I had seen him last and had put on weight, though he carried it well. But his eyes were old and very tired. I was surprised to see him in Paris. The last I'd heard, he was on a hurricane tour of the battlefields in Spain, involved in the making of a film in behalf of the Loyalist cause.

"Are you aware of who I am?" the woman asked as she reached him.

"No," said Hemingway. " 'fraid not, ma'am." And he even went so far as to smile, first at her and then at the reporters.

"Then allow me to introduce myself," she said. "I am the daughter of the Duke of Bilbao; sister of Don Alfredo del Roja; cousin of the Marques of Teruel; wife of the Marques de Sol y Santander—all dead. All dead, Señor Hemingway. And I have come here to do them honour with a public gesture of my contempt for those such as you who have abetted their murderers."

At which point she struck Ernest harshly with her bare hand, fully in the face, but cleanly without employing her nails. And then she spat at his feet, looked him in the eye and said, "*Por España*"—turned away as smartly as a soldier and marched to the doors and out of the hotel.

Ernest, to his credit, didn't lift a finger during the attack, but stood his ground and endured it all like someone in a dream. His expression was mainly one of wonderment that someone not his mother nor his wife—though dressed in female garb—had actually struck him. In a public place.

I overheard one of the reporters, an Englishman, say to Hemingway, "What, may one ask, was that all about?"

And Ernest, fully awake and angry at last, all red in the face except where the livid marks remained from the blows, said; "just some crazy Fascist in a red wig, thinks she's the Queen of Spain. . ." and he turned and began to sweep the reporters before him into the gloomy shadows of the bar. And as he went I heard him say; "my shoes! You fellows see that? Why, she spat on my shoes!"

The following morning, taking advantage of the sheets of rain, I fumbled my umbrella open as I crossed the foyer, held it up like a shield before my face and barged through the doors undetected by the few reporters who hung about— as always.

Nowhere. Nowhere could I find the *Times* of yesterday. I tried six kiosks and three shops and finally gave it up, telling myself by hook or by crook I would find it back at the hotel, even if I had to pay a dozen chamber maids to ransack all the waste paper baskets, room by room.

Later, arriving back at the hotel with an armful of papers— everything but the *New York Times*—I passed the desk and enquired after mail. Checking my pigeonhole the clerk informed me that although there were no letters, there was a copy of the *New York Times*. "Yesterday's." Astonished, I allowed the clerk to place it in my hands and I looked down to see there was a note attached. "Saw you were in the hotel," it said, "and thought you might enjoy the enclosed. Best—Ernest."

The bastard.

I reached my suite somewhat out of breath, with the other papers still tucked under my arm and carrying the *Times* very carefully between two fingers, much the way one carries certain animals—by the tail, so they cannot turn and bite you.

I poured myself a very large Scotch, with just enough water to pale the colour from deadly auburn to narcotic amber. Then I placed eight cigarettes, eight white cartridges all in a row, on the table underneath the reading lamp, and my lighter beside them. When I sat, I even adjusted my clothing in the manner of a suicide who is determined his corpse will flatter him. I lighted one cigarette. I sipped; then I gulped from the glass; then I sipped again and put it down. I opened the paper, leafing through the pages, playing out the role of casual reader even though I, in the mirror, was the only audience.

Nothing. Nothing. Nothing. Nothing. Nothing. Pages one to five.

Page six. There it was. HUGH SELWYN MAUBERLEY: OUT OF KEY WITH HIS TIME. A PORTRAIT—by Julia Franklin.

I gasped and choked on my cigarette smoke. My eyes began to water. For a moment I could not see. I dabbed at the tears with my handkerchief only to discover its cologne was an irritant and thus I watered more. I waited. OUT OF KEY WITH HIS TIME. The one sure way to kill an artist deader than a dodo. . .out of date. . .passé. . .inconsequential. . .out of key with his time.

At last, I could see again. I steadied the page and continued to read. I will not repeat it all here, though one brief passage bears on the story of these walls and must be told.

"The most astonishing thing about this man of letters is the fact that even though Mr. Mauberley currently lives out his exile in Europe, where new fires blaze up every day, he appears to be totally unaffected by the march of events. Instead, he avoids all confrontation with his diminishing talents by spending an inordinate amount of time with the dissolute aristocracy of faded England and with the morally bankrupt crew that mans the élite but sinking lifeboat of a Fascist-dominated Europe. . . .

"How sad that a man once considered to be among the giants of twentieth-century American letters should have passed his zenith by the time he was thirty. And now that he is forty and has ceased to write, it is perhaps even sadder to have to say that his departure from the literary scene is no loss to culture. His works, all along, were paste. They have already been replaced by the diamonds, however rough, of writers such as Hemingway, Farrell and Stratton. . . ."

I read it once. I reread it twice. I read it till I cringed. It was deadly; cruel; precise—and alas—very much of it was true. Not all, of course. Not all. But—oh—the sight of oneself, caught in the eye of one who cannot lie.

The next day, I scanned every page of the Paris papers, thinking for certain there would be mention of the scene between Ernest and his titled attacker in the lobby. Not a word. I looked through them all—twice. It seemed somehow unfair that I must be made to pay for my sins while Ernest got off scot free. And then I remembered. Of course. He had taken all those reporters into the bar and kept them drinking all night long.

At noon on Friday I went around past the bridges and onto the terraces of the Tuilleries. I had forgotten my umbrella and arrived at Tattinger's covered from head to toe with a fine Scotch mist.

Isabella Loverso greeted me in the porches—alone, for she wanted to explain the purpose of our luncheon. My heart did a turn when I saw her. Having completely sentimentalized her, I had forgotten how much strength there was in her height and how real her beauty was. She came along those porches with the energy of Danilova or Karsavina: of someone who had danced all her life. There was a great, wide smile of genuine pleasure on her lips and in her eyes and in the way she took my hand in both of hers and welcomed me. But this was briskly dispensed with. She wanted to come directly to the point.

Under any other circumstances, she assured me, she would

not have swept me quite so quickly off my feet. But recent events (the Abdication, the creation of the Rome-Berlin Axis, certain crises in Germany) made it necessary for her to leap upon what she called my "timely" arrival in Paris, and set up post-haste this meeting with Charles Bedaux. François Côty, the perfumer, was also to be with us at lunch.

Protesting that I did not have a mind for intrigue, I told her I would be glad to hear what either man had to say, though I would promise nothing brilliant in response. This seemed to satisfy her.

Crossing the dining salon she took my arm and said; "we do not trust François Côty greatly, though he can be useful. Be aware that he is somewhat dangerous—and indiscreet."

I mumbled something like "very well", still having no idea why she spoke to me of "we" or of who that "we" might be. And then she said; "Charles Bedaux is extremely important to us. He is the whole reason I have brought you here, Mister Mauberley, and you will not be too surprised, I hope, or think it rude of me if I hardly take part in the conversation. I am really only here to be certain you meet with this friend."

At which point—on the very word—we arrived at the table where Bedaux and Côty were already seated.

"Monsieur Bedaux is born French," said Isabella Loverso while Côty seated her beside him. "But he is also an American like yourself, Mister Mauberley."

"I see." I just kept smiling. It was all like a scene in a film, and I had the distinct impression that Garbo would arrive at any moment. Garbo—or a gun.

Bedaux, having become an American citizen, kept American business hours; none of this two o'clock à la fourchette for him. You ate at noon and were back in the office by 1:30 sharp. If you ate alone, you were back at one. Period. He was a "time-study" man; an efficiency expert who controlled a vast, indeed a world-wide, network of management consultant firms. I was fascinated to note how wide-spread the influence of one man could be, for his clients included (amongst a great many others) Campbell Soup, General Electric, Eastman Kodak, Goodrich Rubber, and Swift. . .and in

Europe, E. I. du Pont de Nemours, the Fiat motor company, the Società Metallurgica Italiana, the Eisenwerke Aktiengesellschaft Rothau-Neudek (steelworks, Czechoslovakia) . . .and in Britain, Crosse & Blackwell and Imperial Chemical Industries of London. . .to say nothing of the Anglo-Iranian Oil Company.

As for François Côty, he had once been the guiding force and inspiration of a militant right-wing group that called itself Solidarité Française, made up mostly of homosexual hoodlums who were given to wearing leather and boots. This fact had given rise to one of the best bilingual puns I have ever heard, when in 1934 it was said that Côty was about to produce a new cologne he would call: "Eau du Cuir!"

True to her word, Isabella Loverso offered little to the conversation other than her attention. She watched both myself and Bedaux with her eagle's eyes all through the meal. Côty seemed to be of no real interest to her. And I wondered how we were connected in her mind.

What confused me most was that having been set up by Isabella Loverso to expect some mighty, earth-shaking scheme, nothing of the sort emerged. All we talked about was Italy, Ezra, my impressions of Venice, and when I had last been in Germany. Aside from that the luncheon was just a luncheon. I had some delicious eggs Florentine and some excellent wine; we discussed a few mutual acquaintances. Côty was morose and preoccupied with a young man across the room and Isabella Loverso ate a double serving of lime sherbet. Consequently, by the time the meal was over, I was greatly confused as to why I had been there at all. "We" did not seem to exist.

But such, of course, was not the case. When the meal was over and the bill had been paid, I was sent away in Bedaux's company to return with him to his offices.

The rain had let up and, though there was a wind, it smelled of smoke and was not unpleasant. The offices were not a great way off. Bedaux was tiny: five-foot seven at the most, and rather rotund. His head was enormous and quite disproportionate in size with the rest of him. Nonetheless this gnomelike figure always moved as if he was running a race. He was also able to keep up a non-stop monologue the whole way, no matter how often the traffic attempted to murder us. In the space of ten minutes I learned a great deal about this extraordinary man.

He'd been born "right here, you know. Just outside of Paris. Place called Charenton. Dumpy. Don't bother. I never go back myself. All the memories too painful. One sister, two brothers. Dull, very ordinary. Father was an engineer. . .mathematician. Worked for the railroad. Best example I ever had of what life ought not to be about; grey all over. When I was twenty. . .I'm fifty now. . .I just took off one day and made for America. 'Go west, young man!' So I did. Landed, New York City—1906. Went everywhere, did everything. Sold horses in the Ozarks. . .dug tunnels under the Hudson. . .ended up in Grand Rapids, Michigan where I made myself a citizen. Yes, sir, Mauberley: Charles Eugene Bedaux made himself an American citizen of his own free will in 1917. Long ago as that. You see, the thing was, Charles E. Bedaux knew what he wanted. And he knew it grew in America. Money. . . ."

At this point we were fending off two trucks, a broken-down Renault and a cabby with a horse. Bedaux just kept putting up his hand and walking through like a matador. I was terrified.

"I was a millionaire, you know, by the time I was thirty-nine. That's right. You believe it. Charles E. Bedaux was a millionaire by the time he was thirty-nine. How old are you?"

"Thirty-eight. Nearly thirty-nine. My birthday's on New Year's Day."

"Thirty-nine, hunh? Same as I was."

"That's right."

"You a millionaire?"

"Not yet. No."

"Unh-hunh. Well. You can be. You have the look."

I doubted it. And wondered what "the look" might be.

"Now I'm going to let you in on the secret of my own great success. The secret of Charles E. Bedaux's millions. The thing is," he said, going through the gates from the street into the courtyard that led to his offices, "what nobody ever organized before Charles E. Bedaux came along was the concept of the distribution of energy." He was opening doors now. "Human energy, you understand." We got into an elevator. "Everybody has an hour. See what I mean? You have an hour. I have an hour. And that fartass Côty has an hour. We all have the same hour. Right?"

I was given no time to say yes.

"Three men—one hour. Three potential units of energy. And in that one hour we all ate lunch. We all ate lunch and we all got up and left. But look here, Mauberley. . .I said something and you said something. . .you and I got to know one another. See? While fartass Côty only sat there with his mouth open. Silent. See what I mean? Didn't even really eat his lunch. Three men—one hour; but only two of us used it to its maximum, filled it with our maximum of energy and got the maximum return. We came away fed, fat and fortified. And therein lies the secret of Charles E. Bedaux's millions. Because I've learned how to take the limp-wristed Côtys of this world—and turn them into Charles Atlas Bedaux!"

He laughed so hugely the elevator doors began to shake.

"Of course," he roared, "I don't mean that literally. I wouldn't want some faggot to carry the name of Bedaux."

His offices were on the fifth floor at the top. In the foyer, there was a secretary, Mademoiselle Liage, who sat at a large round desk, very modern. Everything was white and glass and chrome and all the "paintings" on the walls were posters, advertising Bedaux clients. The posters were gigantic—framed—and I had the impression many of them were the artists' originals. One that particularly caught my attention showed a monstrous blue train speeding straight towards the viewer, with a small yellow racing car just beginning to pull ahead, determined to win the race and be the first to break through the glass. Underneath, there were only two words: FIAT—VINCITORE! And I had no doubt of their veracity, given the "fiat" just delivered by Charles E. Bedaux.

We swept into Bedaux's inner sanctum, Bedaux barely acknowledging the secretary's presence just as he had barely acknowledged the presence at lunch of Isabella Loverso.

Women did not account for much in his scheme of things, I gathered.

Beyond Bedaux's door, there was a large, iridescent room. Two sets of windows overlooked the *Place* and the walls and ceiling were inlaid with smoky, gold mirrors. All the furniture, even the top of the desk, was covered in Venetian leather: faded, leaf-coloured, cool as a forest. One brass lamp with a copper-green shade was lit in the darkest corner.

Bedaux went behind his desk and did not sit down, but indicated that I should be seated in one of the leather chairs nearby. For a moment, there was a silence while he fingered the opened mail on his blotter. Then he spoke, as if to someone hiding in the room, not me.

"Pay attention. I have only time to say this once, Mister Mauberley. Once—and once only."

I was so unnerved by the tone of voice and the fact he refused to look at my eyes that I turned and looked over my shoulder to make quite sure we were really alone. We were. The words "pay attention" had also thrown me since they were patented by Ezra.

"For reasons I cannot explain," Bedaux said, "I am about to visit America. I shall be there for some time; months. The international situation is changing by the hour. In the past weeks alone, General Franco has received the official recognition of Italy and Germany. At this very moment, he sits at the gates of Madrid. There is every possibility, now they have conferred official recognition, that Hitler and Mussolini will actively enter the contest on his behalf. And if that were to happen, Baldwin and Roosevelt might feel compelled to take up arms. In other words. . .war."

Absent-mindedly he offered me a cigar and lighted one for himself. It was much as if, having mentioned war, Bedaux required some immediate manifestation of this theme and had chosen fire and smoke.

"War, Mister Mauberley, is bad for business."

I blinked, having long been convinced that quite the opposite was true. He could see I did not agree with him. "War breaks down the lines of communication. . .shuts down the frontiers. . .scrambles the labour force. . .sends money off in all the wrong directions. . .and, above all, it offends alliances built up over years of negotiation. So I trust you see my point: war is bad for business."

I nodded. Fascinated.

"Yes. Well. Now then, I'm given to understand you are not, or at least that you don't consider yourself, a 'political' person. Is that correct?"

"More or less, yes."

"But you do vote?"

"No. As a matter of fact, I don't."

"Ah? Is there a reason?"

"Well—I'm an American citizen. Born American. But I'm never there."

"Mister Mauberley," he said, and cleared his throat. "For the sake of this conversation let us pretend you do vote. And let us pretend that you vote in America."

"Very well."

"And let us pretend—again for the sake of argument—that you vote for the Democratic Party. . . ."

"You go too far!"

He laughed, "Nonetheless, let us say so."

I shrugged compliance.

"Very well. The Democratic Party has a leader: Mister Roosevelt. And you don't like Mister Roosevelt. . . ."

"Indeed."

"But remember we are pretending here. You *do* like the Democratic Party. What you *don't* like is how it's being led: you do *not* like its leader: you do *not* like his political machine: you do *not* like the men—or, let us say, you do not like most of the men around him. All right so far?"

"Yes."

"All right. . ." Bedaux's figure edged its way along the mirrors, and I noticed that he ran his finger along the glass as he walked. "So you have this party you want to vote for— but you can't, because of its leader; and you can't get rid of the leader because the men around him wield too much influence and his political machine cannot be made to break down." He stopped, mid-wall, his finger still poised, his finger on the glass. I was watching all of this reflected and he was watching me through the back of my head. "What do you do then, Mister Mauberley, when you come to such an impasse?"

It occurred to me to say "You shoot Mister Roosevelt," but suspected that was not the answer he wanted. Therefore, I said; "I don't know. I should probably do what I have done: leave the country and give up my vote."

"Ah, but that's not good enough, is it, Mister Mauberley? Not when, in terms of our pretence, it is vital that the Democratic Party stay in power. No. Not good enough. We need another answer."

Ignoring the assassination plot in my mind, I confessed that I had no other answer.

"But you have, Mister Mauberley. You have." (I could see that he'd stopped walking altogether.) "You wrote about it all, last spring. You put it all on paper and published it, just last spring in the *Daily Mail*."

My mind opened. And the "Democratic Party" became the Nazi Party and Roosevelt was Hitler and Roosevelt's "machine" was the Fascist underpinning holding Hitler and Mussolini in place.

"And so now," said Charles E. Bedaux, "you may begin to grasp why it is I have asked you here."

. . .and what it was Isabella Loverso had meant when she said to me, "you are one of us."

I sat very still.

"Alas, for those of us who believe in. . .this 'Party' " (he would still not name it—maybe still did not trust me) ". . .there has been a loss of faith in its leaders."

"I understand, Mister Bedaux. I do understand what you're saying. Please stop talking in riddles."

This was very hard for him to do; but he tried.

"What do such people do as we who have lost this faith? How are we to make certain the party is not destroyed and above all—if one is a businessman like myself—how do we make certain it continues to be useful to us? Well let me tell you, Mister Mauberley." And here, at last, he came and stood before me. "You find someone else inside the party who believes as you do. And, if you're smart, you set up a kind of network through which you continue to do business and through which you assure the integrity of the ideals upon which the party was founded is not destroyed. And you bring all the best people into that network you can find, and, once you have done that—you begin to make your own world."

He was transported, and swept me with him. Because he meant it. He meant that what had been a mere idea was becoming a reality. *You make your own world.*

"And that is what we're doing, Mister Mauberley, and that is why you are here: because we want you, Mister Mauberley. We need you."

Finally, I spoke.

"You say 'we'."

"Yes."

"Am I to know who?"

He did not even consider his answer: "no. Not yet. Let us say merely. . .us. A. . .cabal."

I could feel my expression alter. I did not appreciate his distrust of me in that moment, after all that had been said. Either I was suitable to belong to this network or this cabal or whatever, or I wasn't. If I wasn't, then I should not have been told of its existence. And I said so.

"Very well," said Bedaux. "But I'm afraid I must return to my riddles, in order to satisfy you. You see, we none of us ever. . .and I stress this. . .we none of us ever mention the cabal in conjunction with its members' names."

"I see."

"However, in the delicate international situation that exists at present, what with the loss of kings and civil wars and the comings and goings of armies—and the breaking of certain treaties, luck is on our side for the following reasons, none of which, by the way, has yet been announced to the public. *One:* as of January 1st, 1937 His Excellency Joachim von Ribbentrop will replace Joseph Goebbels as the number three man in the Nazi hierarchy."

I held my breath.

"*Two:* on the same day, His Excellency Count Galeazo Ciano is to become the Foreign Minister of Mussolini's Government in Rome and the Master of the Rome-Berlin Axis."

Bedaux sat down.

"*Three:* I have here in my hand, the rough draft of a cable I intend to send from New York when I arrive there late next week." He put on a large pair of tortoise-shell reading glasses and shook out a piece of paper from his inner pocket and read: " 'To Mister and Mrs Herman Livingston Rogers: at the Villa Lou Viei, Cannes.' "

Dear God. He had reached into the very heart of my world—for I knew now what was coming and precisely why I had been called into the circle. I stood up.

Bedaux went on reading: " 'You are under siege. The press surrounds you like a pack of jackals. Would it not be best if you and your guest were to seek asylum elsewhere? May I humbly suggest the Château Candé, my home in the valley of the Loire? It is yours for the asking. My sympathetic regards to your honoured guest: my affectionate regards to yourself. Charles E. Bedaux.' "

He removed his spectacles and folded both the cable and the glasses into an inner pocket. I began to breathe again—but only just. For of course the honoured guest at the Rogers' Villa was Wallis Simpson, there since by law she must remain apart from the King until her divorce was final: otherwise there would be no divorce.

The silence extended for some minutes while I thought about what Bedaux had just told me and while he got up and crossed to a cabinet and poured two glasses of brandy.

von Ribbentrop must then be very high up in the cabal. Also Ciano. It made sense—since they both had diplomatic access to practically every door in Europe. But Wallis? The thought was staggering. A King had just renounced his throne for this woman. Did it mean he had renounced it for the cabal as well?

"I trust I need say no more," said Bedaux, handing me the brandy.

"Only about the 'honoured guest,'" I said. "I can't quite make that real."

Bedaux sat on the edge of his desk.

"Why not?" he asked.

"Because the implications are. . .staggering, to say the least."
I took a good sniff of the brandy. It was my turn not to look
at the interlocutor. "Are you saying she's one of these people?
One of this cabal?"

Then I did look at him, very quickly, to gauge his un-
guarded reaction.

He smiled.

"Put it this way," he said. "We're working on it. And that
is where you come into the story." Me. At last. "All very
well for me to send this cable from New York," he said.
"But I do not know the lady and the lady does not know
me. But you, so I understand, have known the lady many
years. . . ." He tipped the brandy forward in his glass and
turned it round and round. I nodded. "A word from you
would assure her, don't you think, that my offer made a
good deal of sense—and, of course, if she knew you trusted
me then. . .Well." He drank.

So I was to be his emissary.

"Am I to mention the cabal?" I asked.

"No, no. Not yet. All that comes later. What we need just
now is *liaison*, Mister Mauberley. Liaison. One of *us*—in
her pocket, so to speak. You can offer her assurances, of
course. Now the King has abdicated, she is feeling, so I'm
told, rather defeated. A little lost. But you can hold out hope.
Be sure you hold out *hope*, Mister Mauberley. And connect
that hope with me. With me and with our unknown friends.
Though you mustn't mention other names than mine. The
thing is to give the strongest impression possible—always
remembering, of course, there are echelons in this that even
I can't name. Echelons above and beyond, shall we say, those
names I have already let out of the bag. And in time—you
may tell her she will know how very strong her allies are."
His eyes were glittering. He could see the future; and the
future he could see was glorious, since it held so much in
store for Charles E. Bedaux. "Put it this way," he said. "You
may tell her there are larger kingdoms than the one she's
lost. That ought to catch her attention."

The goblets had just been emptied and abandoned on the
leather surface of the desk. Beyond the windows dusk was

coming on and the winter lamps had all been lighted on the bridges along the river. The Palace of Deputies was lighted up too as if they meant to sit all night. Snow was falling.

Settling into my overcoat, I asked if Isabella Loverso had taken up permanent residence in Paris. Had she deserted the Palazzo d'Aquila forever? And if so, had it to do with Wyndham's ghost—or with the urgency of what was now afoot?

Bedaux lowered his eyes, thought about his answer for a moment and then said; "surely, Mister Mauberley, you cannot imagine you are being drawn into a world, by joining us, where one is not endangered."

I did not reply to this for a while. I removed my gloves from my pockets, the silk Paisley scarf from my sleeve. Finally I said; "Baronessa Loverso is surely not in *physical* danger."

Bedaux smiled. "Is there any other kind?"

"Perhaps not in your world, Mister Bedaux. But in my world there is a dreadful danger in words.". . .Julia Franklin.

"Just so," said Bedaux—and looked at his watch, indicating it was time for me to leave. I did up the buttons of my overcoat. Picking up my homburg and putting on my left glove, I began to cross the floor towards the exit.

"As we went into lunch today," I said, "the Baronessa indicated some concern about the trustworthiness of François Côty. . . ." I looked at Bedaux. "If that is the case, then perhaps you should tell me what he was doing at our table?"

"A perfectly legitimate question, and one I'm glad to be able to answer because the answer may be of value to you some day."

I put on my other glove.

Bedaux said; "you have heard of Monsieur Côty's organization, Solidarité Française?"

"Yes. Thugs."

"Precisely."

"And. . .?"

"And, Mister Mauberley? *And*? You mean you have to *ask*?"

"Yes, I do mean that."

Bedaux sighed. "Put it this way," he said. "From time to time, Monsieur Côty and his friends are useful to us. It is that simple."

I bit my tongue. "Oh," I said. "I see."

He opened the door into the outer office. The clatter of a ticker-tape machine splattered rifle-fire from behind a glass partition.

"Good fortune on your journey," said Bedaux.

"I thank you. I will do the best I can," I said.

In the mirrors, Bedaux was now effectively lost; just a voice with many deflections. "I need hardly tell you how grateful. . ." he began.

"No. Please don't say so," I said. "I am only too glad to be of service."

As I turned in the direction of Mademoiselle Liage and her huge round desk, I almost collided with a young man standing there who was about to enter Bedaux's office.

Alligator eyes.

I stood transfixed.

"There you are, Harry," said Bedaux. His tone was no longer the same. It was wary now, and flat. "I was told to expect you."

The young man walked straight past me into Bedaux's office. The door closed. Bang. And the ticker-tape fired off another fusillade.

I stood there, quite unable to move. It was the same young man who had stood behind Diana, so insolently staring at us all while Ned was buried. My mind was unable to deliver any reason why he should be here in Bedaux's office. I turned to Mademoiselle Liage, only to discover she too was transfixed. With fear.

"Would you be so good as to tell me his name?" I stuttered, taking my cue from the ticker-tape.

Unblinking, she said; "he is Mr. Reinhardt."

Harry Reinhardt.

One of us?

La Méditerrannée was the overnight train that ran between Paris and Nice. The whole point of taking this particular train lay in the convenience of being able to sleep through the journey and arrive refreshed. But I could not sleep.

Instead, I sat in my pajamas and robe, holding my attaché case in my lap, staring out through the streaming windows at the pouring night with its smouldering towns and its drowning cities dishevelled at the edges of the dark with their lights all guttering but not gone out. Other trains passed us, heading northward, dragging their screaming cars along the tracks by the hair and I would wince and close my eyes. But I could not keep them closed. For every time I shut them Reinhardt's alligator eyes stared back from the dark inside my mind.

La Méditerrannée is blue—like the train in the poster in Charles E. Bedaux's office. At times during the night ride I felt as if I were in a dream watching myself, even to the point of seeing my own figure, robed and immaculate in pale blue silk and spanking white cotton, seated in the lighted window with my hair precisely parted and the collar of my pajama jacket open at the neck, with each point laid in perfect place: Hugh Selwyn Mauberley—an advertisement for insomnia.

And chastity. Like a priest who has taken a vow but who lives out his life with a Priapus in his lap. I would not—could not bow to my desire for women or for other men. It is far too simple, I suppose, to say this had to do with my father's leap and my mother's madness. But something of my fear of physical contact and commitment had to do with that. Something to do with the fear of descent and the fear of being powerless in the presence of desire. Such as the desire that rose against my will when I saw Harry Reinhardt's inhuman eyes. Inhuman and, therefore, without the impediment of moral choice. There was nothing—nothing one could not imagine him doing.

But this was dangerous. This was appallingly dangerous.

At last, after passing Grenoble, I slept—very slightly fallen over, resting against the glass. In my dream, the only dream that night, the small yellow Fiat from the poster crashed against a wall. I could not see who the victims were. But the driver emerged unscathed: Harry Reinhardt.

At Nice I hired a Daimler with a chauffeur and was driven out along the Antibes road to the besieged and beautiful Villa Lou Viei. It was surrounded by an encampment of reporters and photographers—whose fingers were particularly long, so I felt it would be wise to hide my face behind a newspaper. Thus the famous photograph of a Daimler passing through the gates at the Villa Lou Viei with what appeared to be the late King Edward VIII riding in the back seat. In fact it was nothing more than his picture, blown up to cover the entire front page of *Le Monde*. Smiling.

Waiting in the gardens, Wallis looked like a ghost. She was thin and drawn, even plain in her appearance. She had wept, it seemed, for weeks.

"Well," she said, "it seems we are back in China and another man has left us stranded here with empty hands."

"Yes."

"Either murdered—or a suicide." She was trying, I think, to smile.

"Yes. But we will never know. And it's senseless to conjecture, now it's done."

"Is it?" No more smiling now and no more attempts. There was a sense of rising anger in her voice. Of rage. But constricted.

"Yes. And you know it is."

"Do I?"

"Yes."

I knew I must be very careful now. The edge of her voice was dangerous. She could be lost, not only to me, but to us, if I failed to say precisely the thing she needed to hear. Or

if I cut her off from saying precisely the thing she needed
to say.

"I am still expected to marry him. . . ."

"Yes."

She turned aside, with both hands clenched. "It is vile,"
she said. "Unfair and vile what they have made him do."
She looked at her hands and raised them so they swept out
through the air around her, charged with inexpressible ex-
asperation. "All the promises," she said. "The promises,
dear God." She looked away. "I was going to be Queen. Did
you know that?"

"Yes."

"What was it, then? A lie? A hoax? Or. . ."

Now she looked down at her shoes. "I hate him," she said.
"I do," she said. "I hate him."

All I could do was wait.

Finally, she lifted her gaze and stared at the sea beyond
the wall and shouted; *"hate."*

Very quickly I turned her and she threw her hands up to
strike me—me or anyone would do—and I pressed her hand
very firmly against her lips to silence her, allowing her the
impression she had silenced herself and was growing calm.

Still holding onto her, I told her why she must marry the
King. I told her about the centre of the world and that it was
always a free arena there; anyone could hold the stage who
had the power. *"Be visible,"* I said. *"Be unavoidable."* I
said. *"Be there,"* I said. And I said, "There's a banker now
who will stake you all the way."

I could feel her slowly subside. And I could feel her read-
justing her weight so she finally carried it all herself. And
I let her go.

Then I told her who the bankers were and I said, "There
is nothing now that is impossible. Only so long as you marry
the King."

She thought about it for a moment—only for a moment—
and then she burst out laughing. "You're aware, of course,"
she said, "this means I will have to spend the rest of my life
wearing low-heeled pumps."

Six months later, on Thursday, June 3rd, 1937, the newly created Duke of Windsor married Wallis Warfield of Baltimore in a ceremony at the Château de Candé, forty miles south of Paris in the valley of the Loire.

The Duchess was attended by her close friend, Mrs Herman Livingston Rogers of Cannes. The wedding dress was crêpe silk with a jacket, created by the American couturier, Mainbocher. The dress, designed as a two-piece gown, was the epitome of simplicity with a long, slim skirt and a high-collared neckline. The jacket was corseted and closed with nine small buttons covered in the distinctive blue of the dress itself. This particular shade was created especially for the occasion and had already been dubbed "Wallis Blue". It was slightly darker in tone than "pastel".

The Duke's best man was Major Edward D. ("Fruity") Metcalfe. Both wore the traditional cutaway with boutonnier. None of His Royal Highness's family was present.

The guest list numbered less than twenty, and among them were Mr Hugh Selwyn Mauberley and Mr and Mrs Charles E. Bedaux, whose home provided the wedding site.

A wedding is not my favourite ceremony. The predominant image has always been of my parents standing side by side—darkened by the shadow of their future. And when it is said "be joined together. . ."all I can see is my mother's hand, withdrawn—her precious hand that must not be held too tight for fear its fingers would be crushed and the music in them destroyed. But what my father had wanted was to have her and to hold her all the rest of his life. And after the refusal to be joined—the leap into space and the fallen mind. . . .So this was all I could see as I stood there watching the King and Wallis take their vows.

In the garden, after, there were pictures taken—some official; most just snapshots. "Do stand over there!" "Do smile!" And Wallis going away to change and the sound of barking little dogs and the champagne glasses smashing against the wall. Waiting for Wallis—now the Duchess of Windsor—to return, we all dispersed into private places, no one wanting to be forced into confrontations and comments—everyone feeling emptied, somehow. At which point I went in along some corridor, noting that Bedaux ducked inside a room at my approach, disdainful, perhaps, of having to thank me for making his moment of glory possible. And then I saw another man—way off—towards the end of whatever corridor it was in which I walked—and this other man appeared to be a retainer, perhaps. A quiet, lingering figure, not quite certain of what might be expected of him next.

He was hovering there at the farthest end of the corridor and all the light was beyond him in the garden. Near him there was a marble stand with a porcelain vase and the vase was filled with peonies and pale blue delphinium. The retainer's hand went out toward the flowers. It was so tentative, this gesture—like a child who's been told not to touch. Then he did. And sighed. I just kept walking on towards him, though he failed to notice I was there. I was making for the garden, pausing to remark how beautiful "his flowers were."

But they were not his flowers. The "retainer" was the Duke of Windsor, and all his lights had dimmed so far I could not even see his face till I was near him. He did not see me at all. He was too engrossed in waiting and in not being there.

I went out—shocked.

I had not even felt the impulse, in passing, to bow. And I thought—he has already leapt.

Or jumped.

Promoted and arranged by Charles Eugene Bedaux, the Windsor Tour of Germany took place in mid-October, 1937. It was a thunderous success.

They were accompanied everywhere they went by Doctor Robert Ley who was Head of the Nazi Labour Front (as boorish and crude a man as any Wallis had ever met. She did not at all enjoy his company).

They were shown through vast industrial plants and every kind of factory from steelworks to the Meissen Porcelain Works. They were driven through the streets of the working class districts in every city they visited, showing themselves to the people—and to the international press—riding in an open Mercedes touring car. Thousands saw them in the flesh and the Duke returned the uproar of the crowds with the Fascist salute. The mayors of all the cities bade them welcome. Little children curtsied to "Her Royal Highness", gave her flowers and marvelled at her beauty. After all these triumphs, they were finally introduced to Göring, Hess and Hitler—in that order.

Hess stayed much in evidence all through the latter meeting, though for an hour the Duke and Hitler were alone. Hess remained with the Duchess during this hour in an antechamber and, later, she remarked that she had found him "handsome—charming—most persuasive and a courtly gentleman. . . ."

The Duke's reaction to the tour was well summed up in the words he spoke to a meeting of the National Labour Front in Leipzig. "I have travelled the world," he told them, speaking in German; "and my whole upbringing has made me familiar with the great achievements of mankind. But that which I have seen in Germany, I had hitherto believed to be impossible. It cannot be grasped and is a miracle. One can only begin to understand it when one realizes that behind it all is one man and one will."

He meant, of course, Hitler—for the Duke in no way knew of the other forces at work around him.

Sitting on the dais beside him, Wallis looked down at her hands and smiled.

* * *

Quinn left the room and closed the door behind him.

Someone had been busy rigging lamplight along the corridor and down the stairs. He noted the picket, seated now and dozing on a broken chair. Rudecki was nowhere in sight.

Quinn was not eager to find Captain Freyberg but knew he must. The German Tour and all it implied had been quite an alarming read. Not that it was news the event had taken place. But the implications in 1937 had only to do with Hitler; only to do with the grave miscalculation of what the Duke had done in allowing himself to be used. But now it was clear that a force more potent than the fleeting Nazi forces of that moment had been involved in using him—and though it was clear both Bedaux and von Ribbentrop had pulled the strings for whatever that potent force had been— and *was*—someone, too, was pulling *their* strings. And the reach of the cabal was becoming truly alarming—precisely because its edges could not be seen.

There was one good thing, however, over which Lieutenant Quinn could relax. Mauberley's only role had been to play the messenger. And for that Quinn was grateful.

If Freyberg could be kept from his damned speculations, and made to read the walls as they were, all might still be well.

Or would it?

There. You see? Quinn thought. For every hope I raise, another crashes down to the floor. Still. It was his job to assess what was there and to pass that assessment on to Freyberg. And nothing in the rule book said his assessment could not be his own.

He kicked through the snow drifts covering the carpet. A light was burning in the room where Mauberley's corpse still lay in its corner and Freyberg was sitting there on a windowsill.

Quinn went up to the threshold only.

"Maybe you'd better come and have a look at what I've read so far," he said.

"Oh?" said Freyberg. "Any more cats on roofs?"

"No sir."

"You seem depressed," said Freyberg, smiling. "Isn't your hero turning out to be the whited saint you thought he was?"

Quinn was trying not to see the body and therefore not

to enter the room. But he wondered what it was that Freyberg was doing in there all alone, unless he was simply gloating.

"I never said Hugh Selwyn Mauberley was a saint, Captain Freyberg, and he never pretended he was a saint. No one ever said he was a saint except you. The thing is, sir, I think you're missing the point of this entirely."

"Which is?"

"Well, sir, from what I've read so far, he hasn't lied."

"So?"

"Well it seems to me that your whole premise has been that what I would find would be a pack of lies. But when you read it, sir, I think you might just change your mind."

"The point of this exercise, Quinn, is to change your mind—not mine. Yes: I will read what you've just read. But I won't be fooled by it. Not the way it appears you have been fooled."

Quinn stood back to let Freyberg pass into the hall and Freyberg said; "no. Before I go, I want you to come in here."

"I'd really rather not, sir."

"Come in, Quinn; that's an order."

Quinn went in. Freyberg stood behind him and turned him, holding him by the arm, so that he could not look away from Mauberley's body lying in its corner. "Now listen," said Freyberg; "look at him and listen."

Quinn looked down at the twisted arm and tried not to see the face. And Freyberg said; "he walked with Mussolini. He sat down with von Ribbentrop. He befriended a gang of murderers. He wrote Fascist garbage: anti-Semitic, pro-Aryan; anti-human, pro-Superman garbage. He even won prizes for it. Prizes, Quinn. *Peace* prizes. . . ."

Quinn was looking at Mauberley's hand.

Freyberg said; "so you see, it's you I'm concerned about. You—and the millions like you, Quinn—who cannot wait to forgive. And forget."

Freyberg let go of Quinn's arm and stepped away from him.

Finally, Quinn turned around and went again to the door. He felt ill. Freyberg was watching him.

"He's beginning to smell, isn't he," the Captain said.

Quinn looked down at the floor.

"Well," said Freyberg; "there's something you can do while I'm busy reading. I want some men up here to cover him with snow. Exactly as he is, not a muscle moved."

"In snow, sir?"

"Yes." Freyberg pointed out the windows. "There's a lot of snow out there—in case you've been so busy reading you've forgotten we're in the mountains here. They can bring it up in buckets or in bags. Just see he's buried."

Quinn said; "but—that's grotesque."

Freyberg said; "yes. It is, isn't it." And he went into the hall. "Nonetheless, that's what I want. Now."

"Yes, sir."

Freyberg went off down the corridor beneath the bags of chandeliers alone. Quinn had assumed he was meant to go with him.

"Captain?" he called.

Freyberg already had his hand on the doorknob to the first room.

"Yes?"

"You remember what he wrote about mythology, sir, at Dubrovnik."

"Yes?"

"It's just. . .Mythology can have two meanings, that's all. I mean. . .I mean—*The Iliad, The Odyssey*. . .I mean. . .there *was* a Trojan War. The Trojan War did happen."

Freyberg opened the door.

"I know that, Quinn. It's not the Trojan War I don't believe in. . .it's the Trojan Horse-shit."

Quinn looked into the room.

There was a smell. It was true.

He went downstairs to arrange for the snow.

Quinn had put Sergeant Rudecki in charge of covering Mauberley's body with snow and once the job was done, the Sergeant went into Annie Oakley's bar to get drunk.

"Tell me the honest truth, Sarge, eh?" said Annie Oakley.

"You ever hear of him? *Before*, I mean. . . ."

"You kidding?" said Rudecki. "An' you call yourself a movie nut? You never seen Bette Davis in *Stone Dogs*?"

"You mean where she plays the piano in the looney bin?"

"Yeah. Her son locks her up in the god damn asylum when all she ever wanted was to play Rachmaninov's Second Piano Concerto. . . ."

"And Claude Rains acts her husband and she pushes him off the Brooklyn Bridge. . ."

"No. The George Washington Bridge. . ."

"That's right."

"And he deserved it, too. Son of a bitch. Everyone's always so mean to her." Rudecki got out his handkerchief and blew his nose.

"*What did I do,*" Annie suddenly sang, "*to make you treat me this way?*"

"Poor Bette Davis. Oh. . ." Sergeant Rudecki had to dab at his eyes.

"So what's the guy with the stick in his eye got to do with it?" Annie asked.

"He wrote it, dumbass. Don't you pay attention? He wrote the god damn thing."

"The movie?"

"The book. The book. God—and that poor woman. All she ever wanted was to play Rachmaninov's Second Piano Concerto. . . ."

So it went. And Annie sang, ". . .what did I do, that I should be so blue. . .?"

When Quinn finally came back upstairs, he had been fed. The Hotel Elysium still had no heat but it was warmer than it had been, just from the human activity humming all around him. Freyberg's section of clerks was uncrating files and tables and even a safe. Everything you could think of, Quinn thought, except a sign for Freyberg's desk reading PRESIDENT.

The detail of men working under Sergeant Rudecki had brought up forty cartons of snow and dumped them over

Mauberley's corpse—whose elbow could still be seen: but that was all. And the smell had lessened.

Walking along the corridor, Quinn heard the faintest whisper of music. Freyberg must be playing the gramophone. Damn. It would have been nice just to go to bed and not to have to face another confrontation with the Captain until the morning.

Standing outside the door, adjusting his scarf and the collar of his greatcoat, Quinn realized his hands were shaking. Quinn had never seen a person reach so far for vengeance as Freyberg was reaching here in this hotel. It was almost as if he wanted Mauberley to pay for everything the Nazis had done and it made Quinn shiver when he remembered the look in Freyberg's eyes as he'd said he wanted Mauberley covered with snow. Surely that had to be crazy.

He opened the door.

Captain Freyberg was staring out the window and the music on the gramophone was Schubert. Obviously, Freyberg did not hear the Lieutenant enter, so Quinn was able to watch him for a moment. He had never seen the captain look so relaxed and for the briefest moment he thought it must be someone else who was standing there.

"Sir?"

But Freyberg did not hear him.

Finally, Quinn went over and lifted the needle off the record.

Freyberg turned—white as a man who has just been shot at.

"Why did you take it off?" he said.

"I couldn't make you hear me," said Quinn. "And I was afraid I might. . ." He did not know how to finish.

"Startle me?" said Freyberg.

"Yes sir."

Freyberg moved away from the windows and sat on the cot. Quinn did not like this. He really did want to be alone. He decided to put the record back in its blue paper jacket and maybe then the captain would take the hint.

"I don't even know what music that was," said Freyberg.

"Schubert."

"Schubert, yes; but what?"

"A piano sonata, sir," said Quinn, putting the record back very carefully on the surface of the desk. "In B-flat major. Opus posthumous."

"Wouldn't it be nice," Freyberg said, "to have a mind like yours? To know and remember things like that. Then when you want that music you know where to find it."

"Yes sir."

"I suppose you know a lot about music?"

"Not really, sir. This particular sonata is rather well known." And the minute he had said this, Quinn regretted it, knowing how priggish it must sound.

"Rather well known, hunh?"

"Yes sir."

"May an ignorant slob ask why?"

Quinn walked right in: "yes, sir," he said. And reddened immediately. Damn.

"Well," said Freyberg. "Tell a person. Why is it rather well known?"

"Because, sir, it was the last thing Schubert wrote."

"Oh, really, fascinating. The last thing he wrote before what?"

"Before he died, sir."

Freyberg got off the cot and crossed to the desk which held the gramophone and records. He fingered the records lightly, wearing his gloves. His back was now to Quinn.

"I've finished reading the walls up to where it says they were married."

"Yes sir."

"And I've noted it doesn't say they lived happily ever after."

"No sir."

"Isn't that kind of odd—for a fairy tale? Not to say they lived happily ever after?"

"Maybe, sir. But this isn't a fairy tale."

"Oh, yes. I forgot. It's mythology." Freyberg had now picked up the Schubert sonata in its jacket and was looking at its label.

"Poor old Wally Simpson." Freyberg's voice was like a

candy melting in the throat. "Mauberley sure pulls all the stops out on that one. She sure was quite a dame.. . ."

"I thought so," said Quinn.

"She's a whore," said Freyberg.

"And you're a bastard, sir, if I may say so, sir, for saying that, sir."

Freyberg was genuinely taken aback. Quinn automatically stood at attention waiting to be reprimanded. But it never came to that. Freyberg gave a slight cough and then smiled.

"You know, it's fascinating," he said, "the way you lay yourself on the line for these people. I could have you brigged for what you just said. But don't get all worked up about it, Quinn. I'm not going to do it. I'm simply remarking. . .I find it fascinating, the way you lay yourself on the line."

"I haven't said I think what's on the walls is a pretty story, sir. I've only said I think I understand what he's trying to do."

"Whitewash the truth?"

"*Tell* the truth. About himself. Including the mistakes he made. And. . ."

"And. . .?"

Quinn said, "It's just—there are more people guilty than just these people on the wall. And. . ."

"And?"

"And you keep trying to make it seem these people here were the only guilty people in the whole world."

Freyberg smiled. "Well yeah," he said. "I guess there was Hitler too."

Quinn said; "all I mean is—they weren't alone. Damn it! You'd blame the whole war on Mauberley, if you could."

Freyberg only smiled after this and then said, "Lieutenant Quinn, I would like to ask you a question."

"Yes sir."

"Can you tell me why it is your heart goes out to all these people here?" Freyberg made a kind of a dancer's turn that took in all the walls. "I really do need an answer, Lieutenant. I really do. Because, you see, my heart does not go out to any of these people here. And I want to know why. I want to know why, because it makes me feel somewhat less than adequate that I cannot spare them any feeling."

Quinn was hoping this would be followed by one of Freyberg's smiles. But it was not. Instead, Captain Freyberg said; "do you think it could be that I cannot spare that feeling for them because they cannot spare that feeling for me?"

Quinn said; "yes, sir"—very carefully. "It could be."

"You sound doubtful, Lieutenant."

"It's just that we haven't finished reading, Captain. And it doesn't seem fair to condemn a lot of people whose stories have only half been told."

Freyberg looked at the walls. "Does your heart go out to me, Lieutenant, the way it does to all these others?"

"That isn't fair, sir. And you know it. I never said my heart went out to anyone. You did."

Freyberg looked at Quinn and now—at last—he smiled. " 'I never said my heart went out to anyone,' " he said. "Unquote."

"Yes, sir."

"I'm very glad to hear it, Quinn. Believe me."

"Yes, sir. I do believe you."

"Good." Freyberg studied the record still in his hands. "You know, when I was reading I kept thinking: any minute now we're going to meet one of these Fascist bastards that Mauberley doesn't like. And it hasn't happened, yet. Do you think it will?"

Quinn did not answer.

Freyberg said; "oh—it probably will. By the time we've finished reading. Like you said, the story's only half been told." He looked up at Quinn. "By the way—I'm assuming you mean we've only just *read* half; not that he's only told us half." He smiled. And snapped the record in two, handing one of the pieces to Quinn. "Half isn't good enough, is it?"

"No, sir."

Freyberg tucked the other half of the record under his arm in its blue jacket. "Goodnight," he said. And went away.

Quinn looked down at the jagged thing in his hands and was sorry. And he wondered why men like Freyberg were compelled to be the way they were.

Just before he blew out the lamp. Quinn looked at the animals

over his head—and the moon and the stars and the hand—
and he remembered something long forgotten. Mauberley's
mother, so the story went, had lost her mind because she
was obsessed with perfection she could not achieve as a
pianist. That no one could achieve. Just as Freyberg was
obsessed with perfections of another kind that no one could
achieve. Because—if they could—there would be nothing
written on the walls at all. And Freyberg would love that.
He would rejoice in all that white. Then Quinn arranged the
pillow so it wouldn't muss his hair—and blew out the lamp.

FOUR

1937-1940

In the nightmare of the dark
All the dogs of Europe bark,
And the living nations wait,
Each sequestered in its hate;

Intellectual disgrace
Stares from every human face,
And the seas of pity lie
Locked and frozen in each eye.

W. H. Auden

Spain: 1937

The famous raid from the air on the town of Guernica had taken place in April of 1937. All that spring and summer.

German warplanes continued their support of General Franco
with more bombardments along the Biscayne coast of Spain.
Not long after the fall of Bilbao I went into the northern
provinces of Navarre and Asturias with Isabella Loverso.
We travelled by motorcar.

Isabella Loverso was going on a "mission"—the object of
which remained unspoken, though I assumed it had to do
with the cabal. In June, when I returned to Paris—unsettled
in the aftermath of Wallis's marriage to the Duke—Isabella
had indicated to me she would be glad of my company
during this journey. "It is never good to travel alone through
the regions of war," she had said. "If one is by oneself, one
disappears too easily."

It was not, I must confess, for Isabella alone that I agreed
to make the journey. In the back of my mind I also thought
it might provide the subject matter, or at least the stimulus,
for some new thing to write. My publisher had been prodding
me with cablegrams and notes—very terse—reminding me
I had not published since 1934. I remember how, in one of
his notes, he said: "in this age of political malcontents the
still, sane voice of Mauberley would be most welcome."
Somehow, I doubted this—in the face of Ernest's incum-
bency and the rising star of Steinbeck, both of whom seemed
to have cornered the market, if not in "still, sane voices"
then certainly in voices that were still considered sane.

Nonetheless, for reasons of my own, I thought it was imperative to try for another book. On the one hand, I needed
to exorcize the sting of Julia Franklin's remarks; on the other,
I had to overcome the crippling fact that putting pen to paper
had become anathema to me. At home in the Meurice or at
the Grande Bretagne and Bristol, I had been filling two and
three waste paper baskets a day.

When you pass into the north of Spain from France, there
is little chance you will not encounter something that re-
minds you of the past. Your own or everyone's. The names
of Biarritz, St. Jean-de-Luz and Navarre ring all the bells of
English Kings, crusades and chivalry. But the furthest past

of all is rung by the caves of Altamira, where the painted walls reverberate with the cries of Ice Age animals and men that have been dead two hundred thousand years and more.

Castille and Aragon lie to the south, and to the north—the sea, the sun and the yellow glare of the Biscayne Bay. It is all a place of umbered soil and whitewashed stone and the sound rides over it of insects, even through the night, and of storms that never come and of songs you will never forget. It was to that place we made our way, midsummer of 1937. Seven years ago and a half.

In the midst of that journey, I discovered what it was that put Isabella Loverso in jeopardy, providing the edges on which she walked and the fear she had expressed when she said she was afraid she would disappear. It had to do with her past and with her marriage, of which, till then, I had never heard her speak.

At the outset, she and her husband, Barone Masimo Loverso, had been part of the coterie surrounding Mussolini. They had worked for him tirelessly in the early days, devoting not only their time and money, but the prestige of their name when Mussolini was still the relatively unknown editor of *Il Popolo*. During the First World War, they called themselves Socialists. But in 1919 they proclaimed the Fascist Party, whose name was derived from the groups of workers—known as *fasci*—brought together under the hand of Mussolini to agitate for a change in the social order. Very soon they were a major political force, gaining fame and support for their opposition to the rising threat of Communism. They broke up Communist meetings and demonstrations, wrote and published editorials against the Communist ideal and, during the civil wars of 1921, took to the barricades. By the fall of 1922, the King himself sent out a call for Mussolini to take the Prime Ministership and save the country from the Communist menace.

Isabella smiled when she recounted these events.

"They called it *The March on Rome*," she said. "But the truth is, we rode in a private railway car from Milan and were met at the gates of the city by a military escort. All told, we 'marched' no more than a mile—and *il Duce* sat in the rear of a motorcar! It is all a legend, you see? A story—though people who were there and *saw* him riding *tell* you that he walked.. . .''

Perhaps it was seeing Mussolini riding in that motorcar that laid the foundations of Isabella's rebellion against him. His back was all she saw—and all her husband saw—for the next four weeks, and then, in November of 1922, Mussolini assumed dictatorial powers. What had been a shared ideal became a single man: a god.

Over the next two years, "constructive criticism" was still allowed. But in June of 1924, the door was finally shut on "constructive criticism" when Barone Loverso's best friend, Giocomo Matteotti was murdered. Matteotti had long been an outspoken opponent of fascist violence—and in 1924 he made the mistake of publishing his views in a book called *The Fascists Exposed.* His murder, of course, exposed them openly for all to see. But the effect was silence—the all-pervading silence of fear. The press was censored. Silenced. The non-Fascist members of Parliament protested by seceding; thus being silenced. And the people finally lost the right to freely exercise their vote—silenced—when the Fascist Grand Council was established in 1929, putting forth a single party slate of candidates from which the people had to choose their representatives.

As for Isabella's husband, Barone Masimo Loverso, he died of a gunshot wound that was said to be self-inflicted. This was on June 11th, 1924. His friend, Matteotti, had been killed by a gang of thugs the day before. *Il Duce's* explanation was that Isabella's husband must have played some part in Matteotti's death, and afterward regretted it. His murderers attended his funeral; and Isabella, Baronessa Loverso, sought her retirement at the Palazzo d'Aquila in Venice.

For the next two weeks she spent every waking moment destroying every word her husband had ever written. Essays, articles, poems—even his letters written before they were married. And then she drew down all the shades and closed all the doors.

Silenced.

So it seemed.

"What saved you," I asked, "when your husband died?"

Isabella stared from the back of the Daimler in which we rode. "Harry Wyndham," she said.

I had always wondered how Diana's father had entered Isabella's life.

"Harry Wyndham found me in mourning," she said. "And he found me greatly afraid."

For a mile or more of dusty road, this was her only answer.

Finally the silence became so oppressive I asked if she had any children.

Isabella didn't answer. Instead she settled into her furs—light summer furs to keep off the chill after sunset. The road was giving off dust: yellow dust which powdered the windows. The chauffeur drove at an ox-cart's pace, for now we had begun to encounter refugees on their way to the border towns of Irun and Henlaye, and the freedom—if they could achieve it—of St. Jean-de-Luz and Biarritz.

"Look! We are coming to San Sebastian," said Isabella.

"Yes. But your children. . ."

She closed her eyes.

"They were buried with my husband," she said and lifted up her hands to spread the furs around her ears, as if she were afraid to hear the words.

It was minutes before she spoke again.

"Harry Wyndham was like a patient, loving father," she said.

"Yes."

"It was wonderful," she said. "Wonderful to be a child again, for a while, when your children have died. He was very good to me: Harry Wyndham. Very good *for* me. I regained my confidence. I regained my will to live. I was not unlike a little girl whose dolls have all been smashed. For a while, she weeps—and then she walks across the hall and puts on her mother's make-up, her mother's tall shoes and her mother's dress, and she puts up her hair and moves from the nursery into the centre of the salon—and all the adults say: *you have now become a woman.* Yes? I became Harry Wyndham's mistress then—but I never lost sight of the fact that I was something more."

"Which was?"
"The spoils of war."
Andromache.

In San Sebastian we stayed overnight in a hotel called the Bilbao. In Bilbao, our hotel was called the San Sebastian.

"And if we stayed in Heaven," I said, "it would be the Hotel Hell." This made—at last—Isabella laugh.

But no matter where we stayed it might as well have been the Hotel Hell. There was never any glass in the windows; never any water in the taps; the beds were always full of lice and the telephones and electricity were always dead. The worst of all was at Santander, where the war was still in progress and the hotel's name could not be ascertained because its signs had all been blown away by a bomb on the previous afternoon and half the building didn't exist; the hallways giving way to space and the stairways marching out into the sky.

We did, however, procure a suite where I slept on a Regency settee in the salon. Isabella gave me her furs to keep me warm and all night long a convoy of men and mules and trucks moved through the rubble in the street below. The Loyalists were in retreat, their progress steady and unending. I wondered if the chauffeur would have to defend our Daimler with his life and if he had a gun. And then I wondered if the chauffeur was himself a Loyalist. So many of his class were Bolsheviks. What if we should be stranded—undefended—before the Insurgents arrived: would our chauffeur denounce us? Isabella, after all, was Italian; all Italians were universally hated by the Loyalists. Where could we reach for safety?

I was thinking all of this when I heard a noise in the bedroom. Isabella had gone to bed so early—almost as soon as we arrived—and had said to me, "I hate the world at night. It frightens me. The sooner I'm asleep, the better." And now there was this noise. A fierce, whispered muttering.

Alarmed, I arose and, clutching the furs at my neck, I approached her door.

"Isabella?"

Suddenly—silence. All the whispering died away.

"Isabella?"

Nothing.

Out in the streets the great retreat continued—and now for the first time since we had arrived in Spain I heard the faraway booming of gigantic guns that might have been somewhere offshore. These noises heightened my alarm. There was so much movement, so much violent, distant light in contrast to the present dark. Every shadow was a menace.

I went into Isabella's bedroom and struck several matches—each one extinguished by the draught from broken windows. Giving up all hope of seeing her, I called her name.

"Be quiet," she said.

Her voice was like a knife and I backed instinctively away from it. "What is it," I said. "Were you dreaming? What?"

The offshore guns were booming. Shells were beginning to land about ten blocks away along the waterfront. Fires had begun to catch at this or that building, mounting very high so that light of a kind had begun to flicker on the furthest walls of the room. I could see Isabella sitting on the bed with her hands in fists pressed in against her cheeks. She rocked back and forth, but still she was silent. I could see there were tears in her eyes and spilling down across her knuckles. Slowly, I sat on the bed beside her.

"Please, please tell me," I said. "How can I help if you will not tell?"

But all she did was shake her head and go on rocking back and forth in what appeared to be a sort of lullaby—as if she could put the fear to sleep by soothing it and shushing it and rocking it like a mother.

I took her hand. Or attempted to.

"Don't," she said. "Please don't."

So we sat. And I waited. While she stared into the dark and the city moaned with the noises of one army leaving and the gates going up to receive the next. We sat for hours like that, until I slept. And when I woke, she had not moved, but was sitting still the same in her trance of fear.

The menace that had plagued her from the moment of her husband's death did not, it appeared, have any intention of

letting go. And I wondered—of her mind and of her past—
what else I did not know. And of her activities: her mission
there in Spain.

Later that morning we made our escape.

"Where are we going?" I asked the chauffeur.

"San Vincente de la Barquera."

But we never got there. At nine the road was attacked by
aeroplanes and we were thrown into a kind of war I had
never experienced before. This was the war where civilians
were exclusively the victims and where you never saw the
enemy. All you could see was his machines.

The three of us were scattered—Isabella, myself and the
chauffeur—running with a hundred others through a field.
Other fields and olive groves had hundreds of their own.

Behind us and before us there was the smack-smack-smack
of machine-gun bullets striking the earth. The road on which
the Daimler sat amongst a horde of broken old carts and
panic-stricken horses had been hit with so many bombs it
looked like a river filled with islands of smoke. This river
sat up over us with all the people spilling down into the
fields.

The thing I remember most vividly about that bombing
raid was the sense of having fallen from the earth. Nothing
had any real or human context. Everything was upside down
or inside out and it seemed we were all in the air and the
earth was above us.

Finally, we all fell down together: falling onto stones and
stubble with our mouths full of dirt and our fingers clinging
to the earth as if the earth could save us like a raft at sea.

We lay there maybe ten or fifteen minutes—mute while
the storm of bullets blew around us—folding our hands
across the backs of our necks: shutting our eyes as children
do in the crazy hope the blind cannot be seen. And at last
the squalls of machine-gun fire began to fade away until
there was nothing left but the drifting down of dust to cover
us. Dust and sand and even stones. The aeroplanes were
gone.

For a moment, I remember, there was not a trace of sound or movement. Then all at once the fields stood up. Or so it seemed. And the dead were left where they were, face down and immovable as rocks, while those of us who had survived turned back towards the road and simply walked away. This is all I recall. We just kept moving forward—and our feet, which seemed like miracles, were all that we could see. Certainly, no one looked at the sky. The sky was now a traitor; part of the conspiracy against us. It could deliver death without a warning, and it shamed us not to know how to save ourselves or where to hide. I had never felt this humiliation before—which is to say, the indignity of being terrorized by something you had trusted all your life.

The following day we stayed in a nameless village where the chauffeur had engaged a blacksmith to help him manufacture whatever parts were needed to repair the Daimler.

All that afternoon I sat with Isabella in the blacksmith's yard on a bench beneath the vine. The walls of the yard and the buildings around us were white and the vine's new leaves were rainy green. The air was filled with the smell of olive wood and smoke and sun-hot stones. A woman came and brought us wine and bread and pears. The pears were dry and small, but very sweet.

Isabella sat with her legs straight out and crossed at the ankles, showing bruises on her shins I had not been aware existed. These were doubtless from the bombing raid on the road, but combined with the haunted expression in her eyes, the effect was of a torture victim sitting incongruous in the sun.

Isabella said, "They took him from his office into a courtyard such as this—with vines and trees. . ."

This was a complete non sequitur.

"What?" I said.

But Isabella hardly seemed to know I was there. She was sitting somewhere else, I suppose; in the past.

"My husband was only thirty-eight years old," she said, "and all he had done was express his opinion. All he had

done was put some words on paper. But they killed him—
shot him—propping him against the courtyard wall—and
they placed the gun in his hands, and they laid my children,
all of them dead, around him. As if he had killed them."
She was peering through the heat, as if to see the scene she
described.

I waited.

In a moment she spoke again. "When our friend Matteotti
died, he was beaten first. With stones. Were you aware of
that?"

"No." I had only known he was shot, and told her so. I
was watching her carefully. She was perspiring; running a
fever; ill—and the words were coming out of dreams.

". . .and when I dressed my husband's corpse, I found his
back was bruised. But the fingers in which they had set the
gun were as fine and clean and manicured as they had always
been in life. Not a mark. Not a mark. Not a visible mark."
She opened her eyes. "These men—Matteotti and my husband—were writers. Only writers, my friend. Only men of
words.. . ." And she looked at me, informing me of something that I did not know, perhaps about the dangers of
writing.

And I did not. Know.

"My husband was a poet. Just a poet. . ." She looked at
the wall. "But Mussolini's people took him into a courtyard.
Under the trees. . ." She spoke as if the trees had been dis-
graced. "And they killed him. You see? Our friends, my
friend. Our friends. They killed him." Reaching down, she
drew her skirt across the bruises on her shins. "And now,
in Spain I am constantly thinking of my husband and his
death," she said. "How they killed him. With their boots.
And I am thinking all the time of Matteotti, too: and how
they killed him. With a stone. And I am thinking of my
children.. . .I am thinking of the wall and of the trees. I am
thinking of human beings. I am thinking of how it can be
that mere human beings can be so afraid of the written word
they will kill to be rid of it. In a courtyard such as this. On
a day such as this—with the vines and the trees and the
stones as their witness. How can that be?" she asked me.

"Tell me. Tell me. How can that be?"

I did not know.

"And now," she said, "we are here in Spain. Twelve years have passed—and we are here in Spain and the stones and boots that killed Matteotti and my husband, the bullets that killed my children, have become the bombs on that road and the shells from the ships offshore. And nothing is for the better. Nothing is changed for the better. Everything of which we dreamed is gone and all that we feared would happen has come to be. Are you afraid, my friend? Are you never afraid of what we do? Of the meaning of what we do and who we are?"

We were in Spain that summer six more weeks, and then again in the autumn two more weeks and a half. Isabella's commission this time took us along the Mediterranean coast and I remember that during our visit to Valencia late in October, the Loyalist government made its retreat to Barcelona.

I remained completely in the dark as to why—precisely—we were there. Nothing was hinted at and the cabal was never mentioned. My discovery of what it was that Isabella had been doing came about completely by accident.

It was at Valencia shortly after General Franco's troops had entered the city. Isabella and I had remained behind to recuperate from the violent shelling the city had undergone. Isabella's health had been failing. For three whole days she remained in her room at the Hotel Alcador, begging me not to be concerned and urging me not to keep appearing every time I achieved the triumph of an egg or the miracle of figs or the coup of a quarter pound of coffee. "It is enough that I can rest," she said. "It is all I want—to be alone."

But she was not alone.

One early evening, I had been wandering through the ruins of a seminary, talking with the first of the brothers who had dared to return in order to salvage his Order's relics and bury its murdered dead. His story had given me the over-powering urge to write again and I remember that fact as being salient. The breakthrough had finally come and I was in a state of tremendous excitement, actually shaking as I entered the Alcador's lobbies.

Each hotel that had survived the bombs—and this was true of any Spanish city during that war—automatically became the meeting place for the local intelligentsia, the local police and the local contingent of foreign correspondents. The Alcador of Valencia was no different. Consequently I was used to finding its lobbies crowded and used to the presence of men in uniform.

But on this particular evening the lobbies of the Alcador were virtually overrun and the patrons, the police and the foreign correspondents had spilled out into the street.

"What is it? What is it?" I said as I tried to make my way inside. "Please tell me what it is!" There was something in the way they stood and something in the way they behaved that prompted a dreadful and overpowering sense of apprehension.

"There has been a suicide," they said. "Someone has killed themself in the lobby. Standing up in front of everyone—they shot themself."

"Was it a woman?" I asked. "Was it a woman?"

Visions of Isabella's illness, her exhaustion and her history certified my fear that it must have been her.

But no one could say.

"There is a body." That is all they said.

I was angry, then.

The streets of Valencia were full of bodies. People had been dying violent deaths on every doorstep. I myself had just been witness to the mutilated bodies of a dozen priests. Why must there be such a crowd—such a crush at the Hotel Alcador when it was vital I get inside and discover whether Isabella lived or was dead? Could they not go out and stare at the corpses in the square?

"But this," I was told, "was *suicidio*."

Someone had done this terrible thing to themself. And this, I was told, was different than doing "some terrible thing upon the selves of others"—whether with guns or bombs. Thus, *suicidio* was suddenly unique in a world where murder and slaughter were the commonplace—though why I should be surprised or upset by this in the land of bullfights I do not know.

It took me a quarter of an hour to reach the other side of the lobby. The suicide's corpse was lying on the makeshift catafalque of the registry counter. I could only see it was a man: with his brains blown out and his arms hanging down.

When I got to our suite the doors were all locked and I had to swear to Isabella I was alone before she would let me in. I found her packing her steamer trunk—and I could see there had been a fire in the metal waste paper basket.

Isabella was pale and weakened but decisive.

"We must leave," she said. "You must pack at once and we must leave as soon as it is dark. If anyone comes to the door, we are not here."

"There has been a suicide in the lobby," I said, like a child who will not be denied the privilege of telling whatever gruesome news there is to tell.

"I know all that," she said. "I know."

I waited—thinking she might go on and explain what our departure had to do with the corpse. But she was playing a different game.

"Any news of who it was?" she said. Her tone was that of a very bad actress who had been told to throw the line away.

The only thing I had heard was that it was someone whose passport had been revoked—and so I told her this.

"Ah, yes," she said. "The game of invalid passports. So soon."

I asked her what she meant by that.

"In Italy, shortly after the regime became a dictatorship, a great many passports were revoked. Though it took a good deal longer to happen than this. After all, General Franco's troops have only just arrived. There is not even yet a proper government here."

I thought of Dmitri Karaskavin and the long, long wait for passports and sisters that never arrived. But they were murdered. This—in the Alcador lobby—was *suicidio*.

Isabella then did something I had never seen her do before.

She withdrew a bottle from one of the drawers of the steamer trunk and poured herself over half a tumbler of Calvados. She then leaned back against the edge of the desk and, picking up one or two sheets of paper, she carefully set each one on fire with a match and let them fall on top of the ashes in the wastepaper basket.

"May I ask what you're doing?" I said.

"You may," she said, "but I shall not answer."

Oh.

She looked at me.

"Do you trust me?" she said.

I nodded.

"Then do not ask what I am doing."

The silence that followed was among the hardest I have ever endured.

At last she was finished with her burning. "We must take these into the lavatory and flush them down the W.C. No matter how fine the ashes may be, a person with the proper skills can read them."

This I found very hard to believe—and said so.

"Come here," she said and selected, at random, a piece of burnt paper three or four inches square. Even as she lifted it, part of it fell away. But what remained was large enough to have contained a phrase or more of writing. Very carefully, Isabella held this up beneath the lamp and tilted it this way and that until she had achieved a particular angle—slanting away from the light. "There," she said. "Read."

I looked; and read.

The ink, very shiny against the charcoal colour of the fragment, was brown that had once been blue. But the words were as distinct as if they had just been written: *sangre del honor*. And then Isabella crumpled them and swept them back into the basket.

Flushing the ashes down the toilet, I was alarmed to discover they were so light in texture all of them would not go down the chute.

"What shall we do?"

"Put something heavy in on top of them. Here..." said Isabella. And she handed me a fine lace handkerchief. "Wet it first and lay it over them."

I did so—and flushed the toilet one last time. Every remaining trace of the ashes was carried away into the sewers of Valencia. And when I analysed the incident, later, for myself, I thought Isabella's advice had been the advice of an expert. How many ashes had she flushed down the toilet, I wondered. And why?

We "escaped" from the Hotel Alcador later that night in the dark. There was a blackout, due to the threat of retaliatory raids by the Loyalists—which never came. But this was not to say they could not create chaos and confusion, even in spite of their lack of air power. The war in Spain that year, and the next (and, in fact, right up to the end of 1939) took on the character of an amoeba: dividing and subdividing, spreading out here and there, never still, always shapeless, but always vital and alive and self-sustaining right to the very end when, like a creature having fed too long upon itself, it convulsed one final time and shrivelled. And died. But its shape in the closing months of 1937 was still in motion—and the changes could occur so rapidly you could go to sleep and wake in a Loyalist Hotel that in the middle of the night had been the Insurgent's H.Q.

After we left Valencia that night, it was necessary to return a week later in order to retire from Spain on board a ship and run the blockade to Palma.

It was there, on Mallorca, that I read in the papers of the death of the young Spanish poet Luis Quintana, who committed suicide in the lobby of the Hotel Alcador at Valencia. The most disturbing aspect of his suicide, so far as I was concerned, was revealed in the concluding paragraphs of his obituary. Here, where the print was finest, there was a quote from Quintana's final communiqué to the world which had been "smuggled out of Spain by an unnamed friend". The quote that caught my attention was short and pertinent and ran as follows: *"El amor por la verdad es la sangre del honor."* Love of truth is the blood of honour. When I saw the words *sangre del honor*, my heart stopped.

Quintana's "unnamed friend" was Isabella.

Quintana himself was an anti-Fascist.

Of Spain, there only remains one thing to say which I have
left until the end because it overrides the whole of that time.

I have spoken already of the caves at Altamira. My visit
there with Isabella had been in the early weeks of our Spanish sojourn. The Insurgents were shelling the coast from
offshore and every day there was a ration of terror starting
at 2:00 and lasting through the afternoon till 4:00. A person
could set all the clocks by the precision of this event.

So it was that Isabella and I went down into the caves—
with others—during one of these bombardments. Now the
others are only shadows in my mind. I cannot give them
faces. All I know is they were there, and we were not alone.

Some of the local peasants had taken up residence there.
Others made it their daily shelter during the raids. As a
consequence some had brought candles while others had
commandeered lamps from the local public buildings, setting them out in rows along the floor. It was a muted, gentle
atmosphere and all the talk was in whispers, falling away
at the height of bombardment into silence. The air was cool
and far, far away you could hear the sound of water. Somehow, the presence of that sound was a comfort. Everyone's
patience flourished and we sat in rows, while some even
slept.

And there above us, clustered in juxtapositions the meanings of which are lost beyond the barricades of time, were
the drawings of all those animals whose shapes have long
since been altered and disappeared from the view of men.
"Bison" I knew they were called, though little enough like
any bison I had ever seen; and "deer" that were recognizable
as such, though longer of leg and more delicate of hoof than
the deer I remembered passing over *Nauly's* lawns; and
"men" as simply drawn as any stick men made by the children of the human race since the dawn of time and pencils.
And waving blades of grass—or were they trees?—and con-
stellations here and there of fingerprinted stars: black dots.

And out of the corner of my eye I caught a glimpse of
something irresistible above my head, seen in the ebb and
flow of the swinging light: the imprint of a human hand.

God only knew how long ago it had been put there. Maybe

ten—and maybe twenty thousand years before. *This is my mark*; it said. *My mark that I was here. All I can tell you of my self and of my time and of the world in which I lived is in this signature: this hand print; mine.*

I saw these animals. I saw this grass. I saw these stars. We made these wars. And then the ice came.

Now the stars have disappeared. The grass is gone: the animals are calling to us out beyond this place—the frozen entrance to this cave.. . .

In days or hours we will have died. We cannot breathe. The lanthorn flickers. All the air is gone. I leave you this: my hand as signature beside these images of what I knew. Look how my fingers spread to tell my name.

Some there are who never disappear. And I knew I was sitting at the heart of the human race—which is its will to say *I am*.

In January of 1939, Isabella Loverso and I came up here to the Grand Elysium Hotel. Our journeys, for a while, were over and we needed rest. Isabella stayed in this very room.

One day, we were leaning on the parapet staring down into the valley of the Adige. Isabella wore her sables, and I was dressed in Harris tweed, woollen scarves from Ottingers on the Ringstrasse and a pair of fleece-lined boots that were sold exclusively in a little shop in Linz. The Anschluss was over. Germans were everywhere, including many soldiers. There were charabancs full of people down from Munich and up from Italy to spend the holidays. Herr Kachelmayer's hotel was filled to overflowing. This was the golden age of the Fascist powers. All of Europe was in thrall of Hitler and of Mussolini and the air was alive with excitement and anticipation.

Slowly, this day, as I stood there pressing my elbow close to Isabella's, I became aware I was being watched.

Turning, I saw a slight young man who was leaning, like us, against the parapet.

"Lorenzo! Lorenzo!" Isabella called.

She waved and the slight young man came over through the snow.

"Lorenzo de Broca," Isabella smiled at him. "How can it be? Everyone says you have gone to America."

"No."

For a moment, he did not move, but stood and stared at Isabella, then at me, and then at the ground.

"Don't be shy, Lorenzo." Isabella touched him on the arm and laughed. "Don't be shy of us. Please say hello." She spoke to him very like a chiding mother to a favourite child. A prodigal child. "This is Signor Mauberley, whose writing I am sure you know."

de Broca looked up and nodded. Only nodded. But looked at once away.

"Dear Hugh," said Isabella, taking my arm. "This is Italy's youngest genius: Lorenzo de Broca."

"Yes." I stuck out my hand. "I've read your work. It's very fine."

de Broca had blue eyes. He was slim and perhaps consumptive. Something was wrong with the way he stood and the way he breathed. It seemed a tremendous effort just to be there: alive.

He regarded my hand and finally removed his own from its pocket. But instead of shaking hands with me, he reached across and lifted Isabella's fingers to his lips, and bowed.

"Baronessa."

"Signor Mauberley and I are here for the Nativity. And you?"

de Broca scowled.

I drew my hand back through the air.

"I am merely passing through," the young man said. "I should not even be here, now."

"Is it true, then? *Have* you gone to live in America?"

"No, Baronessa. I have gone to live in Paris."

"Ah. . ."

He was lying, and it showed. He was not very good at hiding what was passing through his mind.

In a moment, after an extended and embarrassing silence,

he excused himself and started toward the hotel portico. But all at once he turned in his tracks and made his way very slowly back until he could reach out—if he had wanted to—and touch us both.

"I am sorry," he said. "I cannot go away without I tell you something very closely to my heart." He was speaking English, whereas before we had all been speaking Italian. He turned to me and spoke directly into my eyes. For a moment I thought he was going to strike me. But he didn't. He need not. His words struck for him. "I am always a student of your books," he said. "I am always your lover—of your books. But I am not your lover now, Signor Mauberley. Not any more. You used to have been a great good man. As I saw you first in my student days. A genius. But now you have gone away from all the good and genius I saw before and I am thinking, when I see you a moment ago, that you were throwing down your good words and breaking them below us in the valley. And I ask of you: why have you left from us? Why have you gone away from your self?"

I waited, astounded. Isabella's fingers had tightened on my arm. And I thought of the Marquesa spitting on Ernest's shoes, and I knew de Broca's passion was the same as hers had been. And I knew—and was shaken by the knowing—he was telling me the truth. But I still could not speak.

"Over all the world," de Broca said, "there is darkness now. And where are you that was, who made in all your writing words to make a light?"

He looked very hard at me. So hard I wanted desperately to look away. But I refused. I admired this young man. I had read his poetry and I thought very highly of it. How could I look away, no matter what he said. Ernest had not looked away from the Marquesa. For a reason. If we are brave enough to put our words on paper, then we must be brave enough to have them turn on us.

"It is not my pleasure to have your company here." de Broca turned and extended his rebuke to include Isabella. And then he looked at me again and said, "I am sorry to be your enemy. But am."

And went away.

The war, which now is in its closing hours, began with silence in the dawn of September 1st, 1939.

Some soldiers lying on the ground looked out across a Polish meadow from a German wood and listened for the cock to crow. And when it did, the soldiers turned to one another and said; *shall we begin?*

Four weeks later, Poland fell.

"The War"—like any other war—will come and go and be parenthesized by dates in history books. A war is just a noise—the stench of death—a view, however wide or brief, of rubble—and a cause for lamentation.

After the lamentation: praise. Over the rubble: shrines. After the stench of death: the sweetness of flowers. After the noise: the diminishing echo. Then all the shops will open and the first gold coins go down. *"One dozen postal cards of war memorials, please. The coloured ones, if possible."* And all the figures cut in stone.

A war is just a place where we have been in exile from our better dreams.

Madrid: June, 1940

I was at the Ritz on the Gran Via.

Madrid, in spite of its scars, was beautiful as ever; but the Madrelinos were not so gay as I had remembered. There was a pinched and ponderous look that ran like a common piece of news through all their faces. My suspicion was they had not yet decided how to tell their stories: how to relate what had befallen them. Some had been on one side; most had been on the other. Now, they must be reconciled and learn to live with one another in a state of mutual defeat and victory. Though I did not envy them this I could not help but envy them the ending of their wars. General Franco was victorious. Life could now proceed.

The other news was all of the fall of France. Madrid was inundated with refugees from far away as Antibes and Nice and Marseilles. Every second face belonged to a foreigner.

In Spain they had a most dreadful practice of blaring the news over speakers in the streets. You could not escape it anywhere. The British were at Dunkirk, the Germans were about to invade the south of England, the Government of France had taken to its heels and was embarked on a fleet of sinking ships from Bordeaux. Reynaud had been deported, replaced by Pétain—surely some kind of madness—or a joke. Pétain was eighty-three years old. Charles Eugene Bedaux, of course, would be in his element, since Pétain and his cohort Laval were both in Bedaux's pocket.

But I was in Madrid with Isabella Loverso. So was Wallis, with the Duke.

The circle closed around us there, though it still had the look of a bracelet set with diamonds. Three or four times we met together, telling of our escapades and escapes. We drank a lot of rich red wine and sat on balconies. The Duke had yellow teeth. Wallis was called Her Royal Highness, then. Isabella used a parasol to shade us from the sun. I wore the first new suit of whites I'd worn in over a year. One night, Wallis told the story of her life and left out China. I was very hurt. Then the Duke told the story of his life and left out having abdicated. Wallis was very pleased. Nonetheless these stories told the temper of the times and the motto we had adopted: *the truth is in our hands now.*

Three occasions we met like this. Or four. And by the end of it, we knew each other's lies. The conclusion of this time came suddenly. The Duke and Wallis were called away. Or perhaps it is more realistic to say, they were beckoned. Their initial destination was Lisbon, but the rumours already abounding of other destinations after that made it impossible to tell where they might turn up next.

A reception was given on the eve of their departure and I believe there must have been at least a hundred and fifty guests. Franco's brother-in-law was host. There was an orchestra. And thirty footmen. The Duke of Alba came—a cousin of the Duke of Windsor and as "British" as they come. And the Infante Alfonso—dressed as an air cadet—also a cousin, with the brass-coloured hair of a German prince. The implications of regal incest are truly alarming. How have the Royal Houses of Europe not all bled to death?

But the most prestigious guest of all, outside of those I have named, was von Ribbentrop himself. We had never met, and I was surprised at how nervous his presence made me.

There was so much saluting and shaking of hands and bobbing and "heiling" I wondered where we were. It was almost impossible to grasp a single word of English from the air, though all of this was ostensibly taking place in honour of an English King. And that "King" himself spoke German all evening long. Diplomacy.

The whole reception reeked of intrigue and wine, and I knew to the very perfume of the clothes and the acrid smell of guttering candles—thousands of them—what it was to sit in the presence of Cesare Borgia, wondering who would be the first to fall into a poisoned plate.

Someone, somewhere had been busy; Isabella and myself were to share a table with von Ribbentrop. Isabella now seemed taller than ever, possibly because she had lost much weight and begun to pile her hair in the newest fashion, up from the back of her head to the front, exposing her neck. She was dressed, as so many of the women were, in white, with jewels across her bosom, each of the facets catching every candle's flicker. She also carried, and used, a fan. The heat in Madrid that summer was the worst in thirty years and the night of that reception was the hottest of the month.

von Ribbentrop wore his whitest of uniforms, with a silver globe surmounted by eagle's wings sewn to his sleeve. I could not help but think of Isabella's Palazzo d'Aquila, with all its eagles being adored by a medieval crowd of princes peeling from the walls.

There was a rustling sound. And a murmur.

Everyone turned. Even the candles burned in a new direction. All eyes were levelled. Everyone fell.

The Duke of Windsor was standing—suddenly all alone in a doorway. Smiling like a boy. We bowed and curtsied. But every mind was spinning in the same direction: where was *she*?

The Duke was pale. But his hair was still the same, entirely spun from gold, and his eyes, though somewhat dulled with quite legitimate fatigue, were still that magic shade of blue one thinks he's taken out a patent on.

Still facing him, we rose. And then, as one who cuts a ribbon, or reveals a painting on a wall, the Duke of Windsor made a magician's gesture with his hand, opening its palm towards the ceiling, just as if Wallis might appear by magic out of nowhere, standing on his lifeline or his heartline. Every gaze turned upward.

There she was: resplendent. Wallis descending in a gold glass cage.

Her hair was elaborately piled as I had never seen it used before and held in place with lethal pins, and her body was sheathed in cerulean silk over which she wore a Mandarin's robe embroidered with a flight of birds. Her cage, of course, was a lift embossed with gold but every wall and even the floor was glass and it fell, like a flake of ice, without a sound. Her eyes, as she descended were triumphant. Something about her made me afraid.

Isabella sat between myself and von Ribbentrop. The chef had outdone himself: our meal consisted of salmon; grouse and pheasant; marinated onions and oranges; roast suckling pig; an aspic of truffles, garnished with sprigs of watercress and coriander leaves; a coffee and caramel "custard" the English call a Spanish cream; a water ice of lime—to Isabella's joy—and finally, a host of nuts and oranges in a myriad of silver bowls and then, without the dread formality of men and women separated, snuff from horns, cigars and the Duke's Madeira shuffled up and down the tables while the guests were free to rise and mingle, seating themselves in new combinations. Isabella was beckoned away by the Marques de Estella and Wallis came across to sit in her place between von Ribbentrop and me.

That night I overheard a conversation between them that lifted me almost from my chair.

In 1936 I had written in the *Daily Mail*: "*what is needed now is a new kind of leader—someone like a flag, whose very presence makes us rise. Not a Mussolini, of whom we are afraid. Not a Hitler, who drives us to our feet. But an emblem whose magnetism pulls us upward.*" And now I was to learn how well my words expressed the cabal's intentions. There we were, in the very room with the very leader who had been chosen. And his wife.

So this is history as she is never writ, I thought. Some day far in the future, some dread academic, much too careful of his research, looking back through the biased glasses of a dozen other "historians", will set this moment down on paper. And will get it wrong. Because he will not acknowledge that history is made in the electric moment, and its flowering is all in chance. At the heart of everything that shakes the world, there need be nothing more than a casual remark that has been overheard and acted on. There is more in history of impulse than we dare to know. Yes, they will get it wrong. They will write that Wallis created her world in six premeditated days—alone, like Almighty God. And that on the seventh day, she rested, still alone. It was not so.

If what I mean is not yet clear, then think of God as being Himself created by another being who one day whispered in His ear: "begin".

von Ribbentrop sweated. His eyes were grey and deceptively cool. His lips were extremely sensuous. Wet. His hands were never still. His blond hair thinning. The cleft in his chin very deep. His manners—imperious; sexually intimidating, careful, smiling. He exuded the promise of a secret vice.

There was something said about "how much Her Royal Highness has tragically lost."

Wallis looked at the table. Yes.

von Ribbentrop moved one hand a little closer over the cloth, like a crab, moving sideways. I thought I had never seen such enormous fingers. I was spellbound, wondering if he would dare to touch her.

"Things go so well for us now," he said, meaning the Germans and the War. "Many, many kingdoms falling into our lap. And crowns."

Wallis looked up at this. And smiled.

"Not the crown of England, Excellency," she said. "I believe that has fallen into another lap than yours. A rather knock-kneed lap, if I recall."

von Ribbentrop smiled and shrugged. "There are other crowns," he said, "than the one your sister-in-law is wearing. Not, of course, that England's crown is irretrievable. Still. . .Your Royal Highness perhaps does not understand there are crowns that have never yet been worn by anyone." von Ribbentrop looked away. The whole room glittered. He was drawing her attention to the circle of which she was the centre.

"You have won great success these last three years," he said. "All these people now look up to you—many of whom looked down, in their time."

Wallis sobered. It was so. There was no one in that room who had not kissed her hand. Excepting the Infante of Spain, who need not—yet.

"How long do you think we might have to wait?" she asked.

"Does it matter?" von Ribbentrop said. "We should not be too anxious. After all, we are now the masters of time. The sequence is what counts. Be patient, madam. Never run before the event. Be patient. We have time. *Wait*."

Wallis lifted her fingers into view. Not knowing where to rest her eyes, she gazed at her hand and turned her rings. I could feel her shudder as she fondled her wrist, her veins, her pulse. And then her eyes, inadvertently, fell on mine and she swallowed very hard and looked away at her husband.

von Ribbentrop was already looking at the Duke, who

must have sensed our concentration for he turned and waved in our direction. Wallis gave him a dazzling smile.

And this was how I came, inadvertently, to name our enterprise. Something had fallen into place with all the talk of "patience" and of "waiting", I guess, and it clicked when Wallis smiled at the Duke. It was the Crown she had married—we all knew that—only to have it whisked away. And for the longest time, it had completely disappeared. But Wallis had now seen it hoving into view again—distant, it was true, but there: within her sights.

"You're just like Penelope," I said. I was only joking. "You've had every kind of suitor—me included—but you've turned us all down. Because you're still waiting: for the one true love of your life to return. Not Odysseus, of course. . ."

Wallis laughed and reached across and tapped my hand affectionately. "He's right, you know," she said to von Ribbentrop. "I am still waiting."

von Ribbentrop did not appear to have heard precisely what we were saying. "I like it very much," he said. "We shall adopt it as our *nom de guerre. Penelope.* Yes?"

Yes.

So there we sat: von Ribbentrop, myself and Wallis. Three lean cats and one bowl of cream. The Crown.

"Our motto," von Ribbentrop said; "shall be 'we wait.' "

The whole of Madrid was like an empty room. von Ribbentrop had gone; the Duke and Wallis had gone. The long pale gowns, the ropes of pearls, the medals and the decorations had all been laid away in whatever vaults and drawers and cupboards kept them safe. The diplomatic corps returned to its desks and its intrigues; the secret police went about their business, screening and interrogating refugees from France. The heat was more oppressive than ever. Out in the streets whatever leaves were left—on whatever trees remained after all the years of siege Madrid had endured—turned brown and fell into the gutters. There were even clouds—but never rain. It was like a perverted autumn. Only it was still July.

Isabella and I remained at the Ritz for roughly three more weeks. There was "business" to conclude, she said. But all the business excluded me—which only gave me time to worry by the minute, instead of by the hour, about Wallis and the Duke. One day I asked Isabella point blank what the business was. Of course, it was none of my affair what she did; but her more or less constant absence had begun to wear on my nerves. Who, for instance, was she always leaving the hotel to see?

"It wouldn't interest you," she said.

"But I'm telling you, Isabella, it does interest me. That's why I'm asking."

"But you don't even know the man."

"Well, damn it all, the way you hot-foot it out of here every morning. . . .What is he? Some kind of Latin lover?"

"Hot-foot?" she said.

"It's just an expression and don't change the subject."

"If you will tell me what *hot-foot* is, I will tell you where I go."

"Hot-foot means to exit with undue haste," I said rather testily. "In other words, you cannot wait to get where you are going."

She shrugged. "I could wait," she said. "But he can't."

"*Who* can't?"

"The Marques de Estella." She turned away and looked from the window.

"But he's a toad!" I said. "You can't be having an affair with a toad. I. . ." (I was going to say 'I won't allow it' but I caught myself in time.) "Well: at least now I know whose Mercedes that is you get into every morning. Dear, dear. The Marques de Estella. Of all the men in Madrid. . ."

Isabella was still looking down into the Gran Via at the dying trees and the soldiers sitting in the *cantinas* drinking their wine and the rows of dusty French cars disgorging suntanned refugees from Biarritz in front of the hotel. "Of all the men in Madrid," she said without turning around, "he is the one who can help me most."

."Thank you," I said. "What a piece of news. Delightful."

"Oh. . ." she said. And then she turned. With a smile. "You mustn't think for a moment I'm talking about romance. How ridiculous. Though, I must admit I think you've gone a bit too far in calling him a toad. . . ."

I waited. "Is it political, then?" I asked. "The cabal?"

Isabella crossed the room and picked up a pair of long white gloves. She was on her way to meet him again. "I shall not be long," she said. "And, if it will set your mind at ease—I suspect I shall not be seeing him after this."

She was making for the door.

"You haven't answered my question," I said. "Is there not something I should know—I mean if he has to do with the cabal?"

Isabella pulled the open work veil from the rim of her hat down over her face. "I assure you," she said. "The Marques de Estella is not one of us.. . ."

"Then why?" I said.

"Because he can help me," she said. "And you will have to make do with that as your answer. And now if you will forgive me, my dear friend, I must make a hot-foot to the car." And she was gone.

The subject of the Marques de Estella was closed. She never mentioned him again. When she returned that afternoon, her whole conversation had to do with the fact that in a few more days we could at last return for an extended stay and rest at the Palazzo d'Aquila. Venice beckoned. We would be there the whole of August.

With the Windsors gone into Portugal, I never ceased to wonder what von Ribbentrop's plans for them might be. I could not forget the excitement he had engendered, both in Wallis and myself, before he'd left. But apparently von Ribbentrop had engendered something else besides excitement in Isabella and she told me of this one evening over plates of clams and squid brought over from the coast especially for the patrons of the Ritz. She said she had spent some time alone with von Ribbentrop the day before he returned to

Berlin, and I had not been aware of this. I don't know why, but it disturbed me. It had also disturbed Isabella.

"Did his Excellency speak of the immediate?" I enquired. I was thinking of Wallis and the Duke. "Did he say what would happen next?"

Isabella appeared about to answer "yes" to this question. And then she said, "No." And waved her hand and allowed me to pour her another glass of wine. "Our talk was mostly of your friend, the Duchess, and of her ambition. 'Without the element of personal ambition,' von Ribbentrop said; 'there can be no daring. And what we need now is all the daring we can muster'."

Then Isabella said; "daring I can understand. But ambition is a sickness, is it not?"

When I thought of my mother, whose ambition had been her downfall, I knew the answer to this was yes. But I could not say so to Isabella. I wanted her, for once, to feel there was safety in the world we moved in, that she need not always be afraid. So I said; "sometimes ambition is the only thing that keeps us alive."

But Isabella was ready for this, and she said, "The only kind of ambition that keeps one alive, my friend, is the kind that kills." Then she smiled and said, "You come from America and do not know this?"

I laughed—but as much with relief at the fact she had smiled as at what she had said.

We began to talk of Venice then, and of the month ahead of us.

But it was not to be.

In the morning when I went along the corridor to collect her for our journey, she was gone. And there was not a trace of her having been there. The hotel staff were genuinely confused. They had no idea where she had gone—or when—though it must have been after midnight, which is when we parted.

I never saw her again.

But I did find something. On her bureau, neatly folded

and weighted down with an empty bottle of Calvados, there was a fine lace handkerchief. And in the waste paper basket, traces of a fire.

This was the 20th of July. I would be unable to fathom the meaning of her disappearance until the following October.

Berlin: July, 1940

On Wednesday, July 10th Major Walter Schellenberg left the offices of the *Reichssicherheitshauptamt* (more conveniently known as R.S.H.A.) on the Prinz Albrechtstrasse in Berlin and was driven to a military aerodrome on the outskirts of the city. He was dressed very much like a man going on holiday. He carried the most mundane of luggage—a suitcase and a Gladstone bag—and his clothes were carefully chosen: an ill-fitting cotton suit and a Panama hat that needed cleaning. He was on his way to Madrid. As he nodded good-bye to the S.S. sergeant who had driven him from the Albrechtstrasse, he flashed a handsome and even beguiling smile and said; "when I come back you had best be prepared for a trip to the tailors, Keppel. This Major that you see departing will unquestionably come back a Colonel." Keppel saluted and Schellenberg climbed inside the Junkers-88 that would deliver him to Madrid.

All the way west over France and all the way south over the Pyrenees and into Spain, Major Schellenberg hummed along with the engines of the plane. He was on his way to fulfill a commission handed down from the Führer himself—and there was not the slightest doubt it would be the *coup* of the decade if Schellenberg could pull it off.

Schellenberg thought of the ramifications—best of all for his own career. Himmler, who undoubtedly prized him, must be quaking in his boots at how quickly Major Schellenberg was shooting up through the ranks. He was the local *Wunderkind*, and every exploit had brought him rank and decorations. To say nothing of his share of being feared.

Next, he thought of what this current exploit would do for the reputation of the Albrechtstrasse and of how furious von Ribbentrop and all his gang on the Wilhelmstrasse would be. The "war" between the Central Security Office under Himmler and the Foreign Office under von Ribbentrop was being waged for the highest stakes. Whichever office could score the greatest number of *coups* in this war, would achieve the greatest number of merits in Hitler's eyes. And the "winning" chief would rise to sit at the Führer's right hand. Schellenberg wanted that power for Himmler, mostly because one day S.S. Führer Himmler's job would be his.

Lastly perhaps the greatest pleasure of all would come from the acting out of the commission itself. Schellenberg not only had a talent for his work—he lived for it.

Taking out his checklists, he approved the final details. He would remain for three days in Spain, making certain of all his contacts and especially the Marques, and then would be flown into Lisbon where he would set the necessary machinery in motion.

Schellenberg began to eat the onionpaper on which the checklist had been written. What a great shock it would be to von Ribbentrop and the Wilhelmstrasse when they realized the Albrechtstrasse had done it again. Courtesy of Major Walter—no *Colonel* Walter—Schellenberg, whose job it now was to kidnap the Duke and Duchess of Windsor and bring them back into Spain.

Portugal: July, 1940

It was already evening when Major Schellenberg's flowers arrived. The sun had not set; the stars had not risen; but the sea beyond the Estoril was dark and the western windows of the town appeared to be on fire. At the top of the hill music from a wind-up gramophone floated out across a terrace:

> . . .Though my world may go awry
> In my heart will ever lie
> Just the echo of a sigh,
> Goodbye. . .

It was the cocktail hour and the sound of glasses filled with ice proclaimed the presence of at least one American at the Villa Cascais.

In the courtyard there were several motorcars, including an armour-plated Mercedes, a much travelled Buick and a low-slung Renault. The Mercedes, even now in the gathering dusk, was being polished by a Spanish chauffeur in his shirtsleeves. The fact that he wore a revolver at his waist was in no way surprising. Everyone at the Villa Cascais went armed. It was a precaution against the treason of the times as much as against the intrigues of the house. This was July the 27th—a Saturday—and the Villa Cascais, though situated in neutral Portugal, had become a fortress due to the presence of the Duke of Windsor and his duchess from Baltimore.

So far as the flowers were concerned: the bouquet in a box was brought up the hill by a child whose name was Maria da Gama. The girl had been carefully chosen. Maria was ten and a peasant who could neither read nor write. Unlike everyone else, she had no trouble getting past the guard at the gate. Her sister Alida happened to be the guard-on-duty's *noiva*, or betrothed, and Maria often carried messages between the two.

The girl knew nothing of what she was doing. A box containing flowers must be taken up the hill and delivered at the door. Nothing could be less sinister. So far as Maria was concerned, if she was lucky she might receive the bonus of a glimpse of the ex-King of England. She might even see the famous American harlot, whom everyone said had snared the King by making love in ways unheard of by the common folk of the town. Had the Lady Simpson not resided many years in the Orient? Had she not returned with a secret potion which, when applied to the thighs, made centaurs out of men? And was it not a fact the King wore a dress called a kilt in order to accommodate the transformation of his lower self. . .?

The guard and Maria exchanged their usual pleasantries and she was allowed to pass beyond the gates and enter the courtyard.

Passing the Spanish chauffeur, Maria was not in the least intrigued by the gun nor even by the motorcar being polished. She was looking in the flowerbeds for hoofprints and listening for the cries of centaurs. All she saw was dahlias. All she heard was Noël Coward. "Just the echo of a sigh. . ."

She made her way across the stones and stood before the door. For a moment she looked from side to side in an effort to see through the windows. Nothing presented itself but a human hand that pressed its fingers on the glass. Not a sign of prancing horsemen. Finally, she pulled the chain that rang the bell. From far away she heard approaching steps— all too human and brisk, as if the *policia* were answering her call.

The door was opened. Maria saw a wide, bright foyer hung with paintings and a tall grand staircase. The foyer was so large the whole of her father's house could be fitted inside.

"Sim?" a masculine voice enquired.

Now came the moment of her speech. Maria gulped and spoke: "*Flores. Para a duquesa, faz favor,*" she said, exactly as she'd been told to say. Then, again precisely as rehearsed, she thrust the box of flowers in the direction of the nameless figure before her and fled. She must not be questioned once the box was delivered. That was the final rule. No one was ever to know who had placed it in her hands. Many escudos had guaranteed this procedure. Some had already been given; others awaited her return to the foot of the hill. So in spite of her great disappointment not to have seen the King in his kilt and centaur's haunches nor the Lady Simpson with her Oriental potion in its jar, Maria ran like a whirlwind across the stones and through the gates.

The Villa Cascais was the summer home of Doctor Ricardo de Espirito Santo e Silva, one of Portugal's richest and most influential bankers. Due to "considerations", about which he shrugged and refused to comment, Doctor Ricardo had taken upon himself the task of playing host to the Duke and Duchess of Windsor.

As guests, the Duke and Duchess were hardly a pleasure to entertain. To begin with, they could not go anywhere unnoticed and therefore had to remain within the confines of the villa.

The Villa itself was the essence of Iberian decadence: castellated pink stucco. It was surrounded by terraced gardens and thick stone walls. The Duchess had never liked confinement and she hated the Villa Cascais. Inside its precincts, every kindness—including Doctor Ricardo's generous hospitality—had to be weighed against the possibility of fraudulence. Even the simplest of gestures might contain the seeds of treachery. Treason itself could no longer be defined. Loyalties everywhere were being eroded and blurred.

France had fallen: Holland, Norway, Belgium, Denmark, Luxembourg. The debacle at Dunkirk had left the British Army decimated, unarmed and powerless. Italy had "plunged the knife into the back of its neighbour" and was now at war with France and England. The British had turned against the French, attempting to destroy their fleet at Oran in North Africa and the French had turned against themselves with the creation of Pétain's government at Vichy. Winston Churchill had been made Prime Minister of England and, so far as the Windsors were concerned, had turned against them. Once their friend and ally, he was siding now with their enemy the Queen, refusing the Duchess her rightful titles and threatening permanent exile.

At the Villa Cascais "The Lady Simpson" no longer knew what her husband was up to. At night, he did not always follow her to bed, but lingered in the salon—sometimes alone; sometimes not. Sometimes she heard his voice, with its strange falsetto anger, rising against some unknown adversary on the telephone; probably the British Ambassador. Maybe even Churchill himself. Or the king—God knew. She would see him from her window, leaning on the terrace, deep in thought. The slimness of his shadow never failed to catch at her heart. The shape of his head, the set of his shoulders: he was just a boy—unless you could see his eyes.

His eyes—somehow—had gone out. As if they had been disconnected. The Duchess was—and she knew it—the centre of his life. Her wisdom, her advice, her presence were the food on which he fed: *feasted* whenever the tide of public opinion flowed against them. But now, his back was turned— and what she saw was just his clothes—with no one inside. A shell. Now, too, for whatever reason, there were secrets. The Duke called them "matters of little or no importance". She knew better. She had so many secrets of her own.

She was more and more afraid. July had been like a sojourn in hell. There was a heat wave. For three weeks it didn't rain, and then when it did it came down in sheets. After the rain, it was humid. Red dye oozed from the stucco and killed the roses. More and more gin, more and more brandy and Madeira were consumed. The Duke's mascara ran. The make- up tables were covered every morning with mosquitoes drowned in cold cream, their corpses whitened by talcum powder. Drunken flies crawled up the sides of old martini glasses and fell to the tiles, where they spun on their backs in an ecstasy of euphoria. Lucky flies, the Duchess thought, as she watched them spinning long after midnight when she went in to take her pills. Lucky, lucky flies—with someone to squash you so quickly with mercy, roll you up in toilet paper, flush you down the drains. And she'd wait, with her wrists held out beneath the tepid stream from the cold water tap, staring at her face. The face she saw in her private mirror was a face no other human being had seen. It was her mid- night face, and mostly in her mind. The true face—lifted and lacquered—was the one she showed to others and the world. But *this*, she would tell herself, as she watched in her private mirror, is the face of Penelope—who waits.

As for her husband, she questioned his judgement. She always had, of course. But she'd always been there in the past. The only time she'd ever left him alone in a crisis had been when she'd fled to the south of France in the fall of 1936. Within a month, he'd abdicated. Now he was in flight himself but she had no inkling where he was going. She only knew it was her job to prevent his escape. So she waited, frightened and aloof from everyone. She played her gramophone; drank her gin; wrote many letters—and put them all in a drawer. At first, her letters were addressed to her husband. "Where are you going. . .and why?" And then she discovered to her horror she'd begun to write to total strangers: "Dear Greta Garbo. . .Why don't you write. . .?" "Dear Deanna Durbin. . .Please." She took her pills. She looked in her mirror. And prayed.

There was virtually no one she could talk to about her husband and it was during this time that she suffered the first of the strokes that would plague her in years to come. Its outward effects were minor: a slight hesitation in the choice of words; a frozen nerve beneath her left eye. Inwardly, a gently harboured part of her mind was lost to her forever, in which were contained all her memories of haven and of peaceful rest; of the Blue Ridge Mountains of Virginia, of the genteel voices of her aunts: "Come home.. . ." And the music of her first cotillion: "My! How many partners Bessie Wallis had. . .a dozen beaux at least.. . ." All gone. The stroke was not even diagnosed as such. It was merely thought she had gone to earth.

The flowers in their box had now reached the stairwell, carried in the hands of a richly dark-haired woman whose name was Estrade. Estrade was *secretária temporaria* to the Duchess, a Spaniard injected into the household two weeks before the Windsors' arrival, on a warm afternoon when Doctor Ricardo's back was conveniently turned. She was about to climb to the Windsor apartments, when she saw her new mistress at the end of the hallway, passing towards the terraces. It was the ice in the Lady Simpson's glass that caught the *secretária*'s attention.

"*Duquesa*. . .?"

"Yes?"

"These have arri-ved for your High-ness."

"Flowers?"

"*Si, Duquesa.*"

Neither the Duchess nor Estrade had moved. Each had a view of the other standing at the nether end of a long, cool hallway. One held a box of flowers, the other a glass of gin and ice. One was endowed, in the order of things, with the power to command the other, but for a moment it was not clear which was which. This was what the Duchess feared in Estrade: the menace in the pause before response: the lethal possibilities contained in the dead, black gaze. Estrade had the look of certain dogs that have been trained to kill. Now, there was an insolent break—a fracture in the flow of her obedience—before she turned and walked towards her mistress. The Duchess took the bull by the horns.

"Well," she said; "it's good of you to have taken the risk, Estrade. Thank you. If there had been a bomb inside that box, I'm sure it would have gone off by now."

She could see there was a note. The corner of its envelope angled up from among the rose leaves.

She took a breath. She wound her rings. She must make a deliberate show of courage. *Noblesse oblige*—god damn it.

"There seems to be a note," she said. And snatched it out, like someone pulling a weed.

Nothing happened. The flowers did not explode. The box did not burst into flames. Her hands were still intact. She laughed.

Estrade did not laugh. Perhaps to some, survival is no laughing matter.

"Put them in something tall," said the Duchess, fanning herself with the note, picking up her glass of gin. "They have such lovely stems, we might as well make as much of them as we can. Remove the roses; put them out of my sight." (The Duchess of Windsor could not abide a rose.)

Estrade departed. She walked very hard on her heels to the stairs and the Duchess could hear her climbing all the way to the second floor. *Perhaps*, she thought, *there will be a poison on the thorns.*

She read the note carefully. Once. Twice. Three times. The brutal simplicity of what it said was heightened by the fact the message had been phrased by someone whose knowledge of English was scanty and formal. Dictionary or Cook's Tour language, utterly stilted and utterly direct: *"Death*

beware from British friends," she read. ,"From one your interests in heart." And that was all.

Cascais is west of Lisbon, facing south on the Costa de Roca.
The sand on the beaches has a reddish tinge: magenta. The
rocks are dangerous. It is not the best place to land from the
sea. Nonetheless, a small rubber craft made its way towards
the shore on the night of July the 27th, determined to reach
its destination against all odds. The wind had risen, a storm
was brewing, the dinghy was overburdened and none of the
seven occupants had any knowledge of the terrain they approached. Also, the tide was against them.

Behind them, looming in the dusk, was the shape of a
military flying boat, its engines silenced, its light extinguished. It bore no insignia. By daylight, seen from above,
it was the bleak steel colour of a winter sea. It was armed,
but its guns were retracted. Resting as it was, in neutral
waters and being a military aircraft and foreign, its very
presence was a contravention of all the rules of war. But its
journey had been sudden and made in great haste. Two days
before, the need for such a journey had been so remote it
had only been the subject of nightmares. Now, men barely
competent to punt on the Isis were rowing ashore against
the Atlantic ebb tide. Men whose previous adventures were
confined to petty theft and visits to Paris were making their
way towards a rendezvous with kidnap and murder.

Darkness fell. The storm broke. It rained.

The guest that night at the Villa Cascais was the Spanish
Marques de Estella, Miguel de Rivera: Falangist hero of the
Catalan Front and son of a former Spanish dictator. He was
an old and trusted friend of the Duke's; a hunting crony from
happier bachelor days. He was small, dark and wiry—"wound
up", as the Duchess said. His laughter came in short, sharp
bursts, like the laughter of a doll controlled by a ventrilo-
quist. But he was graceful and athletic, too. He boxed with
great skill and was also one of Europe's finest equestrians.

It was said that the true cause of de Estella's bravery on the Catalan Front—which is where Franco's troops broke the siege of Madrid in March 1939—was the firing of his stables by starving Loyalists who slaughtered his horses and ate them. For days, it was said, de Estella lost his reason and it was during this time he performed so many daring exploits he became a legendary figure. Many believed he could not be killed, for he was seen to walk through sheets of gunfire unscathed. The Duchess of Windsor disliked him intensely. He spent all his energies, much to her chagrin, leading her husband down the garden path of memories from which she was excluded. Most of these memories had to do with "the kill".

The Duke was prone to the "glorious past" and particularly prone to anything reminding him that once he had been happy. Stories of the hunt brought back his sense of fresh air and freedom and also his sense of command. He and de Estella recalled their victims the way other people recall the victims of an accident. Groupings at the kill were vividly recalled. The shape of each scene—some of them twelve years past and more—was evoked with its silhouette imprinted, dated and filed; a precise parade of ten-point stags and bristled boars and countless birds laid out in bloodless rows. When they spoke of all the paws and tails, fox trophies held up over leaping dogs, the Duchess thought of the Spanish General who cried out; "long live death!" before he fell in battle. de Estella's catalogue was filled with such images. "I stood here," he would say to the Duke, "and you were over there to the left. Someone stood beside you. Who was that?" The Duke could not remember. He would struggle with the name and fail to catch it. Yet he could recall the number of their party, even how many of its members were mounted, how many beaters there were on foot and how many dogs were involved. But the faces of his comrades were too subtle to be conjured. So many had been smudged by disloyalty; blurred and obliterated by acts of unfriendliness and treason. They were like the faces in photographs where you look and look and look, the Duchess thought; and cannot think whose arm that is around your waist;

whose hand that is you hold or whose lips those are that press their secrets in your ear.

She felt alone and threatened. There was something deeply sinister about this man, de Estella. Had he not been present at that reception in Madrid? Could it be that he knew of von Ribbentrop's plans—or had overheard their discussion of *Penelope*? She spent the early part of the meal with her hand near her throat. She lapsed into silence and forgot to smile. She had difficulty swallowing her trout. What unnerved her most was the hold de Estella had on her husband. This old friendship must have run very deep and she wondered what sort of obligations it entailed. If David had talked so often and so late at night on the telephone, perhaps he had been talking to de Estella. And if this was so, they might have devised some plan to bypass Churchill's schemes—and this plan, in turn, might thwart whatever rescue von Ribbentrop had in mind. Oh, why had she been forbidden to speak to David about *Penelope*? If she could only caution him. If she could only warn him they must wait for von Ribbentrop. . .But she knew she must not. If David had "secrets", he did not have them long. His mouth, it seemed, was not made to contain them.

Less and less food was eaten. More and more Madeira drunk. The combination was deadly. The Duchess made note of the fact their host, Doctor Ricardo, had fallen as silent as she. And was as watchful. And nervous.

There were two ways up from the beaches to the Villa. One led through the town, the other over rocks and through an olive grove. The olive grove gave way to meadows full of yellow grass and daisies where a goat was allowed to wander, wearing a bell. These meadows rose towards the Villa's walls and the walls led round to the left towards the gate and to the right towards a Martello tower.

In the dark, through the rising storm, the goat had made its way down the hill towards the olive grove, seeking perhaps to get out of the wind in amongst the trees. Its bell made a dull, hollow sound.

All at once, the bell sound stopped and the goat began to bleat. There was a scent down close against the ground of which it was afraid. For a moment, it stood stalk still and then it began to rummage in the daisies. What it found, though of course it did not know it, was the body of the Spanish chauffeur whose neck had been broken and whose gun was missing.

Some men were walking up through the olive grove, veering as if by instinct to the left towards the Villa's gates. The goat lay down as far away from these events as it could get. In the morning, the goatherd would come. In the meantime, the storm would break; the darkness would thicken and the goat would sleep.

In the centre of the table, there was a low, brass bowl filled with late-blooming peonies. The Duchess was the only woman present. She wore her favourite colour: blue. The men, of course, wore black. The room was lit with many candelabra—augmented, perhaps in honour of the Duchess, with ruby shaded lamps—all of which cast a warm theatrical aura, flattering and intimate.

At nine o'clock, they paused before the sweet for cigarettes. The Duke was a heavy smoker and demanded these pauses between the courses at every meal. He called them "intercourse ciggies" and smiled like a wicked child who was passing a rude remark in the presence of adults. His elbow slipped from the edge of the table. He was drinking too much, smoking too much, talking too much. The Duchess was sitting back in her chair, watching him like a Chinese doll: expressionless. The conversation, ever since the trout, had veered in and out of danger zones, like a car being driven by a drunk through the dark.

"Wallis, dear. . ."

"Yes, darling?"

"Tell wha' you said when you heard 'bout Bermuda. . . ."

"Bermuda, darling?"

"Ba'mahs."

"Yes. The Bahamas," Doctor Ricardo interjected. He knew

the Duke of Windsor meant the Bahamas and not Bermuda. He wagged his finger at the steward and the steward motioned the footman forward with wine. Everyone's glass was refilled.

The Duke of Windsor turned to de Estella and shouted at him. "Wallis and I are being shunted off to some damned Island. Wins'on wants to be rid of us. I'm to be Gov'nor, can you believe it of some coral isle! Sand and stuff. . .'s' graceful! But the Duchess said. . .she was so funny. . .when the 'pointment came she said. . .well: tell'm, Wallis. Listen to this!"

Wallis toyed with her fork and looked at the tablecloth while she spoke. "His Royal Highness makes too much of my wit," she said to de Estella. "All I said was; 'it's not an appointment, David, it's a disappointment.' "

The laughter flared, then faded.

" 'Course we're not going!" said the Duke. "We're fighting Wins'on every inch of the way. Aren't we, darling. . ." He looked across at his wife, beyond the pink haze of the peonies. The Duchess tried not to show her alarm that her husband was tipping his hand so openly. The negotiations regarding the Bahamas appointment were delicate enough as it was, without rumours of drunken recalcitrance being spread through the network of spies that must surround a man like de Estella. Royal recalcitrance—drunken and sober—had been the historical seedbed of every beheading she could think of. Besides which, the Marques had not yet laid a single card on the table. And for all she knew, this evil, ochre-coloured little man might even somehow be an agent of Churchill's—playing on David's drunkenness to discover how deep his treason ran.

The hotel was partway up the hill. Major Schellenberg had chosen it with all his usual fastidious care for detail and had registered under the name of "Fritzi Schaemmel". Some years past its prime, the hotel had garnered just the right tone of degenerate decline. The awning was frayed; the stones were chipped; the marble cracked. The glass had not been cleaned for a month and the doorman's uniform was hitched and pinched and pinned. The price was right and some judicious winking and underhanded tipping let the desk clerk know that Schaemmel's "holiday" was a private *mardi gras*—a week of risqué days and naughty nights. His collection of nudist magazines was carefully exposed to the prying eyes of maids and bellhops. Here, they would smile, is the perfect amateur of vice, as eager and unsophisticated as any they'd ever bilked. Throughout his stay—exactly as he'd hoped—he was offered a plump and pleasing selection of "sisters" and "cousins" who would help him spend his money and giggle their way through sessions of sexual exploration that always ended up with quite well acted "indignation" that "the gentleman should have thought he could take such liberties!" Consequently, by the time he was engaged in the depths of his espionage, Schellenberg had successfully established for Schaemmel a reputation for free-flowing cash and boundless sexual naiveté. He was just another harmless German tourist and a happy financial fool into the bargain.

On the morning of July 27th, Schaemmel had made the acquaintance of Maria da Gama. It had taken days to discover the girl's existence and relationship to the guard at the Villa Cascais. There had been a few little hints of monies and pleasures to follow—but first, would the child take part that afternoon in a "game" Uncle Fritzi's playing with the guests at the pink villa? Oh yes. So the flowers had been delivered. And history took its course.

Now, at nightfall, he watched from his window as the storm collected its forces to batter the town. But the storm did not disturb him. It would be his ally. In fact, he could not have asked for better circumstances in which to achieve his ends. Storms, he was well aware, provoke their own psychological atmosphere and serve as the perfect foil for operations such as the one taking place at the Villa Cascais that night.

Schellenberg had been out in the early rain. He had watched from the cliffs above the beaches as the men came ashore in their dinghy; he had seen them land; he had taken note of their number; he had watched as they deflated and buried their craft and had seen them disappear in the gathering squalls of darkness to perform their task. After this, he had waited only long enough to ascertain that the military flying-boat had taxied further out to sea where, doubtless, it would mask its noisy departure in the sounds of the storm. Disgruntled by the fact that the soldiers had arrived at all, he was nonetheless satisfied that he had already undercut their effectiveness. He returned to the warmth of his room where he changed into pajamas and awaited the arrival of Maria da Gama. The girl's return, with whatever news she would bring of the flowers' reception, was to be the high point of his evening. If that went well, then all would go well. The flowers; the note; the flying boat; the seven men on the path, even now going up the hill—all these must fall precisely into place. Only then could the final ingredients be added to make the whole operation a success: the Marques and his other agents inside the Villa must then take over and bring it to a close.

The Duchess laid her arm along the table. Her sleeves were buttoned at the wrist. Tight against her skin, she could feel the card that had come with the flowers. She had kept it with her, telling no one of its contents—not even David, for which she now thanked God as she saw how very drunk he was becoming. *Death beware from British friends.* She could feel the words against her pulse. What British friends? She thought. As if we had any British friends at all. . . .

The doorbell clattered.

The sound was quite far away, but made more apparent by the fact that it rang again and again and again, not unlike an alarm.

Doctor Ricardo motioned to the steward. Something must have gone wrong. The house was overrun with servants. Surely one of them should have responded by now. The steward left the room.

The Duchess of Windsor had her back to the door, a position she did not enjoy. As the bell continued to ring, she looked at the other faces around the table, hoping one of them would speak. None of them did. Everyone sat stony still in his place, while the smoke from the Duke's cigarette curled upward through the candlelight above the peonies.

The ringing now became a banging.

The only two remaining servants, both of them footmen, sifted through the shadows making for the kitchens.

The Duchess looked at Doctor Ricardo. There was something wrong with his reactions. He should have been on his feet. After all—it was his house; but he didn't budge.

de Estella, too, was reacting strangely. He dabbed at his lips with his serviette and then, very carefully, laid it across his lap. When he had done this, his hands did not reappear on the table but remained out of sight below the cloth.

The banging stopped.

There was a dreadful silence.

From a distance they could hear at first voices; then footsteps. The voices were raised in protest and complaint but soon died out. The footsteps quickly followed. Not running, but walking briskly with a military gait.

de Estella suddenly became extremely nervous, as if the footsteps told him something. His hands were under the tablecloth still, unseen. He looked at Ricardo and the Doctor coughed.

All at once the Duchess of Windsor felt a draught. The doors to the dining-room were thrown wide open behind her.

If this is death, she thought, *I should rise.*

But before she could stand, a strangled voice—as "British" as any she had heard—spoke from the doorway. "Please no one move," it said.

The Duchess looked at the Duke.

He was ashen. His hands were laid on the table beside his plate and his head was slightly bowed. It was entirely evident he was expecting to be shot.

Doctor Ricardo had finally risen to the fact that his house was being invaded. He stood with his face in the shadows, his body leaning towards the table. All the Duchess of Windsor could see was the front of his evening clothes, his white shirt spotted with three small rubies.

As for the Marques, he was staring at the doorway with his mouth slightly open. The ochre tone of his skin was drained and dead. Whatever was happening, it was neither what he expected nor wanted. Quite the opposite, the Duchess surmised. She narrowed her gaze.

The Marques looked at the Duke. At the door. At the Duke. He began to rise.

All at once, the Duchess of Windsor knew why he'd really come and what his hand was really doing out of sight in the pocket of his jacket. Her mind leapt forward and the whole dreadful scheme flashed before her eyes: Estrade; the sinister Spanish chauffeur; the Doctor's numb hospitality; and the guest with the forced invitation. . . .Before de Estella was even completely risen, she was on her feet and yanking at the tablecloth. Kidnap. Assassination.

"He has a gun!" she cried and swept the cloth with all its plates and cutlery, glassware, peonies and candles onto the floor.

Instantly, the room was filled with British soldiers. Or seemed to be filled, since they moved so rapidly in order to get between the Marques and the Duke and to wrest the gun from the Spaniard's hands. As it turned out, there were only seven soldiers, but they might as well have been fifty, they made so much noise and threw such gigantic shadows.

For a moment, once the Marques was pinioned and disarmed, and after the clatter of china and glass and silver had been stilled, all that could be heard was everybody's breathing and the sound of the sizzling candles guttering in wine. The Duchess sat back down. Outside, the wind blew hard against the windows and the walls. The vines rattled.

"Might I ask," said the Duke, "who the hell you are? And where the hell you've come from?"

A blond young man stepped forward and saluted smartly. "Major B. M. Gerrard," he told the Duke. The G in Gerrard was hard, as in *eager*. "British Military Intelligence, sir."

The Duke was incredulous.

"At whose instigation?"

"Not at liberty to say, sir."

The Duke almost had a fit. "Not allowed to *say*! Bursting in here—manhandling our guests. . .! And not allowed to say!"

"If your Royal Highness will permit. . .?"

"The only thing I will permit, Major Gerrard," said the Duke, "is an explanation."

"Yessir."

"Well, then?"

"Not before the enemy, sir. Cannot explain before the enemy."

"What enemy?"

The Duchess held her breath. Doctor Ricardo sat down. Gerrard was rigid, at attention.

"Well, Major?"

Gerrard bit his lip. The Duchess admired his firmness. He was going to obey his orders, no matter what happened and no matter who bullied him to the contrary. Finally, she spoke in the Major's behalf.

"Perhaps you should take Major Gerrard aside, sir," she said, addressing the Duke with the utmost formality. "It is obvious he considers one of us to be the enemy."

"Thankyou, ma'am," said the Major.

"Is this true, Major?" asked the Duke. "That you consider someone in this room to be the enemy?"

"Someone. Yes, sir. Excepting, of course, Her Grace."

"You mean, I take it, Her Royal Highness?"

There was just the slightest pause before Major Gerrard replied. "Yessir," he said.

"Then say so, Major."

"Yessir. Excepting, of course, Her Royal Highness."

"I see," said the Duke. "In that case, we shall use the study." He began to lead the way, but paused to survey the scene. "I should prefer," he said "not to leave my wife in the presence of all these guns."

"Yessir," said the Major. And then, to one of his cohorts in uniform; "Dennison!"

"Yessir!"

Dennison, drenched to the skin, squelched forward from the shadows and saluted. As he flung up his arm, droplets of water flew in all directions.

Major Gerrard turned to the Duchess and spoke above her head: "Your Royal Highness, I present Lieutenant Dennison. Would Your Royal Highness be so good as to allow him to. . .to. . .uhm. . ."

"Accompany me to my quarters? Of course, Major."

The Duchess, having spent her first marriage on a Naval Base, knew the dialogue by heart. She rose and played it through like a consummate actress. Her performance was matchless—and drew every man in the room to full attention as she passed.

Dennison saluted the Duke and squelched down the hall behind her.

It was not until she was halfway up the stairs that the Duchess remembered the note in her sleeve. "Dear God," she said out loud, stopping dead in her tracks.

"Is there something wrong, ma'am?" Dennison asked.

"No," she said. "No. I just felt faint. But I'm all right, now."

She continued to climb. The Lieutenant, revolver in hand, was only three steps behind her all the way to the top.

What have I done? the Duchess was thinking. *What have I done? I've played right into their hands. David and I are separated now from all the others, each of us alone with an armed English soldier. British. British.*

British friends.

An hour passed. Two hours. Midnight approached. Along every hallway and corridor, every door was closed.

Major Gerrard, who was in charge of the whole operation, was in the study with the Duke. Upstairs, Lieutenant Dennison was standing on call by the door which led to the Windsor drawing-room where the Duchess was safely ensconced with her secretary taking care of her needs.

Outside, the storm had already done its worst, having tried

its strength against the house and the trees and brought down nothing but a few dead branches. Now, it was reduced to squalls and rain, the rain intermittent. Dennison noted that from time to time, the moon made a brief appearance. He could see it through the windows out beyond the stairwell.

de Estella and Doctor Ricardo had been removed to the library. As host, the Doctor was allowed to serve his guest from the whisky decanter on the reading table. He was most distressed and kept apologizing.

The "prisoners", for so they were termed, were in the charge of Lieutenant Harold Asquith Mudde, whose plaintive voice had been raised all through his life with the cry: "My name is not Mud—it is *Muddy*!" No one ever got it right. He lived, perhaps because of this, in a constant state of frustrated fury and he barked at everyone.

Doctor Ricardo was very shaken by what had happened. He drank a great deal of whisky. He spoke extensively in Spanish to the Marques, and the Marques merely nodded and stared at space. It was clear that de Estella's mind was somewhere else; more than likely down the hall in the study— with his friend the Duke of Windsor.

In the study, the Duke of Windsor made certain he stayed in the shadows. He disliked intensely the feel of bright light when he was alone with a stranger. Major Gerrard could only see the shape of his head and the lights in his buttercup hair. Also his hands, which gripped and ungripped the arms of the chair in which he sat. There was a glass nearby, and a decanter, but the Duke resisted.

The Duke's reaction to Gerrard's story was strangely muted— or so the Major thought, since the story contained sensational elements that might have led to the Duke's being dead at this moment instead of sitting there alive and relatively safe. Certainly safe so long as Gerrard and his men were in charge of the Villa Cascais.

What had just been thwarted was a plot to kidnap the Duke and Duchess and to hold them as political prisoners in Spain. What Major Gerrard did not tell the Duke of Windsor was that B.M.I. had been forewarned the attempt was to take place that night.

"Has Your Royal Highness been acquainted with the Marques de Estella long?" Gerrard asked.

"Years," said the Duke. "And I think you should know I consider that question to be the height of impertinence."

"I beg your pardon, sir. I was merely trying to ascertain. . ."

"You are suggesting, Major, that one of my dearest, closest and *oldest* friends has just attempted to kidnap me and my wife."

"No, sir. I am not suggesting it, sir. I am stating it."

The Duke's hands flew about his pockets until he had located his cigarette case and lighter.

Major Gerrard stepped forward with a match.

"Sod off," said the Duke, and lighted his cigarette with a flame that would have done a flame-thrower justice.

After two or three revivifying inhalations of smoke, the Duke at last was prepared to continue the conversation.

"You realize, of course," he said, "I shall have you up on charges—coming in here *argy-bargy*—accusing my best friend. . .And what, might I ask, would a Spanish Marques do with an English Prince? Not as if the bloody Hispanics were in the war, you know."

Major Gerrard was gallantly patient. He knew his story. He told it well and without embellishments, either patriotic or emotional.

"The Germans have wanted you for some time, sir—as Your Royal Highness must be aware. The idea was that the Marques de Estella would play upon your friendship. . .".

"Acquaintanceship," said the Duke.

"Yes, sir. He would play upon his acquaintanceship with Your Royal Highness and persuade you to cross back into Spain where you and Her. . ."

". . .Royal Highness. . ."

". . .would join the Duke and Duchess of Avila at their hunting lodge in the Sierra de Gredos."

"And this would be *kidnap*?"

"Yes, sir. Because you would be held there under house arrest."

"I think you mean 'hunting-lodge arrest', Major."

Gerrard smiled. "Yes, sir. Hunting-lodge arrest."

The Duke tapped out a message of impatience with his fingers and then said; "the buggers."

"Yes, sir."

"And the Germans. You said this was a German plot."

"In time, an arrangement would have been made to transfer Your Royal Highness into German hands."

"And then?"

"Presumably ransom. Maybe blackmail."

The Duke of Windsor was silent for a moment. Then he said, "Well. At least it's gratifying to know one has some value."

Gerrard did not respond to this.

The Duke said, "You chaps at B.M.I. seem awfully up to date on all of this. May a person ask just how you came to know of it—and how in hell you came to arrive in the nick?"

"It's delicate, sir. And there are details I don't even know myself. But I think it's fair to tell Your Royal Highness we received the news of de Estella's move only two days ago. We were only just able to get here."

"I see. And now what?"

"Well, sir. . ." Major Gerrard blushed.

"Yes?" The Duke of Windsor narrowed his eyes—so that all he could see was a mascara view of the red-faced soldier.

"Our first objective has been accomplished, which is to say, we have thwarted the Marques."

"And your second objective?"

"*Excalibur.*"

"I trust that doesn't mean you're asking me to fall on my sword like some absurd Roman general."

"No, sir. Hardly, sir. No. *Excalibur* is a ship. And you and Her Royal Highness are to be on board when she sails for. . ."

"England?"

"No, sir. Your destination is the Bahamas."

The Duke of Windsor's reaction to this was to break ranks

with discipline and reach for the Calvados.

"That bugger. . ." he said.

"I beg pardon, sir."

"The bugger, Winston!" The Duke was spilling brandy—more of it onto the table than into the glass. "Sends you here on the pretext you're preventing kidnap by the Germans and all the while you're out to kidnap us yourself!"

"Hardly kidnap, Your Royal Highness. All we're meant to do is to see that you reach the ship in one piece."

There was a knock at the door.

The intruder was Lieutenant Dennison, looking rather pale. He saluted the Duke and turned to the Major. The Duke was busy spilling more Calvados over the arm of the chair.

"I beg your pardon, sir, but I think this ought to be seen to." Dennison presented Major Gerrard with a small, white card. "It was given me by the *secretaria.. . .*"

"Estrade?" said the Duke.

"Yes, sir." Dennison turned back to Gerrard. "The *secretaria's* instructions were that this was to be presented to His Royal Highness."

"Then why the hell have you given it to Major Gerrard?" The Duke leapt up to his feet.

Gerrard was just as quick with his explanation. "Señora Estrade is under suspicion, sir. We cannot allow her to freely communicate with Your Royal Highness."

The Duke made a move towards the door. "Where is she? Where is Estrade?" he demanded of Dennison.

"I left her with the Duchess, sir."

The Duke turned, completely livid. He shook as he shouted at Major Gerrard, "You bloody sodding fool! One minute you tell me Estrade is under suspicion and the next I'm informed she is with my wife! Give me that bloody card. . .!" and he snatched it from the Major's hands. The Major, too, had gone as white as a corpse. "What does it say?" the Duke raged, thrusting the card beneath the nearest lamp. "Some kind of ransom note, no doubt!"

He read. He looked at Major Gerrard. He read again. He completely lost his voice. He then tried to run. But he fell.

The Duchess of Windsor was standing in her bedroom. She was wearing her slip.

On returning to the royal apartments, she had decided to change her dress, since the blue one with the long buttoned sleeves had been spattered with wine and food. It was also quite unbearably hot. She had given the dress to Estrade and Estrade had disappeared with it into the dressing-room with instructions to bring back a sleeveless evening gown of a lighter colour. Lighter shades were best in this kind of heat.

But Estrade had not returned as quickly as she might. She had lingered far too long in the dressing-room. Nor could the Duchess hear her, and on going to discover what might be happening, she had found herself entirely alone in the apartments. . .and locked in.

She also discovered something else: something curious that sent a chill down her spine. Some of the clothing had been removed from her cupboards and closets and placed in suitcases. Shoes, dresses, lingerie, gloves and night-clothes. . .everything a person needs for a journey—except her jewelry, which was kept in the Doctor's safe downstairs.

Quickly she went to the door that led to the hall and knocked. She thought, *if the Lieutenant answers, I'm only wearing my slip—but to hell with it. This is real danger.* She knocked again.

"Lieutenant. . .Lieutenant. . ." She could not remember his name. "Lieutenant. . .Please. . .Hello. . .? Hello?"

But there wasn't any answer. He must not be there.

Yet who, if not the Lieutenant, had locked the door? And where was Estrade? Where was. . .?

Automatically, she felt her wrist. The note was not there.

She ran to the dressing-room. There was the blue dress worn at dinner: spotted. There were its sleeves—she fumbled with them, one and then the other. Where? Where? Where was the note? She fell to her knees and searched under all the shelves, over all the surfaces, inside all the cupboards.

Gone. Oh God. She raised her arms against her face. The card. *Where was the card?*

The Duchess of Windsor turned and stared at all the open closets. There were her shoes, dozens of them, bagged like dead birds hanging from the doors. There were her tea dresses, evening gowns, peignoirs, wraps and robes and coats and capes. Blue. Blue. All blue. And there were the suitcases—packed.

In the other room, she heard the door being opened; shut; relocked.

The Duchess watched the mirrors.

There was Estrade: dressed in a mackintosh and wearing a beret.

"Duquesa?"

The Duchess did not answer.

"Duquesa?"

The Duchess placed both hands, like the hands of a corpse, on her breast.

"Duquesa?" Estrade came to the doorway, still in the mirror, but their eyes met. The Duchess remained silent. Estrade's hand was in her pocket. She removed it. There was a gun. A Luger automatic.

The Duchess of Windsor turned and walked, her hands still folded, out of the dressing-room into the bedroom. Her jewel cases—three of them—sat on the bed. She sat down beside them.

"Where are we going?" she said, not looking at Estrade.

"Into España," Estrade said.

"At gunpoint. . .?" The Duchess looked at Estrade, not only alarmed but confused.

"But of course, Duquesa."

Estrade smiled. Her teeth, the Duchess noted, were rotted and black with decay. The Duchess of Windsor went into the bathroom and took half a dozen pills. But nothing happened. They did not help. Where, where, where was von Ribbentrop? What had gone wrong? Who was Estrade working for?

But before she could even begin to think, her window was broken. Stones were being thrown, glass was being shattered. Servants and soldiers were rushing to the terraces. A figure could be seen running back and forth, but then the darkness hid him, mixing with the trees. Long brass arms of light leapt out and flooded across the lawns from opened doors. Both Estrade and the Duchess ran to the windows. One of the

Doctor's houseboys was standing near the balustrade above the steps. He was pointing down at the trees and he was shouting, *"vai ele! vai ele!"* And then; *"o assassino!"*

The Duchess heard Estrade mutter *"bueno"* and caught her looking at her watch.

"This has to do with you," the Duchess said, withdrawing from the lighted windows. "Hasn't it? *Tell me.*"

"I do not know what the *Duquesa* means."

The Duchess pointed at the windows and shouted at Estrade. "He is saying there is an assassin!"

"*Sí, Duquesa.*"

The shouting out of doors continued. *"Vai ele! Vai ele!"* and there was the sound of much running. . .more glass breaking. . .and then a gunshot.

The Duchess ran across the room to the bureau and, taking up the bottle, flung a great deal of gin in Estrade's eyes, meaning to blind her.

She succeeded. Estrade dropped the gun and groped for her eyes.

The Duchess ran to the gun, took it up, and ran for the door. She was still in her slip. She fumbled with the key which Estrade had left in the lock. . .and flung the door nearly off its hinges. In the hallway, she fled towards the stairs.

"Vai ele! Vai ele!" The voices were everywhere.

And then the lights went out.

The Duchess decided to make for the dining-room. She was certain to find some candles there, and it was central. She was glad of Estrade's Luger. *Squeeze* the trigger, she remembered Ernest, her second husband, telling her. *Squeeze the trigger, Wallis. Don't ever snap at it with your fingers.*

When she got to the dining-room, she discovered the cloth and all the dishes were still on the floor and she had to walk very carefully, finally crawling on her hands and knees in order to find the candelabra. Once she had found them, she set them carefully in place on the table and lighted them with matches also found on the floor. She then sat down

with a large chipped glass of port to await whatever horrors
would unfold. She wrapped the table-cloth around her
shoulders, not unlike a robe of state, and, huddled inside
it, she proceeded to get quite drunk. She even smoked some
soggy cigarettes. To hell with it. Whenever they were ready,
whoever was out there would come and find her. Her
candlelight would tell them she was there. In the meantime,
she composed a whole new correspondence in her mind.
"*Dear Amelia Earhart* ..." it began. *I know how you feel* ..."

The Duke made his escape from Major Gerrard quite easily
the moment the lights went out. Gerrard had pushed him
against the wall when the first stones were thrown and in
the confusion of all the coming and going and breaking glass,
the Duke had simply crawled beneath a table. When Gerrard
had reached, in the blackout, for the Duke of Windsor's arm
it had been Lieutenant Dennison he had captured. By which
time the Duke of Windsor was halfway down the hall.

The Duke's first thought was of Wallis and he made for
the stairs. In the dark he missed her entirely—being unaware
she was already feeling her way along the walls towards the
dining-room.

The Duke heard the words and the whispers: "*tenho
medo. . .da escuridão. . .espalhar-se.*" Three people—four,
perhaps—fumbled their way down the stairs against the
opposite bannister and while they passed, he paused, afraid
to breathe. Slowly their whispers faded around the corners
and were gone. He was suddenly alone.

Instead of climbing, however, he sagged on the steps. Way,
way off in the gardens someone was calling; "*vai ele, vai
ele!*" He runs. But the Duke could not have cared less. He
looked up into the dome of darkness.

For one brief moment he was entirely in charge of his own
life. No one could see his expression—he didn't have to act,
perform, equivocate. In the darkness all his dissembling lay
unravelled at his feet and he knew that for months he had
worn his face like a garment. A woollen mask in which he
had begun to suffocate. The image came to him of skeins

and skeins and yards and yards of wool on the stairs at his feet and he found himself laughing: *Thank God mother taught me how to knit!*

He wiped his tears away with his knuckles. Be serious, he thought. There's a man out there who's trying to kill you. He sniffed. He desperately wanted to blow his nose. Be serious, he told himself again; there really is a man.

Seconds later the Duke of Windsor had completely disappeared.

Some time afterwards there was a series of gun shots on the second floor. Almost at once, Lieutenant Mudde appeared on the staircase. He was bloodied and dazed and fell the last ten steps into the hall.

The Duchess hurried from the dining-room to help him. Dennison stumbled out of the dark, attracted by the Duchess' candles. Mudde was not all that badly hurt, but he was raving, his speech weaving in and out of sense. "Up—up," he kept saying, "go up." And when the two of them started up the stairs he shouted after them, like a man convicted of a crime he did not commit, "It is impossible!" he cried. "It is impossible! He can't—he can't have meant it."

Dennison had to restrain the Duchess, she was so eager to reach wherever their destination might be. But she wrenched herself free and spun away from him, rushing past all the doors, throwing this one and that one open until at last she came to the end of the hall where the doors gave way to the Martello Tower. And then, all at once, she experienced fear—came to her senses and fell back.

Therefore it was Lieutenant Dennison who first confronted the scene.

There was a table, several chairs and a tapestry. A half dozen mirrors and stacks of empty picture frames, each one with glass, were lined up along the walls.

Candles burned. Six of them. Seven.

One of the commandos was standing, with his rifle at the ready, off to one side of the doors. Another was crouching on the floor unarmed. His hands were on top of his head

and he looked like a man who was waiting out a bombardment. He had apparently lost his powers of speech, though
noises issued from his mouth and tears from his eyes. The
reason lay on the floor beside him.

Dennison snatched up a candlestick and stepped forward.
Underneath his feet there was a flood of broken glass and
he almost fell.

The commando by the door stopped him with a hand on
his arm. "You'd best not look, sir," he said. "You'd best not,
I think. There's an awful bloody mess."

"I can see that," said Dennison. "Thank you. Is he dead?"

"I think so."

Major Gerrard then stepped out of the shadows, putting
his automatic pistol back in its holster. Dennison was somewhat surprised, not having known Gerrard was there.

"All right, Lieutenant," said the Major. "You stand off.
I'll do this." And, Dennison having fallen back, Gerrard
stepped all the way forward and looked at the Duke of Windsor's body on the floor. Its face was turned away from the
light. There were shards and slivers of glass all around it.
Gerrard crouched down, giving half a look at the kneeling
soldier who was directly opposite. "Somebody come and
take that man away."

There was enormous quantities of blood—more than Dennison had ever seen.

Gerrard turned the face quite gently with his fingers the
way he might disturb a sleeper. And then, without a word,
he pushed the face away so as not to see it any more. Finally
he stood up.

The Duchess, who all this while had been silent, spoke
from the doorway.

"Please," she said, drawing the tablecloth tight around
her shoulders. "Tell me."

Major Gerrard took a deep breath and turned to face her.
"I beg of you not to look, Your Royal Highness. Please,
Ma'am," he said, "he isn't dead; but you mustn't look."

The Duchess was helped from the room and put in a chair
outside the door with her back to the wall.

Dennison was kneeling by the Duke of Windsor. "Who

215

the hell did this?" he whispered. "Who the hell shot him?"
"I did," said Major Gerrard.

Not quite dawn—but the rain had ended and the stars, at last, had emerged. Estrade made her way down through the olive grove to the town, where she had a rendezvous. With her she carried all her possessions in a single suitcase. Her Portuguese sojourn was nearly over. One more thing to do.

Which brings me to the end of Maria de Gama's story. Having delivered the flowers the girl returned as instructed to Fritzi Schaemmel. Schaemmel then paid the child the escudos still owed her and invited her into his seedy little hotel room to share some chocolate and wine.

All Portuguese children drink wine and children everywhere love chocolate. The wine was local, but the chocolate came from Switzerland and tasted very good. It was the last of anything Maria was to eat. Once she was finished, Schellenberg-"Schaemmel" struck the little girl behind the ear and while she was unconscious, he gagged her and tied her to a chair.

When Estrade arrived in the morning, there was light enough in Schellenberg's room to see the child in the corner; see her—and see her eyes light up with the brief, bright hope that all would be well, now a woman was present.

But Schellenberg simply said, "The child must be killed," and Estrade, pausing only to remove her skirt in order to have more freedom of movement, crossed without a word to Maria.

Maria's death was made more difficult by the fact that she wanted so much to live. She fought against Estrade with all her strength and kicked her several times in the stomach. But Estrade barely felt the kicks and carried the child across the room and drowned her in the sink. She did this very quickly, pressing down with her thumbs behind Maria's ears.

It was done and over in five minutes.

Estrade sat down and lighted a cigarette and accepted a small glass of Schnapps.

Schellenberg said to her, "I presume because you have come alone, our friend the Marques has relieved us of our royal guests?"

No. Estrade had to admit they had failed in their mission.

She told him the English had arrived as anticipated, but the Duchess of Windsor had kept the contents of the note to herself, which had caused Major Schellenberg's plans to backfire. On the other hand the house-boy and the gardener had played their roles extremely well—shooting off the gun; throwing stones and breaking windows; crying *"assassin!"* And the lights had all gone off precisely on cue. But. . .Now Estrade had to tell him she had been bested by the *Duquesa.* "With gin she blinded me," she said. "So I lost vital moments in the dark." Still she was able to report there had been an extraordinary occurrence.

"Oh?"

Estrade told him Major Gerrard had shot the Duke of Windsor.

Schellenberg fell silent. If the Duke of Windsor died, they would all be out of pocket. On the other hand. . .

Schellenberg sat down.

Ten minutes later, Estrade had to remind him of the body in the corner.

Maria da Gama's body was found a day later by her sister Alida where it lay enmeshed in kelp on the sand. It was presumed she had been drowned in the sea. The bruises shaped like thumb prints just behind her ears could be explained by rocks. There was no investigation. She was buried on the hillside, halfway up to the Villa Cascais. In the grave-yard there were roses, lilies, delphiniums. *Flores para os mortos.*

By chance, Maria's funeral was taking place at the very moment when the Duchess and her party made their dash for the ship. The mourners kneeling in the grass lifted their heads to see the passing motorcade through a veil of red dust—the Buick, the Mercedes, the Renault all laden with luggage, much of it tied to the roof. Inside the cars, the bandaged and sedated Duke, the Duchess, Major Gerrard and others crouched with their heads below the windows, expecting to be ambushed.

This was the afternoon of Thursday the 1st of August. The Windsors' destination was Lisbon. That evening the American liner S.S. *Excalibur* sailed from the mouth of the Tagus and out along the coast of the Estoril. The sun had not set; the stars had not risen; but the sea was already dark and all the western windows on the shore appeared to be on fire. In one of the staterooms a gramophone was playing:

> ...*Though my world may go awry*
> *In my heart will ever lie*
> *Just the echo of a sigh,*
> *Goodbye.* ...

FIVE

1940

End fact. Try fiction.

Ezra Pound

Captain Freyberg's Operations Centre (*Project Elysium*) was set up next to Mauberley's suite in the rooms once occupied by Greta Garbo. There Freyberg had installed his filing cabinets; specimen collections; photographic equipment; and hung the American flag above his desk. His desk was a metal thing with shallow drawers and locks that were always jamming or freezing. The contents of these drawers were mostly old and mouldy Tootsie Rolls and Beecham's Candy-Coated Gum—hard as gravel—but there were also sheets of foolscap scrawled with shouts and exclamation points. There were typewriters (three), telephones (not yet connected), a black-board crudely nailed to the wall and a map of Europe show-ing where the death camps were. The field telephone, whose range at the best of times was less than a mile, was set on Freyberg's desk so he could check with the larger commu-nications system down in the town. Freyberg's cot was also in this room (the salon) since the bedroom had been com-mandeered for another use.

In the bedroom—strung with white hot lights as if he expected to grill Al Capone—Freyberg had laid a tarpaulin over the floor and there were shovelfuls of ashes dotted like a kid's toy mountain range along one side. Each of the piles was numbered—"shovel one", "shovel two", "shovel three" etc.—all the ashes having been removed from the bathtub next door in Mauberley's suite. From "one" to "twenty-eight" the shovelfuls denoted top to bottom.

When Quinn went in this particular night, Freyberg ap-peared to be playing with a set of cut-outs on his desk. The only other person in the room was Dufault, a typist who was pecking at requisitions, probably for specimen bottles in which to display the ashes.

"So," said Freyberg, "your Duchess got away."

"You know as well as I do she didn't 'get away'," said Quinn. "In the last resort she did her duty."

"Unh-hunh. Duty's such a lovely word, isn't it Quinn? Covers almost everything."

"Almost. Although I can't believe it covers what you're doing. Sir."

The clerk stopped pecking.

Freyberg shot him a look and the pecking continued.

"You hungry, Quinn?"

"No thankyou, Captain." Quinn hated chocolate bars. They rotted your teeth and stained your tongue.

"Sit down," said Freyberg.

"My feet are cold," said Quinn. "I'm better off standing, if you don't mind, sir."

"Sit down."

Quinn sat down.

"I want you to see my newest collection: just completed.

And I thought maybe you—being so 'artistic'—might help me make an arrangement so they can be framed."

"Oh, yes?"

Quinn tilted his head so he could see the cut-outs spread across the desk between himself and Freyberg—Freyberg pushing them around like pieces in a puzzle. All of them were cut from cloth. Each was a different colour: each in the shape of a triangle. Maybe insignia: regimental badges maybe. Maybe just a game that Freyberg had invented.

"Each of these triangles," Freyberg said, "was cut from the breast of a prison uniform."

"Oh."

"That's right. From Dachau."

Quinn couldn't help but sigh. He was so sick of Dachau— sick of its stench in his mind, so sick of the very word, that he wanted to scream. Now Freyberg wanted his artistic judgement so he could frame these sick, crazy patches on a wall. "Well—the pink should be mounted next to the violet," he said "and the green next over from the red, and the yellow. . .well. . .it would look okay with the black."

In a way, he wasn't kidding. He was just delivering a colour scheme that wouldn't clash. But in another way, he walked on glass and knew it, sensing that Freyberg might reach out and strike him, even with Dufault the typist in the room.

But nothing happened.

For for a moment, anyway.

Freyberg pushed the pieces of cloth in a row and sat back nibbling the end of his chocolate bar. When he spoke, at last, it was not to Quinn but to the air between himself and the small faded things laid out before him.

"Violet stands for Conscientious Objectors," he said. "Green for common criminals. Pink for homosexuals. Black for 'antisocials'. Red for politicals. Yellow for Jews. And you see. . .two yellow triangles make the Star of David. Fascinating, hunh? Methodical; concise; no wastage. Even a moron can remember them. . .memorize them. Morons, by the way—the mentally deficient—weren't accorded or awarded colours. No time to sew them on between arrival and departure."

Quinn was watching the patches of cloth and could see

where the stitching had come unravelled or been clipped—
more than likely by Freyberg himself, walking amongst the
victims, stooping every once in a while to add to his collection.

There was a clicking sound in Freyberg's throat and Quinn
looked up to see the Captain staring at him; sweating.

"What do you want me to do, Captain Freyberg? Choose
a colour and wear it?"

Nothing was forthcoming. Nothing. Just the clicking in
Freyberg's throat.

Dufault gave up pecking altogether and even the pretence
of looking at the keys. He swivelled in his chair to watch.
What he saw was Freyberg sweating—with his mouth clamped
shut—and Quinn's perfect haircut, razored on his perfect
neck above his perfect collar.

Then Freyberg said; "I don't think your colour's there,
Lieutenant Quinn."

"Oh? What colour's that?"

"I'm not quite sure. Whatever colour you like, I guess.
Maybe brown for asshole; maybe purple for prick. Take your
pick."

Quinn didn't bother to answer. He debated standing up,
but he thought; *why should I? It will only make him think
he's won.*

"Well at least you're lucky, sir," he said. "No trouble
picking the colours for you. Like I said—the yellow and the
black go together okay."

Freyberg's tongue made a foray over his bottom lip and
then retreated in behind his teeth. "I'm not a Jew," he said.

"Oh." Quinn could not help smiling. Freyberg had fallen—
tripped—but not where Quinn had thought he would. He
had thought the good Captain would deny being anti-social.
"Anyway, sir," he said, "you can still wear the black triangle.
It shouldn't clash with your uniform."

"I am not a Jew," Freyberg repeated; speaking to the desk
and to the decals.

"Does it matter?" said Quinn.

* * *

Berlin: August, 1940

Walter Schellenberg was a graduate of the best academies and held a university degree. He was poised; he was educated; he was charming. He was also a killer. As one of Himmler's bright young men, he was a master of deceit. He never relied on physical disguise. Instead he became the characters he played, much as an actor trained by Stanislavsky might do. He had played the character of Schaemmel entirely from the inside. Fritzi Schaemmel lived. The ears and eyes and hands were Schellenberg's, but what was heard and what was seen and what was touched was Schaemmel's.

Schaemmel had walked down English streets; parlayed information face to face with British agents; sat in the inner circles of the Dutch, the French and the Danish Undergrounds. He had slept with men and women, boys and girls and made them all believe he loved them. Schaemmel was an expression of Schellenberg's genius—a genius that was to propel him all the way to the top until Major Schellenberg had become a Major-General: Chief of Bureau IV (Gestapo) Counterespionage of the Reich Central Security Office.

On Friday, August 2nd, Schellenberg and Estrade returned to Berlin where a meeting took place between them and the German Foreign Minister, Joachim von Ribbentrop. von Ribbentrop had requested the meeting. Schellenberg had insisted Estrade be present. They met after lunch on the 3rd. von Ribbentrop came to them. He seemed most anxious the meeting take place at the Central Security Headquarters on Prinz Albrechtstrasse. The impression given was that von Ribbentrop was being considerate, though Estrade had her own impression the Foreign Minister preferred that Schellenberg not be seen on the Wilhelmstrasse quite so soon after his return from Portugal. Perhaps there was more to the Windsor conspiracy than met the eye.

Throughout the early part of the interview. Estrade merely sat to one side and listened. It was her first encounter with anyone so high in the order of things as von Ribbentrop. Here she was in a room with a man who sat everyday in a room with the Führer. She was discreetly appalled by what she saw. A man wearing spats. A man who carried a walking stick. A man who perspired. A human man. Most interesting.

Schellenberg and Ribbentrop spoke in guarded detail about the plot to kidnap the Windsors. Estrade, knowing her place, was silent. The fascination was all in watching two intelligent men sitting down to complete a jigsaw puzzle whose pieces were patently invisible.

The salient facts were known to both players. Sometime in the fall of 1940 or the spring of 1941 a full-scale invasion of Britain would take place. This operation would be difficult but not impossible. On the other hand, there were certain cards that—if they could be played—might save a great many German lives and reduce the loss of sophisticated equipment and expended energies—energies and equipment better saved for the inevitable war with Russia.

One of these cards was already in the works and would soon be known as the Battle of Britain. Another of the cards was the infusion of hundreds of German agents into the American political scene—financed with massive German funds—whose job it was to prevent the re-election of President Roosevelt and to foment strife on the labour front. This card, too, was paying off handsomely. Henry Ford, who kept the Führer's picture framed on the wall above his desk, played it from the side of management, refusing to let the workers' union into his factories, bringing the whole of an industry to a standstill. John L. Lewis, on the other hand, playing from the side of Labor, had effectively shut down most of America's coal mines. Roosevelt conceded he was "in trouble" and if he were to lose the election, Britain would lose its most effective ally.

The final card to be played would be the kidnapping of the Duke and Duchess of Windsor.

When the directive came down from Hitler ordering the Windsors be detained in Europe, it had automatically been sent to both the Foreign Office and the Central Security

Bureau. Presumably the theory was: if you tell two men to do precisely the same job it is more than likely one of them will succeed in doing it.

Himmler for his part had dispatched Walter Schellenberg. And von Ribbentrop. . . .Well, it was not yet known.

Schellenberg's plan was as Major Gerrard had told the Duke of Windsor; the Marques de Estella would persuade the Windsors to return to Spain, where they would be the guests of the Duke and Duchess of Avila at their hunting lodge in the mountains along the Portuguese border. Once in Avila's hands, they would be betrayed and placed under house arrest.

But Schellenberg also had a back-up plan.

If the Marques de Estella could not "persuade" the Windsors to cross into Spain, they would be taken at gunpoint by Schellenberg himself, with the help of Estrade and other servants in the villa who had been bribed. Avila's role in all of this was to be the same whether he received the Windsors as willing guests or as unwilling visitors: he was to turn the key and hand it over to Schellenberg.

This, then, had been the plot formulated by the Albrechtstrasse.

"And the Wilhelmstrasse. . .?" Schellenberg smiled at von Ribbentrop, who looked into his lap and brushed away some luncheon crumbs still caught in the folds of his trousers. "Surely, now it is over and we have both proved the losers, your Excellency can give at least a hint of what he had in mind. . .?"

At last von Ribbentrop had gathered all his crumbs and he placed them, rolled in a tiny ball of dough, into the ashtray on Schellenberg's desk. "My plan was your plan, Major. Point by point; step by step—the very same as your own."

Schellenberg's smile did not retract a fraction. "Point by point; step by step, the same as mine?" he said.

"That's right."

"But who was your Excellency's agent? Who was acting in your Excellency's behalf?"

von Ribbentrop took great satisfaction in giving his answer. "You were, Major."

"I?"

"Yes."

Schellenberg was still smiling.

"Well, well," he said. "So I have been working all this time for you."

von Ribbentrop made no reply to this. Schellenberg would have to draw whatever conclusion he was able.

One conclusion, however, von Ribbentrop prayed the Major would never draw—which was that the Duke of Avila, far from being prepared to turn the key on the Windsors and hand it over to Schellenberg, had instead been prepared to turn the key on Schellenberg and hand it over to von Ribbentrop. For the Duke of Avila was the very centrepiece of *Penelope*'s Spanish wing.

So von Ribbentrop left Major Schellenberg with the impression that, indeed, he had been working "all this time" not only for the Albrechtstrasse, but also for the Wilhelmstrasse. And it was true. He had been: though no one else on the Wilhelmstrasse knew of it.

Both now sat back and played out whatever remained of their smiles.

A white coated orderly appeared just then with a copper urn of ersatz Turkish coffee and its complement of tiny cups and a pyramid of sugar loaves.

von Ribbentrop went to the windows, looking out at the summer trees, forcing an imposing posture so his back obscured a whole block of light from reaching into the room. It would not have done for the orderly to quit the major's office under the impression the Minister was seated like a suitor. Standing stiff with authority—his walking stick dangling down from grey-gloved fingers—His Excellency presented the very image of a man who had come to lay down the law. Schellenberg was left at the mercy of appearing to have fallen into his chair under the weight of some accusation.

The orderly's retreat was suitably subdued and when the door had clicked and he was gone His Excellency noted the brightness of the day and returned to his place as suitor before the desk.

"There are all these stories one hears," he said as he laid two loaves of sugar neatly on the plate before him and began to remove his gloves. "Such as the tale that His Royal Highness left the Villa not only under guard but 'under wraps', as the British say. Is it true he was bandaged?"

Schellenberg placed a sugar loaf between his teeth and drew the heavy liqueur of the coffee through his lips with as raucous a hiss as any Turk or Levantine.

His Excellency was more refined and merely dipped his sugar loaf in the European fashion and held it poised and stained and slowly disintegrating above his cup while he waited for the answer to his question. When it came, though it stopped his heart, it did not prevent the sugar from reaching his mouth.

"Yes," said Schellenberg. "His Royal Highness was bandaged. But who wouldn't have been? Apparently he had been shot in the face."

"Shot?"

"In the face."

"But surely such a shot would have killed him."

"Yes. One would think so. But it didn't."

Schellenberg sipped once again at his coffee and bit through the centre of his sugar.

"Shot. . ." von Ribbentrop muttered, as if the word had only just been coined and he was trying every variation he could find of inflection. "Shot. How extraordinary. Shot. . ." and he looked at Estrade.

Estrade drew an entire cup of coffee through her teeth and finished with a loud intake of breath. von Ribbentrop perhaps was waiting to hear that Estrade had pulled the trigger.

"He was shot by a Britisher," Schellenberg said.

His Excellency stared.

"A handful of British soldiers, wading out of the sea, not only managed to abduct our Prince, but to wound him and render him incapable."

"Are you saying, then," His Excellency said, "our quarry has been kidnapped and removed from Europe by Mister Churchill?"

The thought of Winston Churchill plotting against the Duke of Windsor was too alarming to encompass.

"Perhaps," said Schellenberg. "But how can a person know for certain? We only report what it was we saw. The British Commandos arrived. There was a shot and the sound of much breaking glass and as we know, the Duke and Duchess were removed together to the ship."

"With the Duke in bandages?"

"Yes, Your Excellency. With the Duke entirely wrapped of head and hands in bandages," said Estrade.

"Hands, too."

"Oh, yes. Very much of the hands. And all the face."

Estrade sat back. Schellenberg, watching the Minister, bit very hard into another sugar loaf.

"These British Commandos." His Excellency said, using one of his dove-grey gloves to dust the long dark edge of Schellenberg's desk. "Their arrival was so timely."

Schellenberg nodded. "Yes."

"But you say you knew? You were prepared for their coming?"

The Major nodded again.

"May one ask how it was you knew?"

Schellenberg-Schaemmel shrugged.

"Very well," said von Ribbentrop. "May one ask—at least— why the Wilhelmstrasse was not told of their imminent arrival?"

Estrade flicked her gaze at Schellenberg, who said: "We did not dare to warn the informant, Excellency. And the slightest activity on the part of our agents would certainly have done so."

von Ribbentrop withdrew his gloves into his lap. "You are saying, I presume, that someone in Portugal who knew of our plans got word to the British and. . ."

"Not necessarily in Portugal, Minister." Smiling now, teeth and all.

von Ribbentrop smoothed his gloves into a pair of hands that rested on his knees. "Then you are saying someone on the Wilhelmstrasse is not to be trusted. That someone on the Wilhelmstrasse informed the British of our plans to kidnap the Duke and Duchess of Windsor?"

Schellenberg did not reply.

von Ribbentrop shrugged. "I see." And he too smiled. The

"war" between the Foreign Office and Central Security would never end.

von Ribbentrop had his own mask to wear—though not so elaborate a mask as Schellenberg-Schaemmel. For many years the international charmer, the champagne salesman who sold his magnums of bubbly Facsism during his days as Ambassador to Britain in the 1930s had appeared to be an innocuous dilettante, seductively arrogant but harmless.

von Ribbentrop ran his own information service, independent of the Wilhelmstrasse, independent of the R.S.H.A. Schellenberg was aware of this, but not on whose behalf the information was garnered.

But now von Ribbentrop wanted every bit of information he could get; wanted it so badly he was sweating with desire for whatever Schellenberg could tell. He smells of anxiety, Estrade thought.

His Excellency said, "So—however it was possible—you intercepted this message, saying the British Commandos were coming, and you sent along that note to Her Royal Highness which read; *'Beware of British friends. . .'* "

The silence that followed this was terrible, for von Ribbentrop had overplayed his hand.

Schellenberg was quick to take advantage. "Your Excellency seems to know the wording of my note by heart."

Luckily, von Ribbentrop was able to use a riposte that had once been used on him when the shoe was on the other foot. "The wording of your note, Major Schellenberg," he said, "is known by heart from here to London."

Schellenberg was forced to retreat, and von Ribbentrop was well aware it must be passing through the major's mind that one of his agents in the Villa Cascais had played the game on more than one side.

Estrade shifted in her chair.

von Ribbentrop, now having regained the upper hand, decided to press for more advantages. His tone was that of a man who knows a good deal more than he will admit—and who muses aloud in order to put the fear of God into his adversary. "You know," he said, "I am still intrigued and I am still wondering how it can be that Fritzi Schaem-

mel—sitting in his sordid room at the Hotel Barcarena—
could have known to the very hour when these British Commandos would arrive. I am still wondering how it could be
he would not only know of their arrival, but also what their
intentions might be. *'Beware of British friends. . .from one
your interests at heart.'* How charming. How quaint the
phrasing. How considerate the sentiment. And to send such
a thoughtful message with a gift of flowers. So touching.
And yet—there was nothing done to prevent the arrival of
these *British friends.* Just Herr Fritzi with his nudist magazines and his binoculars and his own private scheme up
his sleeve. . .And his own league of cohorts inside the Villa
conniving and conspiring to. . .what? Collect perhaps a private ransom? Perform a little blackmail? Or a lot?''

von Ribbentrop was rolling up the fingers of one grey glove
and then the other, creating a pair of soft, cloth fists which
he laid out flat on his knees.

"And this agent. . ." von Ribbentrop shrugged ". . .this
informant. Must it not have been someone who knew the
British were coming because they had *told* the British to
come? I mean—these Commandos cannot have come by
chance. Certainly not by chance on the very night before the
Marques de Estella might have crossed the border with the
Windsors into Spain. And if not that contingency, then your
other, Major Schaemmel. . .forgive me! Major Schellenberg,
whereby the Windsors would have been transported by gun.
How exquisite that timing was. And based on so much intimate knowledge of what it was we were up to."

von Ribbentrop now looked directly at Estrade. His tone
changed completely. Hardened into contempt. He pointed
at her. "Who is this woman, Schellenberg? Tell me who she
is."

Estrade sat with her knees pressed together. von Ribbentrop looked at her eyes. Quite dead. Such eyes were a gift
to one whose work was in the ground. Some of the secrets
they contained were even—apparently—hidden from herself. "Well?" said von Ribbentrop.

Schellenberg rose from his place behind the desk and
wandered out into the centre of the room. For a very long

moment he refused to speak, but stood instead first here then there with his hands in his trouser pockets, in and out of his pockets as if he might be counting his fortune in lint. And when at last he spoke, it was so very quietly von Ribbentrop had to turn his head to hear him.

"I will strike a bargain with you, Excellency," he said—and at once von Ribbentrop's back went rigid. *Bargain* was perhaps the most dangerous word in the current lexicon. "I will strike a very special, perhaps somewhat foolish, bargain with you. Foolish because I might be prepared to pass on a piece of information I have not yet had the chance to analyse.

von Ribbentrop looked across at Estrade. Her lips were parted as though there was a sudden lack of oxygen in the room.

Schellenberg said, "I will tell you more; if you will agree to bargain with me. Yes?"

von Ribbentrop sat further back in his chair. One hand was resting on the head of his stick, the other laid out flat on the edge of the desk, where by now he had made a display of his perfect gloves.

He considered the situation briefly. He needed more information regarding what had gone on in the Villa. He needed—desperately—to know whatever Schellenberg might be able to tell him about this agent who had warned the British. His own information concerning events in the Villa had come from the steward—and the steward had been helpful. But he had not been everywhere in that stormy night. He had not heard everything.

And what, after all, did von Ribbentrop have to lose? There was nothing Schellenberg could ask that would do much more than make the moment awkward for him.

And so he said yes.

Schellenberg stood directly behind him. "For three weeks and more, at the Villa Cascais," he said, "as I'm sure you're aware, my agent Estrade played the role of private secretary to the Duchess of Windsor."

von Ribbentrop pressed the small of his back in hard against the chair before he spoke. "A most extraordinary coup. I congratulate you. But yes; I knew of it already."

Schellenberg then said, "During all that time, Estrade had access to the Duchess of Windsor's wardrobe, her luggage, even to her handbag. . ."

von Ribbentrop felt as though he might faint.

"I would like to show you something, Excellency," Schellenberg said, and went around behind his desk, taking a single sheet of paper which he withheld for the briefest moment before he passed it across for the Minister's perusal.

"I don't know what to make of this," the voice of Fritzi Schaemmel drawled from Schellenberg's lips. "And I thought—I don't know why—you might be able to help me unravel it.. . .So this is my bargain, Excellency. I will show you this, if you will tell me what it means."

von Ribbentrop stared.

"It was removed from the Villa by my friend Estrade. . ." Schaemmel said. "She attaches much importance to it, and I wondered perhaps. . .do you?"

Slowly—very slowly—von Ribbentrop turned the sheet of paper in his fingers and watched it as it slowly—very slowly—exploded in his face.

On it, written in the Duchess of Windsor's schoolgirl hand, was a single word:

PENELOPE.

And underneath it, she had drawn—though crudely, as if only absent-mindedly—the image of an eagle surmounting the globe. Which was, of course, von Ribbentrop's personal insignia. But; "no," he said. "No. This means nothing."

On the street level, von Ribbentrop hurried to find a washroom. He entered, inspected the cabinets for any indication he might not be alone, and then went into one of them, locked the door, took off his hat, bent over the toilet and threw up his lunch and his breakfast.

In the half hour that followed, he threw up twice more and took some pills to counter his anxiety. Sitting there, with his trousers down around his knees and his feet drawn back so his shoes and spats might not be recognized, von

Ribbentrop considered the possibilities of how much Schellenberg knew.

If the cabal had been exposed, then everything was lost. The pact they had made with the future would be null and void—and that was unthinkable. *Unthinkable.*

Hess must be warned at once. And then the others. But not the cabal's upper echelons just yet. Not yet—and—pray God—never. They had chosen von Ribbentrop to orchestrate *Penelope* and if he had blundered—they would cut him off. Before Rudolf Hess could be faced, however, there was one other contact von Ribbentrop must make. Dangerous, but mandatory. He must speak with Air Vice-Marshal Sir Alan Paisley, the only man who could tell him how the British had come to know of the German kidnap plot—and from this man he must discover whether there was even the slightest chance that *Penelope's* role in that plot had come to light in England.

Retreating into the inner sanctum of his private office at the Eden Hotel, von Ribbentrop placed his call. The trunk lines led from Germany through Luxembourg and France into Switzerland—and from Switzerland to London. The call was scrambled.

Though brief, the conversation revealed far too many hints of danger. To make matters worse, Paisley was forced to be maddeningly terse and not a little ambiguous. "Winston, across the hall you see. Why in hell did you call me here? Do make it short." von Ribbentrop asked about how the British had been tipped to the Windsor kidnap and was told: "can't say in detail. Simply don't know, you see. 'cepting this—seems the original word came through to Buster in Madrid. Got that?"

"Yes." Madrid.

"And it was Buster passed it on to Teddy in Lisbon. Got that?"

"Yes." Lisbon.

"Teddy got it up to MI-6 and that's really all I can say. 'cept. . ."

"Yes?"

"Well. Seems if you go back to Buster in Madrid, St. Teresa says. . .got that?"

"Yes." St. Teresa was the Duke of Avila.

"St. Teresa thinks Buster heard it from a woman. An' that's all I know, you see. Sorry."

von Ribbentrop then asked whether or not the Duke and Duchess of Windsor had in fact been kidnapped by the men from B.M.I.—and what sort of state the Duke was in. What did it mean that he had been shot?

"*Shot*, you say?"

"That's right. Shot in the face by one of *your* men."

"No. No. Not shot. Bleeding fool walked straight through a mirror. Gashed himself terribly. Lost a whole world of blood, but he's alive. Just walked straight through a mirror. Bloody fool."

"But I'm told there was a gunshot."

"Yes. There was. One of our men. Dreadful fright it gave him. Thought he'd killed the Duke."

"And were they kidnapped?" von Ribbentrop said.

"Well—put it this way, you see. They have been *persuaded*."

And the line went dead.

In Berlin Rudolf Hess, who was Hitler's Deputy, was behaving badly.

von Ribbentrop hadn't dared do more than indicate the barest bones of what had taken place at the Villa Cascais and what it might be that Schellenberg knew. Hess was all too easily frightened; the greatest care must always be taken not to alarm him. He was the kind of man who would jump from his window if someone shouted fire in the building next door. Nonetheless, the Deputy Führer must be cautioned. The fact was, betrayal might come at any moment and the only way to handle it was to be prepared. The word *Penelope* scribbled on that sheet of paper "crested" with von Ribbentrop's personal symbol of the eagle and the globe could be explained away, perhaps. But only if everyone told the same story. Only if everyone treated it as a joke. And Hess had never told a joke in his life. Or laughed at one.

Consequently, von Ribbentrop would withhold all news of the piece of paper from the Führer's Deputy. The rest.

unfortunately, must be told. But the word, the word. It haunted him. What could the Duchess have been thinking of—writing it there on that piece of paper?

And wouldn't it be the supreme irony if, when that knock on the door were to come in the middle of the night—as von Ribbentrop had so often imagined—the man on the other side were to be Walter Schellenberg, the pride of Himmler's hyenas? Grinning, no doubt. "Ah, yes," Schellenberg would say, "that *word* you were so worried about, Excellency. I think I have tracked its meaning down." And the axe would fall.

But it mustn't. And it wouldn't. Not if von Ribbentrop could pull himself together and act so decisively everyone would be stopped in the tracks. And first he had to discover who it was in Madrid who had passed on the word to the British agent. A woman.

Hess was stony afraid and deathly still when he received the news the Windsors had been whisked away from Europe. He stood at attention, just like a man receiving the penalty of death. He had been outside in his garden when von Ribbentrop arrived. His son, his only child, was playing there still and the sound of laughter came in through the open windows.

von Ribbentrop skipped the bloodier details regarding the Duke of Windsor and his injuries. He forced himself to sit down. He looked away when he said that Schellenberg was poking around and that Hess was not to be alarmed. But Hess was not taken in. von Ribbentrop could see this in his eyes. He knew immediately Hess had gone to the depths of panic, just as he himself had gone to the depths when the news had first sunk in. They were both so afraid of Hitler. They remembered all too well the Night of the Long Knives. And Schellenberg was too ambitious to retreat from his pursuit, if he could prove there was any hint of a conspiracy.

Hitler's vengeance had grown more awesome than Caligula's. His enemies were now strangled with piano wire, which separated their heads more slowly from their necks. Other victims were suspended from meat hooks while they died. And there were deaths far worse than these. . . .

"And what are we to do?" said Hess.

"Jump faster," said von Ribbentrop, regretting the analogy the minute he'd uttered it.

Hess gave his well-known hangdog look, with the eyebrows almost obscuring the eyes. "Jump where?" he asked.

"Forward," said von Ribbentrop. "Forward—faster—more decisively. And with greater calm than ever."

"Calm. . . ." The word had no meaning for Hess.

von Ribbentrop watched him carefully.

Hess was looking into the garden. A child's voice rose and fell. And a woman's voice, after it.

von Ribbentrop had not been chosen to play his important role in the cabal for the simple reason of his high office alone. Or for his name—or for his charm. He had been chosen because he was a craftsman in a field that was thought of more as an art than a craft. Diplomats must, of course, be prone to inspiration as artists are—and daring enough to rely on it from time to time. But most of von Ribbentrop's work was performed with the same honed skill of the practised craftsman who must eschew inspiration altogether for nine-tenths of his professional life. There is too much at stake from moment to moment to sit back and give a mere "performance".

Such a moment had now arrived with Hess. If only the upper echelons of *Penelope* could have been persuaded to minimize Rudolf Hess's role, von Ribbentrop's job would have been made a good deal easier. But the upper echelon had made its decision and von Ribbentrop must abide by it. So he leapt in now with all the skills at his command to pull Hess back from the edge of his paranoiac despair.

He did this by bolstering Hess's confidence in the larger schemes and the wider activities of the cabal. He told of what great successes were being achieved abroad. And at the end of it all, he came around through the word "success" to the child and the woman in Rudolf Hess's garden.

Pointing through the window at Hess's laughing son and wife, he said, "And what greater hope for all our futures could there be than our desire for the success of everything we do in behalf of the new generations?"

Hess was very moved by this.

"We mustn't give up," Hess said. "We mustn't."

Hess turned. His hands shook.

"Hitler must be killed," he said. "He must. And we must do it. . . ."

"We will."

"But when?"

"When it's time. When all our men and women are in place."

"You always sound so calm," said Hess.

von Ribbentrop smiled. If he was calm, he did not know it.

Hess said, "When I was afraid in the old days as a child, I would say to my mother 'will the hammer fall?'"—whatever the hammer was—an illness or whatever. . .and just like you she would say to me: 'I doubt it'. It used to give me such reassurance. And it meant she never had to lie to me."

"And I won't lie to you either," said von Ribbentrop. "Never."

Liar.

"I believe you," said Hess.

But he didn't.

von Ribbentrop rode away in his chauffeured Mercedes, clutching his walking stick between his knees, putting his homburg over it and looking at it as if it were a severed head. His own.

A woman in Madrid. It would drive him mad. And the Duke and Duchess of Windsor riding away from him aboard the S.S. *Excalibur*. Where would it take them first? he wondered. The Azores? And then Bermuda? He tried to draw an imaginary line between the coast of Portugal and the Bahamas. Yes. The Azores and then Bermuda. Such a long, long way away.

Excalibur: August, 1940

On the ship, *Excalibur*, the Duke went into a decline. He seemed in constant need of something or someone to hold him upright. He began to walk with his shoulder or elbow pressed against the walls of the corridors. He developed a phobia for edges and if Wallis (or anyone, for that matter) started across the decks in the direction of the railings, he would whisper: *"stop!"* He sat with his mouth shut tight, jaws clenched and his throat constricted, not even able to swallow his saliva. His eyes were in constant motion, darting everywhere like two blue fish that were trapped in his head, coming back and back to the same two holes to peer through the glass—alarmed and wary, least some hand or hook or claw break through and pluck them out.

His favourite place was the corner of his private salon, where he could sit with each of his shoulders touching a separate metal plate while the ship made a purring noise that hummed up through the hull and seemed to give him comfort. If anyone came too close, he would say; *"don't interrupt. . ."* Only Wallis was allowed to approach beyond the barrier he kept about his person, maintained at precisely the reach of an outstretched arm and gauged according to the knowledge that a snake can only strike the distance of its own length.

Part of the barrier the Duke maintained was the "mask" he wore of bandages. Sir Alan Paisley had been quite right. The Duke had "walked through a mirror" at the Villa Cascais. He had not only walked through a mirror, he had fallen on top of all its glass. A Portuguese doctor was rushed to the Villa as soon as it was known what had actually taken place in the Martello Tower. He was paid a gross amount of money—some of it supplied by the Duke's Spanish host—to treat the wounds and was paid even more to keep his mouth shut regarding the whole affair.

The wounds were more or less superficial but had required some stitching. They had bled profusely as all wounds do where the face is involved and the veins are close to the surface. Even when fully healed they would leave a tracery of scars the Duke would have for the rest of his life. The palms of his hands, a place on his neck and the leading edge of his left thigh had also been gashed, though it was only the thigh that required closing. The doctor had provided a regimen of dressings, ointments and surgical powders and had said; "sea air will do the rest. The salt is excellent for wounds, though His Royal Highness must avoid the sun."

Day by day the dressings were less and less painful and the subsequent bandages were little more than double layers of folded gauze. Before the voyage was over they were dispensed with altogether. Excepting, of course, the bandages on the thigh and the palms of the hands. Anyone the Duke was forced into contact with was told there had been an accident involving an automobile and that nothing was being said because, until the Windsors arrived in the Bahamas, nothing was being said about their whereabouts or even their existence.

The Royal suite was one of two on the uppermost deck. It consisted, besides the salon, of separate staterooms and bathrooms for the Duke and Duchess and a cabin for Major Gerrard. Across the passageway, the former American Ambassador to France, Anthony Biddle, and his wife had a suite of equal size though not of equal opulence, the chintz being faded and the carpets worn. Together, the Windsors and the Biddles commandeered an entire rear section of the deck. The Biddles had lifted a brace of potted palms from their hotel in Lisbon and these, together with an awning, provided cover from prying eyes whenever the Windsors dared the daylight—and provided "comfort and convenience" for the Biddles' harlequin Great Dane.

The Duchess played her gramophone. She was preoccupied with paranoic thoughts concerning Major Gerrard. Major Gerrard never gave them a moment's privacy once they stepped outside their suite. If the Duchess so much as crossed the passageway to borrow a magazine, Major Gerrard was there in his doorway watching her. If she wanted a breath of air at night she noted the burning eye of his cigarette in the dark. Every move she made was monitored. Of course, she realized it was his job to guarantee their safety. On the other hand, who could guarantee their safety from him? Hadn't they been warned: *"Beware of British friends?"* How did she know, for instance, the Duke had not been pushed through the mirror? And Gerrard firing his gun. . . .It alarmed her. Who was he firing at? She was also dreadfully afraid at having lost all touch with von Ribbentrop. The last real contact she'd had had been a month ago in Spain. After which—not a word.

The Duke, meanwhile, played "doctor" to himself. He fiddled endlessly with his bandages and scabs. He also began to tipple. Scotch as well as the ever-present Madeira. Wallis at first put the drinking down to fear and frustration. So much had happened: all of it so alarming. Anyone would take to drink for a while just to survive the shock, let alone being caged in the prison of this ship. She even began to drink a little more herself, mostly martinis. But she couldn't get drunk. Not even drowsy. The Duke, on the other hand, was increasingly prone to staring at space through the smoke of his endless chain of cigarettes and cigars with the glass set out before him like a buoy in the fog; ringing its edge with his fingernail: tap-tap-tapping—always out of sync with the rhythm of her music.

> *Frankie and Johnny were lovers,*
> *Oh Lordy, how they could love!*
> *They swore to be true to each other,*
> *True as the stars above. . .*

One day she tried to look directly into his eyes. But they were spooked and fled.

"David. . .?"

Nothing.

"David, please. I can't stand this any more. I can't do this any more. I'm worn down. Lost. I don't know where you are. It isn't fair. We have to get each other through this—whatever this is. So please. . .Either come out here and join me—or at least let me in so I can hide with you. Please."

"Don't interrupt."

"God damn it!" she shouted at him—and stood up so

quickly her chair fell over. "Come out! Come out of there! Stand up! STAND UP. Don't you remember who you are!"

The little blue fish came round towards her and settled, suddenly calm, suddenly still.

"*Was,*" he said.

"Oh no," she said, her voice lowered, deadly. "Oh no you don't. You can't get away with that with me. Never. I won't let you." She stood right in front of him. "You are, and you will always be, the King."

The fish went into hiding again. The blinds were drawn. He wept.

Wallis spoke quite calmly now. She didn't even tremble. "Cry all you want," she said. "Nothing will be changed. You don't understand," she said. "You have never understood. *I have a job to do.*" She looked at him, frozen; wishing she could freeze him, too.

She turned around and picked up the chair and set it carefully, deliberately, precisely back in place: just as if there had been stage marks to set it on.

"And just in case it might have slipped your mind what that job might be—it is to keep you alive. You—the King, David. You—who can still be anything. And will be." She turned away from him just so as not to see the tears. They alarmed her, because they made her so angry. "I have the advantage over you, David," she said. "Because what I want is something I've never had. And wanting something you've never had makes all the difference in the world."

"Does it?"

"*Yes.*"

"You think I've never wanted something I couldn't have? Just because I was King?"

"You've done pretty well," she said. "Just because you were King."

"Have I?"

"*Yes.*"

He put more whisky into his glass and stared at it for a moment before he spoke again. "I wanted you," he said.

"Yes. And you got me, too."

There wasn't any reply to this; so she turned around and looked at him.

He was staring at her; ice at last.

"Did I?" he said.

But even this didn't hurt her. In fact, she smiled. "Good," she said. "Very good, David. Excellent." She made sure the smile was fixed before she spoke again. "You're learning."

When the S.S. *Excalibur* put into port in the Azores, there was a ban on going ashore. The Duke would not have gone at any rate. He was hiding in his cabin, sitting in his corner. But Wallis went out on deck and stood underneath the awning with Anthony and Margaret Biddle and watched the new passengers coming on board and the stevedores loading crates of oranges and wine.

"Look down there," Margaret Biddle said. "There—over there. Isn't that someone we know?"

Wallis and Anthony Biddle looked.

"Down where?"

"Over there, by those enormous packing cases. The thin young man in the alpaca suit."

Wallis looked.

The thin young man was directing the loading of four wooden crates, two of which were twenty feet long and one of which was almost forty feet long.

"What on earth do you think they can be?"

"I don't know. But whatever they are, he wants them treated like glass."

"And you think we know him?"

"Well, I don't quite remember. . .but he *is* familiar. Don't you think?"

"Maybe he's a movie star," said Wallis.

"He could be. Certainly handsome enough."

Anthony Biddle suddenly said, "It's an aeroplane."

"An *aeroplane*? In boxes?" His wife was incredulous.

"Yes. You see there?"

"Oh yes. . .The propeller."

The propeller was not in any kind of wrapping. And it looked as if the young man might be going to bring it onto the ship himself.

" 'tisn't Lindbergh, is it?" said Margaret Biddle.

"No," said Wallis. "I know him very well—and he's much, much taller than that."

"You've met him, Peggy," Anthony Biddle said. "How can you possibly think that's Lindbergh?"

"Well. . .the aeroplane."

Wallis laughed.

Then Anthony Biddle said; "look. You can see the name of the 'plane on the crate just coming up."

All three leaned out towards the swaying box.

ICARUS, it said.

"*Icarus*," said Wallis. "What a strange, strange name to give an aeroplane. I mean—didn't Icarus fall?"

"That right. He flew too close to the sun."

Wallis looked at the thin young man.

"He's very handsome. Very. I wonder who he is."

"We can ask the Purser."

"Yes. And maybe—" said Wallis, grinning "—maybe we can get him to sit at our table."

But he could not be made to sit at anybody's table. All his meals were taken privately in his stateroom. The excuse he made was simple enough. He was a writer, and he had a book to finish.

His name was Lorenzo de Broca.

Wallis had now tried every ruse in the book to extricate her husband from the depths into which his accident and his exile had thrown him: all but one.

One mid-Atlantic afternoon, there was a storm and Wallis said to the Duke; "do come and bundle up with me. We can keep each other warm."

Surprisingly—though perhaps because of the drink—he was meek as a child. She was even able to lead him by the fingertips.

Outside the waves began to pile up over the prow of the ship and the sky turned a kind of tropical green and the water black. The air was filled with a howling noise and the plates of the hull gave off a cracking sound, as if *Excalibur* might break apart in long curved strips of steel and sink into the sea.

Wallis removed her dress and her underclothes and her dark silk stockings and climbed beneath the sheets and blanket wearing only her slip. The Duke stood watching her, his sea legs splayed to hold him up, his cigarette in one hand, glass of Madeira in the other; and all the time she was undressing he was "undressing" too. But all he removed was his bandages, dropping them down into a brown paper bag, one of the many brown paper bags thrown every evening after dark into the wake of the ship. Once his wife was in and safely out of sight, he climbed in after her, as one who climbs aboard a lifeboat terrified of drowning, but claiming he is calm.

For a moment, once the Duke was in his place against the hull, they were silent. Wallis was the first to speak. "All right?" she whispered. He nodded. "Now?" she whispered. "Yes." "Good"—and she reached out sideways and pulled a photograph there beside her closer over the top of the table. "Now," she said, and turned to the Duke, "it's your turn."

The Duke of Windsor—rising to an elbow—reached across his wife for the photograph and made the last adjustment. Then he lay back and sighed.

"Is she watching?" Wallis whispered.

"Yes."

"Can she see us both?"

"Indeed."

"Good." Wallis smiled. "Then—shall we?"

"Yes."

The photograph was the one that Wallis always kept by her bed, no matter where they were. It rested on a velvet mat, with purple facings, and it showed Her Majesty Queen Mary, the Duke of Windsor's mother, dressed in mourning. And what is more, she could not close her eyes or turn away as her son and his wife began their ritual.

In the aftermath of their battle on the bed, the Duke of Windsor slept. Drugged with pain and alcohol and perspiring profusely as one who is ill with a rare, incomprehensible disease, he began to dream. Darkness fell. The storm broke. It rained.

. . .the lights went out. . .

. . .the Duke heard whispers. . ."*tenho medo. . .da escuridão. . .espalhar-se. . .*"

Three people—four perhaps—fumbled their way down the stairs against the opposite bannister and, while they passed, the Duke of Windsor paused. Slowly the whispering faded round the corners and was gone.

He was alone.

The dream and the event were melded into one, except that in the dream the darkness widened out in all directions. Everytime he dreamt, the dream was edgeless and the bottom of the stairs on which he sat could not be seen or imagined. Perhaps there was no bottom. Maybe there was nothing there but a drop into space. Sometimes in the dream there was a sudden tilting of the stairs and the Duke was forced to cling to the railings, fighting gravity and dizziness in order not to fall. And he would hang there with his eyes closed, sometimes it seemed for hours, until the stairs were righted again and he could breathe.

It had not seemed real when it happened: now, as he dreamt, it was real as knives.

He was alone.

Wallis was somewhere, lost in the house. Soldiers had broken in from the sea and told him there was a kidnap plot. Now there were voices crying "*assassino!*" It would never end.

But here he was alone in the dark and none of them knew where he was. None of them could find him and, if he wanted to, he could take this moment to disappear completely.

That would show them, he thought. If I disappeared. And sent them a letter from the moon, saying *here I am! Look up!*

He laughed.

But, at once, he clapped his hand across his mouth, lest he be heard. Overheard.

If only I could laugh out loud, he thought.

Do anything out loud.
Fart out loud.
Be me out loud.
Be me.

But no. It's not allowed, aloud. If you cross the will of the world, it takes away your crown. And throws it in your face. It would serve them right if I was lost forever. Sitting there all smug and telling me I can't have the woman I love to be my wife. And me the King. How dare they? But they did.

And what if I did disappear? There'd be no one then to tell me what to do; what not to do; no one to tell me who I am and who I'm not. I'd be on the moon, and they couldn't get at me at all. Not even Wallis. . . .

That was when he decided to go to his secret place and hide.

His secret place was the Martello Tower, which Doctor Ricardo used as a storage space for old trunks and boxes, furniture and paintings, no longer wanted but too good to throw away. The Duke had discovered the Tower early on in their stay, when he'd opened a door and there it was: an old musty room with a high-raftered ceiling and dirty stone walls. It had caught his imagination at once and he used it, rather the way he had used Fort Belvedere when he was King, as a place to retire into and take off the face. He had not even told the Duchess of its existence.

It was a boy's place—perfect as Fort Belvedere had been: a place to go and bolt the door and do forbidden things and dream. A place to drink that extra bottle of Madeira, smoke those especially thick cigars and refuse to regret the past as everyone expected him to do. The joy of Fort Belvedere had been its gardens and its walls. Here in the Martello Tower, the joy was in his dreams.

He found it, now, without much trouble: falling forward down the blackened hall to the very end and feeling along the wall until the iron ring that served as a handle struck his wedding band. Turning it very slowly, fearing it would yelp and give him away, he raised the latch and let himself in through the little door that always made him think he was playing *Alice in the Looking Glass* the way he had done with his sister and his brothers hundreds of years ago at Sandringham, thousands of years ago at Balmoral, a million years ago at Windsor.

Once inside, and the door safely closed behind him, he fumbled for his lighter, struck it with his thumb and made his way up the steps to the table in the centre. On the table there was a candelabra in which he had set three fresh candles that afternoon. Behind him on the wall there was a sconce with two more. Having lighted all five, he flicked the lighter closed and into his pocket and marched to the trunk where he kept his supply of wines.

"I'll show them," he said, more or less aloud. "This ought to give them all a good scare. Barging in here with their tales of kidnap and mayhem. Assassins. And my friend de Estella. How dare they?"

And he poured himself a very large glass of port.

Seated at the table, smoking—dreaming—he gazed heavy-lidded past the candle flames at the room with its great stone walls and its piles of ornate picture frames and its stacks of paintings and tall Baroque mirrors leaning back against the stands which barely supported them. A worn-out—exhausted—tapestry had long ago been suspended between the table and the door, presumably to keep the draught from blowing out the lights in another age. The tapestry itself was a threadbare map of the ancient world with all its names in Latin and all its insignia meaningless now, its great gold crests, its crowns and coats of arms almost effaced by time and its seas eaten through by moths, its continents plundered by worms and mildew.

The Duke of Windsor took wry note of the presentations of himself depicted in the mirrors. There were three of him— tricked out in light and shadow—each one completely at odds with the others: something, he supposed, to do with the way each glass was set and the way each glass received the candlelight and threw it back.

In the furthest mirror he saw the Prince of Wales—with all his golden features intact and not a single line on his face. In the middle glass he saw himself precisely as he was: the very man who sat and stared with forty-six years of lines and pouches marking his eyes and mouth—though still some traces of the golden lad could be seen. But in the third mirror the shadows fell wrong somehow, and all he could see was a hunched old man without a face. It made him cringe.

At once he was uncomfortably aware the images were staring back at him, could *see* him, so he took a good long pull at the drink and settled the glass very quietly in front of him before he dared raise his eyes again. When he did, what he saw was his own apparently severed hands with their perfect fingernails and curious knuckles and yellow tobacco stains laid out before him. And he thought of everything they had touched and held and dallied with, and of everything they had willingly—unwillingly—relinquished. Wilfully sometimes; sometimes letting go completely unaware. *Sad*, he thought. *I have sad hands.*

"No don't. You mustn't weep," said the Prince of Wales from the furthest mirror. "No weeping allowed."

"He's right," said the King-Duke of Windsor in the centre of the triptych. "If you do they'll hear you somewhere. Then we'll all be sunk."

The huddled man—the faceless man—said nothing.

The Duke looked up at the Prince of Wales.

"I'm sorry," he said. "I haven't wept since I was a child."

"You forget," said the Prince of Wales. "How quickly you forget. . ."

The Duke took a drink of port and said: "forget what?"

"How afraid you were, when you were me," said the Prince of Wales.

"When I was you? But I am you."

"Oh no," said the Prince of Wales. "Ask anyone. They'll say you gave me up a long time ago."

"When? Why?"

"I can't really say precisely when—but I felt you letting go sometime around the ending of the War. You were having such a good time. And you'd learned not to cringe any more and how to stand on your own two feet and all my uses had become passé. Excepting, of course, my face. And my insignia. Clever you. How you learned to trade on what I was! How you learned—in my name—how to get what you wanted! *Everything!*"

"But I worked for you," said the Duke. "I worked so hard for you."

"Yes. That's true," said the Prince. "And I admit I profited, to some degree. I grew in stature, I suppose. The world came running: that I know. But the truth is, you kept most of the spoils. *You* had all the fun—and I was left to moulder."

"Moulder? What a dreadful word."

"Of course it's a dreadful word. But it's apt. I mouldered. I crumbled. Our father hated you. But it was me that paid. It was me that was curtailed, while you went off and had a good time at the Fort."

"But. . ."

"No. Don't interrupt," said the Prince. "I'm telling you the truth. The fact is, that was when we lost the throne. Because you destroyed my credibility. If ever I needed anything after that, I found it increasingly difficult, if not impossible, to get it. Everything you inherited when you inherited me, you spent. On yourself. And when the moment came for me to assert myself—not you, but *me*—they said; well you can't be trusted any more. Imagine! And our father, lying on his death-bed, saying; *do not let the Crown fall into David's hands*. . .When the Crown is what I had been born for, raised for and had suffered for, you destroyed every vestige of chance it would be mine. And when the moment came, and *you* needed *me*, and you said; *I want the Crown— and Wallis too*, I didn't even have a voice any longer. I was just a thing in the cupboard, hung up on a nail and taken out for parties whenever you thought it would be fun to play."

"I'm sorry."

"Yes. But the trouble is it's you, not me, you're sorry for," said the Prince of Wales. "You hated me—and you hated being me. And you got away from me as fast as you could. And when you left, you absconded with all that was mine, including the Crown. And you gave that to Bertie. As if he wanted it!"

"I know. He didn't want it at all. . . ."

"But I did. And—look what you've done. When I think of what we had," said the Prince of Wales. "And how it ended. . ."

"We have Wallis," said the Duke, with a note of hopefulness.

"You have Wallis," said the Prince of Wales.

"I'm sorry," said the Duke.

"You've said that," said the Prince of Wales.

"But I am!"

"Prove it."

"How can I?"

"Get back the Crown."

"But I don't want the Crown!"

The Duke of Windsor staggered to his feet, knocking over the glass of port as he veered around the end of the table towards the Prince of Wales. And the Prince of Wales loomed up, huge, before him, all his features distorted and ugly.

"Be quiet," said the old, old man, whose face could not be seen. "You'll give us all away. . . ."

"And you," said the Duke of Windsor, turning on the old, old man. "I don't even know who you are."

"You will," said the old, old man. "You will."

The Duke of Windsor became sarcastic, as he so often did when drunk, and he said, "Who are you, then? *The Ghost of Christmas Yet-to-Come?*"

"Come here," said the old, old man. "I want you to see me as I really am."

The Duke of Windsor righted his glass and filled it again with plum-coloured port. He picked up the candelabra then and approached the shrouded figure in the mirror.

"Put away the candles," said the old, old man. "Put them away. Come closer."

The Duke of Windsor did as he was told and set the candelabra behind him on the table. He walked up closer then to the old, old man.

The old, old man was wearing evening dress—very like the Duke's, but darker: dustier and without the rich, thick sheen of the Duke's lapels. It was a suit of clothes as old, it seemed, as the tapestry across the room. The Duke's first impression that the old, old man was faceless had not been quite correct, for looking at him now more closely, the Duke could see there was a nose, a shadowed brow and the merest hint of two black holes where the eyes should be. These holes contained, like wells, the watery reflections of wavering light. And all around the old man's head there was a blaze of glassy fire.

The Duke stood looking in at the old, old man and after a moment they each took a mouthful of port and savoured it before they swallowed.

"Well," said the Duke at last. "Here I am. What is it you want?"

"You," said the old, old man. "You. Because without you I will die."

"Should I care if you die," said the Duke of Windsor, "not even knowing who you are?"

"Look again," said the old, old man. "Is there nothing here you recognize?"

The Duke leaned closer, scanning whatever features he could see, but recognizing nothing. "No," he said. "Nothing."

"Now bring round the lights and look again," said the figure in the mirror, "and you will understand what it is I want of you. Bring them round and look again."

The Duke of Windsor turned and lifted up the candelabra, holding it out arm's length before him and turning yet again to confront the old, old man.

But the old, old man had been transformed.

Before the Duke of Windsor stood a glittering image quite unlike any image he had ever seen before. And yet it was himself he saw. It was himself undoubtedly, in beyond the shimmering candle flames—each flame crowned with its own corona and each corona with its own reflection, and all the reflections surrounding his own reflection floating in the dark beyond the shining surface of the glass. . . .

"Blow out the lights," said the old, old man, "and I will tell you who I am."

But the Duke of Windsor was transfixed. And the old man

smiled because he knew what it was to be transfixed by light. "Blow out the lights and I will tell you who I am," he said.

The Duke of Windsor blew out the candles, one by one.

Before him stood the old, old man, faceless and shabby and worn, as before, with his eyes like wells on a starless night.

"You told me you would tell me who you are," said the Duke of Windsor. "You said you would tell me your name. . ."

"I am. . ." said the old, old man whose voice was already winding down.

"Oh please don't fade away," said the Duke of Windsor. "You said you would tell me your name."

"My name," said the old, old man, ". . .my name is splendour." But his voice was dying inside the glass.

"Vai ele!" another voice shouted. "Vai ele! Vai ele!"

The Duke of Windsor was leaning back against the table. "O assassino!"

Whose voice was that? Where was he now?

He took the lighter from his pocket, fumbling with it, failing to make it work. Out in the hall, there was a lot of shouting now and even the sound of breaking windows.

At last he was able to strike a light and flame the candles. Beyond the door he could hear the soldiers running, knowing it must be the soldiers because of the sound of their boots.

"Help," he said, very quietly at first. "Help."

And then he heard the sound of rifle butts crashing against the door.

"Help!" he said. "Help. . ." Turning from side to side, confused by all the noise, confused by all the wine and brandy he had drunk, confused by all the light and cries everywhere of help and vai ele and o assassino. And he seemed to be surrounded by dozens of figures flickering on and off in the candle-light and the candle-light falling, apparently, sideways as he himself turned this way and that.

And then the door gave way—flew open—and someone shouted at him: There! And the tapestry exploded.

The Duke of Windsor next saw a man—it was Major Gerrard—waving a gun in the air; and Major Gerrard saw the Duke of Windsor and what appeared to be a dozen others surrounding him. The major, assuming one of the dozen must be the assassin, shouted one word: "run!" at the Duke and opened fire.

The Duke of Windsor threw his arms in the air, shouting; "Where? Where? Where do I run?" And he saw some other men come through the door and up the steps and past the tapestry—so he reached out towards them thinking they must have come to save him, and he ran. . .

To their reflection. And his own. Straight through the mirror that only moments before had borne the image of splendour.

And the air was shattered by a thousand brilliant flames and all he could hear was the sound of running water and the stones began to stream with blood.

Then darkness. Silence. And Wallis. With her arms out.
"Wake up."
Where?
"Wake up."
Where?
He woke.
Excalibur heaved.

For a moment, the Duke thought maybe they were sinking. But then he saw his mother watching him, sitting in her silver frame beside the bed. And she was so serene and calm, there was no possibility the ship would sink. None whatsoever.

Wallis said; "you were having your dream again."
"Yes."
Is it over?

* * *

Far off down in the valley, something howled. A dog perhaps. There could be no wolves in Europe anymore. But at home, Quinn thought; it would be a wolf that howled. Or a pack of wolves. One pack would sing and another pack would answer in the distance. Quinn had heard them all through his childhood summers in Vermont, singing down the whole of the Appalachian chain: and he used to try to calculate how long it would take their message to reach from Canada to West Virginia. *I am here*, they would sing. *Are you there?* And their songs had raised the hackles on his neck and even the tiny hairs on the backs of his hands. But this dog under Balkonberg was singing alone. No other dog replied.

Quinn went across the room and drew the shutters closed. But the dog could still be heard.

Quinn lit his candles and set his lamp on the packing crate beside his cot and the writing danced across the walls and Quinn's own shadow spread out over the words and he thought there must have been times when Mauberley lived on Montrechat and brandy, and surely he must have been so drunk he could hardly see and the words must have poured from his brain unedited. They had just come out, the way that howl was coming now from the dog down the mountain.

Quinn rolled off his gloves and lit a cigarette and poured himself a glass of wine. He looked at his watch—it was three a.m.

The poor old dog would die, he thought, and he tried very hard not to hear. If only someone down in the town would let it in. There were soldiers billeted there and some of the civilians had returned. The dog was making such a dreadful sound. Dear God, what a racket it made.

Quinn wondered if Freyberg heard it. Or was he sound asleep across the hall? And, if sound asleep, would his dreams incorporate the dog? If they did, Quinn thought; the dog would have more cause to be afraid than it had down there in the valley.

Dreams.

They were all so violent; bloody; fouled with the mess the war had made of everyone's mind. Nobody dreamt of being alive any more. One dream only he could remember had begun with being alive: a dream in which he lay with his face pressed close against the naked breasts of a girl who was not much older than a child. But she was dead and the beauty of her breasts was thwarted just as they had begun to bud: and as the dream expanded, Quinn had discovered he was lying fully clothed on a bed of corpses whose arms were wound around his back to hold him fast.

And on the wall the dreamer lay bandaged and terrified, huddled under his blankets: lost at sea.

'You were having your dream again.'

'Yes.'

Is it over?

No.

The splendour faded here: faded as surely as the voices of the valley's dogs had dwindled down to one.

Quinn turned and looked at the flickering walls and shook his head. How right it was and wonderful that Mauberley should have his king confront himself in a dream. The kings in Shakespeare did the same. They always met themselves in dreams—as ghosts.

He listened for the dog.

It was silent now—and must be dead.

Quinn sat on his cot and drank the last of his wine. And then it struck him very hard: the dog was silent now. And his only thought had been; it must be dead. And he wondered where that part of him had gone that once presumed when a dog fell silent, it could only be because some door had opened and the dog had gone inside to sleep.

Quinn then got up and closed all the doors around him and slept without blowing out the lamp.

In the morning, when he woke, he drove himself from the bed at once and began to read, at first not even recognizing the words, but only using them to kill whatever dreams he'd had.

*　　*　　*

Italy: August 1940

All through August, I waited to hear from Isabella but nothing was forthcoming. Of course I was mystified—and it made me very unhappy to think she had felt she could not trust me enough to have told me where she was going. On the other hand, she had disappeared before and the messages had been the same: her servants did not know where she was; or they knew, but their instructions had been to say she was incommunicado. I did what I had always done. I telephoned. I cabled. I wrote. I debated making the journey to Venice. I made arrangements to go. I got on the train. I got off. I cancelled the arrangements. I waited.

All this time, I was at Rapallo with Ezra and Dorothy. Ezra was putting Dorothy through hell, but she was stoic and silent and laid out her tea cups and gave a very good performance of the wife who trusts her husband. "Isn't it wonderful Ezra and Olga Rudge get on so well together: so much to talk about: so many interests in common. And the thing I like most is the fact Olga Rudge lives so close by and if I really need Ezra, all I have to do is get the boy to run up the hill and bring him back." She would then—as she offered rose hip tea, or camomile—assure me that Olga Rudge was her own best friend and that was "nice, too, don't you think? The three of us together. . ."

I spent much time alone with Dorothy that August and September.

It was during this time we received the stunning news of Trotsky's death in Mexico. Plastered all over the front pages of the papers—laid out amongst the cups of camomile tea—there were pictures of the great man lying bloodied on a table.

I was both fascinated and horrified. Trotsky may have been the enemy, but still there was something scandalous about a front page photograph of someone—anyone—dying. But this was the age into which we were moving. There were photographs of death on every hand; though most of the deaths were anonymous and somehow failed to reach you with quite the jolt of Trotsky lying on his table. He looked so helpless, lying there, the whole world party to his agony and the agony of his wife, who was shown beside him. She hovered—solicitous—begging, it seemed, our forgiveness that her husband bled so profusely. And, though she tried, she could not hide the bloodied head from the freezing lights of the flashbulbs.

And the reportage was not much better. In Italy, of course, we were shown the death of Trotsky with a sense of triumph. As if *il Duce* himself had brought about the Bolshevist's death. Not that Tio Benito had appointed the assassin— heaven forbid! It was only that, without his great wisdom, the house of International Communism might never have been effectively divided against itself. "While we gain all our victories through unity," he said, "the Communists are breaking up their revolution from within." The assassin had been a "trusted friend"; the murder weapon—an alpine climber's pick—had been driven straight down through the cranium.

The news went on for days and we were made to believe that Trotsky had survived far longer than in fact he did. But this was only to keep the triumph alive. In truth he had only lasted for twenty-four hours. Nonetheless for one whole day he had been articulate, aware and desperate to dictate a manifesto which never saw the light of day. Whoever it was who was meant to be taking down his dying words, somehow managed to burn the notebook they were written in—by "mistake". His wife remained beside him right to the very end—even in the operating theatre (where photographers were also allowed) and then—at last—he suffered a final convulsion and death.

And when Ezra finally came down the hill, he said it was a fitting death; "an alpine axe for one who climbed too high"—a phrase that pleased him so much he wrote it down. And Dorothy did a thing I had never thought she would. She scissored one of the photographs out of the papers and put it in a book beside her bed. This was a picture of Madam Trotsky, staring straight at the camera lens, cradling her husband's bleeding head. "Faith is for women," Dorothy said. "Men don't understand."

In mid-September, still not having heard from Isabella, I played the only card I had left and took the train to Stresa on the shores of Lago Maggiore. I had never been to the Loverso summer home and only knew of it as the setting for the murder of Isabella's husband and children in 1924. It was not a place to which she had ever returned, so far as I knew, but I thought that might be all the more reason for her to go there now to hide. For she must be 'in hiding'—there could be no other explanation for so long an absence and so long a silence. And I was certain it was Mussolini she was hiding from, and always had been: since it was Mussolini who had killed her husband. So I went to the one last place where I thought I might track her down—but all I found was an empty villa with a padlocked gate and a broken eagle mounted on a chipped stone ball surmounting one of the pillars, while on the other pillar there was a great stone wreath that encircled another ball—though the wreath was intact and even the smallest of its flowers had not been worn away by weather.

"Has the Baronessa been seen?" I asked the caretaker.

No.

"Is she expected? Has there been any news of her where-abouts?"

No.

"Might I see the grounds?"

No.

But I did walk around to the open-work fences that separated the gardens from the lake and I stood—with my legs shin-deep in the water—and I looked in through the bars and could see the courtyard where the murder had taken place. And I was rather thrown by what I saw. Because it was so ordinary. Here was the shrine of Isabella's regret and the source of all her passion: and all it was was a plain stone yard with a trellis overhead, supporting an unpruned vine that was running wild and covered with a myriad of rotting, forgotten grapes. And not a sign of any ghosts or of any defiance in the way it caught the light. It was just a plain and shabby terrace, shadowed and damp, with one broken window and a boarded-up door. And I knew then—how?— Isabella was not in hiding, but had escaped. From all of us. But I could not think why.

In October, I was summoned to Rome. In fact, a Mercedes came for me.

My summons had come from none other than Isabella's cousin, the Italian Foreign Minister, Count Galeazo Ciano: though it was not so grand a summons as it might have sounded. I was not to be alone in Ciano's presence—but was only one of five hundred foreign guests who were being treated to a Grand Reception at the Palazzo Venezia, on behalf of "maintaining good public relations with all our resident aliens in this, the mother city of the civilized world".

Our journey through the dark October night was lit by storms and the rain came down like pellets flung against the glass. Thunder, lightning and a great wild wind pursued us all the way from Viareggio, and I thought of Shelley's storm in which he had been drowned. And I wondered, too, if the driver meant to kill another poet—namely myself—he took such chances on the road and he seemed to be riding instead of driving the Mercedes. And, being a German, I thought perhaps he was a male Valkyrie and when I asked him why he had to drive so fast, he replied that his orders had been to get me to Rome without a moment's delay.

He was the most bad-tempered driver I had had in years and finally I got him to admit he hated Italy and would rather be anywhere but here. He was from Bad Godesberg and he missed the Rhine and he used a phrase to describe the world beyond that place where he was born that I have never been able to forget. He said all other places in the world were "ein anderland, nicht mein". And, after that, I forgave him his whirlwind driving and I settled back to sleep. "Another country not my own" is where I had been living ever since I left America.

The following morning, I presented my credentials at the Palazzo Venezia—Mussolini's monumental glorification of bad taste which housed his own offices and also the offices of several of his ministries—and I was finally admitted only after no less than three separate secretaries (each one of higher rank than the one before) had cross-checked my passport against a typewritten guest list. I was then propelled in the general direction of the sound of distant social chatter emanating from somewhere above me. Miles of corridor opened up before me, and thousands of mile-wide steps.

The reception was already in full swing. Going in, I was presented with three red roses—symbolic of the tri-partite Axis—and could see that each of the hundreds of guest had likewise been adorned. I attempted to melt into the crowd, but failed. There were faces I recognized everywhere in the mêlée—and one of the first of these was Julia Franklin. She could, it seemed, be found anywhere, in any company, waiting to sink her pen into the enemy. I hoisted my roses in her direction. She hoisted her fork in mine.

We were lunching in the new Imperial fashion, in which one stands to eat. The "room"—if such it could be called—was the size of a stadium, and was filled with what appeared to be virtually every foreigner of any significance currently resident in Rome. Whether transient, like myself, or more or less permanent, like the clusters of ambassadors with all their under-secretaries and aides. There were others as well: the press, a few film stars; athletes; opera singers; Fascists from abroad attached to Embassies; even a certain recent Nobel Prize winner. Our conversation had just hit its stride when,

"Herr Mauberley. . . ."

It was von Ribbentrop.

"You have not eaten."

"No, I have not, Your Excellency. But. . ." And turning to my Nobel Prize winner, expecting him to protest, I was rather startled to see him withdraw of his own volition.

von Ribbentrop drew me through the crowds towards an

alcove piled with little chairs, all spindly legs and backs;
like children's chairs, or angels': gilded. Here we were—lit
with the light from windows more than twenty feet high,
which gave a view of gardens, fountains, soldiers, trees —
and I had wine in one hand, *fettucini alle vongole* in the
other, and nowhere to put down either my plate or my glass
and no desire for the contents of either. The piles of little
chairs would not support a toothpick, let alone a meal. So
I stood there, hampered, while he drew his head down towards me and spoke without allowing me to trap his gaze.

"I'm sorry to draw you away from your interesting conversation, but the fact is we have very little time to talk and
I have some news to impart, which is why I especially requested your presence."

I brightened, hoping to hear of how things stood with
Wallis. von Ribbentrop had promised her a crown, after all,
and the crown had not yet been forthcoming. "News? Good."

"No," he said. "Not good, Herr Mauberley. Not good news.
But sad."

I watched him.

Sad was a word I should have thought von Ribbentrop
incapable of uttering.

His eyes went on avoiding mine—avoiding everything, in
fact, except his own enormous hands and his glass of wine.

"You will want to know—and need to know—" he told
me very slowly, "that Isabella Loverso is dead."

I wish he hadn't told me in a corner.

I was numb. I couldn't move. The light was so vivid it was
almost blinding and the little chairs were all so delicate and
finely balanced. I thought; *if I breathe they will all fall down.*
And the room behind me gave a roar that sounded like
approval. I tried to make von Ribbentrop look at me but still
he wouldn't.

"Why?" I finally asked.

He looked around the crowded room. He even paused
before he answered me, to smile at someone else.

I waited.

Why?

"She betrayed us," he said to the windows.

And all the windows shimmered.

It could not be so. And I said so, asking for proof.

"The proof is in the fact that she is dead," he said.

And I waited.

"As to why. . ." he said, ". . .I can begin by saying that she betrayed German secrets to the British."

"Begin. . .?" I said.

"You must lower your voice, Herr Mauberley," von Ribbentrop said. "You must lower your voice. And smile."

"*Smile?*"

"Yes. Smile now."

He was looking off at one particular figure. Whose? I looked and saw it was Julia Franklin.

I smiled.

von Ribbentrop continued. "Baronessa Loverso, as you must have been aware, had been verging on a betrayal of the Fascist trust for many years."

I could not deny it. I remember Luis Quintana.

"It came, at last, in July of this year, when you and she were in Spain."

"But you saw her then yourself," I said. "She sat with you. She talked with you. I watched. There was no betrayal then. How can you say this, Excellency?"

"She sat with others, too, you know. She sat with them and talked with them and whether you watched or not—there *was* betrayal then."

"Of whom? To what end?"

"As I said—of the Fascist trust. And also. . ."

"Yes?"

"Of *us.*"

I did not respond. It was all unreal.

"Did she not spend time—much time—with the Marques de Estella?" von Ribbentrop asked.

"She did. Are you saying she told him about us, about *Penelope?*"

"No."

"Your Excellency, please. This game—this corner—it is stifling. Tell me what it was she did."

"You do not then know why she was forming this liaison with de Estella?"

"No, Your Excellency. I have already said so."

"The Marques de Estella was involved in a plot to kidnap your friends the Duke and Duchess of Windsor."

I had not, till then, heard of this.

von Ribbentrop continued. "The Marques, in his cups— as the English say—and thinking he spoke to a trusted friend, was careless enough to let some hint of the plot slip out in Isabella Loverso's presence. And she played him into her charming net and caught him. He told her everything."

"I don't understand," I said. And I didn't.

von Ribbentrop then told me about the plot to kidnap the Duke and Wallis. And told me it had been Isabella Loverso who had informed the British. All of this while she and I were in Madrid only three months before. And then she had disappeared.

"So she did not disappear," I said. "She was taken."

"Yes."

"By whom?"

I expected him to say by Mussolini. But he said; "by Schellenberg."

Dear God.

"But *why?*" I said. "Why did she betray us?" I knew she had been wavering, but—

"I can only have a theory," said von Ribbentrop. "But I'm fairly certain it's right."

"Which is?"

"Which is that she despaired of all of us. Our Nazi friends— our Italian friends—and, yes, even of us. And so to thwart us all, to stop us all, she handed the Windsors back to the British. She prevented their being detained in Europe by Hitler. But she also knew the next and vital step in our scheme was to establish the Windsors as our figureheads."

"You said it was Schellenberg who took her."

"Yes."

"And she is dead."

"Yes. Dead."

"Why couldn't you save her?" I said. "She was yours. She was your agent. Surely you could have intervened."

"You think so, Herr Mauberley?"

"Yes."

I watched his eyes go cold. von Ribbentrop turned towards the windows, warming himself. "Let me just say this and do not interrupt. Within two days," he said, "or three at the very most, Isabella Loverso would have told Schellenberg everything there is to know. Bang. It would all be over. And quite apart from that, Herr Mauberley, you have to understand Isabella Loverso was prepared to die—and I think you must be prepared to know that."

I was staring at the sky beyond the window. Brilliant. Limpid. Dazzling.

"You must always remember what it is we want," said von Ribbentrop. "And that some of us must fall before we can have it."

He reached out to touch the little chairs as if they might respond with music. He was like that—always giving the impression he could evoke a breath from stone. Fingertips like magic wands.

"Every day," he said; "I have to move through twenty worlds, Herr Mauberley. Twenty different worlds or more, being German Foreign Minister. I have to get in—and get out alive: twenty times a day. But at least it is known I have the whole of the Reich behind me. When it comes to us, Herr Mauberley, to *Penelope*, all I have is *me*. And I have to get in and out alive: *alone*. Like you. And just like Isabella Loverso. Except. . ."

"You haven't told me what happened," I said.

He shrugged.

Finally, "tell me how she died?" I said. "I don't mean the details. . .only *how*?"

He looked at me.

"You aren't going to like my answer, Herr Mauberley, except in one detail.

"Which is?"

"She died very quickly. She was shot."
Oh.
"And the answer I'm not going to like: what is that?"
"It was one of us who killed her."
I blinked.
One of us.
"Who?" I said.
"Me," he said. "I did."

Finally I found the voice to ask him why it had been him.
"I was the only one she trusted," he said. "And she knew I had come to free her."
Which, of course, he had.
All I wanted to do was turn around and walk away.
But where was there to go? I had just lost all my safety forever.
I looked at the food and drink in my hands; von Ribbentrop's back; the sunlight and the windows. Five hundred human beings all adorned with roses were standing right beside us, and it couldn't have mattered less. There could have been a million, and the little chairs, like gilded bones, would still be piled around us all. Empty cages waiting to be filled.

SIX

July 4th, 1941

Fascism can only exist because of its excesses. Its excesses are its logic.

Lauro de Bosis

Nassau sweltered in the sun.

The early morning's clouds of rain lay off along the far horizon, bound for the open sea. A perfect day, if you did not have to move. But all through the afternoon, at least until the hour of three, there was a steady stream of human traffic making its way towards the Governor's Mansion. This was to be the site that day of an episode of horror that would go down in history as *The Spitfire Bazaar*—and in *T̶* Magazine as *Wally Windsor's Fiery Fête.*

In the months between their arrival in the Bahamas and the events about to be described, the Duke and Duchess of Windsor had been the house guests of Sir Harry and Lady Oakes, the Islands' leading citizens.

It was not for lack of an official residence the Windsors made their home with strangers. Indeed, the Governor's Mansion had been dutifully modernized and repainted at some cost in order to accommodate a Royal Duke and his wife. But the Duchess had disapproved of the décor and she flatly refused to live in "all those rose-red rooms" and to walk on mildewed carpets of a questionable hue. There was dampness everywhere but in the taps. Every faucet opened, dribbled forth its rusty drop and started to bang and scream. The house was undermined by termites and infested with things that crawl. As for the Royal apartments, they must have been devised through the eyes of the one who saw the world by neon light alone and every counter at the local Woolworth's store had been raided for a new idea. Consequently, the Duchess would be forced to undertake the redecorating of the entire establishment herself and, to this end, the temporary accommodations with the Oakes were arranged.

The job was precisely what the Duchess required. All her energetic ambition for von Ribbentrop's scheme was nicely sublimated by this chance to show off her skills, her genius, as a manipulator of public taste. Her transformation of the Mansion was magical, and when the date was set to open it for scrutiny it was she herself who chose the Fourth of July. This was her personal Declaration of Independence, her break with the provincial society of which she was meant to be the *doyenne*. *Doyenne* was a word she hated. *Doyennes* were mere ambassadors—not Queens.

So here it was—the day itself—when she and the Duke would be unveiled on the lawns and her masterpiece unveiled behind her; with its new French papers and its Spanish tiles and its shades of blue unheard of in these backward isles—to say nothing of her imported cuisine, embezzled from the kitchens of the Waldorf in New York and flown down the night before. Packed in dry ice there was quail for everyone (five hundred guests), Boston lettuce garnished with truffles, pink champagne, lady fingers, raspberry sherbet moulded in the shapes of eagles and crowns, chocolate medallions stamped with the Ducal crest, and huge glass bowls of peppermints and sugar dollars for the children. Her own mouth watered when she thought of it all: the sign of a perfect hostess being that she would make the perfect guest at her own buffet.

The press release—in words most carefully chosen—said the Duke and Duchess of Windsor *"having decided to open their home to the leading members of Bahamian society, wish to use this occasion to call attention to the desperate situation in the mother country of this colony. Therefore, donations will be called for towards the purchase of a Spitfire Fighter Plane, to be presented in the name of the people of these Islands to the people of the British Isles. God Save The King.*

Nassau, New Providence, July 4th, 1941"

Winding upward to the Mansion at the top of Mount Fitzwilliam the Governor's Road was clogged with motorcars and straggling people. Swing music drifted down through the groves of casuarina trees, mingling with the breathless chatter of new arrivals as they poured in through the gates and up the melting asphalt. The atmosphere was almost one of Carnival, but the Duke of Windsor's personal guard of kilted Cameron Highlanders, standing at attention in their scarlet tunics along the drive, forced a note of sober grandeur on the scene.

On the lawns there were five marquees forming a candy-stripe horseshoe. At the open end stood the Mansion itself—L-shaped, screened and shuttered against the heat, with its crowning widow's walk looking out over Nassau Bay, Hog Island and the Atlantic Ocean to the north. The Bay was full of American yachts and other pleasure craft, all blue and white and spangled with fluttering flags and pennants reflected in the pale green water. But the wharves and docks and levees that served these boats and ships were practically deserted. Everyone had come up town to stand against the iron fence and watch the Five Hundred arrive. Impeccable policemen, dressed in white, had to hold the crowd back from the gates and from climbing up too high on the railings, lest a child be killed or an eye put out by the rows of iron lilies that decorated the top. And from climbing, too, on the statue of Christopher Columbus, whose back was to the proceedings and whose shoulders made the perfect roosting place for little boys and birds. The explorer's gaze was on the sea and the place—invisible—from which he had come so long ago. "What have I done", he seemed to be saying, "to deserve this end? That I should be frozen here in bronze: in this of all places. Nowhere. And all these people at my feet, whom I cannot see."

The crowds began to assemble at noon. The Duke and Duchess of Windsor were not expected to appear till three. In the meantime there were games and raffles on which to throw one's money away. "All in a good cause! All in a good cause!" cried the movie-star celebrity barkers—the young Miss Lana Turner among them. "All in a good cause!" There was also a French Café, a Newsreel Cinema and a Fortune Teller's Booth that featured Elsa Maxwell dressed as a gypsy sitting behind a crystal ball. But the main attraction remained the Windsors themselves. Everyone wanted to see the Duchess, everyone wanted to touch the Duke, everyone wanted to kiss and taste her rings and look into his cornflower eyes. "Five hundred cats and a King," said Adela Rogers St. Johns.

At approximately two o'clock, a station wagon recognized by nearly everyone in the crowd attempted to make its way up the drive. Inside was a certain Nelson Kelly—known as

"Little Nell" because he was under five feet tall. Nelson Kelly wanted to see the Duke at once because he had a story to sell. But *at once*, in the press of people and cars, was quite impossible.

Little Nell began to honk his horn, but it did no good. "In the name of God," he shouted out the windows, "let me pass!" But his words and their pompous urgency only made the others laugh. "No passing here, Little Nell!" they shouted back at him. "No passing here—no matter who you are!"

"But I have to get up the hill!" he cried.

"Then walk!"

They were all so mean; they were all so vengeful; they were all so rich. It did not matter to them if they walked. They had their time to take and none of them perspired: not one, in all their blue and white. But Little Nell had a living to make and the only way to make it was to sell his story. That was his job, to delve and to dig for stories and to sell them, always selling to the highest bidder, sometimes selling twice, sometimes not being able to sell at all. Little Nell most often sold to the press, but other times he sold to husbands, wives and lovers; bosses; solicitors and even the Chief of Police. There was nothing about these people he did not know and nothing he would not sell. The trouble was, the people knew it and instead of being afraid, they scoffed. Nell was always saying, "just you wait. You'll see. One day, I'll find a story big enough to make you tremble: then I'll sell it to *Time* Magazine," he'd shout. "The New York *Times*, the Boston *Globe*! You'll see. . .!" The very names were talismans and Little Nell would turn them over on his tongue the way a miser turns his money in its jar.

Nelson Kelly tried to back the station wagon up but since his arrival three Rolls Royces, two Mercedes and a Bentley had all crowded in behind him. Still Little Nell was loathe to leave the car. If left, it might be pushed aside and overturned. There were too many pranksters amongst the crowd— playboys with nothing better to do than show off their skill at creating chaos—and Little Nell had suffered at their hands before. Sometimes he thought that pranks were the whole and only occupation of these people. Merciful heaven—

some of the things they had done! Once, Little Nell had found his Ford full of barking dogs; and another time with rolls and rolls of toilet paper, boxes of pencils and a pencil sharpener. Worst of all had been the prank in which some person had affixed a periscope to the roof and driven the Ford into the Bay. Still. . .a car was only a car and Nelson Kelly's business with the Duke—or with someone in charge—was far more important than that. He would have to chance it.

Honking his horn again, jamming it down with one little hand while he drove with the other, Little Nell shouted "Out! Out! Out! Get out of the way!" while he veered towards the verge of the drive.

Long-gowned women wearing picture hats and walking under parasols; men in blazers, white ducks and panamas; debutantes holding their tea gowns out of the dust and carrying their silver shoes; children playing hide-and-seek between the Royal Palms that lined the drive and policemen in white pith helmets all bolted hither and yon to avoid his wheels. "Out! Out! Out!" shouted Little Nell above his horn. Old men raised their walking sticks in alarm and rattled them across his offending fenders and banged against his doors. Women screamed. One man climbed on the hood of the wagon and crawled right up to the windshield, shaking his fist in Little Nell's face. "You bugger!" he cried. "You absolute shower! What the hell do you think you're doing?" But Little Nell paid no heed to the words. Instead, he gunned the motor and the man slid off and fell to the ground.

At last he brought the station wagon to a stop, having got it partway up the hill and a good way onto the grass. He was sweating profusely, even though he had already taken his jacket off. He was no longer presentable, but he still had his story to sell and someone must be made to pay attention. Little Nell rolled up all the windows and climbed out into the blazing heat. One by one he locked his doors, burning his palms against the handles. Putting on his jacket, he checked its inner pocket to make sure the envelope with its dangerous message was still in place. It was.

Little Nell lurched towards one side. For a moment he

was lost and had to depend on gravity to tell him which way to go. The crowd was not a mob up here, but a slow-moving, silent mass of swimmers breathlessly struggling upward to the air above the swelter on the hill.

Even in spite of the heat, Little Nell kept moving. "Out!" he muttered. "Out of my way. . ." And the horde was parted before him, gaping that anyone should hurry so. But on seeing it was only Little Nell, the horde was unimpressed. "He always behaves as if the world were going to end. . ." they said of him. "He always behaves as if. . ." But surely it did not matter how Little Nell behaved. He was nothing more than a gossip monger, "nothing but a bitch!" This time, however, the horde was wrong. For the world was going to end and the thing in Little Nell's pocket—sealed in its envelope—would have told them so.

Inside the Mansion, the Duchess of Windsor was looking in her mirror. There she was—in white. The white had been her idea. Everyone in the Official Party would be dressed in white from head to toe. The Duke in his white Naval uniform; she herself in this white Schiaparelli; Aunt Bessie Merryman from Baltimore just off white in a tea dress with jacket. And even though Marsden-Fawcett, their aide, must abide by his khaki, she had asked him to bleach it down and now it was a nice pale beige and from a distance "white".

The Duchess sat completely still, not even parting her lips to breathe. Down the hall, in his brand new apartments, the Duke was sipping wine and smoking cigarettes with a large blue bib around his neck. His face was still a mass of scars and he had to spend two hours at the make-up tables every time he made a public appearance. Nonetheless, he sat quite patient while the Duchess did her work—and when the artist departed, he always had to wait another hour to jell, staring at the empty place the Duchess left behind when she was gone.

Marsden-Fawcett came to the Duchess of Windsor's door and spoke to the maid. All the Duchess could hear was his stuttering whisper; nothing important—nothing she could not guess; the imminence of the event; the building up to "now". She heard him go away; she heard the door being closed; she heard her maid say "ma'am?" She waved her hand. She knew. She rose. The buttons must now be hooked on the back of her exquisite dress. She watched herself being closed and battened.

Sweet Marsden-Fawcett, she thought. Marsden-F-F-F- she called him. Not much more than a boy: a pleasant, stammering, eager child with enormous eyes—like a rabbit. Major Gerrard, on the other hand, was hard and solemn. Grim. He was out there now on the lawns in charge of Security....Gerrard, who had fired his gun at the Duke of Windsor, who had "arrested" them for Churchill and brought them here to this dreadful island. Major Gerrard had commandeered a corner of one of the marquees—the one where the Newsreel Films were showing the Fall of France, the Battle of Britain, the bombing of London and Coventry, films that were intended to whip up a frenzy of enthusiasm so the Spitfire Fund would be fully subscribed. The Duchess of Windsor hated these films. She thought they were despicable and had sanctioned Major Gerrard's corner there in the hope, perhaps, the bombs would fall on him.

The buttons were now all done. She was perfectly contained in the white Schiaparelli—and had to shield her eyes in order to see herself.

"I have to see the Duke!" said Little Nell to the man who was barring his way.

"Get away," said the man—a giant to Nell—"We don't need your kind here." And he waved his hands as if to rid himself of a gnat.

"But I have the most important news to sell!"

"They all say that—your kind," said the man, whose job it was to open doors, and shut them. He was dressed in impeccable livery, satin breeches and buckled shoes. His coat was a deep blue velvet trimmed with silver. Little Nell was standing on the crushed shell drive and the liveried gent was standing out of reach of the sun.

"But the news I have is vital," said Little Nell; "it's the most important news of the day. And the Duke—or whoever it is who's in charge—must see it right away. Otherwise. . ."

"Otherwise what?" The giant, who was testy by nature, as becomes a man whose job it is to open doors and shut them, did not care for threats. "Otherwise what, may I ask?"

"Otherwise you'll be fired. Let go. Dismissed. When they hear what you have prevented from reaching the ears of His Royal Highness, the Duke of Windsor—or whoever it is who's. . ."

"*I* am in charge of this door," said the giant, "and *I* am in charge of you and *I* say you shall not enter. Go!"

Little Nell was now very close to tears. "Listen," he said—and he reached inside his pocket.

But the porter cut him off. "If you are about to produce a coin," he said, "I think you should know I have never accepted a bribe in the whole of my career. . . ."

Just then, a young lieutenant with a pleasant face and a faded uniform appeared behind the giant. "What's all the f-f-f-. . .?" he said.

"No fuss," said the porter. "Just this dwarf, that's all."

"Oh, it's you, Nelson Kelly," said Marsden-Fawcett, who had dealt with the little man before. "You always choose the most awkward moments to show your f-f-f-. . .Couldn't you come back some other time?"

"Please, Lieutenant," said Little Nell. "I really do have the most important news to sell the Duke. . ."

"No," said Marsden-Fawcett, who had still not deigned to emerge from behind the screen door, "I'm af-f-f- you're out of luck. Not a chance. Their Royal Highnesses are cloistered and out of reach; and nothing—no one shall disturb them."

"But. . ."

"No," said Marsden-Fawcett.

"No," said the giant—barring the door.

"You'll regret this," said Little Nell. "You will. You wait and see. . . ." And he stomped away.

They were just like all the rest, he thought in his fury,

Careless of every life but their own: arrogant and aloof and selfish. Well: he would make them pay. He would not divulge the contents of his pocket. Not for any price. No, not even for ready money. He would stand aside and watch them suffer the consequences of their foolishness. But—of course—how could someone like Marsden-Fawcett be expected to know about foolishness when he couldn't even say it?

The Duchess, seated now in the salon where the Official Party had begun to gather, was profoundly aware of all the clocks and watches surrounding her. Everything, it seemed, was ticking. She looked across at her Aunt Bessie Merryman—the only remaining relative she had in all the world—and she thought; *thank heaven I will never look like that.* But at once she regretted thinking it. It was Bessie the Duchess had been named for; her mother's sister and her own most loyal and staunch supporter; faithful through every crisis up and down the map of time. Up and down, up and down: all their lives had been up and down, like a wild and dangerous dance where the dancers dance in peril, like a polka danced in the dark. And, even now she noted Aunt Bessie's toes were tapping. . .keeping time.

The Duchess blinked.

My mother died, she thought, of a cancer in her eye. Of a tic. . . .I am so afraid of the dark. And if I blink again, the floor might disappear.

She stared.

Aunt Bessie Merryman's toes were tapping down in the shadows under her skirts. All the clocks were ticking. Time is darkness—time is light. You either dance, or fall.

But the Duchess of Windsor sat very still and she thought; *or you stop all the clocks.*

Out on the lawns, waiting with everyone else for the Windsors to appear, Little Nell was busy with his notebooks.

Wherever he went, wherever he sat—in streets, in bars, in public toilets—Nell made notes. He listened with a stethoscope and he watched through a magnifying glass. He collected graffiti. His theory was that you could sum up the age you lived in by reading its walls. The truth, which loves to hide, had found the perfect hiding place. It was just another bit of gossip in amongst the litter of names and dirty jokes on the partitions of a comfort station.

Little Nell never missed a trick. His eyes were like two wooden discs on an abacus: clickety-click—they moved so fast a pair of Chinese fingers might have been hitched to his brain. He watched and listened and waited. He was very poor. The thing was, there wasn't much of a market for pranksters' tricks and the lazy, unimaginative dreams of part-time whores. But he gathered what he could and he sold what he had—and he waited for the moment when the giants would begin to stir.

In the meantime, he marvelled at what he overheard and at what he found on the walls. Round and round the stories went, and the hands that wrote them were never seen. Who were these ghosts, whose sources you could never check, who could only be identified by what they wrote, but who always wrote it in the dark, like God. The only trouble is, he thought—recalling the eternal twilight of the world's latrines and the rows of feet beneath the cabinet doors—the only way I'd know it's God is if I recognized His shoes.

Due west of the town of Nassau lies the island of Andros—far enough away to lie below the horizon. Not that any vantage point in Nassau would present a view of anything due west no matter how close it might be, since the town itself stood up in the way. But what could not be seen could still be heard—a distant storm; an approaching ship (if it blew its whistles loud enough and sounded all its bells) or the Pan American Clipper flying in from Miami.

Now, in his dressing-room, the Duke of Windsor caught the sound of something deep inside his ear and could not tell if what he heard was real or not.

"Henny," he said to his man, whose name was Albert Henderson, "Is something there?"

"Where, sir?"

"There." And the Duke made a stab at pointing in the right direction, more or less describing a circle.

"No, sir," said Henny.

"But wait. . ." said the Duke and he whispered as he spoke. "Are you absolutely certain?"

Henderson looked. The Duke was standing, centre of the room, transfixed. Nothing else was visible. "I'm sorry, sir, but I don't see a thing."

"Did I say there was anything to see?" said the Duke. "My question was: *is something there*? Do you *hear* anything?"

Henderson was greatly relieved. "No sir," he said quite brightly. "I can't hear a thing—excepting, of course, the crowds outside and the music."

"No," said the Duke. "Not the crowds and not the music. A sort of buzzing sound. . ."

Henderson held his breath and considered what he should say. "Is it possible Your Highness might be referring to the sound of flies. . .or bees, perhaps?" He waited for inspiration. "Or even birds? There are birds that buzz, you know."

"You think I'm mad, of course," said the Duke. "But I'm not. I tell you, Henny—there is something *there*!"

And he pointed due west. And even though his valet still maintained there was nothing to be heard, the Duke of Windsor was quite correct. Something indeed was there, casting its shadow over the island of Andros and making "a sort of buzzing sound" as it headed due east towards the town of Nassau.

Little Nell forayed further onto the lawn.

Bosom high to most of the women, Little Nell made a shopping tour through a kind of heavenly store where all the best that could be had was on display. And the dresses were cut so low. . .the heat, of course, being the cause. . .and the fact it was a garden party. Yes. These debutantes were much too well brought up to want to show themselves in any crass or decadent display of—oh my goodness!—*flesh*.

Little Nell snatched a glass of pink champagne and guzzled

it to slake the thirst so suddenly brought on by all this heat and the press of all these bodies. There. And he left his empty glass on a passing tray and snatched another.

Mopping his chin, he turned in a new direction. Over in one of the marquees he spotted zebra stripes and what appeared to be an orchid-bearing tree. This was the Duchess of Windsor's tribute to the *El Morocco*, one of New York's finest watering holes and a second home to many of her rich American guests that day. Inside, he could see a tropic pool and palms and, wading in the pool, flamingoes. Everything was pink and black and white, a kind of living waxworks: not quite real, but the next best thing. The light was wrong and all the flamingoes must have been extremely tired—or their works run down—since every step they took was a slow-motion parody of walking in their sleep. But the drink at the bar was very real and the band was real and the blonde who stood up to sing was real. And the crowd inside with all their glasses raised.

> . . .*Without your love,*
> *It's a honky-tonk parade,*
> *Without your love,*
> *It's a melody played*
> *In a penny arcade.* . . .

Little Nell turned to wander past a Punch and Judy Show and a large display of the Duke of Windsor's various Coats of Arms set out in lilies, daisies, iris, roses:

> . . .*It's a Barnum and Bailey world,*
> *Just as phony as it can be,*
> *But it wouldn't be make believe,*
> *If you believed in me.*

And then—all at once—Little Nell could see her.

LANA TURNER—KISSES FOR SALE!

This stopped him dead in his tracks. *Dear, sweet*

Jesus. . .Breasts. Lord, bless thy servant. Grant me one kiss and I will give away my secrets free. If only I could touch. . .and he nearly squeezed his champagne glass into a mess of shards. But, no. It was impossible. It would never do. Little Nell stepped back and watched Miss Turner through the haze of his dreams; it well may be there is much in this world so real, so terribly real we dare not unveil and touch it since its reality would only overwhelm us, no matter how lovely, sensuous and gratifying it was. Could any man truly bear the weight of all that Lana Turner flesh in his hands if it were real? Was it not best—in the interest of public sanity— to consign such flesh to magazines and films and to balance it there in the mind: *palms up!* Strawberry nipples dipped in pink champagne and eaten raw in dreams. How could such dreams be exposed to the sweat and callouses of real hands smudged with ink, fumbling with real buttons? Little Nell would never know. The knowing, alas, was left to Tyrone Power and Jimmy Stewart, Lana Turner's movie-star lovers. *And they say,* he thought, *she is only sixteen years old. Sixteen. Fifteen. Fourteen. God! If I had a soul to sell!*

Nell turned away and reached inside his inner pocket. *Just one kiss,* he thought as he fingered the envelope. But no. They had refused already. And besides. . .he turned and looked again at his dream, where she stood dispensing kisses for cash. . .*she's innocent. She'd never understand.* And he decided, then and there, that if the awful moment came predicted in his pocket—he would rescue Lana Turner. All the rest could fry in hell.

The Duke of Windsor finally came down the stairs, where he passed the Judiciary lined up in the hall together with the members of the Executive Council. This was a mere— and dread—formality. Everyone bowed a little and scraped a little and the Duke, in his turn, made a show of being able to converse like an ordinary human being. In the past, this had been his greatest talent; now he could barely look these people in the eye or hear their names without a gun going off that was loaded with accusations aimed at himself. They all think I've let them down, he thought; and I don't even know who they are. . . .Marsden-Fawcett had to guide him through the tour of hands.

There was Lord Chief Justice Sir William Wilmott, puckering his lips, sucking his gums; always looking and sounding as if there was something stuck between his teeth. There was Lieutenant-Colonel Frederick Wanklyn, Commanding Officer of the Volunteer Defence Force. And there was Noel Bingham ("Thingummy") Ross, whose grandmother Lally Bingham-Ross had been among the mistresses of Edward VII, the Duke of Windsor's grandfather. But the Duke was thoroughly distracted all the time they stood there, with his eye on the outer doors and the crowds beyond in the blazing sunshine. And even though he vaguely heard them speak of the latest polo matches at Clifford Park and the racing season at Hobby Horse Hall, he only heard them through the buzzing in his ears, growing by the moment increasingly louder. At last he cut their formal greetings short and he said to all of them; "can you hear that sound?" And they all said; "no."

He made his excuses and wandered away, still pursued by Marsden-Fawcett; and when the Duchess turned and saw her husband enter the salon, she was instantly alarmed. His face was pinched with confusion and pain and she thought he must be ill. "Keep Marsden-F-F-F- away," she said to Aunt Bessie, urging her to join the aide-de-camp on the farthest side of the room.

"What is the matter with you, David?" she said, somewhat testy by the time she got him into a corner. She could smell the wine and she thought; *if he's drunk for this of all events, I will kill him.* "What is the matter?"

"Something is going to happen," he said, with a curious look of anguish in his eye. "Something dreadful is going to happen, Dolly. You think we can make it stop?"

"What is it? Aren't you well? Something 'dreadful'—what do you mean? A heart attack?"

"No. Have you got any cotton wool?"

"Of course not. *Cotton wool*?"

"My ears. . ." He looked around the room. "Even some

Kleenex would do. I could wad it up and stick it in. . . ."

"David." The Duchess used her sharpest edge to cut him off. "There's nothing wrong. And nothing 'dreadful' is going to happen. Nothing. In a moment, you and I are going out there" (he was staring at her; suspicious) "to show those people who we are. That's all. We will simply show them who we are. And I only ask one thing. . ."

"Yes, Dolly."

"All I have in this place is you. And all you have is me. So it's us against them. Do you understand?"

"Yes, Dolly. *Us against them.*"

She looked at him and knew he did not comprehend the magnitude of what they were about to do. But then, the magnitude of admitting he was alive was enough to put him off, these days.

"Here comes Marsden-Fawcett," she said, "to take you away. I'll be with you in a moment. Get him to pull your jacket down at the back. It's riding up. . . ."

Marsden-Fawcett came and, with him, Aunt Bessie Merryman. Marsden-Fawcett took the Duke away and the Duchess set her mouth and narrowed her eyes. She crossed to the nearest mirror. Aunt Bessie tried to follow, but the Duchess cut her off. "I need a moment," she said. "If you don't mind. Please."

Aunt Bessie Merryman understood. It was her belief—and one she had instilled in Wallis Warfield—that the only calm that counted in a high-tension world was the calm that came from being able to retreat entirely into the centre of one's self in moments of stress. And the Duchess of Windsor's way of achieving this calm was through the meticulous guardianship of her own appearance. Whenever tensions became unbearable—as now—she always turned to the looking-glass.

She set every hair in its place. Every hair was a nerve and they must all be tightly flattened to the mould of serenity in which she meant to walk out through the doors and onto the lawns: *us against them.* And when she was ready, she paused just long enough to see her husband through the glass—far, far off in that other world where everything was reversed. His reflection distressed her even more than the man himself, whose weight she had supported with her hands. The mirror-man had no weight at all: no weight— and all white; white in his uniform; white in his powdered face; white in his aureole of refracted light. He was like a doll that had been left unwound.

But the clocks had not been stopped.

In the mirror, it was nine. And at nine o'clock all this that was about to happen would be over. If only she could stay right there, and by-pass the hour that was about to strike.

Three p.m.—and the moment had arrived.

Outside, the Five Hundred had begun to turn expectantly towards the Mansion at about ten minutes to three. The police had closed off the top of the driveway by blocking it with—of all things—an ambulance. There was an air of rippling excitement that exuded from the crowd, almost visible like heatwaves shimmering over their heads. And the singer went on singing in the *El Morocco*:

> *Jeepers creepers!*
> *Where'd ya get those peepers?*
> *Jeepers creepers!*
> *Where'd ya get those eyes?*

An aeroplane was approaching from out beyond the harbour. The sound of it was like a droning bee swelling through the music and the chatter.

Little Nell had wandered off and returned three times with pink champagne to the vicinity of the Kissing Concession, where Lana Turner was still ensconced like a glorious cow in a pen. She was doing a roaring trade. But Little Nell was nervous. Three o'clock was the appointed hour and the undelivered message still remained unsold in his pocket.

Overhead, the aeroplane was making a close, then closer, circle—climbing upward. Probably getting a view and maybe even taking a picture for *Life* Magazine of the whole Bazaar. Nell saw a man make a gesture with his cane towards the

282

sky. Everyone looked at the plane. It was levelling out.

Meanwhile, the doors of the Governor's Mansion were opened and the Duke of Windsor heard the aeroplane.

"That's it," he said—delighted—to his wife and Marsden-Fawcett. "*That's* been the buzzing in my ears."

The Duchess had to admit it was really quite loud. But she was very pleased. It meant there was one less facet of her husband's condition she had to worry about. One less hallucination. One less stroke of paranoia. "*Now,*" she said, "we can go." And she gave his elbow a little squeeze of encouragement. Out they went.

Everyone—all the Five Hundred—took an involuntary step across the grass. The Duke and Duchess of Windsor had finally appeared. White. Tiny. Smiling.

They waved—and a noise like a toppled hive of bees ensued. The Official Party was engulfed in a tidal wave of human backs and extended arms, swallowed whole from the view of the likes of Little Nell and Lana Turner.

Then—all at once—"oh look!" someone shouted. "Look at the sky!"

The aeroplane was making a lazy turn and rolling onto its back. From its tail, a long thin stream of exhaust appeared: blue—and then red.

"Red!" someone cried. "Look! Look! Red!"

The Duke and the Duchess of Windsor were completely forgotten in the centre of the lawns, hemmed in on every side by the crush of people—all of the people looking skyward. The trail of red exhaust had begun to make a loop and the loop began to take on a form that could not be incidental.

"M!" someone shouted. "M! Look! It's writing!"

And indeed it was. . .M and then E very clearly emerged in the flow of inky smoke and the audience below began to sway and twist in a slow, hypnotic circle as the letters followed one another into the sky.

M.

E.

N.

Men.

This caused a great deal of laughter to go up into the air to join the letters. "Men!"

And then, as the letters continued to emerge and to follow one another, forming other words—or what seemed to be other words—the crowd began to chant.

"M!" they all sang.

"E!"

"N!" they all sang.

"E!"

"M!" they all cried—and clapped their hands like children at a birthday party. "M! E! N! E! M!. . .MENEM!"

Every eye was on the sky. Little Nell sat down hard upon the grass and his hands began to shake. And the sweat came down in a torrent over his eyes so he could barely see and his feet were twisted under him in agony.

"What does it mean?" said one old man. "Menem?"

"Wait," said another. "I don't think it's finished yet."

"No," said Little Nell unheard. "It hasn't."

And the aeroplane went on spelling out its ciphered message above them. M.E.N.E.M.E. . . .it wrote. MENEME. It wasn't even English.

"Maybe," said the old man; "if that N was really meant to be another M, he's saying to us: Me! Me! Me!"

"No," said Little Nell, who wasn't even watching any more, "He isn't saying me—me—me."

And then—something fell from the plane. A strange, elliptical shape, like a tear drop: made of aluminium.

"Oh. . ." said someone. "Oh. It's a bomb!"

Major Bunny Gerrard, waving his famous revolver in the air, had leapt onto a table in front of the Parisian Café. It had been his intention to threaten the plane and to try to kill the pilot if it flew within his range. But now, with this object falling through the air that might have been a bomb, Major Gerrard had the chance to take his aim and fire before it hit the ground. And if it had been a bomb, he might have made it explode in the air and saved five hundred lives. But it was not a bomb.

It was the plane's spare tank of fuel.

And now there was brightness spilling down the sky, a great orange chute of flames that broke, mid-fall, and scattered everywhere. Gasoline. It could be smelled.

Everyone fell to the earth as if a muezzin had suddenly called them all to their knees. Men, women, children all fell down. But it was not in prayer. It was to hide.

And Marsden-Fawcett, kneeling with the Duke and Duchess, tried to say for all the others; "f-f-f-. . ."

Fire.

And then it caught.

The word itself leapt everywhere over the heads of the crowd like a flame. Fire. Fire.

Everyone rose and ran. First they went one way. Then they went another. Then another. And then it struck them all at once. They were trapped. There would be no running anywhere. On every side they were blocked by marquees; by the Mansion; by the ambulance at the top of the drive and by the press of motorcars that filled every gap between the trees. Five hundred people and more were entirely hemmed in and there was not a hope of getting out.

Major Gerrard blew three blasts on his whistle.

This brought all the Cameron Highlanders up from their stations on the hillside; running like scarlet dogs to the sound of their names. Some even climbed across the tops of motorcars, with their rifles raised and their bayonets flashing in the sun.

Everyone fell down again.

Out of the aeroplane, now fell bright green paper. A bright green snowdrift, rolling over, falling down as the people fell. And the aeroplane went on with its writing. . . M.E.N.E.M.E.N.E.T.E.K. . . .

People began to rise and to stumble across the backs of others who could not get up. Suddenly the Duke and Duchess of Windsor, white like statues, were revealed in the very centre of the lawn. The Duchess was holding up the hem of her Schiaparelli skirt. The Duke had his mouth open, staring at the fallen circle of people. By now, the marquees were going up one by one in candy-stripe volcanoes causing an enormous, roaring updraught which lifted the remnants of the canvas and the bright green papers into the air like burning flags.

More and more people were rising from the ground. Fire was flooding out around them over the stones and shells and through the grass. There was a second convulsive movement, again *en masse*, towards the canvas enclosures that only moments before had offered shelter from the sun. Now, there was nothing but a wall of flame and a corps of struggling human torches flailing against the holocaust, drowning for lack of air in waves of fire and smoke.

And the bright green papers made a blizzard and the Duchess of Windsor, holding out her skirts, appeared to be gathering them. DEATH TO FASCISTS EVERYWHERE! the bright green papers screamed. But neither the Duchess—nor anyone—could hear them.

Now the people wheeled towards the barricade of cars and the siren on top of the ambulance was wailing. A woman had pushed her children in through the glass and was lying across the front seat, cranking the siren's handle just as if she were winding a gramophone. And all the time she lay there, she was shouting at her children; "Shut up! Shut up! Shut up!" But her children were dead—because she had smothered them.

The crowd became a mob. It had no other choice. Men beat at women with their walking sticks. Women beat at men with their parasols. Children were beaten aside with ice-cream chairs, while others were thrown through the air like parcels—riches thrown from a sinking ship.

In the Cinema Marquee, seventy-five or a hundred people had been watching the Battle of Britain and the Fall of France. Now, in a nightmare calmly narrated by a disembodied Movietone Voice, they were caught themselves in the hordes of struggling refugees who clogged the roads on the screen while the dive bombers strafed them in the ditches down between the rows of chairs. Real flames caught at their hair and their clothing. Real screams mingled with the screams of falling bombs and the rising flames over London echoed the rising flames that leapt towards the sky above the lawns at Nassau. Suddenly the screen was filled with the image of a Spitfire squadron rushing towards the camera. Just as it took off, the whole marquee exploded.

The Duchess of Windsor saw a woman standing before her in flames like a figure in a mirror who kept repeating; "I am dead. I am dead," as her arms flew up to cover her face as if in shame; and the words were perfectly enunciated, spoken without a trace of anguish or agony: simply *I am dead*. The Duchess of Windsor fell to her knees and crawled away across the burning grass. All around her there was chaos, heat and terror. And a great, wild wind that was made by the fire itself. And far, far away—or so it seemed—she could see her husband, lost in a daze, beginning to walk towards the fiery awnings, holding out his hands to the flames as if they were salvation.

The sight of him drew her at once to her feet, and the Duchess went running, galvanized by his image, limping and not knowing why. She had lost one shoe. But even so, she was totally unaware the 'earth' beneath her feet was flesh and she just kept running, single-minded, over the field of bodies towards her husband. "Don't! Don't! Don't!" she was crying, either aloud or in her mind. "Don't!" But all she could hear was the rush of the winds through the tunnels of the fire.

Moving like a figure of glass in a furnace the Duchess turned and turned and turned, only vaguely aware of the thrashing arms and sticks all around her: walking sticks, swagger sticks, stakes pulled out of the ground, pointed parasols, chair legs, table legs, anything with which to jab and batter—and it was in this way she discovered why it was her shoe was missing. It was in her hand and she was using its heel to strike at whoever got in her way.

When she finally got as far as the Duke she had no idea where they were; there seemed to be only herself and him in a wilderness of violence. The Duchess put her arms around his shoulders and drew him close. The naval uniform was smouldering but it was not on fire. For a moment the Duchess didn't even try to move, but stood while the movement of the others flowed around them like a river. Then—very slowly—she began to push the Duke of Windsor gently backwards, both of them moving against the stream.

It was the longest walk the Duchess had ever made. Thirty

yards towards the drive. . .on and on and on. And her partner, catatonic in her arms, without a whimper but alive. And
for days—for weeks—the Duchess of Windsor's legs and
thighs would ache with the effort of it and in her dreams
she would go on pushing her husband across the dance-floor
on the lawns—hearing over and over the crazy song about
a paper moon, a cardboard sea and a melody played in a
fiery arcade.

As for Little Nell, being so tiny he had tried to crawl away
and hide in the Kissing Concession under the counter. But
Lana Turner had to be saved and so he offered to lift her up
as best he could, with his palms beneath her breasts; but she
fell to the ground and was carried off by three tall men in
blue velvet coats with silver trim. And buckled shoes. And
Little Nell was left behind, alone and unable to move. One
of the men—a giant—had stepped on his neck and crushed
it.

The last thing Little Nell saw before he died was the writing high in the sky above him: *mene mene tekel upharsin;*
the final scrawl, the ultimate graffiti. . .*thou art weighed in
the balance—and found wanting.*

God's shoes were size twelve.

All that remained, when the fire had died, were the ruined
shapes of the great marquees, looming in the moonlit smoke
like sunken ships with all their ropes cast off upon the
blackened sea of grass. Soldiers and firemen, doctors and
nurses, policemen and mesmerized survivors wandered over
the scene identifying, trying to identify, the victims. Fifty-
five dead in all: including both Major Gerrard and Lieutenant
Marsden-Fawcett. Gerrard's automatic was welded to his
hand. As for Marsden-Fawcett, he was found, like a child,
with his fingers in his mouth—as if in desperation he was
trying to pluck out "fire".

Aunt Bessie Merryman lost all her hair and had to wear a wig for the rest of her life. And she joined less and less in her niece's company. "Fire," she said, "is the one true terror and the only thing in hell I can't endure." The Duchess of Windsor let her go. Fire, she had surmised, was what awaited them all, though not in hell. And only those who could endure it would be allowed to remain in her retinue.

Far in the depths of the Mansion, the lights began to go out and it seemed there was a kind of will towards darkness.

Soon after midnight one of the nurses, all in white, bent down to see if Little Nell was dead and, finding that he was, she closed his eyes and reached inside his jacket, seeking for some identification. None was there—but she found a long brown envelope and opened it, thinking it might tell his name. Folded neatly inside there was a bright green leaflet of the kind that had fallen from the plane that afternoon and a piece of plain white paper. On the white was written, by hand, the simple message: *For Your Information—Friday, July the Fourth, 1941 at 15:00 hrs.* And on the green, a simpler message in bold, black type—already known: DEATH TO FASCISTS EVERYWHERE.

The fire had claimed its fifty-five victims and three days later the sea yielded up the fifty-sixth: the body of Lorenzo de Broca, the young Italian poet whose words had so embarrassed Hugh Selwyn Mauberley one day when they had met on the steps of the Grand Elysium Hotel at UnterBalkonberg in 1939.

Perhaps it had been de Broca's intention all along to die in his plane—or perhaps it was the result of his naïveté and panache. One thing will never be known, which is whether he carried the extra tank of gasoline to get him home to Florida, whence he had flown, or for the purposes of fire to which it was put—either by accident or design. At any rate, de Broca had not made it very far out to sea before he crashed. The aeroplane the Duchess of Windsor had watched being loaded aboard the *Excalibur* in the Azores had joined the other skeletons of war machines and ships beneath the waves;

while the whimsical currents had deposited its drowned young pilot—who called himself Icarus—on the coral close to a colony of birds whose wings he would have envied, but whose beaks and claws had no respect for mythology—except insofar as they fed on it.

* * *

Fire, Quinn read again, *is the one true terror and the only thing in hell I can't endure.*

He turned around very quickly after that and walked out into the room where the gramophone sat on its desk and the half-moon piece of shiny black Schubert sat propped up beside the pile of other records. *Piano Sonata in B flat ma. . .*he read. This was his *memento mori*: his reminder of Freyberg's will that everyone should die the worst of deaths he could devise.

Well.

They had.

Quinn stuffed his pack of Philip Morris into the pocket of his Eisenhower, buttoned his greatcoat and grabbed the blanket from his cot and threw it around his shoulders.

Out in the corridor there was a smell like formaldehyde which Quinn discovered was coming from the room he now called Mauberley's Crypt. Freyberg was standing, blocking the view, in the doorway.

Quinn had hoped not to see Captain Freyberg in this particular moment. His equilibrium was frail. He didn't want the burning world on the walls to be joined to the caustic world out here in the corridor of the Grand Elysium Hotel. He had the dreadful feeling that, if Freyberg read the story of the Spitfire Bazaar, he might rejoice in the body count. But perhaps he was being unfair. Perhaps it was just the juxtaposition of the sight of Freyberg's back and the over-powering smell of acid.

"Where are you going?" said Freyberg.

"Out," said Quinn.

"Out?" said Freyberg. "There's a god damn blizzard."

"Yes sir."

Freyberg smiled as he gazed at Lieutenant Quinn's attire. "All dolled up, I see."

"That's right," said Quinn, and he pulled the blanket fur-ther around his shoulders. "May I go now, sir?"

Freyberg turned away and said; "no".

It was an arbitrary 'no' and Quinn was sure of it. Just because it was obvious he wanted to get away from the walls, Freyberg was going to prevent him. No better reason. Just the hate. "Come along to my office," the captain said. "I have something I want to show you."

Quinn stood back.

Captain Freyberg was saying something into the Crypt—something to one of the soldiers there which Quinn could not quite hear; though he quite distinctly heard both "bottle" and "brain". And the smell of formaldehyde was very strong on Freyberg's clothing as they strolled along to the Opera-tions Centre in the Garbo suite.

"You're very subdued," said Freyberg.

"Yes sir."

They got inside the room where Dufault was typing and Freyberg went around and sat behind his desk. "Aren't you going to ask me what I'm doing with the formaldehyde?" he asked—not looking up but rummaging through a litter of notebooks and papers, opening and closing drawers.

"No, sir." Quinn could already guess. *Bottle, brain* and *formaldehyde* could only mean one thing—and why did Freyberg feel he had to tell it, say it, spell it out? It was like a sickness in him. Just as Isabella Loverso had said ambition was a sickness, so was this mordant streak in Captain Frey-berg: his dreadful will to force your nostrils into the dirt and your ears into the centre of the scream.

Thank God—the Captain found what he was looking for and the dreadful thing that Quinn had feared was never said aloud.

"Look at this," said Freyberg, shoving an official-looking piece of paper through the litter across the desk at Quinn.

Quinn's hands were still in mitts as well as gloves and he had to take them off in order to pick the piece of paper up. "What is it?" he said.

"Just read," said Freyberg, sitting back with his hands behind his head. "I thought you should be the first to know. I haven't even filed it yet."

Quinn opened the double-folded page. It was an official communiqué from OSS-G-2. Freyberg was watching him—and the sound of Dufault's typing forced the words on Quinn like a hammer driving nails.

Ezra Pound had been arrested at Rapallo. Up on the hill above the town, at Sant'Ambrogio in the house of Olga Rudge.

A reward had been posted: WANTED FOR TREASON. HALF A MILLION *LIRE*. DEAD OR ALIVE.

No one had got the reward, however. Pound had delivered himself into the hands of his captors and now the Americans were holding him in a cage at Pisa.

"Looks like the round-up has finally begun," said Freyberg.

"Yes sir."

Quinn double-folded the page again and handed it back across the desk.

"May I go now, sir?"

"If you like," said Freyberg.

"Thank you, sir."

Quinn pulled his mitts back on and saluted.

Then he wheeled around and was gone through the door before the captain could find some other reason to call him back.

Going down into the lobby, Quinn was nearly knocked off his feet by a large metal plate being struggled up the stairs by a pair of men the size of lumberjacks.

"What the hell is that?" he said, and the lumberjacks, grateful for the chance to lay their burden down, set it against the iron balustrade on the landing and drew aside the burlap bags that covered it.

"Captain Freyberg wants it in his office over his desk," said one of the lumberjacks.

"But what the hell is it?" said Quinn again, tipping his head towards one side in order to read the writing.

"Don't ask me," said the articulate lumberjack, whose friend was so out of breath he was sitting down on the steps with his head thrown back. "All I know is it comes from over the gate at some prison camp—and it's part of Freyberg's collection. . . ."

Quinn didn't even reply. He knew already where it was from and what it was. Dachau. ARBEIT MACHT FREI, it said.

He closed his eyes and turned away.

"What's it mean?" said the lumberjack.

"It means that *work shall set you free*," said Quinn.

And he went down the stairs in his blanket and his mitts and he pulled his scarf up over his ears as he went even further down across the lobby, making his way past Annie's Crystal Saloon and the six wide marble steps that led to the great glass doors with their ironwork design, and out beyond the word *Elysium* into the snow, where he turned to the left and walked across the courtyard and out around the mountain through the blizzard, following the paths of goats and sheep, seeking a place where he could bury the ghosts of the fifty-five dead who lay on the lawns at Government House and the one who was eaten by birds and the one who was crouching in his cage at Pisa and the one whose hand was reaching back towards the past he could not prevent, the one whose silver pencil had burned the walls. . .and with every step, Quinn tried to hate himself for having made the mistake of thinking they were human beings. And for having memorized their names.

SEVEN

1941

Beneath the sagging roof
The stylist has taken shelter,
Unpaid, uncelebrated. . .

Ezra Pound

Mauberley was working in a corner etching the story of the Spitfire Bazaar.

Outside Herr Kachelmayer was sitting out in the sun with his wife. All the smaller children were playing in the snow. Only Hugo was not in the courtyard.

It was almost the end of April. The edelweiss was pushing through the snow on the lower slopes below the hotel and the sound of bird-song came from the valley, rising with the updraught. Sometimes an eagle was seen—but this was very rare.

Frau Kachelmayer noticed the woman first—and she nudged her husband. "Look."

The woman's hair was covered with a woollen scarf, and she wore a moleskin coat and a pair of army boots. She looked, in fact, very much the sort of woman who might have been in the army, were it not that she was limping and had no uniform.

Herr Kachelmayer told his wife to leave things up to him, and not to interfere and not to show the least concern. His reading of the woman in the boots and moleskin coat was that she might be dangerous. A hungry deserter from one of the work groups who were clearing roads in the valley. A gypsy, perhaps, escaped from a concentration camp—or maybe even a spy. The fact that she carried no luggage did not bode well.

Still, he approached her with all his usual charm and expansive hospitality. What could be the harm in showing her how innocent he was.

Hugo was watching from the Kristall Salon—ticking off her features on his fingers: *fur coat; dark complexion; ugly expression*—and as he watched her remove the scarf—*short hair*—"like the hair of a man."

He ran up the stairs and burst into Isabella's suite.

de Broca's aeroplane had just begun its magic writing in the sky when *die weisse Ratte* entered, desperately out of breath and gasping the words: "Quick, quick! She has come."

Mauberley at first was so engrossed in his work he was quite unable to make out what it was that Hugo meant.

"Short hair!" the boy hissed. "What should I do?"

Estrade.

At last. And the story on the walls unfinished.

Mauberley looked at Hugo, all the colour draining from every extremity.

Hugo had the strangest look in his eye. A sort of wavering smile that did not reach out to his lips. His lips were still severe and pale.

"Has she spoken my name?" said Mauberley.

Hugo paused just a second and then said, "Yes. But of course."

Mauberley reached inside the lining of his greatcoat, drawing out the useless nickel-plated revolver.

"Tell me the truth," he said. "Have you bullets for this?"

No.

"Dear God," said Mauberley. "Then how am I to stop her?"

"Maybe I can stop her," said Hugo.

"Then go and do it!"

"Well," said Hugo. "It will be dangerous. And what if I have to kill her?"

"No. You mustn't kill her," said Mauberley. Not that he didn't want Estrade dead. It was just that he could not ask a child to kill. Not even Hugo, whom he knew would kill in ten seconds flat if paid the right price.

"Can you just get rid of her? Get her away? Tell her I was here—and have moved on to Innsbruck. . . ."

Hugo still waited.

The bastard, thought Mauberley. And my life at stake. "All right," he said, "here." And he drew a huge uncounted wad of bills from the lining of his suit and held out half of them to Hugo. "Send her away."

Hugo took the money and weighed it like an expert, balancing the roll of paper without even looking at it.

But still he waited.

Mauberley could hear, quite plainly, Herr Kachelmayer's voice in the lobby below. But Hugo did not move.

And Mauberley said, "I will give you the rest of this. . ." holding up the other half of the wad, "when you return and prove to me she is gone."

Hugo left.

Mauberley barricaded the door when *die weisse Ratte* was gone and knelt and prayed to St Teresa—a thing he had not done since his sojourn in Spain with Isabella.

"Dear Madame—Santa Teresa—" he said, "—I do not ask for this woman's death. But only for my life. A little while longer. Please. . ." And he stayed on his knees for over half an hour.

At last, *die weisse Ratte* returned. He scratched at the door and spoke his name, and Mauberley let him come in by inches.

The first thing that came through the crack was Estrade's scarf, which Mauberley recognized from the train. And this was followed by a pair of boots; first one and then the other, thrown in onto the floor.

Mauberley pulled the barricade aside and Hugo himself came through the door.

"This scarf," said Mauberley, "these boots. This looks as if you have killed her."

Hugo shook his head. His face was swollen and his hands were bleeding and the front of his jacket was torn. But he looked very pleased with himself.

He swore to Mauberley the woman was not dead. But he said, "She is the next best thing—and she cannot harm you now."

Then he held out his hand and Mauberley paid him the rest of the money.

Kachelmayer himself appeared that evening.

It was all too clear that he and his son had discovered in Estrade a vein of gold they meant to mine to the very last speck of dust.

"You are much afraid of this woman. Yes?"

"It is true. Where is she?"

Kachelmayer looked around the room at all the writing and instead of answering, he said, "I suppose she would be most interested in all of this. . . ."

"Yes."

Kachelmayer snapped his head around, smiling openly. "One hundred marks the day. That will feed her and keep her away from you."

"Feed her?" said Mauberley.

"Yes, but of course," said Kachelmayer. "You said expressly to Hugo you didn't want her to die."

"I also said I wanted to be rid of her."

"But you *are*, Herr Mauberley. You *are*. It's just. . ."

"You don't want her to die, either. Yes?"

Herr Kachelmayer shrugged.

"There's a war," he said. "I have a wife and four children. . ."

"*Five*," said Mauberley.

"Yes, yes. Five. So one hundred marks a day. And you will never see her again."

"What proof have I," said Mauberley, "you haven't killed her and aren't just bilking me of money for nothing?"

"You want I should show her to you?"

Mauberley thought about it. "No," he said.

Herr Kachelmayer got his money. As did Hugo. Every day.

But they were true to their word—and Mauberley never saw Estrade again.

Nonetheless, he broke an empty bottle and kept its jagged body with him everywhere he moved. Against Estrade. And against the others, too. One of them must have inherited her razor.

* * *

Rudecki had gone hunting; poking; prying.

Down in the cellars, he heard a tapping noise: the way a rope will slap against a flagpole in the wind—constant in rhythm—all at once stopping, then re-commencing. Tap-tap-tap.

Out beyond the kitchens, in a dark and damp stone passageway, he found a row of lockers, each with heavy slatted doors, and he supposed they must have been used to keep the vegetables in and other things a hotel used that must be cold but not refrigerated.

Tap-tap-tap.

Oddly—even having fought so many battles in the night— Rudecki had no qualms about the dark. He just walked in.

It was not entirely pitch black. There was a spill of light that followed him.

The smell was damp and like an old latrine.

Tap.

Tap tap.

It could be rats. But there was nothing left for rats to eat. Unless they ate the wood.

Tap-tap.

Rudecki ventured half way down the row of lockers.

Nothing. Nothing. Nothing.

Nothing.

Then—all at once—a hand reached out and grabbed him by the ankle of his boot.

He tried to scream. In fact, he thought he had. But all he did was shudder.

Then the hand let go.

Rudecki—stepping back—away, crouched down and looked across the floor to where the hand lay out against the stones.

It was a woman's hand, and filthy black with dirt. Its wrist was pale and blue with veins and the arm, that stretched back in beyond the slats, was clothed in a sleeve that was torn.

"Who's there?" Rudecki asked. "Are you alive. . .?"

His answer was a movement—and withdrawal of the hand.

"Who put you in there?" he said. "What are you doing in there?"

"The fat man and the boy," Estrade said weakly. "The blond boy and his father."

Who could she mean?

Then it dawned on him: the bodies they had found.

"*Bitte*. . ." the woman whispered. "*Wasser. Bitte*. . ."

"Sure," he said. "You wait. I'll be right there."

Rudecki scurried back along the passageway into the brightness of the kitchen. Something was already happening in his mind. This woman was his own. . . .Not to tell the others: not just yet. This seemed imperative. After all, it was him that found her. Why should he share her, just to have her taken away.

He brought a silver bowl and held it under the tap until it was full.

He would give her this to drink.

He would find some food and feed her.

He would bring some rags—a towel—and clean her.
He would fuck her.
God.
The water overflowed the bowl.
Rudecki turned the taps and hurried like a spilling thing himself along the passageway.
"You wait," he said. "You wait. . ." as if he spoke to a dog. "You wait—I'll be right there. And then you'll be all right. You'll be all right. You wait. . ."
He set the silver bowl down out of reach of the hands, on the stones—and set about breaking the lock that closed her in.

Annie was drinking alone in his bar: alone, except for the people in his mind.
It would be nice if someone new should come. He was sick of Ingrid Bergman. Sick of her always moping in the corner. All she did was sit there: waiting. All she ever wanted was the same old song. Movie queens. Sometimes they could really get you down. Some, of course, could get you up. He smiled.
Rita Hayworth? Ida Lupino?
Lana Turner.
Ah. . .Lana Turner in *Ziegfield Girl.*
She was drunk. It was perfect.
Somewhere Tony Martin was singing; "You stepped out of a dream."
And Lana Turner—Ziegfield Girl—was drunk and she was walking down a staircase. That one there. In the lobby.

> *You stepped out of a dream,*
> *You are too wonderful to be what you seem. . .*

Annie Oakley, as he always did while tending bar, was polishing his rifle. All his little cans of oil, his rags and his brushes were laid aside and he snapped the final pieces into place.
Out in the lobby, Lana Turner dragged her mink coat down

the stairs behind her—moving her hips in perfect time to the music.

> Could there be eyes like yours,
> Could there be lips like yours. . .

Annie watched through lowered eyes. The golden hair; the pouting lips; the hand, unsteady on the rail. . .

> You stepped out of a cloud
> I want to take you away. . .

Annie pressed his groin against the bar.

He closed his eyes.

And opened them.

Someone was running. Someone was calling.

"Help! Help! Jesus! Jesus! Help me! Help!"

Annie leapt across the bar.

Lana Turner froze against the rail. She had reached the bottom step. But someone real was falling through the lobby. Someone real. A man. With his hand on his crotch—and his crotch all bloodied—half his trousers torn away—and his hands going mad. He was bleeding. Bleeding and screaming: "Jesus! Help me! Jesus!"

Someone else was running. Someone else.

A woman.

Others were running, too—Freyberg still eating a candy bar and Quinn trying to drag himself from the Duchess of Windsor on her walls.

And Lana Turner hung against the air.

Annie caught a glimpse of all these people standing on the stairs or coming down—or partway down. He couldn't tell. He was watching Rudecki—it was Rudecki—bleeding and screaming and clutching his crotch and falling down. . . .

And the woman. Running. As if she could not find her way—or was blind and did not know where anything was. And there was something silver flashing in her hand.

"Kill her!" Rudecki screamed. "Kill the fucker! She cut my balls off! Kill her!"

Annie stopped dead in his tracks.

Every muscle—every nerve was obedient.

This was his job.

He raised the Browning Repeater, making a short, clean sweep of the woman's path and he fired.

And she fell. In her moleskin coat.

And her razor spun out—whirring like a propeller—all the way across the floor until it stopped at Lana Turner's feet.

* * *

Germany: May, 1941

At exactly 5:45 p.m. on Saturday May 10th, 1941 a Messerschmidt 110 took off from Augsburg, Germany and flew towards the British Isles.

The pilot of the plane was Deputy Reichsführer Rudolf Hess. His destination was the estate, near Glasgow, of the Duke of Hamilton. The journey, apparently, was sudden. Hess did not even take a suitcase. In his pockets, however, he carried various phials of medicine and also photographs of his wife and son. On one wrist he wore a gold watch; on the other a gold compass. He carried a photograph of himself with his name in print across the bottom, afraid he would lose track of his identity before he arrived.

At midnight, von Ribbentrop was called into Hitler's presence at the Berghof and asked to explain Hess's strange "defection". The minister folded his arms and said he could think of nothing. The journey, he told the Führer, was just as much a shock to "myself as it is to you". In the salon where this scene took place were two other men—Leitgen and Pintsch, Hess's adjutants, whose misfortune it had been to bring the Führer the news his Deputy had flown. Hitler raged; screaming at the two men; "how could you have let this happen? England will say a knife has been plunged in my back! My allies will desert me! They will say I cannot be trusted! Think of the secrets Hess has taken with him! Damn you! Damn you! Damn you! To have let him slip through your fingers. . .Damn you!" And then, while von Ribbentrop sat and watched from his perch on a plundered settee (Louis XIV—taken from Versailles), Hitler demoted Leitgen and Pintsch, literally stripping their insignia from their collars and sleeves with his own two hands. He then called loudly into the ante-chamber, bringing the guard, who marched the two unfortunate men away to prison—and piano wire.

After they had gone, Hitler looked in the mirror and smoothed his hair. "Ruin! Ruin!" he muttered. He almost seemed to have forgotten von Ribbentrop was present. Then he turned to him and said; "why has he done this? Why?"

von Ribbentrop languished on the settee, crossing his legs and looking at his fingernails like an ad for nonchalance. "I shouldn't worry," he said. "There's every likelihood that Hess is mad and nothing will come of it but gibberish."

Hitler grunted.

von Ribbentrop lifted a long, grey hair from his lapel and set it free to float to the floor.

Hitler said; "how can you be so calm?"

von Ribbentrop smiled. "My dear old friend," he said. "I long ago learned that one must never react with panic in the face of madness."

The two men looked one another in the eye. As "moments" go, it must have been one of the strangest moments in the history of the war. Perhaps in the whole of history. For there was panic staring at madness personified—and smiling.

Hess was found, with his ankle broken, wandering in a field of maize. McLean, the Scottish farmer who found him, was nonplussed to be confronted by a courteous, wounded gentleman trailing the strings of a parachute and asking the way to Paisley. The famous countenance meant absolutely nothing to McLean, who never read the papers. As for Hess, he just kept saying; "take me to Paisley. I must see Paisley at once." He meant, of course, Sir Alan Paisley. The farmer thought he meant the town.

The constable on duty at Paisley that night was shocked to look across his desk and see a man he instantly recognized as Adolf Hitler's Deputy standing there, looking very angry and asking why he had been brought to the police.

" 'e fell doon," the farmer said. "From up over." No mention of the Messerschmidt was made, since no one had heard it crash so far out in the darkened Firth.

Hess kept rapping on the desk with his knuckles and saying over and over again that he must see Paisley. To himself he kept repeating his litany: *even if you have to play the madman; do so till Sir Alan appears. He is the only one who will understand your message.* . . . The words were welded to his mind.

But Sir Alan Paisley did not come.

Hess began to cleverly insinuate the instability of his condition. At first he merely twitched and drew the backs of his hands across his cheeks.

"You got an itch?" said the constable.

Hess made a noise like a cat, crawled up on the nearest bench, crouched there and began to purr.

The constable soothed him, put him in a cell and telephoned for medical assistance. He had never seen a madman before—any more than he'd seen a Nazi face to face.

Mewing in his corner, Deputy Reichsführer Hess looked out from under his bristling brows. His haunches ached. His ankle pained him and was swollen. Somehow there was a crack in the scheme of things. And before it could be mended, it ran across the floor of Hess's cell and up through his mind. What if Paisley never comes? he was thinking. What if he never comes and I am left like this?

The next morning the telephone at the Eden Hotel was nearly jangled off its hook.

At the other end Sir Alan Paisley could hardly contain his disbelief.

"Did you send him here?" he said. "Did he actually come on your instructions?"

"Of course not," von Ribbentrop said.

There was a pause.

Then Paisley said, "Do you think *they* sent him?"

"No."

Paisley waited, but obviously von Ribbentrop had checked, so there was no point pursuing this line of thought.

"Then what am I to do?" Paisley asked. "Here he is on my doorstep. He's already mentioned my name. God knows what he may say next."

"Then he must be silenced, mustn't he."

"Well, we can hardly tear out his tongue."

"That's right," said von Ribbentrop. "But what about his mind."

England: 1941

Shortly after the First World War, the British Army purchased an estate called Latchmere House near the village of Ham, in Surrey. Their purpose in doing so was to provide a shelter for the most severe cases of what was then called "shell-shock". In time, psychiatry insisted all pretence concerning "shell-shock" must be dropped in favour of calling a spade a spade: the patients at Latchmere House (all of them officers) were "irretrievably insane".

By the time the Second World War rolled around, Latchmere House was officially designated as a Mental Hospital, whose Director was a certain Major Olivor of the Army Medical Corps. Early in 1940, Major Olivor was approached by MI 5 who thought a mental institution with a military cover might make the perfect place to sequester enemy agents whose will they were seeking to break.

So it was to Latchmere House that the supposed Nazi agent, Rudolf Hess, was brought for "treatment" in the summer of 1941. He was suffering, or so it seemed, from a deep conviction that on or about the 19th of May he had ceased to be a human being and was now a cat without a tail.

Hess was delivered into Major Olivor's hands by Captain (Doctor) R. S. "Bingo" Baggot, an agent of MI 5. Baggot had been provided with the credentials of a practising psychiatrist (he was a medical doctor only) so that he might stay with his patient without arousing the suspicions of the staff. No attempt was made to deny the patient was Rudolf Hess: only the nature of his "treatment" was disguised.

Ham was a mix of idyllic scenery, remoteness, village charm and sinister walls. There was, in fact, an entirely fenced-in compound where the more recalcitrant of the German spies were housed in jerry-built barracks under the watchful eyes of bully guards and guard-dogs. Every once in a while (though it was rare) the multiple crack of a firing squad rang out through the woods to announce that another agent of the Reich had refused to break allegiance with his secrets. So far as the inmates at Latchmere House were concerned, the war went on—and so far as the town's folk were concerned, another pig or sheep had been slaughtered for the inmates' tables. This aspect of the institution was directed by a hulking colonial colonel known as "Tin-Eye" Stephens. "Tin-Eye" Stephens was from Rhodesia, the land of Prester John and diamonds, and he wore a monocle.

Stephens and Baggot often took Hess out for walks in the evening under the trees. Sometimes, dogs went with them and Hess was made extremely nervous. But Stephens carried a stick and, so long as Hess kept close by, the dogs did not seem to be inclined to bother him. Baggot carried a small rubber ball in his pocket and whenever the dogs did not accompany the strollers, the ball would be thrown and Hess would chase it and bring it back to Baggot in his mouth. Always Hess would be encouraged to investigate the rabbit warrens and the mole hills, in the hopes that he might consider killing the inhabitants—but Hess seemed to have neither the taste nor the talent.

"You realize, of course," said "Tin-Eye" Stephens—who, as a Colonial, knew a trifle more about animals than Baggot did—"this is the first and only vegetarian cat I have ever met."

"Hmm."

"Won't eat meat; fish; raw eggs; mice; insec's; birds—none of the food of a cat."

"Distinctly strange," said Baggot. But what Baggot really thought was that Hess must be faking the cat act, because "any real cat would defend itself by using its claws or by climbing a tree when chased or threatened by dogs. No real cat would run behind its keeper."

"Just so," said Stephens. "In fac' you may be on to him entirely."

It was decided Hess's convictions must be put to the test.

"We shall overwhelm him with cat desirables," said Stephens, "and see how he reac's. . ."

The first thing Baggot and Stephens came up with was the scheme concerning fish-heads.

Every Friday, fish was served to the patients and prisoners, and late every Friday night the remnants (mostly heads and bones) were disposed of in the incinerator. Now, at Baggot's insistence and with Stephens' help, the fish-heads were gathered up in a barrow and taken around to the hut where Hess was ensconced with his personal guard, and dumped outside the windows.

"The smell of that, to a cat, must be pure heaven," said Stephens, drawing his handkerchief over his nose and walking away.

The town cats came through the trees and made a feast of it and howled all night for more. But Hess was sickened by the stench and threw up several times. Major Olivor had to attend him in the morning.

Other tricks were played: female cats in heat let loose on the premises; mice uncaged in the bedroom; birds introduced by the score—but nothing was forthcoming. Stephens and Baggot finally concluded, as Stephens put it—"this is just an ordinary man like you or I: an undeniable human being and not a cat at all."

The game was up.

Or so it seemed.

In September of 1941, Hess was given a new attendant; a man who said his name was Hart.

Hart was introduced into the ranks of Latchmere's warders with credentials of the highest order. He had been, so his papers stated, a psychiatric orderly for more than five years at Llangho Prison, a place filled to overflowing with the cream of Britain's pathological cases including "The Mad Dog Killer of Tyne" and "Grendel of Botsford".

Hart had subdued them all. Or so it was said.

Within a month, Hart had induced his ward to eat not only meat—but raw meat. Hess was also made to visit the knacker's yard (on the premises) to watch the dismemberment of animal corpses, and to take his daily walk in the vicinity of the incinerator, where he was told to stand for various lengths of time in the fumes and smoke because they would turn his cold blood warm. And, finally, he was led on a chain (with the "collar" attached to his left wrist) deep into the woods, to a certain compound, and made to witness what he was told was the slaughter of a pig. The pig, however, cried out something human just before it died and the word made a noise in Hess' ear that was familiar, though he wasn't sure why. This noise was "Hitler" but Hess could not for the life of him remember how to put the meaning of this noise into words of his own. It occurred to him, at this moment, that a gesture might express the meaning just as well so he raised his hand in the air and smiled at it.

And then Hess brought the hand down as hard as he could bring it—slicing with it, like a knife, at the side of Hart's neck.

Hart was knocked to the ground—but got up smiling.

Hess struck out at Hart's neck again, but this time Hart

said to him; "no, not with the flat of your hand. Use your claws."

Three days later Hart stood in a telephone kiosk next to the local *Boots the Chemist* and placed a call to London.

"Paisley—yes?"

"This is the Keeper."

"Yes. Yes?"

"It's over, now. All done."

"Good," said Paisley. "Excellent."

Freeing himself from the kiosk, Hart looked up the street. Autumn was closing in. The wind was rising.

He began to cross the road.

Hart had enjoyed the work with Hess, although he preferred something more of a challenge than a "push-over". Hess had already been half-way there by the time Hart got to him. All he had to do was urge him over the line.

But he had done his job with brutal efficiency. Hess was entirely helpless. The word *Penelope* would never cross his lips again. Not coherently, at any rate. Nothing coherent would cross his lips again.

Knowing that, Hart walked on up the street and by the time he came to the end and turned the corner, he was himself again:

Harry Reinhardt.

The very next day Hess attacked Major Olivor in his office. Olivor's face, neck and hands were bloodied.

As guards rushed in, Hess crouched against the wall. Noises, quite inhuman, issued from his throat. When Baggot reached the scene, he took one look and realized that, whether or not his patient had been mad when he woke up that morning, now he was mad beyond all rescue.

One week later, Hess caught his first mouse: broke its neck with his teeth and ate it whole while it was still warm. In the next two years, he attempted suicide twice and by the autumn of 1943 he could not remember any human detail from his past. He had become a complete amnesiac—and would remain so, on and off, to the end of his days.

In the Eden Hotel von Ribbentrop read through the speech Paisley had drawn his attention to. Herbert Morrison, the British Minister for Home Security, speaking in the House of Commons, had said; "it doesn't much matter any longer what kind of animal Hess may be; the main thing is that he is caged."

von Ribbentrop smiled and set the paper aside.

Done.

Nauly: November, 1942

I had been seated in Diana's orchard. Bird watching. The arrival of the motorcar rather annoyed me, since it made such a noise it drove away the only green woodpecker I had ever seen in my life.

I watched through my glasses, thinking only that some bothersome local official had arrived to inform us of yet another regulation concerning the air raids that were increasing by the hour. Poor Diana, I was thinking. They have come to tell her one more field has been destroyed by a fallen bomber or one more servant is required for the night-watch or civil defence or whatever. The staff had already been abysmally depleted; nothing left but the oldest of the parlour maids and the youngest of the gardeners and stable boys.

At first there was just this tiny motorcar on the drive. Its driver, for the moment, did not get out and it was impossible to see beyond the glare of the glass. I did see—watching through my glasses—that a boy called Roger came from beyond the manor, carrying a garden fork. He approached the driver's side of the motorcar and some sort of cursory conversation took place. Roger then went away to fetch (I presumed) Diana.

But it was not Diana who returned. It was Niven, the stable boy. What was going on?

The door on the driver's side of the motorcar opened.

Harry Reinhardt.

I only discovered I had risen because I bumped my head on the branch of an apricot tree. This slapstick moment was unfortunate because the seconds lost in regaining my composure and my sight were apparently precious moments in which some verbal message had been delivered to Niven. And when I had fumbled—finally—their figures back into focus through the binoculars, Niven was nodding vigorously and speaking rapidly and Reinhardt was reaching inside his pocket, bringing out papers of some sort: notepapers—envelopes—or five-pound notes, I could not tell which, and handed them to Niven.

Reinhardt climbed back into the motorcar and drove away. I followed the car until it was out of sight.

Niven was walking through the orchard, coming through the tall grass in my direction.

This was a lad I knew. Niven had been born at Nauly. I had always liked him, and had taken great pleasure in hearing him whistle away in the barns. If he saw me he never failed to wave.

And here he was delivering a message from Harry Reinhardt.

"Well," I said to him, "what is it Niven?" fully expecting to be handed an envelope or a sheet of paper.

"I'm to tell you Friday at the Savoy. . ."

"I beg your pardon."

"I'm to tell you you're to spend the next Friday in town and a room has been hired at the Savoy Hotel in your name and you're to wait till the telephone rings. Mister Reinhardt said you'd understand, if I told you it had to do with. . .your first book."

Crowd Invisible.

How clever of Reinhardt to think of that. A description I might have coined to describe the *Penelope* cabal.

"Niven?"

"Yessir?"

I tried to smile.

"Do you like Mr. Reinhardt?"

Niven put both his hands in his pockets. "Well—I've known him so long," he said. "I never really thought about whether I liked him or not. . . ."

My heart stopped.

"How long *have* you known him?"

"Since I was twelve, I guess. May I go now, sir? I have a calf just been born. . ."

"Yes do. And thank you."

As he walked away the only thought that came was that ever since my arrival at *Nauly* since Isabella's death, for one reason or another, Harry Reinhardt had been keeping track of me through Niven.

All through my sojourn at *Nauly* I had been brooding—thinking of everything I did not do and had not done. I did not save Isabella. I had not saved anyone. I did not reach out for Diana. I had not reached out for anyone. I did not write. I did not think. I did not read. And excepting those moments in which I wrote in my journals, I did not have any contact with myself. I was a cipher. Nothing. And since 1941, when my country (only my nominal country by then) went officially to war, I had not even known to whom I belonged. I was like a person lost in drink, to whom the world is nothing but a place in which one wakes unhappily and from which one turns with stoppered ears and blinded eyes. I was useless—not to put too fine a point on it—to everyone. Even useless, so it appeared, to the *Penelope* cabal, whose only acknowledgement of my existence had been to remind me that Harry Reinhardt was watching me and wouldn't let me "slip away". I was even being called to London—and London was "real". But the Mauberley who would go there didn't think of himself as real at all. He was just a man who stood in orchards watching birds.

Very late that night I went outside and stood in the dark with my collar up and I thought: I could walk into Neddy's pond, like Ezra's crazy Chinese poet—embrace the moon and be gone. I could put a stone in my pocket, as Virginia Woolf is supposed to have done—something large enough to pull me down. Or I could go upstairs and lay my head on old Lord Wyndham's pillow and simply breathe my last. Death that simple—just stop breathing. And what would be the loss? I had done my best work. Maybe all my work. And lost my voice. My credence.

Dear God, I thought, the stars are dark and cold and far away. They give no light at all.

And if I were to do this, would it matter?

Well, yes. It would matter if all I did was drown myself. If all I did was drown myself, I should only be slipping my body underneath an envelope of water. Sliding from sight without a sound. Whereas I had always promised myself: before death—height.

And before height, surely some sense of climbing, even if only from this pit.

Friday? The Savoy? Like some dreadful assignation with a tart. If I only had the courage, I would go with a revolver. Isabella, my work and me—I thought. I owe someone a lot of death.

December the 8th was a Tuesday. Six years even to the very day of the week since Neddy's accident.

Late in the afternoon I went with Diana to the churchyard and she carried winter roses—the latest blooming roses I had ever seen at Nauly.

I stood back, removed as far as possible. Overhead there was a river of aircraft. German bombers. By daylight. It had come to this.

Diana set the roses down over Ned. And after a moment she removed a few and set them down over her son Charles

Augustus. Then she moved back, stared as one might look at a difficult painting, almost closing her eyes—with her head on one side.

I thought of all the laughter we had shared—even the arguments—all the enjoyment of one another's mind. And then I thought of Ned saying; "we won't get beyond this awful moment if people like you give in." And I was suddenly glad, in the presence of his death, that I was still alive and had rejected slipping under the cover of the pond he loved so well. What a desecration such a death would be.

Diana stooped above her son and rearranged his roses by his stone and came away quickly, looking up at the droning aeroplanes.

"In a way," she said, "I suppose I'm glad that Charles Augustus died when he did. It saves him dying now. . . ."

And we left.

I had never seen Diana look so grim. It was just as if a pin had been drawn from a grenade in her pocket.

I told Diana I was going up to town in order to visit with my American publisher—a man, so it happened, who was then in England as a Captain in the U.S. Army. This assignation was, of course, a lie—though I wished it could have been true. It would have been good to sit across the table from him then with a manuscript between us, and all those marks in the margins that are like a signal: *work in progress*. But it was not to be. The only work in progress was perfidious and ugly, nothing to do with the careful mind that used to be.

I went up by train. The room at the Savoy was booked, as promised: H. S. Mauberley, Esq. But the clerk at the desk had no idea who I was. Time changes.

All evening and all through the night, the 'phone did not ring. Only the bombs.

At last the call came through—on Saturday morning, very, very early, just as the "all clear" was sounding.

Paisley's infuriating, nasal voice informed me he was down in the lobby. Might he come up?

"Are you alone?" I asked him.

"Do you think I'm mad? Of course I am."

Paisley arrived in uniform. Blue, with excessive ribbons and braid. I disliked him at once. He was arrogant, brisk and dismissive of my past. I was nothing but another courier, so far as Alan Paisley was concerned. A messenger.

What I was told was this:

". . .we have mutual friends in the Bahamas. She is most willing and co-operative. He, to put it bluntly, is a bloody coward and from what I'm told, is more and more into the drink and cannot be made to do a thing. Which is to say, he cannot be made to make up his mind. Now, I grant you, this business of the Fiery Bazaar has been most off-putting. But a real man. . ." said Paisley, brushing some dust from his over-decorated chest, "would get around a bad experience and not let it get him down. After all, look at us. Bombs every night and positively surrounded by fire. Walk through a flaming inferno day in, day out. And do we run? Never!"

I became aware that Paisley would lecture me two or three hours on the subject of manly courage if I didn't prevent him, so I drew him back sharply. Why was I here?

". . .you're a friend of hers," he said. "Someone she trusts, so I gather. Someone who can help her deal with the hubby. He must be brought around to our side. And fast. The whole damn structure of everything we're about to achieve depends on his being in Europe by mid-summer."

And so?

". . .and so we are sending you over there to shore things up. To give the wife the support she requires—and to deliver information regarding their return."

Their return.

". . .but of course. They're to come back over and be made ready to be set in place. But the gen you'll be given just before you leave will explain. Above all else, you're to instill a sense of urgency. And if you must, devise some way to force him back. And she, of course, will help you."

And what if I refuse to go?

". . .dear fellow. You must be joking."

"No," I said. "I'm not joking."

Paisley's blood-pressure red increased. "Look here," he

said. "You're bloody well on your way and that's the end of it, Manderley. . . ."

"Mauberley," I said.

"Well. Well—whatever," he said. The name simply didn't matter. "If you don't comply. . ." and here he had at least the decency to be embarrassed by what he had to tell me ". . .your friend Diana Allenby will suffer for it. And I'm sorry to tell you this so bluntly, sir, but she will suffer the very same fate as her husband. And you don't want that to happen, now do you?"

Ned Allenby had been murdered.

Monday, I went back south by train.

Diana was seated in the morning-room. She was smoking. There was hardly any light, though it was only three in the afternoon. It had been a very wintry day, and cold. It took me a moment to realize she was drunk. Not in any brazen sense, but lost in the liquor the way a person loses her way in the fog. The world looms up with a different shape than it does in the sunlight, and apparently that is how she saw me, for that is how she addressed me—as if I was a shadow or a ghost. But one with which she was familiar, and one for whom she had been waiting.

"Sit down," she said.

I had barely removed my overcoat. I was shivering and damp, and already in a state of shock. Here I was with the widow of a murdered friend and I was the only guarantee she had—though she did not know this—that she would not be murdered, too.

"What is it?" I said.

Diana reached out into the gloom beside her and took up a notebook—one of my own—from a table on which she had also placed a decanter of whisky and the old glass box that had once been Neddy's and was now her own, for cigarettes. Abdullahs.

"I was going to apologize," she said, "for having invaded

your privacy. But I can't even think of how to word an apology, Hugh." She opened the notebook and looked at it. "I was in your room. I'm sorry, but this is my house. You are under my roof. I was therefore in your room. I don't know why. To look out the window, I think. To see which view it was you had of Ned's garden—since Ned is so much on my mind these days—and I got to poking around. I mean, it is my house, and I hadn't been in that room since you arrived. And that was months ago and. . ."

"*Diana. Tell me.*"

She bit her lip.

It took a moment for her to shut the motor off—the one she'd been riding downhill. She gulped from her glass and stubbed out her cigarette and lighted another one and poured more drink and did not offer me one and then she said; "you. . ."

I waited.

She closed the notebook, let it rest in her lap and then, quite deliberately, she threw it down on the floor.

Both of us looked at it lying there. Neither of us moved to pick it up. And looking at it, I realized Diana must have read all—and drawn a most terrible conclusion. The truth.

"Everything Neddy said about you," she said; "is true. You are a traitor to your friends. You have reneged on your integrity. Long, long ago you betrayed your own country. Now, you have done the same to ours—to mine and Ned's. You have consorted with our enemies and you have drawn out knives against us all. . . ."

"Diana. . ."

"If you speak again I will burn you alive," she said.

I waited. God. . .

The fog drifted. Clocks ticked.

And then Diana said, "The other night, Hugh, you wrote about suicide."

Yes.

She looked at me.

"And you are still alive," she said.

Berlin: 1942

There was an air raid.

von Ribbentrop was working late at the Hotel Eden. When the planes came over, the only thing to be done was to concentrate on something else. Air raids had come to be a time—both in London and Berlin—when many people made love, wrote books, gambled for fortune and started diaries. Only the children slept and, in order to achieve this sleep, mothers had begun to drug their babies with I. G. Farben's revolutionary new-strength Aspirin tablets: (half-a-tablet in warm skim milk). They were a miracle.

von Ribbentrop was working alone. He had been there four hours already when the air raid started. It began at ten. His notes were spread out all around him under the brassy light of a single lamp. At the window, all the heavy drapes and muslin curtains had been drawn and, so long as the planes stayed over the outskirts, the noise was not too bad. It was only when the guns in the Wannsee began to pound that the hotel shook and the lampshades tipped.

At ten-fifteen, he decided he was lonely. Picking up the 'phone, he rang downstairs to the desk. The man on duty there was very cold and brisk about it all. Such things had not gone on at the Hotel Eden before the war. In those days, the clientele were all respectable older gentlemen with nieces and ladies with their nephews. The Desk was not involved with anything more clandestine than a bottle of wine delivered at midnight. Now, Herr Minister von Ribbentrop had brought them to this: an actual whorehouse.

His Excellency's woman (whose name was Lisl) could not be contacted immediately, due to the raid. The Desk would have her there as soon as possible. von Ribbentrop was satisfied: he would go on working.

At eleven there was a knock on his door. Unthinkingly, von Ribbentrop didn't even bother to put on his jacket. He rose, with his fountain pen still in hand and slapped across the rug. He was wearing an old pair of slippers made of felt, and the heels were run down.

He opened the door without really looking to see who was

there. "In, in. . ." he said—and was half-way back to his desk before he realized no one had followed him. He had even undone the buttons of his flies.

"Lisl. . .?"

von Ribbentrop peered across the rims of his glasses.

Someone was standing in the darkened hallway. A man.

"Hallo," said von Ribbentrop. "Who is that?" Involuntarily, his hands fell down to cover his groin.

The man was in uniform, with his greatcoat slung from his shoulders in the Prussian style. He was also wearing his cap and appeared, from the silhouette, to be a personage of quite high rank.

"You're creating a draught," said von Ribbentrop, "whoever you are, and I'd appreciate it if you'd shut the door."

He went back over to his desk, from behind which he could see the figure—backlit—still in the hall. He sat down.

"I've come to tune your piano." The voice sent a shiver scudding up through von Ribbentrop's innards.

Schellenberg.

von Ribbentrop tried to laugh.

"Come in." He stood up. He sat down. After all, it was he who had rank, he remembered (in spite of his fear). And it was he whose flies were open.

Schellenberg entered and shut the door behind him. Having done this, however, he stayed where he was with his boots on the parquet.

"My, my!" said von Ribbentrop. "Look at you! A Major-General."

"Yes."

"And what may I offer you?"

"A little wine, if that were possible."

"Of course."

von Ribbentrop busied himself with the bottle and the glasses. He was wishing he'd put on his jacket and shoes. Somehow, he felt defenceless in his shirtsleeves and slippers. Draughty through the middle.

Schellenberg threw aside his greatcoat and cap and finally strode across the rug to a sumptuous chair in the aura of the lamp. His uniform was new and shiny. The nap was not yet broken down.

"Very impressive," said von Ribbentrop. The uniform creaked like cardboard. "Even though I never was fond of black." His own uniform, designed by himself, would best be described as pearl green.

They drank.

"What's all this about your coming here to tune my piano?" von Ribbentrop slipped into the chair behind the desk and reached for his silver cigarette case.

Schellenberg smiled and placed his glass on the edge of the desk. "Nothing but a figure of speech," he said. "Every time there's an air raid, I think of tension. Every time I think of tension, I think of a wire pulled taut." He made a gesture, using both hands. "And every time I think of a wire pulled taut, I think of a piano."

von Ribbentrop swallowed. He stared at Schellenberg. "Really?" he said.

"Yes," said Schellenberg. "My father was a piano manufacturer. He practically invented piano wire."

von Ribbentrop smiled greyly.

"All our pictures were hung with it." Schellenberg hung them in the air as he spoke. "All our mirrors—even the most gigantic mirrors in the hallways, framed with marble. Nothing tougher in the whole wide world than piano wire. *Prosit*." They drank.

von Ribbentrop looked at his lap. His flies were still open. Very carefully, he did them up. Button by button.

"And so I grew up knowing all about pianos," said Schellenberg. "And I really do mean it. I can actually tune one."

von Ribbentrop said, still staring at his lap. "But I have no piano, Walter."

"I know that."

There was an unpleasant silence. von Ribbentrop was forced, at last, to speak. "I don't like games," he said. " 'Specially *cat and mouse*, Walter." He looked at the master of espionage, but the master of espionage was playing with his lip. "Just tell me why you're here," said von Ribbentrop— steadying the glass and drinking the wine.

Schellenberg released his lower lip and drew his finger over the other, like a man who had recently worn a moustache. "Ah, me," he said. "Yes. Why am I here. . .Maybe just to check out what I know against what you know, Excellency, concerning one or two matters."

"Good. Try me."

Schellenberg finished his drink and set the glass back where it had been, precisely in the centre of a ring of spilled wine. "You've heard the news about our old friend Hess, I suppose. Gone quite mad."

"Yes."

"Interesting, I thought—the role that Paisley played."

von Ribbentrop closed his mouth up tight against his teeth. How was it Schellenberg knew? His discussions with Paisley had been scrambled, as always. How *did* Schellenberg know? Unless he had deciphered the code-break and tapped the wire. Or unless—(though this was unthinkable)—Paisley had begun double-dealing.

"And then there's all this new stuff about the Duke of Windsor. . ."

"New stuff?"

"Yes."

"Like what?"

"Well—I don't know. But I can tell you this much: that kidnap plot, where we tried to land him in Spain, was over and done with almost two years ago. . ."

"Seventeen months."

"Yes." Schellenberg crossed his legs. "Seventeen months." His voice trailed off for a second—and then came back like a thrown brick. "Following their escape, you know, every piece of information and every instruction in my department regarding His Royal Highness was stamped, by orders of the Führer, *no longer operable.*" He smiled. He sighed. von Ribbentrop was watching him so intently, the ash on his cigarette had grown by over an inch and was about to fall into his wine. "And in spite of the fact the Führer has instructed me to call off the dogs. . .the dogs have not all come home. *Have they?*"

The ash fell.

It even made a noise, like something drowning.

von Ribbentrop put his hand across the mouth of the glass, as if he could silence it.

Schellenberg was smiling his Schaemmel smile: his alter ego gleaming in the light.

Bombs were falling a mere kilometre away.

von Ribbentrop stood up and walked to the windows, where he pretended to fuss with the blackout curtains.

"You were saying something about dogs," he said.

Schellenberg held out his glass. "Was I?"

"Yes."

von Ribbentrop, looking very white and old, crossed over to the wine and poured a drink for his visitor.

"Thank you." Schellenberg sipped from the glass and then set it out in the light at arm's length, staring at it. "I have come here," he said—so quietly, von Ribbentrop had to lean forward to hear him—"in order to warn you, Excellency, that from now on, wherever your dogs go, my dogs will follow."

"You keep referring to dogs, as if. . ."

"Don't interrupt," Schellenberg said—and immediately Schaemmel smiled and said; "Excellency."

von Ribbentrop sat down.

"I admit I'm not entirely sure what you're up to," said Schellenberg. "But I have a fair idea. We made a bargain once, about a piece of paper. Perhaps you might do well to consider fulfilling your part of the bargain before you have gone too far. You will recognize, I'm sure, that it can only be a matter of time before I catch up. I shall not be unsympathetic, in the meantime, to hearing whatever you might propose. There is never any harm in listening. I can always turn you down, if I don't like the terms. And you, Excellency, can of course always take the chance of turning *me* down. Can't you."

von Ribbentrop did not reply. He was in retreat—inside his head; somewhat in shock—somewhat in wonder of this man's impertinence; somewhat in anger—entirely afraid.

Schellenberg finished the wine in his glass and stood up. He was handsome enough in his uniform to be intimidating just on that account alone. He was also in brutally fit condition, since he was so much in the field. von Ribbentrop, by contrast, felt like a twisted and worn out dishrag. The pressure of carrying the German arm of the cabal more or less alone for the last eight months since Hess's flight had taken its toll.

Schellenberg gathered his greatcoat and cap and stood across the room in the vicinity of shadows. A bomb exploded in the lake and made a great *hissing* noise—even showering the windows with its rain.

"I shall leave you, for now," said Schellenberg, swallowing Schaemmel whole as he put on the greatcoat. "But I do want to say I think you and I might do very well together whatever it is you're trying to do alone. So many plots are afoot. We live in a world of intrigue, don't we. One has to be so careful not to get caught up in the coils of someone else's downfall."

von Ribbentrop made a half-hearted attempt to reach him before he was gone—but the door was closing before he was more than a quarter of the distance. Standing in the middle of the carpet, one slipper on—one off—Schellenberg's last words echoed in his ear. "Everything to gain or everything to lose. Yes? Goodnight."

Two days later, there was an envelope on von Ribbentrop's desk at the Wilhelmstrasse containing nothing but a single loop of piano wire.

From that moment on, time was a hangman.

EIGHT

1943

The Coral isle, the lion-coloured sand
Burst in upon the porcelain reverie...

Ezra Pound

Nassau faces north and is braced against the sea by a low, thin shell of land called Hog Island. The beaches on this island are exquisite: long, curling stretches of pure coral sand. A few of the more exclusive clubs and two or three private compounds enclosing the vulgar mansions of the *nouveau riche*—whose names I cannot recall—were the only buildings there when I arrived in June of 1943. People really only used the island for sunning by day and dancing by night. The natural vegetation was sparse—mostly scrub—

but the club proprietors and the millionaires had planted groves of exotic trees which, having all their growth at the top, afforded shade but little privacy. Privacy could only be attained by erecting walls and these, made of stucco, were surmounted with rows of jagged glass to ward off thieves and "peepers". Hog Island was not a place I adored and I seldom ventured there. My dislike of it stemmed from the fact I could not disassociate the place from my fear of sharks. It could only be reached from Nassau by ferryboat, and on the very day of my arrival someone fell—or was pushed, as a prank—from the decks of this public conveyance and eaten by a shark in full view of fifty or sixty people who all stood by and did nothing.

The harbour at Nassau widens opposite the town, providing mooring space for private yachts and motor launches. There is also room for pleasure ships such as the S.S. *Munargo*, on its weekly run from New York, to manoeuvre freely into port past crowds of fishing boats and tramp steamers bustling about their business delivering cargos of fish and crab. Many of the steamers come up from Cuba and South America laden with tobacco, coffee and rum. Others come from Gulf State ports with oil and gasoline. Boston, New York and Charleston provide even more refined cargo: Scotch whisky, linen sheets, Philip Morris cigarettes and artichoke hearts in tins. And, when I was there, the Pan Am Clipper Service still had its daily flight from Miami, splashing down in the Bay and taxiing through the water traffic to its levee at the foot of Mount Royal Road.

All day long there was a constant clamour of birds and bells and shouts and steam whistles, intermingled with the cries of vendors in the Market Place and the songs of the Negro women clipping and baling sponges under the wooden awnings on the wharfs. By night, there was other music—some of it calypso, drifting out towards Hog Island from the bars and cafés on the waterfront, some of it sophisticated swing, wafting back towards the town from the Porcupine and Paradise Beach Clubs.

Now that America had entered the war, there were not so many tourists on Bay Street as there had been. Nonetheless, the population of the Island had jumped dramatically due to the influx of refugees and airmen's wives. The airmen themselves were stationed elsewhere in the Bahamas with the RAF Bomber Command. Weekends, they would visit Nassau and the streets filled up with blue—and blue being Wallis's favourite colour, she would stand whole hours behind her blinds and watch with binoculars through the slats as the blue parade of fair young men passed by—a river of golden heads.

It was to this place in the season of storms and hurricanes I arrived, June 3rd of 1943, to prepare the Duchess of Windsor for a sudden though undated departure for Europe. Her strength of purpose and her famous patience with fate were finally wearing thin and I found her quite alarmingly "old" and broken. She gave in very quickly to her temper; spoke unkindly of nearly everyone and was making enemies as fast as Ford made motorcars: *one a minute*. Her assembly line of bitchy remarks was begun with perhaps her most famous. When asked, after being introduced to Bahamian society, what she thought of Nassau's *crème de la crème*, the Duchess of Windsor replied: "I cannot answer that, since all I seem to have met is the *lait du lait*."

This venom was returned in kind, if not in words—since no one dared to speak her language aloud. Once while reviewing an Honour Guard the Duchess was made to stand on the ground while the Duke received a helping hand onto a dais raised so high it almost obscured his wife—and all that was seen of her on that occasion was her hat. Her extravagance was bitterly complained of, too, though I know for a fact she gave up many of her favourite foods and only wore so many changes of clothing—four a day—for the simple reason that her system could not abide the humidity, and the bathing and showering facilities of Government House were the worst I have ever seen in a residence that size. It was a nightmare place for anyone devoted as the Duchess was to personal cleanliness and impeccable appearance. Her hair, for instance, began to fill her brushes to such a frightening degree she had to send to New York for someone to come down and treat it once a month so she would not go completely bald. And the Duke. . .

Her concern for the Duke was also taking its toll. This concern ran so deep she did not even voice it to her closest friends: or, rather, acquaintances—since she had no friends. It was because of this reticence—so strongly at odds with her awesome willingness to speak her mind on other occasions—the rumour got started that she and the Duke were parting. He appeared less and less when there were guests and Wallis—searching her vocabulary of lies—could not produce a single explanation that did not veer dangerously close to what she thought was the truth. He had already lost his nerve and now, she was convinced, he was losing his grasp of reality. The fact she could not mention this to anyone, put a strain on Wallis that was monumental.

"Henny" Henderson, the Duke's valet, was born a nervous wreck. He always shook at the merest suggestion that anything or anyone new might be introduced into the world he knew and in which he was secure. This made of him the perfect servant: since neatness, precision and routine were the only means by which he was certain life could be maintained. He adored the Duke of Windsor, and the Duke of Windsor adored him back. "Henny" could do no wrong, and was even trusted with the make-up tables to hide those scars the Duke could not see himself. And there had to be someone, too, who could get the Duke in and out of the new and strangely bewildering supportive clothing he had begun to wear: stockings that held his veins in place; braces that gave him a back; and other things. . . .

Always these "things" would arrive in boxes from foreign places such as Hamilton, Ontario and Echo Valley, Nevada and Hollywood, California.

On the day of this particular incident, the Duke was in his dressing-room making ready for a public appearance of which he was extremely apprehensive. Henderson entered in a state of great agitation, having just returned from meeting the Pan Am Clipper. On board, the Duke had been assured, there would be a long-awaited parcel.

Now that parcel had reached the Royal presence, tied to the wrist of "Henny" Henderson with a thin and painful piece of string.

"You're looking awful fagged," said the Duke.

"Well I ran," said Henderson—petulant.

"Shouldn't run," said the Duke. "Isn't good for the heart. . . ."

"But, sir, you insisted. . ."

" 'Specially not in this dreadful heat. *Heat up—feet up!* That's my motto." The Duke swirled the contents of a large crystal tumbler and took a tiny sip, very neat and careful so as not to stain the edge with the red on his lips.

"Do you think I might sit down, sir?" Henderson asked, quite ashen.

" 'Course," said His Royal Highness. "Sit." And he nodded towards an ottoman.

The Duke, who wore his underclothes and a blue silk robe, went over to the bureau where he kept his whisky and poured himself and his valet a drink. He lighted a cigarette and waved away the cloud from around his face. He was looking extremely handsome: Henderson had already done his make-up.

"Well, well," he said, like a child pronouncing the opening words of a serious and complicated game. "And what have you brought me this time?"

"This box," said Henderson—and began to untie the string from his wrist.

"Hand it over."

The string was proving to be recalcitrant.

"Do hand it over. Do."

Henderson finally broke the string and the Duke set down his whisky, reaching out and taking the box in both his hands. "Don't watch," he said. "You must close your eyes."

"Oh, I don't like this," said Henny Henderson, half in the game, half out. "I don't like this at all. I never did like surprises, sir." He could hear a lot of papers rustling and string being scissored and something falling to the floor.

"Clumsy, clumsy me," said the Duke. Then; "damn. . ." and Henderson could hear the Duke of Windsor scrabbling about on the carpet. "Just keep your eyes shut. Don't need your help."

"Please, sir. Please," said Henderson. "Don't place anything wet in my hands. Nothing live, I beg of you."

The Duke of Windsor laughed.

"There!" he said. "You can look now."

Henderson opened his eyes—first one and then the other.

Before him stood the Duke of Windsor, blue robed and black socked, grinning from ear to ear with his yellow stained teeth. And cradled in his arm was what appeared to be the head of a life-sized doll from the mouth of which a pale, dry stream of sawdust saliva curved towards the carpet while the Duke reached up his hand to caress the white, wavy hair with which the head was crowned.

"A surprise," the Duke said—as if Henny Henderson needed to be told it was a surprise—"for Her Royal Highness. And you aren't to give this game away."

Henderson rose to his feet. Speechless.

The head had been meticulously formed and was made, or rather covered, with white kid leather. And the hair, which must have been human, was marcelled in a most distinctive way. The whole effect created a visage more than vaguely familiar to the valet and therefore more than vaguely disturbing.

"I distinctly told them not to give it eyes," the Duke was saying. "How very disappointing. But I see they're only painted on—so perhaps they can be washed away. . . ."

Henderson opened his mouth and closed it. The Duke was completely engrossed in the head and had begun to turn away, as if to show it to the mirror—and it was only in the mirror that he saw the face was damaged. At first, he looked quite cross—but then he stuck his finger into the drooling mouth to stop the flow of sawdust and muttered; "loose lips sink ships." His eyes caught Henderson watching. "And I might say the same to you," he said.

"Yes, sir."

"Not a word. Not a single word."

"No, sir."

The Duke laid the head very gently back in its box and retrieved his glass of whisky. "Am I right in thinking," he said; "that Her Royal Highness is in possession of what I believe they call a dressmaker's dummy?"

"Yes, sir."

"Is it much in use, do you know?"

"I can't really say, Your Royal Highness. But I can ask the seamstress. . . ."

"Do that. I should like the use of it for awhile. See what can be arranged."

"Yes, sir."

"Without—of course—suspicions being aroused."

"Yes, sir."

Suspicions?

Henderson went away extremely baffled. And not a little on the leery side. And the Duke retreated into the bathroom, where he ran a sink full of warm soapy water; into which he dipped his wash cloth and began to wipe away the painted eyes from the white kid face. And when this was done, he placed a Band Aid over the mouth.

As for me, I had been boarded out, so to speak, in one of Nassau's most prominent houses: *Westbourne*—the home of Sir Harry and Lady Oakes. It was here that Wallis and the Duke had stayed while awaiting completion of the renovations at Government House. But *Westbourne* itself was awful—and more than merely ugly. It was graceless and cluttered and it had no discernible shape. There were stairways running up against the outer walls and closed-in porches that were always damp and terraces that were always dry and verandahs, top and bottom, running all around the house. Constantly, as I recall it, one was being looked at or walked in on by a servant or by one of Oakes' sons who had just returned from boarding school. One of these sons in particular was extremely precocious, and might at any instant take it upon himself to walk through your bedroom, passing from one side of the house to the other without the slightest concern for what you might be doing or how you might be dressed or what hour of the day or night it might be. But it was after all "his house," and Oakes, who was inordinately fond and protective of his children, would brook no criticism, however gentle, of their behaviour. "If he wants to get to the other side and yours is the most convenient way, the thing to do is stand back and let'm pass." It could not be more simple.

As for Oakes himself, Sir Harry and his gentle wife were an odd but somehow endearing couple, perfectly matched as opposites. They·had met while on a cruise around the world in 1922. In those days Oakes was a feisty Canadian millionaire whose money was in new-found gold and she was an Australian beauty whose father worked for the Government at Sydney. Eunice MacIntyre had been a stenographer in a bank and that, till Harry Oakes, was the closest she had come to a million. She was half his age and "towered" above him—"towered" being Sir Harry's word—by more than three inches. She had the manners and he had the money. This story has been told a hundred different ways. Mostly we call it *Cinderella*; sometimes we call it *Goldiggers*. But in the case of Harry Oakes and Eunice MacIntyre, the plain truth was they fell in love. They were married in 1923 and over the years became the parents of five extraordinarily beautiful children—children of a troubling beauty: vaguely disquieting. Eunice preferred not to show them. Harry forbade them certain company. Of course this led to problems. Children grow up and want their own lives.

Oakes himself, although a Canadian citizen, was an American by birth—from the state of Maine. (The Duchess called him "the Baronet Boor from Bar Harbour!") His wealth was in gold, not a nugget of which was inherited. Oakes had strewn the world with his diggings, from the Klondike to the Congo, from the outback of Australia to the Laurentian Shield. He was a self-made man in every sense and had searched the globe with pick and shovel for fifteen years before he made his famous strike at Kirkland Lake, Ontario in 1912. Consequently, Lakeshore Mines became the second largest yielder of gold in the world. Oakes was made a millionaire two hundred times and more. And it seemed he was determined that for every dollar he would have an enemy.

His manner was appalling. His rudeness and meanness were legendary.

He was also enormously ambitious. In Canada he had decided his wealth was worth at least a seat in the Senate. But his enemies blocked him. No deal. No matter what he paid, or who he paid it to, nothing was forthcoming. The seats in the great red Chamber were not for sale. At least, they were not for sale to Harry Oakes.

In a rage, he went to England and there his money was respected. He was able to purchase a baronetcy with large contributions to St. George's Hospital. And when he returned to Canada, now Sir Harry Oakes, Bart., he threw his title into the ring with his millions. "What about now I get to be the Governor General?" he said. But laughter was all he got for this and Harry Oakes had finally had enough. If Canada had slighted him, Canada would be sorry.

He was already paying something close to four million dollars every year in taxes. And what if he died? Death duties alone might cut his enormous estate in half. All for a country that wouldn't even allow him to sit in the Senate. All that power—and nothing he could move. Except himself. And with himself—his gold.

He began this manoeuvre in the accepted ways of business traditions: forming various corporations; scattering his assets abroad in anonymous bank accounts; disbursing his profits amongst a number of specially created agencies. Still he was victimized and overtaxed.

In 1934 he met a man on the *côte d'avarice* of Florida— and this man, whose name was Harold Christie, looked

out across the Straits and said: "there are some islands
there. . ." whispering in Oakes' ear. "Weather adorable
. . .taxes next to nothing. . .death duties nil."

"Are they for sale?" Oakes asked. "These islands?"

Yes.

And so it was that Harold Christie, promising *death duties
nil*, sold Harry Oakes a good place to die and—all unwit-
ting—his death.

The relationship between the Duke of Windsor and Sir Harry
Oakes was difficult to classify. On the face of things, they
should have been enemies: one the epitome of all that is
civilized, genteel and respected, the other a walking sum-
mary of all that is crude, contemptible and mean. But they
had become—for a while—the best of friends and to some
degree, cohorts.

There was talk between them of business deals, something
to do with gambling concessions. Oakes wanted the concessions more than he could say. He had a great vision of stone
white casinos set amidst flowered gardens and amusement
parks. They would guarantee post-war tourism. They would
save the Bahamian economy. He would lend his name to a
number of great hotels. It would all be for charity, bounty
and posterity. The Duke might even have a hotel named after
him.

The Duke's part in this was to be historical. He would
change the gambling laws. Or rather, he would arrange to
have them changed. He would pester here and pamper there
and in the long run, being Royal, he would have his way.

Oakes knew a certain amount of money would have to be
made available—here and there. He knew the Duke of Windsor had expenses. He knew the Duchess had intransigent
tastes in what sort of table she set and what sort of rooms
she could live in and what sort of clothes she would wear.
And he knew the British Government was not inclined—if
indeed it was able—to send large drafts of monies hither

and yon wherever it was the Duke and Duchess might want to spend it. So, in order to gain concessions, Harry Oakes made concessions. In a word—he provided.

But my mission was not with Oakes. He was merely the host arranged for me by Wallis, who thought he would provide the perfect cover.

My first encounters with Wallis were tentative and formal. Neither one of us knew how to play the game. It was impossible to get away from everyone else for any decent length of time, but this was only because of our nervousness at what we were doing. If we were left alone we would no more dare to close the door than dare to flourish a gun.

But there were things one had to tell and things one had to know, and we had to find a comfortable way in which to talk without arousing suspicion. Suddenly I got a call one afternoon, about the second week in June. It was from "Her Grace's secretary"—a certain Mister Howard—and would I be good enough to meet the Duchess and her party at the Porcupine Club, Hog Island, that evening at ten?

This meant I would have to brave my way through the dark above the sharks. But Sir Harry said he would send me in his motorlaunch, which he did, but not before he had reminded me at length I was his guest and I was not to mingle with "the younger crowd. They're an immoral lot—white-feather boys and boobs." His eyes made a shift to the right and to the left and back to me. "I've a son-in-law there—and all his friends. And I don't want you near him. Understand?"

"Yes. . ." (Sir, I almost said.)

The son-in-law was Count Alfred de Marigny—married to Oakes' eldest daughter, Nancy. "But now I've got Nancy up in Boston. Sick with a minor operation. Only way to get her away from him. And you are not to mention her name to anyone. Understand?"

"Yes."

"I don't want her talked about," said Oakes. "I don't want any of them to even breathe on her name."

But her name was practically all I heard—though not at the Porcupine Club. It was from Sir Harry's driver, the man who drove me down to the wharf and, having switched vehicles, over the sharks to the levee on the other side. His whole conversation—a monologue—was based on the news regarding Miss Nancy. She had left her husband, Alfred de Marigny, and was seeking a divorce. This, then, was the "sickness" she suffered from. And the "minor operation" mentioned by Sir Harry was severance. It was all too familiar—and I thought of Wallis in Paris, 1936, denying every rumour while she was setting all the wheels in motion. Nonetheless, the story of Miss Nancy and her Count provided me with some explanation, at least, of Sir Harry Oakes' bad temper and his subsequent behaviour.

At the Porcupine Club there was Wallis, plus a party of twenty. Wallis was beaming and gleaming in a silver gown. I have rarely seen her give a better performance. Goodness, she was gay.

"Come on, Maubie," she said. "Let's dance."

I could not, of course, say no—but I dreaded the very thought of dancing. I had not even dreamed of dancing for years and it seemed unfair that my first appearance on a public dance-floor, after so much time, should be with the Duchess of Windsor. Obviously, I was out of practice with celebrity. When a hundred faces turned in our direction, I cringed. And when Wallis said to me, "Now we can chit chat. . ." I turned beet red. I thought the chit-chat was a form of dance and asked her how it was done.

Wallis threw back her head and laughed out loud. Every eye in the room was on us still, and would be till we were seated again. "I mean," she said "we can talk while we dance. And if the music is loud enough, no one will hear what we say."

She told me then to put my arm around her waist and take her hand. As soon as I had done the latter, she straightened her arm—and mine—and said, "You remember Dmitri teaching us the Castle Walk?"

I did—and we began.

At once the whole room gasped, since no one there had danced the Castle Walk since 1917. And some had never seen it done at all. Round and round the floor we went, with Wallis staring at me, smiling, and me staring back quite blank.

"Smile," she said. "Smile. . ."—through her teeth. "Play it up, Maubie. *Act*."

Slowly, more and more aware of what she was doing, I relaxed and even began to enjoy myself.

I too began to smile.

And all the people watched us—mesmerized, because we stood so straight and held our arms so straight, first down against our thighs then out towards one side, then upward in salute. And we turned and turned and turned.

"You are going away by submarine," I said.

"And how will we know the submarine is here?"

"A ship will come."

"A ship?"

"A silver ship—or white."

"A ship?"

"Not large. And it will sit offshore. And someone on the ship will get in touch with me."

We turned.

"And what am I to tell the Duke?"

"Just tell him: now the word has come and we are going back."

We turned.

"But he's afraid. They told us: *death to Fascists everywhere*."

"Then tell him we are going where it is safe."

We turned.

"This ship—will they be Germans? What?"

"The submarine is coming from von Ribbentrop. The ship— I cannot tell what he's arranged."

"And when?"

We turned.

"I cannot say, but soon. And when I tell you: *now*—then we must leave within the hour. That's all I know."

"But how can I prepare? How can I pack? What can I take? My *things*? The minute I open a suitcase lid, someone will guess I'm going away."

We turned.

"Make up a story. Tell them you're going to New York. A diplomatic mission. Of course the news must not be broadcast."

We turned.

"I think on a submarine I will not be allowed to take very much. It is not an ocean liner."

"No."

"But never mind."

We turned.

"If it comes to that," she said, "we only need ourselves."

We turned.

"And my jewel case, of course. . . ."

We turned.

"And the make-up tables."

Then—we turned—"But what if he will not come?" she said. "He is so afraid. You have no idea."

"Tell him if he does not come, he will be more afraid," I heard myself saying. "*I* am afraid," I said. "Tell him that, if it will help."

"You men," said Wallis. "Isn't it strange? I'm not afraid at all."

The dance was over. Some of the "audience" even applauded.

By the spring of 1943, the war had grown so large it was impossible to gain a comprehensive view of who was winning, who was losing. Everyone seemed to be in the throes of simultaneous victory and defeat. Only one thing was clear: so far as the *Penelope* cabal was concerned, the war had begun to move too fast. Events were clouding the whereabouts of the players. For us, it was not the sort of war where you could afford to lose battalions in a forest or a convoy of troops in a mountain pass. We had no troops. We had no army. All we had was us; and every figure had to be accounted for.

Chess is the best analogy: a stately game, a courtly game

where the moves are never blurred by haste. In such a game there is no indecisive movement. The fingers are never seen to hover above the board. It is only the mind that hovers there. The eyes tell nothing, yet they see it all. And when the moment comes, the hand goes out decisively, unwavering—plays and makes its statement all in one gesture. The figures rise and fall according to their shapes and everything that happens must be inevitable.

Now we had lost Hess. And Bedaux too, whom the French had arrested in Algiers late in 1942. He was charged with treason against France and America, but no one knew where he was being held. One moment, rumour told us he was imprisoned in Africa. Algiers. Next, he was being held in France and would face an Underground tribunal. Some rumours even placed him in Florida—talking, making deals, and bargaining for his life.

In Rome, Isabella's cousin, the Count Ciano, was fretting that unless he was allowed to knock down Mussolini *now*, the Allies would arrive from their victories in Africa. Nothing then could be done to set a member of the cabal—himself perhaps—in *il Duce's* place. All the gains and benefits of years of Fascist control would be crushed beneath the heel of democracy.

The cabal was still poised on the verge of its *coup*. But a grand success was needed and the best would be the recovery of the Duke and Duchess of Windsor. Nothing, now, must be allowed to prevent their being returned to Europe. *Poste spéciale.*

In my room at *Westbourne*, night after night, I could not sleep—or thought I did not sleep. The geckoes mingled with my dreams and I watched them struggling up the walls and creeping out across the ceiling—shadows only, beyond the netting—and every time one made it to the centre, I would count the seconds till it finally let go and fell. The lucky ones might only fall into the net, or be so young and small they had not weight enough to harm themselves or die. But every morning after my single hour of sleep I would push the corpses into a box with the toe of my shoe, and take them down into the service room, handing them over to Mavis Boodle, the only servant in Sir Harry's house who, it seemed, was not afraid to take compassion on the dead. And Mavis Boodle would lift the lid and peek inside and say what pretty colours and wasn't life a trial? Later, I think she would burn them, out in the oil-drum incinerator. Certainly I saw her there, standing in the mid-morning sun, with a newspaper folded over her head to ward off the flies.

Wallis had, early in 1941, established a Thursday night poker game at which the regulars were Harry Oakes, a man called Gillie Laidlaw, and, once every month, Elsa Maxwell, who "popped down" from her suite at the Waldorf in New York more or less on a regular schedule. She had come to be known as the "Waldorf Washerwoman"—always numbering among her many pieces of luggage the six to eight boxes containing Wallis' best French lingerie and on occasion the Duke's dress shirts. Returning to New York, Miss Maxwell would then be encumbered with the same set of boxes neatly filled with the previous month's soiled linen. In the hotter months the number of boxes would double, since Wallis, not being able to abide the feel of perspiration, changed her undergarments three or four times a day. Miss Maxwell, however, was never heard to complain of this errand—perhaps because she could raise, when her purse ran dry, a little something—or a lot—by renting out the famous lingerie at a fee. Her motto for this enterprise was a pun on a well-known song: *"you can dance in the slip that danced next the shirt that was worn by the Prince of Wales."*

The poker game took place in one of the private rooms where the public was never admitted. The only servants allowed at these sessions were the ever-faithful Henderson and the ever-faithful Mister Howard, Wallis's private secretary. Henderson and Mister Howard were barely on speaking terms. It was said their rivalry was based on the fact that while Henderson was allowed inside the Duchess of Windsor's apartments, Mister Howard was forbidden to cross the threshold of the Duke's. Henderson barred the way and once, it is reputed, even went so far as to say: "there are certain things we men don't want the other sex to see..." And Mister Howard had run away and was livid for a week.

The table was set in a corner under a pair of lamps, the heat of their bulbs being dispersed by a battery of humming electric fans whose gently weaving faces (white) created the impression of a small select audience watching a slow-motion tennis match. They were all lined up (about six or eight of them, depending on the humidity) along the top of a refectory table. This table, drawn in close to the players, was always set with an array of bottles and tumblers and buckets of ice. Throughout the evening, Mister Howard and Henderson provided plates of sandwiches, headache pills and—whenever the situation called for them—smelling salts. Gillie Laidlaw, whom I never came to know, was especially susceptible to taking his losses badly. Five hundred down and his hand would go to his forehead; eight hundred down and he would be forced to loosen the collar of his shirt and stuff his chest with a bib of towels; one thousand down and he became distracted, losing track of the ante and being unable to add or to multiply; fifteen hundred down and he had to stick his fingers into his ears to stop the ringing; two thousand down and he would faint. Elsa Maxwell said that Gilbert Laidlaw ought to learn the difference between a simple pass and passing out. I think he was some kind of broker. Retired in 1929.

Poker night, June 17th was one of the hottest nights that season. Everyone said so, and I believed them. Mavis Boodle, leaving that evening to walk back into town—none of Sir Harry's servants slept in the house—got only halfway down the drive and had to stop and untie the strings that held her dress in close against her body. Watching, after my bath, from the upper verandah, I could see the dress swell up with the sweet, hot breeze from the sea and Mavis Boodle sail

340

away like a woman in a tent. But the breeze soon fell and there was a dreadful stillness everywhere. I could not get dry no matter how many towels I used.

I have spoken already of Harry Oakes' precocious son. His name—I believe derived from his mother's Australian background—was Sydney. Sydney was never called "Syd". It was thought unbecoming and lower-class. He was a handsome boy, but troubled in some way. I believe he was then about fifteen or sixteen years old and ripe; very ripe.

Sydney and Alfred de Marigny had been friends ever since de Marigny and Nancy were married. Sometimes the boy went over and stayed with de Marigny even after Nancy had gone away to Boston. This was perhaps nothing more than juvenile hero-worship—an adolescent fixation on an older man. de Marigny, after all, cut a dashing figure not unlike the film star Errol Flynn. He was master of a racing yacht and had been almost around the world and he stayed up late at night—and there was always music on the gramophone and ladies from the Porcupine and Emerald Beach Clubs dropping in for drinks. How could a boy of fifteen or sixteen years resist? Especially when his father wouldn't let him walk downtown alone—or drive the car—or have a girl.

Shortly after eight, I heard a lot of banging of bureau drawers and slamming of doors in Sydney's room. Used to his habits by now I fully expected him to crash any second through my room and out to the verandah on the other side. I stood against the wall and waited, dressed in my shirt and undershorts and socks, with my new white trousers in my hand.

What I got, however, instead of Sydney was Sir Harry Oakes himself, in a state I can only describe as "appropriate". If heat precedes the storm, here was the hurricane. Oakes was soaked from head to toe and I thought he must have been standing in the shower in all his clothes. But the wet was only perspiration. His face was red with fury and I truly feared for his life. He was so enraged he could hardly breathe and had to gasp for air between each phrase of what he said.

In his hands—in both of them—were pieces of paper, crumpled and torn and surely about to burst into flames.

"That—that—that—" he rasped "—god damned pervert Freddy de Marigny! Get—get—get your coat! Come with me! We're going to. . .agh!" He raised both his arms above his head so he could breathe ". . .save my boy!"

"But tonight is a poker night," I said. "We'll be late."

"Late? Who cares?" he gasped. "The Duchess can wait."

"What's wrong?" I asked.

"He's gone. GONE. And my wife found this letter. . ." —waving it back and forth in front of his face, as if to verify its existence.

"Sydney is gone?"

"Yes. And this letter: this letter is horrible. HORRIBLE. . ."

Oakes burst into tears.

"Dear heaven. Please. . ." I said ". . .sit down."

"I can't," he said. "We have to get him. Quick. Before that Freddy. . ."

Harry Oakes turned and bumped into the door as he tried to leave the room. "Come on," he said, still weeping—blind. "Come on!"

He stumbled out along the verandah, squishing the pieces of paper into balls and stuffing them into his pockets. "Hurry!" he yelled at me.

I pulled on my trousers and grabbed my tie and jacket and hurried as best I could.

"What is it? What?"

I followed him into the car.

"That pervert Freddy stole my daughter! Now he's stole my son!"

The motor car leapt forward.

Harry Oakes was driving, still weeping.

From what I could gather in between the dozen fiery deaths we nearly died that night and the blasting of the horn and the screaming of the wheels, Alfred de Marigny had written a letter to Sydney, filled with "horrible, dragatory remarks. . ."—Oakes had also lost complete control of his language. All these dragatory remarks had been about Oakes himself and had been, apparently, inflammatory enough to convince young Sydney he should run away from home and go and live with "that...Freddy." Lady Oakes had found the letter in Sydney's pocket and had fainted when she read the letter. "Read it! You'll faint, too!" Oakes roared. But I could not even begin to decipher what was written on the scrunched-up bits of paper, soaking wet from Oakes' pocket.

At last we arrived at de Marigny's abode—a surprisingly modest bungalow with a wooden exterior step and a porch that might have been stolen from Rampart Street in New Orleans. Every light was blazing and music—also stolen from Rampart Street in New Orleans—was blaring from all the windows. Alfred de Marigny liked his music loud, apparently, and his lights bright red.

"I'm going in to get him," Oakes announced. "You stay here and guard the car."

Aside from de Marigny's music, the street was relatively quiet. But all at once the music stopped and the sound of shouting and banging leapt through the windows—falling, like two men struggling, onto the lawn below. I could hear no other voices save the two: Sir Harry's caterwaul and, I presume, de Marigny's relatively dignified shouts of denial. He must have said: *"I did not"* twenty times in the course of three or four minutes.

At last the front door opened and there was Sydney, hustling—being hustled—down the steps by his father. Alfred de Marigny, hugely tall and thin, was a mere silhouette in the doorway.

"Don't let him lie about this, Sydney!" he shouted. "Don't let him lie about it!"

Sydney, blank-faced and weeping, was pushed into the back of the car and Oakes raised his fist at the house and all its occupants. "Whores! Perverts! Bastards!" he roared. "Child molesters! Monsters of Sodom and Gomorrah! You have ruined my children—and I shall ruin you!"

As he got into the driver's seat he said to me, "Lock all the doors!"

The drive that followed was even more alarming than the first, though we did not speed so fast and Harry Oakes, at last, had his eyes wide open. The only weeping now was Sydney's—not any longer the weeping of a child but of a young incoherent animal flayed of all its protective skin.

When we had driven only a little way, I discovered with some apprehension we were not driving to *Westbourne*, but on to Government House.

In the poker room, the players had foregathered—Elsa Maxwell among them. They were wondering how it could be that Sir Harry Oakes, who was never late, was well over half an hour behind schedule.

"I suppose," said Elsa, who was always saying this, hoping to draw some hint from the Duchess as to why it *really* was the Duke would not come down and play, "His Royal Highness wouldn't consider dropping whatever he's doing, and play a round or two—at least until Sir Harry arrives. . ."

Wallis made a lot of noise with the ice in her glass, pretending she had not heard the remark.

At this point, there was a screeching sound outside of a car being rammed to a halt on the shells of the drive.

"Harry," Elsa muttered through the smoke of the cigarette that dangled from her lips, "has just remembered it's Thursday."

The car door slam-banged and the front hall suddenly filled with noisy activity, as if a troop was being deployed.

One of the aides could be heard, at some distance, informing Sir Harry the others were in their places awaiting him.

The Duchess fanned the cards and set them aside.

Out in the hallway Sir Harry's voice was rising and falling in a tirade.

Everyone waited for him to burst into the room, but he did not come.

An aide appeared in the doorway. "Forgive me," he said, "but Sir Harry Oakes has arrived."

"We gathered that," said Elsa.

I, meanwhile, had been left on the drive not knowing which way to turn or what to do. Sir Harry's behaviour had gone so far beyond the pale already.

Sydney was huddled in the back of the car, staring at his father with a look of hatred quite alarming.

Oakes had marched to the portico, pushed the constable aside and banged through the doors.

Wallis rose from the poker table and went out into the hall. Outside, lightning flashed and thunder crashed and a sudden rain was poured out of heaven by the bucketful.

The hall was empty. So where was Sir Harry Oakes?

Wallis reached up and pulled her ear in order to hear the rest of the house. Far away, upstairs—just as she had feared—she heard the voice of the Duke and then the unmistakeable obscenities of Harry Oakes. Wallis let go her earlobe.

She began to walk—with purpose and speed, but silent—up the steps towards the landing. Her hand on the balustrade was wet with perspiration and she paused to wipe it on her skirt, and to remove the noisy bracelets, dropping them into her bosom before she continued to rise.

The aide came into the hallway below her, watchful, but silent; tactful at least to that degree. Wallis turned, and wordlessly, she pointed up in the direction of the Duke's private suite. The young man nodded. Wallis nodded back and cautioned him, by raising her hand, not to follow her.

Wallis stood, quite unnoticed, in a tiny alcove that served as a vestibule between the Royal quarters and the rest of the house, and luck being with her, she discovered that the door had been left ajar.

Looking in through the crack which made a bright incision straight down the centre of her face, Wallis could plainly see the Duke, who was seated, and Harry Oakes, who was pacing in and out of view. Oakes was wearing his dress shirt and tie and the trousers usually worn with his yachting jacket—trousers of cream-coloured flannel caked with mud and soaking wet. His shoes made a squelching noise as he paced and his hair was plastered flat from his dash through the sudden storm and the tip of his nose was plagued with a steady stream of water pouring down his forehead.

Wallis looked at her husband. He was seated at the dressing table, wearing his kilt and cardigan. Chilly again. She noted the woollen scarf around his neck and the worn-out expression on his face, a man preoccupied with fear and helplessness. And with that thing he was making. . . .

Wherever it was.

Was it there in the room? Would Harry Oakes see it? God— if he did. . .

Wallis scanned as much of the room as she could through the slice of open door and—at first—she was much relieved to discover there was nothing in view that would give the Duke away. But then she saw it: standing back in the shadows. And on the bed—dear heaven!—a long black gown. She caught her breath and put her hand against her mouth. *Oh please, Sir Harry: please stay angry. Don't regain control of yourself. Don't look around you. Don't.*

But she need not have prayed. Sir Harry was apoplectic. Something to do with one of his sons and "that pervert de Marigny. . ."

"I changed my will, of course," he was saying. "Him and Nancy won't get a god damn penny. Not a god damn cent. So there's nothing more I can do on that score. She's married to the twit and that's the end of it. But now. . ." Oakes became incoherent with rage. "When I went in there tonight! There was *ladies* there!" He gave the word 'ladies' a twist of disgust that almost choked him. "*Ladies*. . .and my son! My son was there—and oh—oh—oh! There was boobies everywhere— and men who was touching them: titty-touching in the presence of my son and one of them women was touching *him*. My son. She had her hand on him. Had her hand right on him! I tell you, Duke, if you don't get off your behind and do something. . .do something. *Do* something. Why, there must be millions of ways! You could force a court order. You could banish them; exile the bastards. You could. . .you could. . .Perverts!" Oakes at last sank down on the end of a chaise and put his face in his hands and wept.

The Duke of Windsor finally blinked.

"I'm not the government, you know," he said. "I mean, I'm not the Assembly and I can't create the law. We found that out when we tried to change the books on gambling, Harry."

"But you could make demands. *You could make demands.*" Oakes rose and sat down. "I mean, he's only a child. There has to be some law covers *that*, when he's only a child." Oakes rose again and stood in the very centre of the floor.

The Duke was watching him through the mirror, Wallis watching him through the crack in the door. Oakes was caught between them. For a minute he seemed unable to move. When he spoke again, his voice was tired and weakened by the expenditures of rage and bewilderment. "I can't believe," he said, "that I'm standing here and you're telling me there's nothing you can do. When my son is exposed to. . .when my son. . .when. . .I can't believe there's nothing you can do."

The Duke just waited, looking down and moving rings and cuff-links around the surface of the dressing table.

"Banish the bastards. Exile. . ." Oakes whispered.

The Duke of Windsor smiled. "Harry," he said. "It's *me* that's in exile. Me that's been banished. . . ."

And me, Wallis whispered.

"Can't you understand?" said the Duke. "I'm nothing but a figurehead. I don't have any power at all."

Oakes clenched his fists. "You're the Prince of Wales!" he shouted hoarsely. "You're the god damn Prince of Wales!"

The Duke did not reply, but turned away from the mirror in which Oakes stood reflected.

"My son. . .my daughter. . .and this *place*! This god damn place of which you're the Governor! I'll tell you what: if *you* don't clean them out, *I'll* clean 'em out. I will! And I'll send my kids away from here and my kids will never come back. Never. And I'll have a word with the papers, too. I *will*! I will speak about this—and I *will be heard*! And you aren't going to like that, Prince. You are not going to like what I have—what I *will* have to say: about this place—this place of which you are the Governor; this place where I cannot get myself a legal casino. . . ." Oakes was shaking with fury, ". . .but where my son can get himself laid at the age of fifteen by a bunch of whores on whom you turn a blinded eye! You're god damn right, you have no bloody power! You hen-pecked, impotent twit!"

Wallis paled.

But the Duke did not budge.

Oakes crossed the floor and stood so close to Wallis in her hiding place she could smell the wetness of his clothes and feel the heat of his anger. "And another thing," he said, "I'm calling your credit, Duke. I want my money. *All* of it. *Back.*"

Fifty thousand dollars—in the last year alone.

Oakes pushed the door wide open, making a prison from which the Duchess could not escape. She could not see, but she could feel the power in his hands as he pushed and pushed and pushed against the door as if he knew she was there and meant to crush her. "You're nothing but another human being, Your Royal Highness," Oakes said, with a hint of astonishing gentleness in his voice. "And people ought not to have what you have unless they deserve it. All my life I fought for what I got, and it's people like you I had to fight against. But it's you that owes me, now. You owe me. And I guess that says it all." There was the slightest pause, and then Oakes said, "Goodbye. . ." and was gone. There was no more pressure on the door. And Wallis could breathe again.

She heard Oakes going away and down the stairs. She looked in through the crack at David.

He was seated before the mirror: wool-backed and blond and utterly still. From the shadows, off to the right, the "thing" itself was watching him. And he was watching it, with its pale kid face and its broken mouth with the Band-Aid pasted over its lips. And its crown of marcelled hair. And—on the bed—the dress.

Wallis shut her eyes. *You're nothing but another human being;* she heard Oakes shout in her mind. And then she opened her eyes and thought: *whatever that might be.*

Down in the hallway, to which I had finally been admitted by the nervous aide, I watched Sir Harry make his exit from the scene and heard him drive away with Sydney. The hall, in spite of its chandeliers, its tiles and its modest grandeur, had taken on the feel of a hospital waiting-room.

I was wet and I wanted to delay my entrance to the poker salon. The aide, who had only seen me once or twice before and was not yet sure of who I was, stood over near the door to the portico, looking for all the world as though it was his job to keep the storm outside from entering. I sat in a high-backed chair and made a rainy puddle round my feet. There was silence now that Oakes had gone, and all we could hear was the thunder.

Wallis, coming down, was like an actress in a film. She used the stairs quite consciously and made a scene of dignified bereavement. The "star" upstairs had died, and here came the widow, walking into the future, music swelling up with every measured step she took. The aide and I were watching, he at attention, me from my puddle, rising.

Wallis paused at the bottom.

"Mister Hugh Selwyn Mauberley," the aide announced.

"Yes," said the Duchess. "We've met." And coming across towards me, she put out her hand, over which I bowed in order to kiss the tips of her fingers. But I found no fingers there to kiss.

She had made a fist—and the fist was so tight I had to help her force it open.

"Thank you," she said. And when I looked, I could see the enamel over her features had cracked.

And then she led me away, the two of us walking, all unaware, across the frozen sea of the tiles—and I thought: *if the ship doesn't come, we will walk like this all the way to Europe, with her hand on my arm.*

Sir Harry Oakes' neighbours were now alarmed.

First, he had sent his children away and then his wife. Then he had fired over half his servants—Mavis Boodle remaining. Next thing people knew, he was living "all alone" at *Westbourne* and wouldn't answer the telephone. In the evenings, after Mavis had gone, I had to answer it for him— and some times I could hear him picking up the extension: *click*—and his breathing. Unlike Wallis, he was new to the spying game.

He began to walk around in workman's boots and old fatigues. He ceased to be a gentleman entirely—not that he'd ever been much good at it. Now he was even dirty. He never washed and was always unkempt.

He pulled up the flowers in his garden. He made a great fire and burned them all. He appeared one day with an axe and cut down all the little trees that grew along the edge of his drive. He drove his car around his lawns and chewed up all the grass.

Some years before, when he'd first arrived and begun to buy up all the land that Harold Christie had for sale, the first thing Oakes had done was plant a thousand trees. Evergreens mostly—spruce and pine and other trees that liked a sandy, shallow soil. They had been his pride and joy, these trees— and everyone had said: "a man who plants so many trees where no trees were before can't be all bad." It had been the first good sign that Harry Oakes was civilized. Now he went down to the Public Works and came back out along the road with an army truck and trailer. When the trailer was unloaded, what came down the ramp was a dirty yellow bulldozer.

"What's he want with a bulldozer?" Mavis asked.

One of the other servants answered, "Maybe he's going to build that big hotel and gambling casino hisself."

But this was not the case. For days, what he did was go out early in the mornings, while the sun was still at a tolerable angle in the sky, and knock down trees—all the thousand trees and more he'd planted and nourished and cultivated over the past ten years. He destroyed them—every one.

No one now would voluntarily go near him. I was growing

more and more alarmed. I was afraid. After all, he was sworn
to some kind of vengeance—and now all the trees were gone,
there would only be human beings to turn it against. Oakes
was dangerous and unpredictable. Up on his bulldozer,
screeching its gears and bellowing its horn, he was like a
mad rogue elephant run amok and trampling down the world
around him.

But no one ever got close enough to see the tears that
streaked the dust on his face—and I only saw them myself
through my binoculars. And he wept all the time he worked,
and he cried at night, when he thought that I had gone to
sleep.

He kept this up for two whole weeks, and then there was
a silence.

That was when his neighbours started locking their doors.
And I started locking mine.

Elsa Maxwell, squat as a toad, was not notorious for tact.
There was nothing she would not say or do, if the spirit
moved her. Consequently, it was she who blundered upon
Queen Mary in the course of making a foray into the forbidden area of the Royal apartments.

It was Thursday, July 1st and Elsa had come to spend the
whole week because of the Fourth of July holiday. Early in
the evening she left the poker table and went to look for a
washroom. That week—it so happened—the washrooms in
the public section of the Mansion were undergoing repairs
and the only one of them in service was occupied at the
time of Elsa's need. But Elsa's need was greater than her
trepidation, so she simply marched up the stairs and turned
to the left.

"Afterwards"—as Hemingway would say—she re-entered
the passage and was about to descend the stairs when her
attention was caught by the sight of an open door: and beyond that open door—the sight of a woman in a long black
dress. Elsa now prowled eagerly forward unhampered by
discretion; stepping into the Duke's private quarters beyond

the little alcove where Wallis had stood watching Harry Oakes two weeks before. The door was open; Elsa was there; she sailed in. What could be more natural?

She announced herself with one of her sumptuous coughs. Elsa was slightly asthmatic. And she had her excuses at the ready, like an ace up her sleeve. But she was not prepared for what she saw, and therefore all her excuses dropped to the floor. As she did herself.

"Your Majesty. . ." she said. And hoisted her skirts in order to manage a curtsey.

The Queen was standing just beyond the open door that led into the Duke of Windsor's bedroom. She was wearing black and, also, one of her famous hats.

Rising, Elsa reshuffled her pack of resources and was about to launch into an elaborate story about the Duchess having sent her up to enquire if the Duke would not come down and join them at cards when. . .the door swung closed in her face and the light all around her dimmed.

"How strange," she said to the air. And the suddenly empty room in which she now found herself standing took on a sinister silence. Doors were so seldom shut in Elsa's face—and whenever they were, it was always with some comment or expletive preceding the slam. But this was different. . . .This was the Queen. . . .And. . . .

Elsa retreated hastily.

Down in the poker room, Elsa Maxwell drew the Duchess of Windsor aside and whispered urgently. "Why in the name of heaven didn't you tell me?"

"Tell you what?"

"Your secret. Your secret." Elsa's eyes were dancing into every corner of Wallis's expression—trapping every nuance of the effect her words were having. "Your secret. You know. . ." And Elsa made a furtive gesture towards the upper reaches of the house.

"No," said Wallis. "I don't know. What are you talking about?"

Elsa looked across at the rest of us, seated—innocent—looking at our cards and trying to overhear her conversation with the Duchess.

"Wallis dear, please," said Elsa. "Don't be coy. I *know.*"

Wallis felt an urgent need to be seated, but there was nowhere near enough to sit. It appeared to her stranded reason that Elsa could only have discovered one thing—since only one 'secret' existed worthy of so much excitement and that was *Penelope.* But how? By what means?

Elsa—seeing she had the Duchess on the run—pursued. Her eyes filled up with knowing brightness and she said; "oh—I know it all, now." And then she said and did the most frightening thing that anyone could say or do to Wallis—given the circumstance. She winked—and curtsied and muttered: "Your *Majesty. . . .*"

Wallis—whose lifelong episodes of feeling faint could be numbered on one hand—nearly passed out cold on the spot. Elsa knew. And if that were so, then the very bowels of gossip had been opened and would gush the whole wild tale upon the world.

"How did you discover this," she said at last: resigned but already regaining her command of the situation—thinking ahead and wondering how Elsa Maxwell might be silenced.

"Well—I *saw* her," said Elsa with triumphant simplicity.

"*Saw* her?" Wallis could not quite take this in.

"But of course. Upstairs. Just now. In His Royal Highness' bedroom."

"His bedroom?"

"Yes. The Queen. The Queen. Queen. . ." Elsa looked at us and lowered her voice so far it became *basso-profundo molto sotto voce.* "Mary," she sighed. And smiled. "And oh—you should talk about 'majesty'. The way she stood there. The carriage. The bearing. The dignity. The dress. The hat. . . ."

"The dress. The hat. . . ." Wallis repeated. And then there was an instant flood of relief. "Oh! You mean Queen *Mary.*"

Elsa gave Wallis a look of disdain. As if she could be fooled. "Yes, Wallis. I said 'Queen Mary'."

Wallis took Elsa by the arm and propelled her into a corner.

"You realize what would happen if anyone should discover this. The Queen's very safety depends upon it."

Elsa said; "dear. Do you really think I'd breathe a word?"

Wallis said; "yes. I do. And you mustn't. Or I shall have you arrested."

Elsa stared.

Wallis said; "yes. I would. It's that important."

Elsa sighed. "Well," she said. "At least it explains a lot. I mean. . .about the laundry hampers these last eight weeks or so. And all that strange conglomeration of underthings. The knickers. The camisoles. The corselets. . ." She restrained a guffaw. "I thought they were yours."

This set them both to laughing.

The crisis had passed.

"Dear," said Wallis. "The day *I* wear a corset, you will not."

Nothing was ever quite so satisfying in the presence of Elsa Maxwell as having the very last word.

Later that night, the Duke of Windsor sat on the edge of his bed with his mother's head balanced on his lap.

He had removed the black toque with its dyed mauve sprig of clipped and trimmed feathers and the long strands of pearls that were Queen Mary's trademark and his posture was forlorn and defeated.

He was looking at the dressmaker's dummy borrowed from his wife's seamstress and at the long and elegant gown with which it was adorned.

It was a failure.

Head and body could not be made one. Whatever Elsa might have said to Wallis concerning 'dignity', 'bearing' and 'carriage' there could never be dignity and bearing and carriage to equal those of his mother. Not that he was slighting Wallis. But the head and the body could not be made one: and that was all there was to it.

And so—what now?

What of the mantle of majesty he had wanted so for his wife that he had given up a portion of his reason to attain

it? Gone. He could not—for all his strengths and charm—
attain the very least of it: her right to be called *Her Royal
Highness*—let alone Queen. He would have to accede. And—
in that moment—sitting there on his bed at the approach of
that midnight in July of 1943, he did accede. With his mother's
head in his lap and the shadow of his wife flung up against
the wall, the Duke of Windsor knew he was condemned
forever to be hidden by the shadow of his wife: a shadow
that would lengthen till it all but shuttered out his own: just
as his mother's had in that moment when she made him
feed the birds and had left him there alone to find his way
from a room without the benefit of lights.

Well.

There was still one thing.

The mirror.

And there he sat—waiting. Hours.

When, at last, he could not sit still any longer—he held
his mother's head up close beside his own and stared. Slowly—
very slowly—he withdrew the Band Aid from across her
mouth and watched as all the sawdust fell away into the
darkness, out of sight.

And in the morning, he went out all by himself—and
found a place to incinerate the head: until not a trace of it
remained.

Mavis Boodle had grown up full of wonder that the paradise
she lived in was so filled with death and decay. The shores
of her childhood were littered with the refuse of storms and
far off civilizations. The bones of ships and horses washed
in through her dreams, her only memory of the Spanish-
American war. A convoy of transports had been harried
through the straits by a hurricane and two of the transports
had gone down carrying their cargo of cavalry mounts. The
sharks had done the rest, but the remains of their feasting
had been carried over the reefs and into the lagoons by
stormy tides. Mavis did not remember much of the cause

of all this wreckage, since hurricanes came and went on a regular basis all through her life. But the tangled bones of the ships and the skulls of the horses, filled with tiny feeding crabs had haunted her memory always. They, and the stark bleached icons of her dead parents were the stones on which she stood forever, looking out at life with hand-shaded eyes, scanning the future for some returning figure—any returning figure—ship or horse; mother or father, fleshed in hope. Anything would have satisfied her, just so long as it came back living, or bearing news of life.

Often, during the time when Harry Oakes was knocking down his trees, Mavis Boodle would finish a portion of her work and then, unable to sustain her tolerance of watching so much destruction, she would wander down and sit as near the shallows as she could get. I, through my binoculars, could see her back as she sat far off, and the parasol with which she warded off the sun. Once, I recall she returned with a scowl on her face because her favourite trees had just become the latest victims of Harry Oakes' rampage. "I have been counting the birds," she said, "and wondering where it is they come from when they drop so sudden from the sky. And, where will they sit, Mister Mauberley, now all Sir Harry's trees is gone?" And then she said, the scowl expanding till it even seemed to affect her shoulders; "I took to noticing they never mourn their dead—the birds—but eats 'em." Then she looked beyond the windows to the noise of Sir Harry wrecking trees and said, "There's a lesson there, in the birds, somewhere."

On July 3rd, a Saturday, Mavis came back happy from the shore and she said, "There's a ship out there. A big, long silvery ship way out. You ought to go and take your binoculars, Mister Mauberley, and see. Looks like a ship from a fairy tale."

When I saw it first, that evening in the sun, I could only think of the *Nahlin*, seven years before and almost to the day. It was, in effect, a sort of spirit-ship—a mirror ship, a spectre, lying out beyond the reef—and the last thing lit by the dying sun as it fell behind the island. I knew, of course, it had come for Wallis and the Duke and I prayed it had come for me, as it had before in its first incarnation; me and ten thousand others, surrogates for all the world as we ran and tumbled down that hill in Dubrovnik. Only now there was no one standing; no one hoisted onto another's shoulder; no one crying *long live love!* and *death to darkness!*; no one lighting torches and crying through the streets *Eduardo!* No one carried the moon or put it in the sky. There was nothing, now, but the shaking out of one bright sheet of light that fluttered and fell and was drowned in the sea and the night by which the ship was hidden, falling across us all.

Oakes was seated in his kitchens eating "rations" which included sourdough bread he had made himself. He was weeping all the time he ate.

I have never known a human being to be so incessantly despairing. It was always either too hot or too cold a day. "If only it would rain; if only the sun would shine. I can't stand all these people; where have all the people gone?" It was a tirade of sighs and moans from dawn to dusk. His concerns were not entirely selfish and he cranked and complained as much in behalf of others as he ever did in his own behalf. "The niggers here are dreadful unhappy," he told me once. "Poorest niggers I ever saw outside of Africa. Something's got to be done about it, you know. 'specially the children. Nothing, nothing, nothing to look forward to. And that, of course, is the whole point of life," he said; "having something to look forward to. . . ." His saying that reminded me of my father. And Oakes' face, like Ezra's, was always screwed up around a question—though the question was a mystery. Or was it? It occurs to me that always, always inside of Oakes' head there was a voice to which he paid the kind of heed that drives the saner voices into silence— until its whinings and complaints are the only thing to be heard.

"You ever go to bed with the Duchess?" he asked—with butter running down his chin.

"Of course not," I said. I was tense and testy, having seen the ship and knowing what it meant. I was waiting for the messenger to get in touch and uncertain how this would be done.

"Funny, the way he gave up owning the world to have her," said Oakes. "And what a ride she's given him. All the way up—and all the way down. I don't understand. . ." He belched. "You think she's drained him dry—or what?"

"I don't know what you mean," I said.

"He looks like a man who has to spend all day just getting himself prepared to think about having an erection. All his juice is gone—and I figure she has to be the cause of that.'"

"It's none of your business, Sir Harry."

"Oh? I think it is. I think it is and I think it ought to be, when a man who's supposed to be our leader can't get off his arse because his wife has put the pliers where they'll hurt. Came down a great long fall, that man—and I think it's all her doing."

"Well you're wrong."

"Whose doing is it, then?" said Oakes. "Something's certainly made him incapable—afraid. . ."

The telephone rang.

Oakes did not stir. It was just as though it had not rung at all.

It rang again. Oakes did not appear to hear.

"Someone ought to be doing something," he said. "Standing up for values, decency, the law. . ."

I rose. The telephone was across the room in the housekeeper's office, which was just a glassed-in cubby-hole with shelves, a desk and a chair.

". . .somebody ought to be reminding him of who he is and force him to stand up straight. . ."

I went inside and picked the receiver off the wall.

". . .somebody ought to. . ."

"Yes?"

For a moment there was silence on the line—though not a blank and empty silence. It was the silence of someone waiting to make sure the voice he was hearing was the voice he wanted to hear.

"You have the Oakes' residence," I said, "and this is H.S. Mauberley speaking. *Hello.*"

"You've been waiting for a message," said the voice at the other end, at last. "What is the watchword, please?"

Oakes was completely preoccupied.

"Do you weave?" I said.

"Yes I do," said the voice. "But every night I unravel it."

The voice was coming from a thousand miles away.

"And what am I to do?" I asked.

"In an hour you're to meet the messenger in Rawson Square."

"But it's almost eleven o'clock."

"You're to be in Rawson Square in an hour," said the voice again—and the line went dead.

Hanging up, I realized nothing had been said about how I might recognize the messenger. But then I thought; *of course, he'll recognize me.*

"You going somewhere?" said Oakes.

"Just out," I said. "For a walk. Don't fuss. I may be gone some time."

"I know," said Oakes.

I stared at him, alarmed.

"You're going downtown to pick up one of those whores in Rawson Square."

I blinked.

"Well, I warn you," he said. "You'd better not bring her here. I won't have any more whores underneath this roof."

The air was filled with the smell of bougainvillaea. Down along Prince George's wharf there was music. Other music, as always, drifted back across the Bay from the Porcupine Club.

It was hot, but not unpleasant. Many people were out to get a breath of air, and a few of them were sitting in the oval of the park on benches in amongst the flowers.

I was wearing my whites and my Panama hat, though there

on Bay Street, Nassau, these could hardly be called a trade-mark. Every second man you saw who wasn't wearing uniform was wearing whites of some description—though I dare say mine were the only whites that night from Venice.

Having hired a cab, I was early. Walking round the oval, taking my time and pausing under each of the lamps so I might be seen distinctly, I got no reaction to my presence. Nor did I see anyone I either recognized or who looked a likely candidate. No one even said "hello"—which I thought was a trifle unfriendly. And sad. I had always wondered what it would be like to be middle-aged and undesirable. Now I knew; though of course I could probably make myself "desirable" enough if I knew how to play the predator.

Where were all the whores Sir Harry had spoken of? Not a sign of anyone I would have called a whore. Just a few Airmen lolling on benches in pairs and trios and otherwise couples ranging in age from the very young to the very old.

I went up onto Bay Street then and crossed from the park to the Square. And there they were. The whores—though not a multitude. I sat down fairly close to the street, afraid to penetrate too deeply into the Square lest my intentions be misinterpreted. Watching, every once in a while I could see that one of the Airmen broke away from his friends and plucked up his courage and crossed, as I had, over Bay Street and into the Square. They, however, had every intention of penetrating further into the dark than I.

The promised hour was drawing to a close. Hugh Selwyn Mauberley—poet, novelist, critic, polemicist and winner of prizes, including both the Pulitzer and the Concordia—sat amongst the whores and lighted a cigarette.

Should I write that he sat "amongst the *other* whores"? I do not know. I do know I thought it then, as I sat there on my bench all dressed in white. And it made me smile. In spite of my nervousness that I was there at all, in the dark—or nearly in the dark—with all those strangers, one of whom might be looking for me; watching me; assessing me. . .and in spite of my apprehension of what the messenger might say and what he might expect of me. . .and in spite of my fear of Harry Oakes and the Duke and—yes—of Wallis, too. . .in spite of all the years I might still have to live as me, despised as I was by people I admired, and looked down upon as I was by all, or nearly all, of my peers. . .I smiled. I smiled because I was alive. I still had that. I could smell the bougainvillaea still, and smoke my cigarette and feel the cool white cloth of my suit against my legs—and I could watch the Airmen, still, in the marvel of their youth, the brevity of which they had no inkling of; and I could see them cross the street and pass into the dark and I could feel their fear, their marvellous, sensual fear as they went their way to whatever beds they would find. I still had that. I still had that.

And then he was there.

And it was him.

He said, "There is too much light just here. Get up and go further back. I will join you."

But how could I get up and go further back? How could I go anywhere? I could barely move. I had thought it would be anyone but him. I had thought he was safely out of my life.

Move further off. There is too much light just here. . . .

We sat on a bench and I could see his shoes, his hands, his knees. The shoes, as always, were the sick lime-brown of alligator skins and the knees were still the square, hard knees of an athlete—but the hands were folded into fists and the veins stood out so boldly I could see his pulse.

The only view I really got of his face was when he struck the match and it flared so long I knew he was giving me a chance to look at him. He had still the same damned beauty as before, though now I could not see the eyes. They were cast against the light and hidden by the brightness.

After the match was out, it seemed very dark.

"Who are you, Harry?" I said. "Tell me who in hell you are."

Harry Reinhardt gave what passed, at least in that particular moment, for a laugh.

"No, no," I said. "Please tell," I said. "I want to know."

"I'm the messenger," he said. And it frightened me because it dawned on me all at once what the message really was. It was the message he had delivered to Ned.

Above us, over the Square, there were half-a-dozen nightjars—or more—and all through the time we sat there, one by one they flung themselves down through the air towards us. Just at the end of every dive, they made that strange, low screeching sound that can be so unnerving when you don't know what it is—and is haunting when you do. They do it for the danger, no other reason. Just for the danger. Just to impress. Each bird climbs a little higher than the one before, and flings itself a little closer to the ground. Only the males indulge in this, of course, while the females sit on the telephone wires and watch. At the end of the display, there might be a mating.

"The only thing I've never understood is why they do it in the dark," I said.

But Harry Reinhardt said it wasn't really all that dark. He said the degree of darkness depended on how long you'd been there.

And I thought; no. *It depends on who you are.*

Before he left me sitting there, he said we must meet again Monday at two o'clock. He wanted the Sunday to adapt himself to his surroundings, walk out and see the town and judge the distances between the houses where each of us lived and the ultimate rendezvous. Not that he did me the honour of telling me where the ultimate rendezvous might be.

Just as he was about to leave, I spoke his name. "Harry?" I said—because I wanted to see him turn around and face me in the light. But he didn't turn and neither did he pause. Once he had left me, we were apparently strangers. All I could see was his shoulders and his buttocks and his going away. And I sat there half an hour, unable to move.

I felt a compulsive need to hide and not to speak or hear my

name. I was even leery of taking a cab that night, fearing to
tell a stranger where I lived. So I walked back "home" to
Westbourne, using as many residential streets as I could,
knowing fewer people might be strolling there. But I could
not resist a pass by Government House to see how many
lights were burning. None.

Sunday morning, July 4th, I anticipated correctly Wallis and
the Duke would have to attend the Memorial Service for the
victims of the *Fiery Fête.* Consequently I telephoned as early
as I dared—at 8:00 A.M.—and got the Duchess out of her
bed.

"*Chit-chat,*" I said.

"Good morning," she said.

"I thought I should telephone to say the messenger has
arrived."

Wallis coughed.

"Are you all right?" I asked.

"Oh, yes. It's just my early morning hack. Would you
repeat the message, please?"

"I said the messenger has now arrived."

"And what's the news he brings?"

"Am I seeing you tomorrow?" I asked.

"You're coming to dinner, yes. And cocktails at seven."

"Any news I have, I'll bring you then."

"Can you tell at least this much. *Are we going?*"

"Of course," I said.

Wallis was the first to hang up—which is why I heard the
second "click".

Harry Oakes had been listening.

On Monday at two, I was seated in Rawson Square on the
same wooden bench we had used before. I will say this much
for Harry Reinhardt: he was prompt. On the very dot of two,
as if appearing from the air, he sat at the other end of the
bench.

I don't know how long we sat there, while we finalized
the details of the plan. The S.S. *Munargo* was to leave on

the morning of the ninth for New York. Our story was to be that the Duke and Duchess were making a secret trip for diplomatic reasons. And with the danger of a lurking German submarine, we would say, the Windsors must board the *Munargo* under cover of darkness on the night of the eighth.

It sounded like a cunningly-thought-out operation. The authorities who could potentially prevent the Windsors' escape from the Bahamas would actually be duped into lending a hand—a military escort down to the wharf, a boat ready to take the couple out to the *Munargo*; and no communication with anyone on board for fear the enemy might pick up the signal. The whole departure, in fact, would be kept a total secret, so the authorities were to be told, until the Windsors safely reached New York.

"What really happens?" I asked.

"They will be rowed out to the yacht, of course."

"Rowed?"

"It won't be far. . . .The main thing is to get them on the yacht and the yacht will do the rest."

"The rest?"

"Deliver them to the sub."

"I hope you're impressed with what I've said about the Duke. He's in quite bad shape, you know."

"That can't be helped."

"Of course," I said. "I'm only trying to prepare you. After all, we want to be ready for any eventualities. Can't have something coming out of left field just as we get underway."

I told him then about the Windsors' dogs.

"Dogs?" said Harry Reinhardt.

"Yes," I said. "There are six of them—and the Windsors won't go anywhere without them."

"Well, if we have to," said Reinhardt, "We'll take them along and drown them at sea."

Ever since the Fiery Bazaar, Wallis had been unable to celebrate the fourth of July in any other way but as a sombre public wake. She did, however, have her revenge by creating "The Glorious Fifth".

Understandably, I was extremely nervous on this particular occasion, knowing Wallis and the Duke were to quit the Bahamas four days later and never return.

The dining-room I see in my mind was blue. I cannot recall precisely who was there although I know that Elsa Maxwell was and the Windsors, of course, and myself. What I see is perhaps a frieze of ten or a dozen faces—all of them suspended, hung above the plates. I also see the silver knives and candlelight through glass and all the men in white, their shirts and dinner jackets caught at the neck with black-tie knots, and the women in their evening gowns all blue—I don't know why the women all wore blue; they did, that's all; or they do in my mind—and all their hairdos caught in the updraught from the blazing candles, sweeping back from their faces—every face an oval marked with all the appropriate dots: two eyes, a mouth, a nose and all pulled taut and pinned into place with outsized jewelled ears. I remember the ears so vividly, and the sound around the table of ten, a dozen little mouths being fed—and otherwise the only sound was of the knives going up and down and of Wallis shaking out her bracelets over the cloth and the Duke of Windsor's cigarette lighter clicking through the whole proceedings. All he seemed to do was smoke and I think he hardly ate at all.

There was wine all through the meal and the intrusive arm of the steward pushing past the shoulders with its bottles, pouring out the sound of someone drowning every three minutes or so.

And the smell was of yellow jasmine—everywhere.

Into all this white and blue there was suddenly injected—unannounced and uninvited—the twin black presence of Harold Christie, the real estate man, and Sir Harry Oakes. They had come, so they said, presuming there had been some mistake. They had always been invited before on "The Glorious Fifth".

Wallis lifted her eyes to mine. And then she looked at the Duke. The Duke was drowsing, way off past the jasmine in its bowls and the candles in their glassy lamps. The pouches and the lines beneath his eyes had been whited out, and the blue of those eyes was dangerously sad. It could make a person weep to see those eyes, and think; *poor boy—what can we do to help?* And his fingers reaching down to feed his meal to the crowd of little dogs beside his chair. His heart was very wide, but his mind was not.

Christie and Sir Harry Oakes were seated then, squished in between two ladies each, and I know that Oakes had Elsa Maxwell on one side. The chairs they were given, of necessity, were small, and the pieces of silver set for them were only for the entrée and the compôte coming later of mangoes, melons and Kirsch. And they only received the briefest visit from the steward: droplets of wine that barely wet the glass. . . .

It was a nightmare then to the end of the meal. I don't know what precisely Christie knew. But he must have known his friend had aces up his sleeve and was going to play them one by one till he'd got the effect he wanted. Still, I had the impression he was just as mystified and ultimately alarmed as the rest of us, watching and listening to Oakes as he produced each card and scored each coup.

"How are you, Harry?" said the Duke. "Sorry we went ahead without you. . ." And he lighted his eighteenth or nineteenth cigarette.

"From what I hear," Sir Harry said, "Your Royal Highness means to go ahead without us all. But Her Grace, of course, will go with you. . ."

Wallis passed. I passed. The Duke passed.

Elsa looked puzzled.

"Trips?" she said to Wallis, attempting to sparkle.

Wallis gave warning with a look: the subject was taboo.

"*Trips* is an interesting word, Miss Maxwell," Sir Harry said. "Thing is, some trips are journeys—and other trips are falls." He laughed. The most unpleasant laughter I have ever heard.

"Horses trip," said the Duke. "I've had a lot of falls that way. . ."

"Yes," said Oakes. "I remember one you had. I was there." He looked around the table. "King of England, down on his arse."

The table froze.

Finally, Elsa broke the silence.

"Better down on his arse than on his luck," she said.

All eyes—Elsa's too—looked over at the Duke.

"Yes," said the Duke. "Ha-ha."

I had never, till then, heard a person actually use the words *ha-ha*. It made me laugh. Then Wallis laughed. Then everyone. The ice—for a moment—melted.

After the thaw, however, Oakes went at it again. "Any of you people seen the big silver yacht offshore the last two evenings?"

No they had not—and yes they had. It was roughly half and half.

"Won't come in, so I'm told. Stays out there the legal mile and won't come in. Just sits. Sometimes she sits all night—and I see her in the morning. Other times. . ."

Wallis cut in. "Surely it's just another of those Cuban millionaires. They sit out there and take the best fish and then move off to the Keys and take the best fish there. So I'm told," she added hastily. "They can't get landing papers anywhere, you know. I mean they never come and *shop* and spend their millions—all they do is sit out there and. . ."

"*Wait*," said Sir Harry.

Wallis had walked right in—and knew it. Her complexion reddened.

Then Sir Harry said, "I'd wait, too, if I knew what kind of fish I was going to catch out there. Anyone knows we got the best there is. Unique." He ate a little food and went on talking, chewing with his mouth open. "Night fishing's dangerous, though. Never know what you might pick up on the end of your line. Sharks, sting rays, subs. . . ."

"What's a sub?" someone said. "I've never heard of subs."

It was natural—normal, I suppose. There are fish called "bottles" and "skates" and "stockings". Why should there not be fish called "subs"?

Harry Oakes did not laugh this time. This time he looked across at whoever it was who had spoken and "Madam," he said—or "Sir—if you have never heard of *subs*, then you have never heard of Hitler, either. Or the war."

Wallis laid aside her fork and summoned the steward. "Clear. . ." she said. I heard her. "And have Mister Howard come down."

"Yes, ma'am."

I began to panic in earnest. Everything that Oakes was saying was proof that he'd not only listened on the telephone but had also followed me to Rawson Square and Harry.

The steward set his staff to clearing away the course in preparation for the compôte and he himself went off to fetch Mister Howard.

"I'm sure we don't want to talk about the war," said Wallis. "Let's change the subject to something closer to home."

"You can't get much closer to home than that, Your Highness," said Oakes. And all at once, the anger he had withheld so far, exploded. Rising, he banged the table with his fist and all the little dogs went rushing into the corner to hide. "The *S.S. Munargo* and silver ships and German subs. . ."

Elsa muttered in my ear, "I thought he was going to end with *sealing wax and kings*. . ." and chortled. She was greatly enjoying herself.

"You can't," said Oakes, "get any closer to home than that!" He suddenly pointed at Wallis and shouted, spitting— "And *you* damn well know it!"

Wallis did not even blink.

"Oh, I think we can," she said.

Mister Howard came in and leaned towards the Duchess. Buzz-buzz.

"Yes, ma'am."

Mister Howard left the room.

The compôte arrived.

Then Wallis said, "For instance, you could tell us all about Sydney, Sir Harry."

Harry Oakes' mouth dropped open.

"*Do*," said Wallis, smiling. "It's such an intriguing story."

"Sydney?" said Oakes. He really did seem lost and puzzled. He looked across at Harold Christie. Then at me. And then, again, at Wallis. "What about him?"

But I could see the fear in his eyes. Wallis had touched

368

the one dear thing—and dangerous—in his heart: the subject of his children. I could even see the prayer go up: *don't let her say it, please...*

And then she did. She said it, leaning forward, looking at Elsa. "Sydney Oakes has been having an affair with..."

"*Freddy?*" said Elsa.

Harry Oakes sat down.

For a moment, we were safe.

At the close of the meal, Wallis said to me: come—and it was now I discovered what she had been up to with Mister Howard.

We crossed the hall to the Council Chamber. On the table was a richly shining leather box. Mister Howard, with a pistol in his hand, was standing in front of it. Wallis dismissed him and he went away—though not before he handed her a chain of keys.

Wallis took me closer and unlocked the box. Inside, against a velvet cushion, lay a necklace with pendant, earrings and brooches of the most exquisite emeralds I had ever seen.

"These," she said, "were left to the Duke by Queen Alexandra. Now they are mine—though the present Queen insists they be returned...." She lifted the necklace up for me to see against her neck—and laying it back on the velvet, fingered the brooches and earrings.

Wallis said, "These are the loveliest things I own and it would break my heart to part with them. But, still..." She looked at me and shut the lid decisively. "I am sending Harry Oakes to you here. And if—when he is gone and I return—these emeralds have disappeared, they will have served their purpose."

Quickly, as if afraid she might change her mind, she hurried to the double doors and opened them both.

"Maubie...?"

"Yes, ma'am?"

"Save us. If you can."

I nodded.

Wallis left, and I turned back to gaze at the emeralds. Now,

I thought, lifting the lid, I am playing d'Artagnan. And the Queen of France depends on my finesse.

Oakes, when he entered, was hardly my image of the evil Lady de Winter, but he would do as one whose machinations could destroy a Royal House. On the other hand, I thought I knew him better than to think he could be bribed. I would hold the jewels in reserve for this encounter. Though I might have to use them, I would only use them as a last resort.

I offered him some port from the sideboard.

No thankyou.

Yes; he was going to be difficult.

"I've been asked to speak with you," I said.

"So I gathered," he replied. "But I'm not obliged to listen."

"No. But I think you'd be very unwise—I think you would regret it if you didn't."

"Oh? *Regret* it? That sounds kind of like a threat, Mister Mauberley."

"It is," I said. "But not of the deadly kind." I became inspired. I knew exactly what to say—and how to use the emeralds.

"Listen, Sir Harry," I said. "You've hit upon an intrigue in a most unfortunate way. It is true, the Duke and Duchess are departing. . ."

"Hah!" he roared. "Hah-hah!" And he did a sort of little dance.

I said; "please do be quiet and hear me out. You've no idea at all what you've put in jeopardy here. And you just may be dancing on someone's grave."

This sobered him, at least for the moment.

"All right," he said. "Speak."

"The Duke," I said, "is ill."

"You're god damn right he is," said Oakes. "The impotent twit!"

"He's *physically* ill," I persisted, "and requires a most delicate operation in order to save his life."

Oakes paled. "His life is in danger!"

"Yes," I said. "Imminent." And left it at that for the moment, letting it swim around in Sir Harry's brain.

Then, just at the very moment I could see he was ready

to believe, I went across to the leather box and sadly, with a heavy heart, I lifted the lid.

Oakes stared.

"There's a surgeon in Boston who can save him," I said. "But it's very touch and go. The Duke cannot be flown—and therefore he must go by ship. Of course, it would never do to have it known he was leaving the island by ship, lest the Germans send a U-boat and sink him. Therefore, it's all being done under cover of darkness. Except that. . .somehow. . ." I did not say how, in order to shame him that he had followed me ". . .you, of all people, fell upon the plan and, for whatever reason, misinterpreted. . ."

"Oh, dear me," said Oakes, whose eye was on the emeralds. "What have I done?"

"Whatever you have done," I said, "can only be undone if you promise never to mention it again. The best and only ally we have, is silence."

Oakes sat down. And then I played the emeralds.

"These," I said, "have been donated by the Duchess as payment for the surgeon, but if you will accept the brooches in lieu of what is already owed you. . ." I was gambling, of course, outrageously—but it worked.

I saw Oakes face twist up in the all too familiar prelude to tears.

"I wouldn't take a cent," he said. "I wouldn't accept a penny. Why," he said, "I'll wipe out the debt altogether. What's a little money with a person's life at stake? Oh, God. . ." and here the tears became a flood. "What have I done? What *have* I done?"

When the tears subsided and he'd blown his nose and put away his handkerchief, he said; "I must admit, I never did like *her*. But the Duke, I did. I liked him very much. And I knew there had to be something wrong. He was behaving. . . .Really, he was just too peculiar." Then; "look," he said—and rose and began to cross to the doors. "Don't let her sell those emeralds. Let me pay for this. I wouldn't mind at all, if it will help the Duke." He was now at the door. "Boston, you say?"

"That's right."

"An operation?"

"Yes."

"Get him away in secret—no one's to know. . . ."

"That's right."

"I won't breathe a word."

"Good for you."

Oakes went through the door and looked back in. "Boston's a good place to hide," he said. "That's where I sent my daughter Nancy, when I had to get her away from that pervert Freddy. . ."

"Yes." My heart stopped.

"Boston's a good safe place," he said.

"That's why we've chosen it," I said, barely able to breathe.

"Of course."

He was gone. It took me at least another minute to recover. Then, at last, I breathed an enormous sigh of relief and turned to close the lid on the emeralds. *Done,* I was thinking. *Now there is nothing standing in our way.* And at that very moment, Oakes returned—and I guess I knew he must.

"You son-of-a-bitch," he said. "You lying son-of-a-bitch."

I felt my shoulders give.

"There's no more anything wrong with that impotent twit in there than there was with my daughter Nancy. . ."

And so, the game was up. All the time I had been talking, something had been worrying me—which was that I knew I had heard the story I was telling, before. *Illness—operation—Boston. . .*

And if anyone knew that combination was a lie, it had to be Sir Harry Oakes.

By twelve o'clock the other guests had left. Only I remained and the Duke was asleep, having taken pills and retired to his apartment.

"All right," said Wallis, once we were cloistered safely in her bedroom. "What are we going to do?"

I told her I did not know. And it was true. I was numb. My brain would not perform.

Wallis said, "Do you think he can really harm us? Stop us?"

I didn't even have to pause. "Yes," I said. "I think he can."

Wallis sat on her bed. She looked so forlorn that I thought we were back in China, certainly back in the South of France. I watched her picking at the threads of the coverlet, damaging her nails, trying to contain herself and finally succeeding. When she spoke, her voice was just as calm as if we sat at dinner, drinking wine. "I have only one more chance," she said. "Only one." Then she smiled. "We've been leaning on each other now—you and I—for almost twenty years. . ."

I blushed. I had never thought she had leaned on me, only that I had leaned on her. Wallis was strong and I was weak. It was a fact of life.

"Ever since I was Mrs Winfield Spencer. . .yes? In the lobby of the old Imperial Hotel, Shanghai. . ." Wallis stood up and walked across to the windows, looking down through the slats of her shutters at the lawn where Harry Oakes had stood and yelled obscenities that other night in the rain and where, two years ago, fifty-five people had died in a nightmare of fire. "Everyone wanders off," she said. "Everyone wanders off and is gone before I can catch them, Maubie. *Catch* them?" She laughed. "I make it sound so cruel. And that isn't what I mean." She turned away again. "My father died when I was still a child—a baby. Then my mother. Wandering off into their deaths before I could. . .catch them. Gone before I could catch them up; that's what I mean. And Win—he was so fine and handsome; truly, truly dashing he was. Lovely man he was, all bright and shining in his uniform, all white and beautiful—and sad." She sighed. "*He* wandered off before I could catch him up—into a bottle— China—death. Oh, well. . .And Dmitri Karaskavin. . .need I remind you? You, who loved him, too. Who could ever catch *him* up? Then Ernest. . .*marching*. Oh! How he wanted to be a soldier. Crazy. Me, I mean. I was crazy to have married him. I guess of all my men, I loved him least—if I loved him at all. But I never caught him—never could catch him, either. Such a *gentleman* he was. And dull as a ditch. *Elusive* as a ditch. Does that make sense?"

"Perfect sense," I said. "There's nothing quite so elusive as a ditch. It starts somewhere. . .it ends somewhere. . .and in between it catches little bits of everywhere else. A ditch is elusive as hell."

Wallis laughed. Then sobered. "Now I've lost David. Oh—God—Maubie. Hugh. Dear friend. I can't begin to tell you where he's gone. He's left me so far behind, I don't know where I am. But I do know where I want to be. I've always known that. Always. And this ship, this ship that's come. This promise. . .This is my one last chance. Me, you see, I can catch up with. . ." She stared in the direction of her husband's rooms. She touched her hair and smoothed her skirt. "Of course," she said, "I am the strongest. I have to make him follow. Don't I? He has to follow me. And I never—never, never understood that before. David has me to catch. And we have to help him. . ."

We. Us. We. I looked away.

"Don't, Hugh. Don't look away. This is your last chance, as well as mine."

She stared at me. I stared at her.

"Help me," she said.

"I don't know how," I said.

Wallis turned—but only half—away. "Do you love me?"

"Yes." I sat completely still.

"Hugh?"

But I could not look at her. I was afraid.

"It will always be said," she said, "until the end of time, that the King gave up his throne for me. But you and I are the only ones who know or will ever know that I gave up my throne for him."

It was true.

"And I want it back."

Of course, there was no sleep that night and my room was filled with every ghost I could summon. Every death I had ever seen was played before my eyes. And I thought of Beatrice in *Much Ado: "do you love me?" "Yes." "Kill Claudio. . ."* And I thought of Lucrezia Borgia, Agrippina, Messalina—while the geckoes struggled up the walls and across the ceiling, searching for a fly to kill.

And all the while I did not sleep, I knew that Oakes was

down the hall and knew that he was wakeful, too, and would not sleep. The air was stifling—not a hint of breeze—and the night was filled with the cries of birds and the tick of clocks and the voices of a thousand frogs and insects, scrabbling mice and the sudden barking of a dog that could smell the fear in my room and knew the meaning of the fear. And I rose and pushed aside the netting, braving the corpses on the floor and the sudden convergence of all the mosquitoes round my head and in my ears, and I lunged for the door on my left and locked and bolted that and then went round to shutter after shutter, pulling them down and latching every one of them in place.

In the morning, white on white, and even my underclothing bleached as white as salt, I carried down the box of corpses, wondering how it could be so light, so weightless in my hands, and gave it across the table to Mavis Boodle, noting unavoidably as I did the multitude of oranges she had killed and was squeezing into a glass to keep me alive.

At nine, I left the house and went downtown where I could find a telephone with no extension—certain no matter where I went that Harry Oakes would overhear.

I dialled a number Harry Reinhardt had made me memorize—waiting and waiting a very long time before there was an answer.

"Meet me," I said. And hung up.

I met with Harry Reinhardt late in the afternoon of July 6th in Rawson Square. We sat side by side on our usual bench.

"I need your help," I said.

"Well—I've always known that, Mister Mauberley," said Reinhardt.

Yes; and I suppose he had from the moment he saw my eyes.

"What can I do for you?"

Turning towards him, I tried as hard as I could to look into his face and not to falter. I thought of my father, walking on the roof of the Arlington Hotel. *Those who jump to their death have cause*. . .I looked at Harry's mouth—his lips— his alligator eyes. . .and *those who leap have purpose*.

I leapt.

"I need a death," I said.

A little smile appeared at the corner of his lips.

"All right," he said. "Just tell me where and when and who. . ."

It was done. My fall was over. All the way down.

That was Tuesday.

Two days to go. The plan had been to get the Windsors away in the dark of Thursday night as late as possible. But all at once we appeared to be thwarted. There was Harry Oakes to deal with—and there was a sudden change announced regarding the departure of the *S.S. Munargo*.

Oakes was now a matter entirely out of my hands. He was Reinhardt's affair and I drank myself half blind in order to drive it from my mind. At least I tried—but it didn't work. I have found this almost always to be true. When you need the most to be sober, two drinks will put you under the table. But when you need the most to be drunk, a gallon will not even slur the speech, let alone knock you out.

The *Munargo* was leaving Thursday a.m.—pre-dawn—instead of on Friday. Thus, we had to get the Windsors away, in order to maintain our ruse, on the Wednesday.

Mister Howard and a certain Miss Comfort were to act as surrogates on board the ship and would lock themselves in their cabins all the way to New York. They had no notion why this was being asked of them, but their loyalty was such they looked upon it all as a "lark" and poor little Mister Howard—with his livid pride—was made to feel he had finally redeemed his prestige in the eyes of "Henny" Henderson. Henderson, panic-stricken, was being left behind altogether.

And so, on the night of Wednesday July 7th, 1943, the

Duke and Duchess of Windsor, six small dogs, a great deal
of luggage, Mister Howard, Miss Comfort and a military
escort climbed or were pushed or were thrust into half-a-
dozen motor cars and driven away from Government House
in the early stages of a storm that by 3:00 a.m. would become
a hurricane.

Mister Howard wore the Duke of Windsor's uniform as
a Major General and Miss Comfort wore a dark grey suit and
a tailored coat belonging to the Duchess—plus one of Wallis's
most becoming hats, with a suitable veil. As for the Windsors
themselves, the Duke had almost to be carried, he was in
such dreadful shape—and Wallis, aching with the roar of
triumph she was not allowed to voice was trying her best
to smile a little sadly at the fact they were going away and
would be gone so dreadfully long. . . .

When she came to me in the line-up of those who had
been assembled to say goodbye, she allowed me to lift and
to kiss her hand but then—all at once—she kissed me herself
on the cheek. And she whispered; *"we have won."*

And then they drove away in the rain.

Reinhardt and I were to join them on the silver yacht,
though we were to go there by a different route. Nevertheless,
it is true that in that moment I had said goodbye to and seen
the last of the woman I had loved—as a dog loves its mistress—for the past two decades. Wallis, Duchess of Windsor,
would never be that woman again.

The early hours of the evening had been cloudless and starry.
Now, there was a roaring wind and the first sheets of rain
were blowing across the lawns at *Westbourne* and turning
them into reflecting pools in which the lights of the Staff
Car Wallis had assigned to me were dipped, like fingers
searching for something lost. I could see there was another
motor car—though I did not recognize it—parked in the
driveway.

Reinhardt had told me this would be our rendezvous: and

from here, we would leave together to join the others aboard the yacht. I assumed, therefore, the motor car was his. I got out near the gates and ran the rest of the way to the house.

Once inside the house, my first impression was of silence: then of the emptiness around me, usually filled with the brooding, paranoid presence of Oakes.

"Reinhardt?" I said. Not very loud. "Reinhardt?"

There was no reply.

I was more afraid than I can say.

There were so many fearful images in my mind. The death I had asked for had been so ill-defined I could not make it real. Certainly I could not make it happen in a place familiar as this house had become. "The dark" is where Harry Oakes would die, not here with all these lights and the mess he'd left in the kitchen and the mud he'd tracked on Mavis Boodle's floor and his army boots kicked over by the umbrella stand. Surely he would be out somewhere in the dark; or maybe in the sea; not here.

"Reinhardt?"

I went to the bottom of the stairs.

I knew I must climb. The climbing was part of the nightmare.

Going up, I noted there were smears on the wall; stains on the rug; a broken spindle; mud—or something—on the bannister. Oakes at his best as the grumpy badger in his winter lair. The "something" on the bannister was more than likely jam, and the smears would be made by his elbows, greased as he worked on his bad-tempered partner, the big yellow bulldozer parked on the lawn.

Reaching the top of the stairs, I went into the guest room on my right, beyond which I could see the lights in Sir Harry's room.

I gave the partly opened door a push.

What I saw at first was just the shape of the room. On my left, a curtained window—closed against the storm—and a door that led to the ubiquitous verandah, awash in the rain. On my right, there was a bed and beyond that a painted Chinese screen standing open, hiding the rest of the room from view.

I had only been in Sir Harry's bedroom once before, but I was certain there should be two beds there—though only one was visible.

Harry Reinhardt was sitting, with his back against the headboard. Beside him lay his leather coat. His clothes were wet and stained and his hair was plastered against his skull. Just exactly as I had seen him first at Edward Allenby's funeral. Always—the rain. He held up his hands for me to see and they were smeared with blood.

I stared.

"Everyone get away all right?" he said.

I nodded.

I was watching him. That's all. Just watching him. I wanted to see what his eyes might do.

They were watching me. He was smiling.

"Where is Harry Oakes?" I said.

Reinhardt did not reply.

"Harry?" I said. "Where is he?"

"Everything's taken care of."

He laid his hands—palms up—on top of his knees and shifted along the bed until there was room for me to sit.

"Sit down," he said.

I sat.

For a moment, he studied his hands, curling the fingers— stretching them out. And then the hands lay stilled and red.

"I've always wondered," he said, "why animals lick each other's wounds. . ."

There was a pause.

"Maybe," he said, "they like the taste of blood."

"I beg your pardon?. . ."

I closed my eyes. I was so afraid.

He reached up then and pressed my face into his bloody palm. "That's right," he said. "You lick it clean." And he pressed again—so hard this time that my lips were forced apart and I began to lick because I had no choice.

I do not know for certain how it was I was made to sleep, but I suspect Harry Reinhardt did it by applying pressure to the arteries in my neck. However long I lay there, whether unconscious or asleep, it was long enough for Harry Reinhardt to make his escape. When I first awoke I was not aware of anything being wrong. I could see the Chinese screen and I remember thinking how charming it was with its Imperial Courtyard filled with mandarins and courtiers and its shaded verandahs—so much wider than the verandahs at *Westbourne*. . .And then I knew where I was.

But the air. . .

It was all so curious.

The air was filled with feathers. White, soft, snow-like feathers, gently and relentlessly swirling in the stream of an electric fan that was buzzing on the far side of the room. The room itself was very ill lit but there was light enough to see I was not alone.

The screen had been moved and it now stood six feet further off than when I had first made my entrance. But its removal proved that my memory of there being two beds had been correct. It was just that all the time I had been lying there with Harry Reinhardt, the screen had obscured the other bed—and now it was revealed.

It is very hard to tell the rest of this, I suppose because I've tried so hard to make it leave my mind. But it won't.

In the air, although there wasn't any fire, there was the smell of it. Also the smell of kerosene. Or something very like it. I could not really tell.

On the bed beside the one on which I sat lay the body of Harry Oakes. He was dressed in a pair of striped pyjamas and was lying on his back. One arm was caught underneath his body and the other was flung between his legs in that gesture so often made by boys in their sleep against the atavistic fear that Lilith will come in the dark with her scissors. . . .

Oakes had been battered all around the face and head, but his features were still completely recognizable. Only his blood obscured them—and the feathers floating in the air, escaped from a mangled pillow. Some of the feathers were caught in smears of spittle and gore, and others were fluttering very close to the body, like butterflies afraid to alight where so much death had been spread in their way.

The realization I was alone with this horror drew me to my feet. It dawned on me what Reinhardt had in mind. This murder I had asked him for was to be mine completely, and when the authorities came it would be mine to pay for.

And so—of course—I ran.

In the dark of July the 7th, 1943 in Berlin at the Hotel Eden, the Piano Tuner returned to finish what he had begun.

von Ribbentrop said; "it's too late, now. They're already on their way. Everything's been set in motion."

But Schellenberg said; "you're wrong, I'm afraid. I've called the whole thing off."

"Called it off? How?"

"Your submarine. It will not surface."

"But. . ."

"It will not surface, Excellency, and therefore it will not pick up your cargo."

von Ribbentrop slumped forward in his chair. "You don't understand," he said. "You must let it happen."

"No," said Schellenberg. "We have other plans, now."

von Ribbentrop stared at him.

"We?" he said.

"Yes. We." Schellenberg smiled—and sat down. "Us."

After a moment, von Ribbentrop was able to speak again and said; "you are not one of us."

"I am, now."

"You don't understand what you're tampering with. You can't—or you wouldn't be doing this."

"Listen," said Schellenberg, "you should be grateful. The war is changing everything. The face of everything is changed. Your friends, the Windsors—they would really do more

harm than good. And the good they *can* do is best kept up
our sleeve for now."

"But you don't understand. . ."

"*You* don't understand, Excellency. I am saying you have
lost control of this."

von Ribbentrop could feel his innards giving way.

"As I say, you should be grateful. You've carried it alone
so long. And now you have help. That's all."

"There are others," said von Ribbentrop. "You don't understand what you're tampering with."

"What others. Paisley? Ciano? You will come to understand. The order of your priorities has been changed, Excellency. Please: believe me. You will come to understand."

von Ribbentrop stood up. He was afraid his bowels would
give away completely. Standing was the only way he could
gain control of them.

"And me?" he said. "What happens to me?"

Schellenberg shrugged very pleasantly and smiled in an
altogether friendly way and said; "We're not in any hurry
to decide that."

We? von Ribbentrop looked at his feet. So Schellenberg
had found the upper echelon. von Ribbentrop's feet appeared to be dangling in space, they were so very far away.

"Besides," said Schellenberg, "we don't know the final
outcome of all this yet. I think we should wait to hear what
happens and, in the meantime. . ."

von Ribbentrop looked up. But there weren't any meat-
hooks there. There wasn't any wire, just yet.

Schellenberg sat back.

"We rest."

"Rest?"

"For now. Yes." Schellenberg's eyes lowered. "Sit down,
Excellency."

von Ribbentrop began to fade away in the dark. But he
thought; death is not death until they put you in the ground.
Everything above ground is life. I still have some chances.
So long as I can see the ground. . .

His lips moved. But he was silent.

And he thought; when you die like that: when they cut

off your head—does your head go on living? Is it capable of thought? Even for a moment? And—what if there was something left to say? What if there was something to be told: some warning to be given? And no voice. No voice.

He moved his hand along his thigh towards his knee. He was aware of every finger. Aware of the cloth. The skin beneath the cloth. The sinew. Tissue. Tendons. Muscles. Bones.

The marrow.

Everything still there.

Knee.

Shin.

Ankle.

Foot.

Sock.

Shoe.

Floor.

In the dark—in the storm—they were cast adrift. A motor launch had been with them—but all at once there had been a violent wave—and when the wave had passed, the motor launch was gone. Gone on purpose, of course. The painter had been cut. The last thing Wallis had seen had been a man leaning down to wield the knife.

And the yacht never came. And, of course, the submarine had probably been a myth to begin with.

Only a myth. Or a dream.

Dear God.

They were sitting in the rowboat with their luggage piled around them, when the sun came up.

The Duchess of Windsor was sitting aft—with her arms spread wide to steady her, the Duke more or less in front of her—turned away.

The storm had departed in the dark and now the sea was

calm, though the groundswell was terrific and with every rise the Island slithered into view and slid away with every fall.

They were drifting. Waiting. Listening. Six little dogs were lying at their feet. Wallis shaded her eyes and scanned the whole horizon. Nothing—but the Island.

Wallis sighed.

It was over. She looked at the Duke and her mouth twisted down. Whatever they were—here and now—the two of them—was exactly what they would be forever. She looked away towards one side and then the other, counting her pieces of luggage. Twenty-six.

The back of her neck was rigid. She was perched very still on the edge of the seat. Her hair, pushed back and up, was severe yet elegant. It was covered with a pale blue veil and the veil came down to her chin. Her mouth was very red; her eyes, though blue, had darkened against the intrusion of so much light. Her whole face had frozen and now must carry, even through the veil, through the rest of time.

If only David would speak. But his mind was in the water, trying to wash the past away—and the future, too, she supposed—if he could get his way.

He was holding onto the gunwales—desperately—just as if the boat were the only reality left.

"David?" she said.

He closed his eyes.

"David," she said. "Let go." And she reached across her knees and his and began to release his fingers from their hold. "Let go," she said. "Let go."

There. He relaxed. He even looked up at Wallis.

It's Thursday, she was thinking.

Cards.

The Island held them two more years. And every evening the Duke went walking with Wallis and the six small dogs. The perimeters of their empire—newly defined—were the borders of their lawns. The Duke took to wearing hats with wide, white brims in order not to see the sky or let the sky see him. And when seated, Wallis holding his hand, he would stare at the roses in his garden and cut off their heads in his mind. It's good for them; he said. And it serves them right. Sometimes he verged on the place where he kept the memory of being the King, but he always tried to veer around the corner and miss it. He was careful, too, not to approach too closely any windows, doors of glass or mirrors. All the rest of his life he was faithful to Wallis. All the rest of his life he found his comfort in her shadow. All the rest of his life he pitied those around him who would never know what it was to have given everything away for love.

And sometimes, of an evening, they could both be spied as silhouettes at the top of their hill, on the bench made of stone, reserved for them alone. And when the breezes stirred the brim of his hat, the reflections could be seen of an Empire going out and setting in his eyes.

Every night at nine o'clock, Wallis would rise and take him by the hand and say; "it's time, now, David. Let us go." And they would wander off towards the comforts of the dark and the blessings of sleep—with all the little dogs on a string behind them, snuffling at their feet.

*　*　*

April, 1945

Mauberley was standing on his chair.

It was now so dark, so shuttered everywhere, and all the clocks had stopped—he could not tell the time.

Hugo, earlier (whenever that had been), had told him of the armies moving up against the edges of the valley: one from the south, another from the north, and all the Germans—trying not to look like soldiers, trying not to be an army (armies were being slaughtered)—caught in the middle, turning circles on their backs like flies about to die. And the Russians moving in from the east.

Thank God for Switzerland, from which direction only spies could come, singly and in pairs, perhaps, but not in armies. Never an army of spies.

Mauberley could hardly see. His eyes were weighted down with plaster dust and lack of sleep. And his fingers, drained of their blood since he had to hold his hand above his head to write, could barely any longer hold the pencil. Sometimes he held it like a knife and carved the letters into the wall. Other times he had to use both hands to hold it up, while yet again he simply had to stop and, while his mind rushed on across the words, he tried to hold them back until his hands could master them.

By now he was reaching the end.

Had all the truths been told? Had everything been said? He gazed around the walls. Not bad. Four rooms completed. Isabella's rooms, at that. And even though his words weren't eagles, her eagles were there. He had put them there so long ago, it seemed. All her life Isabella had believed above all other things in the value of the human mind. And she had placed her faith in the currency of the human mind, the written word. Her husband had died for the written word, and her children because of it. Nothing he knew of Isabella Loverso was more profoundly moving than that. And yet, in spite of those deaths of family and friends, and in spite of her terrible fear, she had remained determined to salvage what she could of words and hold them up against the sword.

Mauberley got down off his chair. Now would be a good time for music, moving him through to the end. Schubert's "last words" would do very nicely. This, after all, was Schubert's country—not only the place, but the ending of things.

Mauberley shuffled through the rooms with his candelabra in hand, until he came to the salon. All along the ledges of the windows, even in spite of the shutters, there was snow.

He placed the opening disc of the sonata on the Victrola, turned the crank and lowered the heavy arm with its precious needle—the last—into place. He lit another *Kavalier* cigarette and washed away its cardboard taste with a great long swig of brandy. Looking across the room, he read: *Wallis is sitting in my mind as I saw her first in the lobby of the old Imperial Hotel in Shanghai. . .*

He raised the bottle.

"Prosit."

Done. He could see himself in the mirror. Not a happy sight. Ah, well. He straightened the line of his pinned-up coat and even went so far as to match the ends of his scarf and push them neatly back inside against his chest. Using his knuckles, since his fingerends were in pain, almost raw, from holding the silver pencil in the cold, he whisked away the plaster dust and the cigarette ash and the little bits of glass—his rhinestones from all the broken windows he had failed to mend.

And all this while the perfect music, played by the perfect fingers of Alfred Cortot, made its perfect rhythms and made its perfect impact—Schubert's last words—endings.

Summations. Yes. There was one last thing for Mauberley to say.

Think of the sea, he began to write and went on writing until the music ended.

Damn.

Mauberley got down off the chair and, still with the pencil in his hand, he made his way to the Victrola, lifted the arm and turned the record over.

Last movement: *Allegro ma non troppo.*

He cranked the machine accordingly: sprightly, but not too quickly. And smiled. It was excellent advice, with the end in sight and a good night's rest and. . .

Who was that?

He moved towards the door.

"Hugo?"

No answer.

Mauberley looked back into the room. The candelabra's candles were guttering. He put it back in its place and before he blew them out, he took up another candle and drew a light for it from the others. Then, closing the door behind him—always his safety precaution—he moved off down the hall towards his own room.

"Hugo?"

Still no answer. It must only have been the chandeliers he had heard, going through one of their midnight dances in the wind.

He was tired. He would sleep.

"Hugo?"

Nothing. So when he reached his door, he turned and looked back down the corridor and saw that Garbo's door and Isabella's door and all the other doors were closed and all his lights extinguished.

"Goodnight," he said out loud.

And the chandeliers jangled. Draughts from somewhere. Never mind. Bed.

In the morning, Hugo would come with an egg, perhaps. And perhaps the wind would die away and the sun would shine. You never know. A person never knows.

It would be such a pleasure, he thought, to sit in the sun and to eat an egg. Just to sit there. Just to be there.

Mauberley turned the corner into his room.

"Hugo?"

There was someone.

"Kachelmayer? Is it you. . .?"

No.

It was Harry Reinhardt.

As, of course, it had to be.

Mauberley's struggle was mostly a struggle not to be slaughtered. The death itself was welcome. But he wanted not to be slaughtered. Please. He put out his hands. He even offered the silver pencil. Anything, not to die like this. If one could only pay the executioner, the way that kings had done: be quick. Be quick.

But it was not to be.

And worst of all, in the final moments of his struggle, with his arms both broken and his fingers locked at the ends of his hands, he was turned by Harry, long enough to see the figure of Hugo, *die weisse Ratte*, standing apparently passive; watching.

Just as the ice pick entered the eye, Mauberley's very last thought was: the brain itself can feel no pain.

And cannot bleed. It can only die. And death is rest.

Reinhardt's final act was to get the boy to help him burn the notebooks. All of Mauberley's journals and papers and letters, poured into the bathtub and covered with kerosene and set ablaze. It was marvellous to Harry's eyes. The complete destruction of the man he had been sent, by Schellenberg, to kill—and of all his words.

The boy, when the fire was over, put out his hand for payment.

"Once we're downstairs," said Harry.

"But you promised," said Hugo.

"Yes. And I keep my promises," said Harry.

And they went out into the corridor.

Hugo started down the stairs. He was debating whether or not he should tell this man about the writing on the walls. In fact, as they got to the landing, he turned to say so. "There's. . ." he said.

But that was all.

His body was found where Harry Reinhardt felled him. The others also. The ratty father; the terrified mother; the running, squealing children.

It was over.

Out beyond the shutters the wind was bringing down the last great blizzard of the winter from the mountain. All the shutters banged and the snow crept through into the rooms and all the candles guttered and went out and drifted over the bodies in the courtyard and the silent gramophone wound down.

All the light there was, was grey. And the air was filled

with crystal noise and a blowing avalanche into which Harry Reinhardt disappeared.

* * *

Quinn finished reading at dawn.

Crossing to the windows, he opened them and pushed the shutters wide.

Outside, there was a hush, and the air was scented with the smell of freshly fallen snow and the warm green smells from the valley far below. Two worlds: and now the horror was over in both of them.

Quinn turned back into the room and went down the hall, thinking he would get some coffee or some tea and a biscuit. But he was stopped by Freyberg at the door of Garbo's salon.

Freyberg was drunk.

"Come in," he said. "I've been up all night."

"So have I," said Quinn. "I was just going down to get some breakfast. . ."

"I have lots of breakfast," said Freyberg. "Come in."

Quinn could smell the wine from the corridor, even before he entered; but the smell of it inside the room was dense as a fog.

"I've been working," said Freyberg "and I want to show you. Over here. This. . ."

He was the sort of man who was formalized by drink. His gestures widened and became almost graceful. His words came out in single file, each word very nicely rounded off before the next word began: no slurring—only elocution. It was the syntax that suffered.

"Breakfast" was a red, nameless wine offered up in coffee tins and a chocolate bar for bulk.

What Freyberg had to show Lieutenant Quinn was a set

of scrapbooks whose covers—having been designed for children at play—were incongruous lambs and calves and ducklings in barnyards; Mickey dancing with Minnie Mouse; a clockwork band of shining toys; and a smiling doll with a bow in its hair.

Inside: Dachau.

"Why are you showing me this?" said Quinn. "I was there."

He was very tired and very angry.

"I know you were there." said Freyberg. "But do you remember?"

"Yes; I remember. God damn it, sir. And I don't want to see those things again. I can see them in my mind. I don't need any bloody photographs."

"Everyone needs photographs, Quinn. You see this here. . .?"

Quinn tried not to look—but Freyberg forced the picture up in front of him.

There was a man being set on fire. The man was still alive.

"Experiments," said Freyberg. "Eh? Remember?"

"Yes. I remember, Captain."

Freyberg turned the pages.

"You see this?"

Quinn looked.

There was a man inside a pressure chamber. Screaming.

"More experiments. Yes?"

"Yes. I know that, Captain."

Freyberg picked up the scrapbook showing Mickey and Minnie Mouse dancing on the cover. He flipped through the pages.

"Here," he said. "You see this? Look."

There was a picture of Quinn himself. He was standing beside an open oven door—and inside the oven twenty bodies, or thirty, unburned.

"Yes. I know that, Captain. Can't you see I'm standing right there."

"Yes. But do you remember it?"

"Yes."

"And this. . .?"

The book with the doll.
Children. All the children.
"Yes."
"And this?"
Calves and ducklings: lambs.
Inside: the living—starved.
"You see this? You see this? You see this? You see this?"
"YES!" Quinn screamed at him. "Yes, God, damn you!"
"Yes," he whispered.
They sat.

Freyberg shoved the scrapbooks back across the top of his desk and knocked his tin of wine onto the floor.

The sound of it dripping was like the residue of rain that falls from the corners of roofs when a storm is over.

Finally, Quinn stood up.

He went around behind the desk and picked up the coffee tin and set it carefully out of harm's way.

Freyberg was beginning to sag. Quinn looked down at the top of his head: just like the head of a boy; a child.

Quinn reached out to lay his hand on the back of Freyberg's chair: letting it fall with a sideways motion. All that touched was the edge of his little finger.

Freyberg didn't move a muscle.

Then Quinn went away.

Later, Quinn went in to look at Mauberley—just to make sure there was snow enough to cover him. The room was like a refrigerator.

All Quinn could see was the back of Mauberley's neck, and the tail of one of his scarves. Wanting something—anything—he drew the scarf away and held it in against his chest. And then he put it around his neck. And turned and left and closed the door.

That night, he lay on his cot and stared at Mauberley's stars. All he could think of was: *they are there. And they will not go out. Like other stars.*

Freyberg and Quinn were both preparing their summations when the news came.

They were to vacate the hotel. *Now.*

Quinn didn't understand. But Freyberg did. He was apoplectic with rage.

"It's the same old story," he said. "The same damn story all over again."

A colonel had been sent from Munich to enforce the evacuation. Apparently Captain Freyberg's attitude towards the Nazis was a matter of concern.

"We are leaving," said Freyberg to Quinn, "for no better reason than the fact the Russians have occupied Vienna."

"So?"

"So we have a *new* enemy, Lieutenant. Understand? Nazis are out. And Commies are in." Freyberg threw his pen across the room. Quinn considered picking it up. But didn't.

"What will be done about the walls?" he asked.

"Defaced, I suppose. I don't know. Blown up. Does it matter?"

"Of course it matters. All the people. . ."

"Precisely, Lieutenant. *All the people.* Every last man jack of them is going to get off scot free. Not, of course, that it's going to worry *you.* God damn it! Scot-fucking-free."

"I can't believe that, Captain. . . .The very fact that Mauberley's put them there means they will not go free."

Freyberg looked at Quinn: amazed. "You know," he said. "I think you just may be the dumbest man I've ever met. You really think the people on those walls won't be absolved?"

"No, sir. I don't think *anyone's* going to be absolved."

"Bullshit, Lieutenant. Bull *shit.* And you know why? Because, even in spite of everything you've seen and read— you yourself—I can see it in your eyes—are already turning away to look at something else: to find some other place to lay the blame for the hell we've all been living in this last five years. It's written all over you: Mauberley himself has already been forgiven."

Freyberg was shaking.

Quinn could think of nothing to say.

But Freyberg could: and he said; "look. Come here a minute."

Quinn stepped forward.

Suddenly Freyberg struck him: very hard in the stomach.

Quinn fell down on his knees.

Freyberg looked at him without a trace of passion.

"What are you doing down there?" he said.

Quinn had to fight for his breath—but he said; "you hit me."

"No I didn't," said Freyberg. "The wind did it."

And he walked away.

Quinn was the last to leave the Grand Elysium Hotel.

He preferred not to ride and requested he be allowed to follow the others on foot. He wanted, he said, to walk down the mountain. The Colonel from Munich had no objection to this: his whole concern was with Freyberg.

Mauberley's body rode by itself in a small, three-quarter ton truck that followed the ambulance which carried the crates of Captain Freyberg's Dachau Collection. Captain Freyberg himself sat up very tall in the Colonel's Jeep and appeared not to hear a word that was said to him. Quinn could not help but think the Captain looked like a prisoner. In all, there were seven vehicles, the rest being six-wheeled "Deuces" and the single armoured car that went with them everywhere.

Quinn went out and stood on the steps to watch them leave. He caught the briefest glimpse of Private Annie Oakley, who was sitting in the rear of one of the "Deuces". He noted that Annie's eyes gave a flick as he was driven past the portico: one last look—then away. A dead look, impossible to analyse; except, Quinn thought, Private Oakley's final shot of the war had been fired in the lobby of the Grand Elysium Hotel.

Mauberley's body was driven past, moving towards the emerald waters of the Ötzalsee. And looking out from the parapet Quinn could see the valley of the Adige and the rising mists of the spring of 1945. It made him feel very sad and he wished that he did not know how much that view had meant to Hugh Selwyn Mauberley.

The hotel was empty.

Like Annie Oakley, Quinn was forced to take his own last look.

And, like Captain Freyberg, he would take away his own collection. Around his neck, the scarf he had lifted from Mauberley and in his kit the two dusty halves of the Alfred Cortot recording of the Schubert Sonata.

In time, the remainder of the stories were concluded. Hess and von Ribbentrop were convicted of war crimes at Nuremberg in 1946, Hess sentenced to life imprisonment and von Ribbentrop to death. Hess, it is said, has moments of what appears to be sanity, claiming that if he could speak with Alan Paisley, much would be explained. But Alan Paisley died in 1954, and Hess cannot, it seems, be made to believe this is so. von Ribbentrop struggled for twenty minutes, hanging at the end of his rope, but his executioners were deaf to the sounds he made. It was said this death was his due.

Count Galeazo Ciano was shot by a firing squad in Berlin—1944.

Charles E. Bedaux was murdered in his cell at Key Biscayne in Florida in February of 1944, while the Duke and Duchess of Windsor were still in residence across the Straits in Nassau. His killer has neither been found nor identified, although it is thought that it might have been a man who worked for a very brief time in the prison infirmary, since

Bedaux was killed by an overdose of drugs and the man in question disappeared shortly afterwards. This crime remains unsolved, as does the murder of Sir Harry Oakes. Alfred de Marigny was charged with that murder and put on trial, but was acquitted in the fall of 1943, and upon his acquittal, the case was closed. In spite of entreaties from interested parties, the Duke of Windsor, acting in his capacity as Governor of the Islands, declared that no further investigations or inquiries would be tolerated.

Ezra Pound was convicted of treason and sent into prison, although he was ultimately released into a mental hospital and in the end, was pardoned and allowed to return to Italy where he died in 1972.

Walter Schellenberg was also put on trial at Nuremberg; convicted and sentenced to life imprisonment.

Three years later he was free.

Before he left the Grand Elysium Hotel to walk down the mountain, Quinn went upstairs one last time to look at Mauberley's epilogue.

Think of the sea, he read.

Imagine something mysterious rises to the surface on a summer afternoon—shows itself and is gone before it can be identified.

The people on the shore sit beneath their umbrellas, comfortable and dozing. Half of them are asleep. Of the other half, perhaps only two or three have seen the thing. None of them points: none of them shouts. None of them dares. After all, one could be wrong.

By the end of the afternoon, the shape—whatever it was— can barely be remembered. No one can be made to state it was absolutely thus and so. Nothing can be conjured of its size. In the end the sighting is rejected, becoming something only dimly thought on: dreadful but unreal.

Thus, *whatever rose towards the light is left to sink un-named: a shape that passes slowly through a dream. Waking, all we remember is the awesome presence, while a shadow lying dormant in the twilight whispers from the other side of reason; I am here. I wait.*

And Quinn dated it: May, 1945.